TriQuarterly

TriQuarterly is

an international

journal of

writing, art and

cultural inquiry

published at

Northwestern

University

TriQuarterly

issue 123

Editor
Susan Firestone Hahn

Associate Editor
Ian Morris

Operations Coordinator
Kirstie Felland

Production Manager
Siobhan Drummond

Production Editor
Greta Polo

Cover Design
Gini Kondziolka

Editorial Assistant
Samantha Levine

Assistant Editor
W. Huntting Howell
Sarah Mesle

TriQuarterly Fellow
Joanne Diaz

Contributing Editors
John Barth
Lydia R. Diamond
Rita Dove
Stuart Dybek
Richard Ford
Sandra M. Gilbert
Robert Hass
Edward Hirsch
Li-Young Lee
Lorrie Moore
Alicia Ostriker
Carl Phillips
Robert Pinsky
Susan Stewart
Mark Strand
Alan Williamson

CONTENTS

Editors of this issue:

Susan Firestone Hahn and Ian Morris

Cover: Born in the Wind #1, encaustic on panel,
18 x 22 inches, by Felicia van Bork, 2004

John Koethe

21.1

What I remember are the cinders and the starter's gun,
The lunging forward from a crouch, the power of acceleration
And the lengthening strides, the sense of isolation
And exhilaration as you pulled away, the glory at the tape.

I never really got it back after I pulled my thigh my sophomore year.
I still won races, lettered and was captain of the team,
But instead of breaking free there was a feeling of constraint,
Of being pretty good, but basically second-rate—

Which Vernus Ragsdale definitely was not. When he was eligible
(He was ineligible a lot) no one in the city could come close—
No one in the country pretty much, for this was California. We had
     our
Meet with Lincoln early in the spring, and he was cleared to run.

I was running the 220 (which I seldom ran) and in the outside lane,
With Ragsdale in lane one. *The stretch, the set, the gun*—
And suddenly the speed came flowing back as I was flying through the
     turn
And all alone before I hit the tape with no one else in sight.

Friends said he looked as though he'd seen a ghost (a fleet white one).
The atmosphere of puzzlement and disbelief gave way to
Chaos and delirium when they announced the national record time
Of 21.1 and I stood stunned and silent in a short-lived daze—

Short-lived because the explanation rapidly emerged:
They'd put us in the quarter-mile staggers by mistake, to be made up

Around two turns, not one. I'd had a huge head start on
Everyone, on Ragsdale on the inside most of all. By the meet's end

Lincoln was so far ahead they didn't even bother to rerun the race,
And so we ran the relay, lost, and everyone went home—
Leaving me wistful and amused and brooding on the memory
Of my moment in what was now a slowly setting sun.

There's a story that I read my freshman year in college
Called "The Eighty Yard Run," by Irwin Shaw. It's about a football
    player
Who makes a perfect run one afternoon and feels a heightened sense of
Possibility and life: the warmth of flannel on his skin, the three cold
    drinks of water,

The first kiss of the woman who is going to be his wife. All lies before
    him,
Only he never measures up: gradually at first, and then more steeply,
It's a long decline from there, until he finds himself years later on that
Football field again, a traveling salesman selling cut-rate suits.

I'm not immune to sentimental cautionary tales: the opening door
That turns out to have long been shut; the promissory moment,
Savored at the time, with which the present only pales by comparison,
That tinctures what comes later with regret. I'm safe from that—

Track wasn't everything, but even minor triumphs
Take on mythical proportions in our lives. Yet since *my* heightened
    moment
Was a bogus one, I can't look back on it with disappointment
At the way my life has gone since then. Perhaps all public victories

Are in some sense undeserved, constructed out of luck
Or friends or how you happened to feel that day. But mine took off its
    mask
Almost as soon as it was over, long before it had the chance
To seem to settle into fact. I'm human though: sometimes I like to

Fantasize that it had all been true, or had been *taken* to be true—
The first of an unbroken string of triumphs stretching through to
    college,

8

Real life, and right down to today. I ran that race in 1962,
The year *The Man Who Shot Liberty Valance* was released,

A film about a man whose whole career was built upon a lie.
James Stewart thinks he killed—and everyone *believes* he killed—
Lee Marvin, the eponymous bad guy, although he never actually killed
    anyone at all:
John Wayne had shadowed him and fired the fatal shot,

Yet governor, senator, ambassador and senator again
All followed on his reputation. He tries at last to set the record
    straight
—The movie's mostly one long flashback of what happened—
But the editor to whom he tells the real story throws away his notes:

"When the legend becomes fact," he orders, "print the legend,"
As the music soars and draws the veil upon the myth of the Old West.
Print the legend: I'd like to think that's what *my* story was,
Since for a moment everyone believed that it was true—

But then it wasn't anymore. Yet it's my pleasure to pretend
It could have been: when Willis Bouchey at the end affirms the fairy
    tale
With "Nothing's too good for the man who shot Liberty Valance,"
I hear in my imagination "who beat Vernus Ragsdale."

Susan Stewart

Dialogue in San Clemente

Soul

When the world was too hot to touch, you carried
me into the crypt where the bulls had been slain,
a labyrinth of bricks, woven down
below the human god.

Body

There was my match in limbo, circled
by nowhere's cloud. That was the August,
the end, of the moon's long draw
and tumult—the force of my own last hold
over you, and your first flight and dream.

Soul

Limbo was a fresco, and blameless.
You stuck me fast to the keyhole,
a speck in the eye, a splinter, this
clenching cramp, a limp, a blister—all
in all, sore and fester. Deaf
to regret, you always chide me.

Body

In truth, I rarely give you a thought;
I'm really not a drape around

a promise. You can try to fill me
with your flitting light, but I'm
water all the way through—
your shoreline at your service,
the cat's last sack, a ruin.

Soul

Pity has a swerve when it's real.
All you can think of is the climate
of your thinking and that's not
thinking at all. Without you,
I'd be raw in the weather—
my thanks for that, I'm not complaining.

Body

If I could wander as you do,
if I could uproot and fly,
a sewer could serve as a wishing
well, a mine yield stars
that shield a mine.

Soul

Little wonder there's little wonder
then. I'll wait here under
the stairs. By day I'll sweep
them up and down, by night
I'll weep beneath them.

Body

No voice, no light, are we thrown to the beasts—
or is it that they once were thrown
to us? I climbed the same stairs
and came back down, and what I saw
remains, my firmament.

Soul

What knowledge, what knowing, what knowledge—
what knowing then bars us from
what fear? I was glad the bright day
when we met. Will I be twice
as glad in darkness when we're parted?

Three Geese

snow thaw
    red haze
dusk-bent harvest
the wild geese
    vying in
one line wavering
    then fast down
close and
    closer
        thwacking
            air
    above the creek bed
one splash
    splash of
        another
            splash,
                and
                then another
        glide and
gliding, three
    circles
        rippling out
in sequence
    swelling and receding
on the
    swirling
        dark
        water, coursing
        fast through sliding
            silts of snow
      March now
    thaw
    and glow silent
    out of
last light
red haze, promise
    over maples, oaks, and poplars

Day-lily

Unrecognizable now, a mash
of airy sweet—
ness stuck
to itself, an orange smear
dank across
the book where it rests.
At dusk you
had brought it from
the ditch bank
to the desk—
three waves, three
sepals, each dashed
maroon above
the stem, all
in all, thick
as cloth.
The stamens
sprung up, antennae:
June dusk,
dusk for
listening.
Now at dawn
an ant, determined
undertaker,
makes his way
like a cursor,
diagon-
ally over
the page,
the lily
of the day
is fairer
far in May,
fairer far
in May,
the lily of the day.

Donna Seaman

A Conversation with Stuart Dybek

Stuart Dybek is a poet and a short story writer whose work is inspired and shaped by his memories of growing up in Chicago, and by his love for music. Over the course of writing his five books—each exquisitely crafted, indelibly lyrical, arrestingly urban and down-to-earth, devilishly funny, and ravishingly erotic—Dybek has conjured a mythic city of brick and asphalt, desire and dreams. Dybek's Chicago is a checkerboard of ethnically defined neighborhoods in which human life in all its striving, absurdity, and beauty dominates, while nature, in all its determined wildness and glory, persists in the city's weedy seams and in the vastness of Lake Michigan.

Dybek's stereoscopic vision of the city's steely reality and penchant for risk-all romance underlies his two poetry collections, *Brass Knuckles* (1979) and *Streets in Their Own Ink* (2004), and his three works of fiction, *Childhood and Other Neighborhoods* (1980), *The Coast of Chicago* (1990), and *I Sailed with Magellan* (2003). Dybek's linked stories and poetry are as essential to understanding life in Chicago as works by Theodore Dreiser, Nelson Algren, James Farrell, Gwendolyn Brooks, Saul Bellow, and Leon Forrest, and yet Dybek transcends his earthy precincts, spiriting readers away to more mysterious, archetypal, and profound realms. Not only does Dybek masterfully evoke the intricate, singing web of urban life, he also elucidates the complex symbiotic relationship between people and place in painterly descriptions of city streets, morning glory-wreathed chain-linked fences, the chimerical great lake, and the white-cap-raising and trash-spinning wind, thus elucidating our ability to discern and be transformed by beauty, however unlikely its manifestations and harsh its settings.

Dybek's work has appeared in such distinguished venues as *The New Yorker*, the *Atlantic Monthly*, *Harper's*, *Poetry*, the *Paris Review*, and *Tri-Quarterly*, and he has been the recipient of many awards including a Whiting Writers' Award, a Pushcart Prize, several O. Henry Prizes, and a PEN/Bernard Malamud Prize. A professor of English at Western Michigan University, Dybek was in his hometown in late May 2004 when we spoke, making one of many appearances associated with the selection of *The Coast of Chicago* for One Book, One Chicago, a citywide reading and discussion program sponsored by the Chicago Public Library.

DONNA SEAMAN: Your stories are so poetic. The imagery and metaphors are so rich, and so fully integrated into character and story, I'm curious as to what form you started writing first, poetry or fiction.

STUART DYBEK: They were always simultaneous, and continue to be written in tandem, so to speak. I kind of "collect" in poetry. Writers often keep little journals, and I call mine "A Great Thoughts Notebook," with tongue firmly planted in cheek. In there a lot of stuff gets recorded in a sloppy verse line, and imagery is emphasized. Then I loot that stuff for both stories and poems.

DS: In talking about the early stages of writing when you aren't sure what form a piece is going to take, you've referred pieces-in-progress as "unidentified written objects."

SD: Yes. It very seldom happens that a piece starts out as fiction and ends up as a poem, but it has happened to me frequently that a piece starts out as a poem and ends up as a story. Ray Carver wrote both fiction and poetry. People, most of whom much preferred his fiction, used to say that he didn't think he could write fiction if he didn't write poetry, no matter what anyone else thought about his poems, which, I hasten to add, I do like.

DS: There's an intriguing tension in your stories between what we call reality, or observable life, and other dimensions of being. And I think you bridge the divide between the tangible world and the unconscious, or the hidden world, with images. *I Sailed with Magellan*, for instance, is brimming with images of water, birds, and flowers. Is this is a conscious artistic choice? A deliberate strategy?

SD: I don't think it started out consciously. And to this day, I remain a big believer in taking advantage of accidents—which are often an indication of what your un-reflected-upon-instincts are—but without drawing it out too much. What happened, for instance, in my first book of stories was that I had written a bunch of stories and they didn't seem to have much coherence. I really hadn't even thought of them as a book. Then a local library asked me to do a talk, and they asked me to give them a title for the talk. And while I was happy to do the talk, I hated the notion of giving it a title. I always have a hard time coming up with something snappy. So I worried about that excessively, and somewhere along the line I came up with *Childhood and Other Neighborhoods*.

Initially I was just proud of myself for having succeeded in coming up with a title for my talk, but later on I became kind of fond of it. Then I realized that it could be a title for a collection of stories. So that was kind of an accident. The second accident that I wanted to talk about in relationship to your question was how, once I had this title, it made me realize that out of the stories I had, I could sort out neighborhood stories, which also meant Chicago stories, because I had several stories I had written that didn't have a darn thing to do with Chicago. So all these many years later people kindly rank me in the Chicago Tradition, but it was only an accident that I decided to gather Chicago stories around this title.

The other problem I had at that time was that a bunch of my stories were what you might call realistic and several were unrealistic, and I had never thought about putting them together. But when I looked at what I had, now that I was going to do Chicago stories for the first book, I realized that I had almost equal amounts of each, and that by just completing the design and writing a couple more "unrealistic stories" I could have a sequence: an unrealistic, a realistic, an unrealistic, a realistic. So there never was an overarching strategy, a conscious decision. Instead there was this feeling that you're way into what might cohere as a book. But once that I did that, it made me aware of the whole notion of counterpoint in writing. I was very aware of how important counterpoint is in music, but it never really occurred to me before that it was a tremendously important mechanism that writers of all kinds use in order to create compression and resonance. That when you take two things that are unlike and you put them side by side, a current jumps between them, as in positive and negative, and that this current is often what the reader supplies where there is silence. So the reader is participating in bringing these two things together, and what's happening is that stuff is getting said that you haven't had to write in language.

You're able to say it by just the arrangement of two images, or two stories, or two whatever.

So I became very conscious of the notion of counterpoint, so much so that when I was working on my next book I was looking for another kind of counterpoint. This time I had written all of these short-shorts, these prose-poem-like stories. So the counterpoint in *The Coast of Chicago* became the counterpoint between the little vignettes and the longer stories.

DS: Music is a key element in your work. Not only is your writing musical, but music also plays a part in your characters' lives, and music is part of the cityscape in which they move.

SD: Yes, it's become a real subject for me, and an unavoidable one because of the role music plays in my own life. In my personal life aside from writing, music has an almost religious aspect to it. So it sneaks in and bleeds into the writing the way a person's religion might. Music is transformational, transcendent. A lot of what we ascribe to religious experience any number of people find in music, and so as subject matter in a story it often signals that there will be some transcendent moment, or at least a reach for a transcendent moment.

DS: A profound sense of place is also key to your work. You grew up in Chicago, and you're considered a Chicago writer, part, as you say, of the Chicago Tradition, which includes Theodore Dreiser, Nelson Algren, James Farrell, and Saul Bellow, a literature known for its gritty realism and focus on the underdog. Yet if you look closely at Chicago literature, you do find poetic prose, highly imaginative interpretations, and surrealist, or magical, or otherworldly passages. You detect the writer's awareness of the fact that this pragmatic city is actually a land of fantasies and dreams. I wonder if you perceive of this aspect of Chicago literature, and if you feel that Chicago-based literature has changed over the years.

SD: My perception of it now is certainly different than what my perception was when I was a younger guy at any earlier point in my own writing, when I was still in a kind of apprenticeship. My perception then was that the Chicago Tradition was, in fact, a realistic tradition. I could see where Algren tried to make departures, and certainly Bellow was capable of tremendous lyrical flights. I mean, he's a spectacular stylist and he can write any way he wants. But the tradition itself seemed to be pretty much linked to social realism and that was something I admired it for. I never ever sat down and thought of myself as a "Chicago writer" by the way. I was just trying to write stories. But the stories I wrote initially were imitative in that they were realistic stories, and I found it very hard to have what seemed to me to be an individual voice writing in that totally realistic mode. I had a nagging feeling about this lack of distinctive voice, but I didn't know how to get it. Finally, what happened was yet another accident. I ended up writing a story I hadn't sat down to write, and it had to do with music.

I've told this antidote before, so I feel a little sheepish about repeating it, but I always write to music, and I always have. It's a way of heightening concentration and "getting in the mood." When I first started doing it I listened mostly to jazz, which was the first music that I really truly fell in love with. But by this point in my early twenties I was writing to anything that interested me, and what was interesting to me at the moment was Eastern European composers, Bartok and Kodály in particular. I absolutely love cello. So I was listening to their cello stuff, and I had taken on a loan from the library a very beat-up LP record of Janos Starker playing Zoltan Kodály's "Suite for Unaccompanied Cello," which still amazes me to this day. And under the spell of that music, I wrote a kind of unrealistic Chicago story. At that point the only writer I knew who even nodded in that direction was Bernard Malamud. So that was a little personal breakthrough for me.

At this point, speaking now in the present, sure, I don't think that Chicago writing can any longer, or in any sense, be strictly identified as coming from social realism. There are just so many independent voices of different ethnic and racial backgrounds, and a lot of them bring the folkways of the culture that their parents or grandparents lived in into their work, and all of that has enriched the palette.

DS: I agree, and yet so much of Chicago literature is rooted in the city itself. The neighborhood is a theme of Chicago life that most contemporary writers continue to be inspired by, from John McNally and Joe Meno writing about the far South Side to Sandra Cisneros writing about Mango Street, Ana Castillo writing fiction about neighborhood gentrification, and Joseph Epstein and Adam Langer writing about Rogers Park. The neighborhood is a crucible of the self, even as young protagonists dream about discovering the wider world, which is often associated with Lake Michigan. You write about the lake and other aspects of nature so evocatively, which reminds me of a line in a story titled "Blight" in The Coast of Chicago, a line that I think can serve both as your credo as a writer and as a key to your questing characters. Deejo, the guy with the car, tells his friends, "I dig beauty." This turns into a big joke, but it truly is a reason for living, and your characters often find and treasure beauty in the most unbeautiful of circumstances.

SD: I think that's really accurate. I still feel that, even though we live in this postmodern world, art in general, certainly literature in particular, can be beautiful without being ornamental. So as a writer it's often a goal to try and risk writing something beautiful. In the stories themselves, imagination often becomes a survival skill for characters in a world of sometimes severe limitations due to class. One of the reasons that Chicago neighborhoods are interesting is that they are paradoxical. There is an enormous amount of richness in this little unit called neighborhood, but at the same time there are dangerous limitations inherent in it as well. So how does one enjoy the richness and make that part of life without also suffering the limitations. For many of the characters, and as you said, a lot of them are young, imagination helps them survive, and it's imagination that also leads them to a perception of beauty.

DS: And this perception of beauty provides an unexpected portal into other realms.

SD: That's right.

DS: In *I Sailed with Magellan*, Perry, the main character, loves what he calls the "unsanitary canal." It's actually a harshly industrial spot, but because he's an imaginative guy, he transforms what's in front of him into a place of strange and haunting beauty. Of course this vision is difficult to share, which makes him feel like quite the misfit.

SD: Yes. I think that's true. In the earlier story you mentioned, "Blight," one of the things that happens is that the neighborhood has been made an official blight area, but in all different ways the story tries to demonstrate the notion of beauty as being in the eye of the beholder. Well, I suppose I've just reduced my story to a cliché, but what the heck. I wrote it, I guess I can destroy it, too. So to continue, one element of that is the ecstatic. These kids are always looking for the ecstatic moment. And, in fact, when Bijou utters that line, "I dig beauty," a remark that he then gets maligned for for the rest of his days, he utters it in a total ecstatic moment, when he's just carried away. Then there's a story in *I Sailed with Magellan* called "Orchids," in which one of the ways the guys make fun of each other is to keep telling each other, "You're getting carried away," or "Don't get carried away." But, of course, what they want to be is carried away.

DS: I'm interested in the evolution in your fiction, from *Childhood and Other Neighborhoods* to *The Coast of Chicago* to *I Sailed with Magellan*.

SD: In the first book, *Childhood and Other Neighborhoods*, the kind of stories that were providing the nonrealistic side of what I talked about earlier as counterpoint, are, to my mind, essentially grotesque. Grotesque is frequently identified by the merging of humanity with something else, often the beast. And there's actually a story in there called *Visions of Budhardin*, in which a guy is merged with a papier-mâché elephant. So while I also wanted to imply counterpoint in the next book, I didn't want to repeat the grotesque-realistic counterpoint. And what was kind of interesting to me at that time goes back to your earlier question about poetry. I kept asking myself what the difference is between verse and poetry. And one of the things that occurred to me is that when people ask me about "poetic fiction," a lot of the time what they are really talking about is the fact that something might happen in a story that would earn for you, or trigger for you, a lyrical moment. And in order to express that lyrical, or even ecstatic, moment, you change modes. You go from the realistic mode to the lyrical mode. Without going too much farther on that, I will just quickly say that in our society we mainly associate poetry with a lyrical mode. That is, it is associative, it isn't cause-and-effect the way a story is. If you put a story in a chronological line and you say first this happened and then this happened, there is an implicitness in that, a cause and effect. Whereas if you go from the image of rain to the image of a lake, because of the association of water, you're thinking in an associative way, as you do in dreams. And lyrical time is different from narrative time.

So as soon as I began thinking along those lines and realized there were different modes a writer could write in—even though I hadn't articulated this quite clearly to myself—I realized that I wanted the counterpoint to the realism in *The Coast of Chicago* not to be grotesque but to be lyrical. And so what happens in that book is that there is all kinds of different versions of lyricism. "Chopin in Winter" has one kind of lyricism, and some of little interconnected vignettes, like "Lights," have a prose poem-like lyricism, and "Pet Milk" has got a very romantic lyricism. One of the things you do in a lyrical mode, or one way you can use a lyrical mode, is to eroticize the city. And that book has various versions in which the city itself is eroticized, whether it's a kiss going across the city in "Nighthawks," or on the El train in "Pet Milk." The city is constantly being eroticized there.

The basic reflex was similar in *I Sailed with Magellan*. I wanted to continue to explore writing about this city, and I wanted to continue to explore writing about this neighborhood, but I didn't want to continue repeating these kinds of formulas. I don't want to repeat the lyrical-realistic counterpoint anymore than I wanted to repeat the grotesque-realistic contrast. So I was looking for sameness and yet difference. I also wanted to try to write a book that was more unified in conventional ways because, for me, there were underlying unities in those first two books. I mean, unities were present in the kinds of choices I made with the first two books as to what to include and what to exclude. And once I had decided what to include, what I then needed to write in order to complete it felt, on a gut level, like some kind of design. Now, I didn't necessarily expect that the reader would tease that out, but I did hope that the reader would feel that there was a coherence.

In *Magellan*, I really wanted the reader to be a little bit more aware of what the coherences were. So how could you not be aware of the fact that a character named Perry Katzek appears in every story, or that each story has within it a song? So there were what I would call conventional unities in it, unities that approach a form that is sometimes called a novel-in-stories. Some critics debate exactly what a novel-in-stories is, but I have no huge desire to join in that debate. And I really did still want some interplay between the real and the non-real. So the last story I wrote for the book was "Breasts" because I really wanted to add that one underlying counterpoint moment.

DS: Your writing is full of music, but it's also gorgeously visual, and I picture each of the books you've just discussed as works of art, with the first being a collage in which you've juxtaposed many images and styles. *The Coast of Chicago* is more patterned, fit and jointed together like an inlaid floor rather than pasted together. And *I Sailed with Magellan* is a radiant tapestry, each tale woven seamlessly into a greater whole.

SD: One thing that I mention to students when I teach, and which I've always enjoyed saying for the sake of pure mystification, is that I find literature to be a really odd art form. And that I live in a state of total envy toward all the other arts. I would give anything to paint or to play a musical instrument. It's the lack of the sensual. All the other arts come right through the senses. We see a painting with our eyes, but how do we read? Where does that all take place? It doesn't take place on a piece of paper or a computer screen. The medium, language, is the most abstract of all the mediums. And that mystery extends to the point at which if I read a story by Dickens or Eudora Welty I say, Eudora Welty told me this story or Dickens told me this story, but who tells the writer? In other words, even though I could tell you that "Breasts" includes a few factual incidents, the story itself is not a recounting of those factual incidents. It's just so mysterious how stories piece themselves together.

I was in a hotel room in New York City just after 9/11. I had gone to New York to do a benefit. There were benefits all over the place at that point, and it was just a few days after and the city reeked of death. The ruins were still smoldering and smoking, and I don't know, maybe it was under the spell of all that violence, but suddenly, just totally unbidden, the scene in "Breasts" in which Joey Ditto kills Johnny Sovereign just came out of nowhere into my mind. I wrote feverishly on hotel stationery.

The same thing happened with the wrestler in that story. I was sitting on a curb with a great photographer, Paul D'Amato.

DS: One of his photographs is on the cover of I Sailed with Magellan.

SD: Yes, he did the cover. I think he's brilliant, a genius. So Paul and I had gone down to a summer fair in Pilsen, where I grew up. Paul had spent seven years taking pictures of that neighborhood. We were hanging out together. It's always fun to hang out with Paul. I just loved watching him take photos. I was sitting on the curb eating a taco, and Paul was right up on the action. They had erected a wrestling ring on 19th Street right under the El by St. Ann's church and I was watching these two guys with masks wrestle. And I was watching Paul photograph them, and suddenly one of the guys got tossed out of the ring right on top of Paul. For a moment I was afraid he broke Paul's neck, then the next moment I was thinking, "Well, Paul still has his neck intact, how's his camera?" But Paul is a tough guy. He picked himself up and laughed and dusted himself off. At that moment I suddenly knew that there had to be a wrestler in the story "Breasts," which didn't even have a title and wasn't even written. I'm talking about process now, not writing, and I'm always a little suspicious when the conversation turns to process because it's so very different than actually creating a thing. It always take place in

Dreamsville. You can talk about process, and then the actual thing never gets written, so what good is it?

DS: But it's essential. Lots of people have the chops. Lots of people can make sentences, but they don't have the stories to tell. They don't have the images.

SD: It was just so oddly mysterious. I guess I'm back talking about accidents. Why would that come into your mind and why would you know it was for a story that you hadn't even written yet?

DS: I think you're talking about the artist's profound receptiveness to the world, their openness. I think of it as an aesthetic readiness.

To go back to the abstraction of writing, I understand what you're saying about writing's lack of sensuousness, but writing is a physical practice. You are making things out of words. You do use your hands and your eyes to build words out of letters, sentences out of words, pages out of sentences. To my mind, writing encompasses every creative act. It does all that painting can do and all that music can do, and more. Language is the universal medium. Almost all of us have language, almost everyone can get hold of a book, or an audio-book, a pencil and a piece of paper. You can read and write anywhere with the minimum of equipment. And literature's reach is infinite, its subjects and points of view limitless.

SD: Well, one of the things I've tried to do to emulate the other art forms, which I'm admitting to envying, is that I've tried to become very aware of the craft of writing. Because what I really want is a stained up old box of oil paints, and things like color wheels. When I first got interested in all this, one of my best friends was a painter. He was going to the Art Institute of Chicago, and I envied the way he bought himself a pair of real soft suede pants to impress girls. But that wasn't enough. He then had to take these pants that he had just paid some obscenely expensive price for, money he couldn't afford, and he had to spatter them with his paints so that he looked like an artist. What am I going to do, walk around with a piece of paper?

DS: Ink stains.

SD: They'll just think you're an accountant or something.

DS: You're explaining something that mystified me in the story titled "Nighthawks," in which the library becomes some sort of miserable hell and the art museum is heaven.

SD: There it is. That's it. So one of the things I've done is try to pretend that all these things like metaphors and scenic construction and counterpoint and blah, blah, blah are like easels and canvases and canvas stretchers and gesso. Because I do perceive abstraction in language and concreteness and sensuality in all the other art forms, I've been attracted to writers who swim upstream against abstraction. That is, writers who set out to make an abstract medium as essential as they can. And sometimes they do it and play both sides of the fence, and those are often my favorite writers. The writer who comes immediately to mind would be somebody like Eugenio Montale, the Italian poet, and Yeats, another poet. Writers like that really intrigue me. In the great Yeats poem, "Sailing to Byzantium," he talks about "hammered gold and gold enameling." By the time you finish that poem it feels like a poem written not of words but of gold. So as an unreachable goal for me—the attempt to turn a story into music, which of course you can never do, or to turn it into a sensually visual object, which of course you can never do, leads to the emphasis of imagery and rhythms and so forth. Not that those things aren't already a part of writing. Of course they are, but by energizing them and keeping your mind on them, one draws on one's love and emulation of other art forms. And I think it's really important. A lot of times writers are asked, Who are your influences? Who are you reading? The question needs to be expanded to, Who are you looking at? Who are you listening to? Whose performances are you going to see?

Wang Xiaobo

Translated from the Chinese by Hongling Zhang and Jason Sommer

2015

1

I've wanted to be an artist since I was a little kid. An artist wears a corduroy jacket, leaves his hair long, and squats down by the wall of a police station—Lijiakou police station had a bare brick wall, deep gray in color; my young uncle often squatted by it, blowing air into his cheeks until they puffed up. Sometimes, the corduroy jacket he wore would puff up too, like the sheepskin rafts ferrying across the Yellow River. Then he would look fatter than usual. This image left me with the impression that artists were something like sacks. The only difference between the two is that when you get tangled up with a sack, you have to move it away with your hands; when you stumble over an artist, you kick him and he will move off by himself. In my memory, positioned at the base of a gray and shining vertical plane (that's the wall) is a brown ball (brown was the color of the corduroy jacket)—that was my young uncle exactly.

I could find my young uncle at the police station. The station had a courtyard circled by a wall of whitewashed gray bricks. A red light hung in the doorway, which would only be lit after dark. Once the people there saw me, they would shout, "Ah, the great painter's nephew is here!" It felt like home. At noon, the policemen cooked noodles in the reception room by the door. The smell of the noodle soup made me feel doubly warm. I could also find my young uncle in a nearby coffee shop called the "Great Earth." The inside was always pitch-black since the electricity wasn't on, but candles filled the air with the choking smell of paraffin wax. Looking at people in the coffee shop, you could only see the lower part of their face, and these faces were all dark red, like barbecued baby pigs. He often did business with people there, and also often got arrested there on a charge of selling paintings without a permit. My young uncle often committed this kind of error, because he was a painter but didn't have the mandatory painter's permit. After he got arrested, somebody had to bail him out. There was a block of shops near the police station, and most of them, built in the fifties of last century, were houses with steep tile roofs. Under the two rows of small gingko trees on the sidewalk, people built fires to barbecue lamb tips on spits, which burned the leaves yellow and made it an autumn scene year round; later all the trees died. The place he lived wasn't far from there, a one-bedroom apartment in a tall building—the building had a square box-headed look, fairly ugly with trash-strewn hallways. Whenever you went to see him, he was never home, though that wasn't always true.

My uncle was a painter without a permit, but what made him different from others was that he was so industrious: sometimes he painted, sometimes he sold his paintings, and therefore at other times he squatted at the police station. When he painted, he would lock the door and put on soundproof earphones, so that he couldn't hear if someone knocked on his door, and he wouldn't pick up the phone either. Alone, he faced his easel like a man in a trance. Since he lived on the fourteenth floor, nobody could lean over to the window to peek inside, so nobody had ever seen him paint except a burglar. The burglar, climbing into his apartment from a balcony on the thirteenth floor, had planned on stealing something. But after he walked into my uncle's living room and got a glimpse of his painting, he was shocked. He walked over, tapped him and said, Hey, buddy, what the hell are you up to? My uncle had gone into his painting trance, so he snarled, Don't bother me. I'm painting. The burglar crossed to the other side of the room, squatted down and watched him for a while. Then he couldn't help walking back over to my uncle, lifting up his left earphone and saying, Hey, you can't paint like that! My uncle, fierce as a wolf, shoved him to the floor and went on with his painting. The guy squatted on the floor for a long time, waiting to discuss painting issues with my uncle, but he never got the chance. Finally he opened the front door and walked out, taking my uncle's camcorder and several thousand yuan along with him. However, he left a note with a solemn warning: if you keep painting like this, you'll commit errors. Though he stole things himself, he couldn't stand

closet to cupboard. If he came across a lot of cash, he would write a letter of accusation to the public prosecutor's office, reporting the victim
on suspicion of embezzlement; if he came across very little money, he
would send a letter of commendation to the victim's work unit, praising
the person's integrity. He also prepared many mottoes and philosophical
adages on life: you take something from the house—you leave something
for the house. If the family had videotapes, he would check them one by
one, confiscating the obscene ones so that the owner wouldn't be cor-
rupted. Some families had too many videotapes, but he would still watch
them one by one; as a result, the owner would come home and catch
him. From the police station to the neighborhood committee, everybody believed he was a good burglar and didn't want to send him to
prison. But unfortunately he stole too much. Finally they had to execute
him, which made the policemen in the station and the old women in
the neighborhood committee all weep for him. Before the execution,
the burglar made a will, donating his body to the hospital. One of my
classmates attended medical school there, often seeing him in the
formaldehyde trough. The guy has a big tool, my friend said. He even
looks handsome in the formaldehyde trough. No one can tell that he
used to be a burglar. He took a bullet in the back of his head, but you
couldn't tell if his body wasn't turned over. Every time they had
anatomy class, the girls would fight over him.

My uncle's crime was just a misdemeanor, but it really got on people's
nerves. This was because his paintings, with their riot of color, made no
sense to anyone, and no one could tell what his paintings were about.
Once, I saw a policeman hold up a painting and bawl at him sternly,
Young fellow—Stand up and tell me—what is this? If you can tell me
what this means, I'll squat there instead of you! My uncle turned and
looked at his own work, then squatted down again, I don't know what
it is either. I'd better do my own squatting. In my opinion, he'd painted
something that resembled either a huge whirlpool, or a squirrel's tail. Of
course, if a squirrel grew a tail like that, it would be a real freak. Because
of paintings of this sort, the permit he used to have was revoked. Before
revoking his permit, the department concerned tried their best to do him
a favor by printing out a list that read as follows: Work 1, "Sea Horse";
Work 2, "Kangaroo"; Work 3, "Snail"; and so on. The words in quota-
tions were the titles that the leaders supplied for the paintings. They believed that people could understand them once the titles were given. Of
course, the sea horse, kangaroo, and snail in the paintings all looked

strange, like they were crazy. As long as my uncle agreed to use these titles, they would let him keep his permit. But my uncle refused to use the titles; he said he didn't paint sea horses and kangaroos. The leaders said, It's OK not to paint sea horses or kangaroos, but you have to paint something. It would have been better if my uncle hadn't breathed a word, but he argued with them, calling them silly cunts. That was why he got kicked out of the painters' union.

As you know, I'm a professional writer. Once I wrote a story about my elder uncle, saying that he was a novelist and a mathematician who had all kinds of fantastic experiences. That story got me into trouble. Somebody checked my census register and discovered that I had only one uncle. This uncle had attended elementary school at seven and middle school at thirteen, graduated from the oil painting department of an art school, and now was an idler with no profession. They also checked his grades from elementary school through middle school; the best grade he got in math was a "C." If he had become a mathematician, it would have definitely stained the reputation of our country's mathematical circles. For that reason, the leader had a talk with me, assigning me a plot along the following lines: when my uncles were born, they were twins. Because my grandparents were poor and couldn't afford raising them, the older one was sent to another family. This older one had a talent for math, and could make up stories and write, too, very different from my young uncle. So he and my young uncle had to be twins from different eggs. The plot also offered an explanation for this: my deceased grandmother was a native of Laixi in Shandong province, where the water has a special ingredient that makes women produce lots of eggs. So, just because my grandmother was from Laixi, she was turned into a female yellow croaker fish. The leader intended to make me revise the story according to his plot, but I refused to do it—my grandmother raised me and I have deep feelings for her. And I also believed that as a writer I could have as many uncles as I wanted. It was nobody else's business. Therefore, I committed an error, and my writing permit was revoked—I've written about this in another story, and I don't want to get into it again.

At the time I'd go to pick up my young uncle, my mother was still living. My uncle had this divergent strabismus problem; both of his eyes looked outward at the same time, but they were a little better than a carp's. My mother's eyes had the same sort of problem. Looking at her reflection in the mirror, my mother thought herself beautiful in every way except her eyes. She blamed this on my young uncle. Since she was born before my young uncle, it was hard to say who was to blame. She was a schoolteacher, and the subject she taught didn't have much to do with art. However, as my young uncle's sister, she thought she ought to understand him better. One day, she told my uncle, Let's see some of your paintings. But my uncle said, Forget it. Even if you see them, you wouldn't be able to understand. My mother particularly hated when someone said there were things in the world she couldn't understand. So she flung her plate across the table and said, Fine, I won't look at them even if you beg me. You'd better be careful. Don't ask me to bail you out when you get into trouble again. My young uncle stayed silent for a while, then walked out of our house and never came back. It had been my mother's responsibility to pick up my uncle from the police station, and afterwards, she refused to do her duty. But my uncle still got into trouble, as always. When he got into trouble, he would be put in the police station, and, like our mail in the post office, pick up had to be on time, otherwise we would have to pay a late fee. So I had no choice but to go there.

I have longed for love since childhood. My first sweetheart was my young uncle. Even today, I still feel embarrassed about this. My uncle was very attractive when he was young; he had dark, shiny, thick hair and smooth, taut skin; his body was bony but muscular; when he stood naked, he looked like a thoroughbred, with his broad shoulders and small hips; his penis was big but firm—I didn't really know about this last matter since I'm a man, and I'm not gay. So you should check with my young aunt.

I had skinny arms and legs when I was little; my knees could bend backward, so could my elbows; I had a pointy mouth and a monkey's hollow cheeks, and what's more, I still had my foreskin, although it was hidden in my underwear, out of view. One day I picked up my young uncle from the police station. It was a hot day, and we were both sweating like pigs. He stood by the road, trying to flag down a cab. He said he was going to take me swimming, which made me so happy I started to daydream. Just then, I got a kick at the back of my knees. Stand straight, my young uncle said. That meant my knees were bending and I was getting shorter. They tell me that when I bent my knees, I looked almost three inches shorter. After a while, I got another kick, which meant I was shrinking again. I didn't understand why it mattered to him that I got shorter, so I stared at him. My young uncle said ferociously, You look really obnoxious that way! I did love my uncle, but the bastard was not nice to me. That really hurt my feelings.

My uncle had divergent strabismus. I suppose in his eyes the world must look like a wide-screen movie, which should have helped his career; from the scientific perspective, if two eyes are far apart, their depth perception should be more acute, and they have greater precision in gauging distance. In the early twentieth century, before laser and range radar were invented, people had already used this principle in measuring distance; they installed two camera lenses on the ends of a pole, about ten yards in length. Since a human being's eyeballs can't be that far apart, the improvement to vision by inducing divergent strabismus would be limited.

After a while, a cab came to take my young uncle and me to Yuyuan Lake. The lake water gave off a fishy smell that came from the mud. My young uncle said that every winter several human skeletons would be found in the mud after the water was drained. It made me feel that below my body, on the lake bottom, corpses were swelling like sponges, and then dissolving into the dark-green water. For that reason, I was afraid to put my head under water. Having scared me sufficiently, my young uncle swam off and began eyeing the figures of the girls on the shore. From what I saw, the girls' bodies were average; the ones with really first-rate bodies didn't come to the lake. No matter how unhappy I was, I finally got the chance to see my young uncle's body. He did have a big tool. After he got out of the water, the top of his penis was water-logged and pale as a mushroom. Later, that pale penis was imprinted on my mind. In my dream at night, my young uncle kissed me. I scrubbed my lips after I woke up—it was a nightmare, of course. I believed that pale penis was a kind of threat to the world. When my young uncle got out of the water, his lips had turned dark purple and his eyes were blood-shot. He threw me a ten-yuan bill, telling me to take a taxi back on my own, and then staggered away himself. I pocketed the money and carefully followed him, walking towards the Great Earth coffee shop, towards danger. Because I loved my uncle, I couldn't let him take the risk alone.

My uncle often went to the Great Earth coffee shop, and so did I. Built in the mid-twentieth century, it was a tile house with a steep tile roof and barred wooden windows on three sides. People said it used to be a grocery store. After it was turned into a coffee shop, red curtains with black linings were hung on all the windows. That was why the room was so dark; if you fell asleep inside, you woke not knowing whether it was day or night outside. Only when you sat in a booth by the wall and lifted the curtain, could you see the light outside, as well as the dust covering the windowsill. On every table a cheap white candle burned, with dark smoke curling up and spreading the bitter smell of paraffin wax. If you stayed too long, your nostrils would have a layer of black stuff. But, if you came to a table lit with a yellow candle that had no smoke and no smell, that was my uncle's—like me he couldn't stand the smoke of the paraffin wax, so he always brought his own candles. People said he made these candles himself, blending them with beeswax. He always ordered a cup of coffee, but never drank it. One of the waitresses knew him very well and even had a crush on him. Every time he came, she would give him the real brewed Brazilian coffee, but only charge him for the instant kind. Still my uncle didn't drink it. She was very sad and cried in the dark.

Hoping to see for myself how my young uncle sold his paintings, I put a lot of effort into tailing him. I crawled on the dark floor of the Great Earth, wearing holes in all my sleeves and pants. When the waitresses came over, with coffee in one hand and a flashlight in the other, I had to crawl out of their way, too. Every now and then, I wasn't fast enough and tripped them. They would drop the trays and scream, Ghost! Then my young uncle would come over to grab me, pointing to the way home and spitting out a single word, "Scram!" I pretended to leave, but would sneak back a moment later and continue dragging myself along the dark floor. In the dark, I could tell there were roaches, rats, and some other animals in the coffee shop; one of them was very fluffy, like a weasel. It bit me and left a bite mark, smaller than a cat's but bigger than a rat's. The bastard's teeth were sharper than an awl. I couldn't help shouting, "Fuck!" So I got caught again. He dragged me all the way out, and then I came back. We would go around like this several times an afternoon, till even I got tired of it.

Finally, the person my uncle had been waiting for came. Stocky and bald, he constantly bowed to my uncle as if apologizing for being late. I thought he was a Japanese, or a Chinese person who had lived in Japan for years. They began talking in whispers, and my uncle even showed him some color photographs. I believed he was hammering out a deal, but I saw neither paintings nor money—the two things I really wanted to see. Otherwise, I couldn't claim that I had seen through the artist's tricks. After they walked out of the coffee shop, I went on tailing them. Unfortunately, my uncle always caught me at that point; he would hide by the door or behind the little street vendor's stand, grab my collar in one motion, and beat me half to death—the guy was very alert. They were about to close the deal, which could be a risky moment for both the people and the booty. That was why they kept checking around. While trailing my young uncle, one had to consider his carp-like eyes. With a wider field of vision than ordinary people, he could see behind him without turning around. But one thing I never figured out: how did the police get him? They must have been more observant than I was.

One day, I ran into that Japanese guy on the street. He wore a striped suit and held a tall woman's arm; the woman wore a green silk cheongsam and had a straight figure and a vigorous way of walking. But her skin seemed rough and a little old-looking, too. I glanced at her face, noticing that the space between her two eyes was very wide. Struck by this, I decided to follow her. She squatted down to fix her high heels, and grabbed me as I passed. Out of her mouth came my young uncle's voice, Shithead, how come you're following me again? Besides the voice, she also gave off my young uncle's special body odor. I'd suspected she was my young uncle from the beginning, and now was completely sure. I said, Why are you doing this? He said, Cut the nonsense! I'm just selling my paintings. If you keep following me, I'll strangle you! As he said this, he squeezed my shoulder hard, his fingers clamping my flesh like two steel hooks. Anyone else would have shouted at the top of his voice, but I could take it. I said, OK, I won't follow you anymore, but you better not get caught dressed like this. After he loosened his grip, I suggested that he put on a pair of sunglasses—his appearance really worried me. Honestly, if he'd brought me along, I could at least have kept an eye out for him. But my young uncle preferred taking his chances on his own rather than getting me involved. If he'd gotten arrested that time, it would not only be illegal trading, but also a case of perversion. I also heard that once my young uncle hung four pieces of cardboard on his body and squatted on the street pretending to be a mailbox; the Japanese guy, dressed as a postman, went to do the deal with him. But I wasn't an eyewitness—a policeman told me. Another time, he pretended to be a high school student, volunteered to sweep the floor at a McDonald's, and hid his paintings in a trashcan; the Japanese disguised himself as a garbage collector to pick up the paintings. These were the times they got caught, which was how I heard. But my young uncle didn't get caught every time; otherwise, he'd have had no income and would've had to live on air.

Once I took a trip to Mount Hundred Flowers, and saw some locals standing by the road inviting sightseers to tour the mountain on their little donkeys. A weird idea flashed through my mind: if my young uncle disguised himself as a donkey and the Japanese were a tourist riding on his back, they could bargain as they toured the mountain. So whenever I saw a donkey, I slapped its butt—I believed if the donkey were my uncle, he would definitely not allow me to spank him. He would stand up like a human being and fight me—the donkeys didn't respond much, so it seemed none of them was my uncle. But the owners were hot to fight me, and said, Hey kid! Where did you get to be so free with your hand? It looked like my uncle hadn't come up with the idea, which was good. I wouldn't like anybody to ride my uncle. I didn't tell them that I was looking for my uncle; they wouldn't have believed me anyway. That was how I toured Mount Hundred Flowers.

For a while I really wanted to open up to my uncle: You don't have to dodge me. I love you. But I never spoke up—I was afraid of his fists. Besides, I also felt these words would be too shocking and unconventional. My young uncle's two eyes were wide-set, and his gaze was sleepy-looking, which fooled people about his reach. Of course, only someone regularly tricked by him would understand this. I often thought I was out of danger, but still he would trip me with one kick. I heard that twentieth-century Kongfu master Bruce Lee was also good at this, but I am not sure whether he had divergent strabismus or not.

Uncle Policeman said that one good thing about my uncle was that he never tried to run away when he got dragnetted. Instead, he would walk towards the flashlight and say: Well, you got me again! They would say: Your young uncle deserves to be called an artist. He's an honorable man, not petty at all. The phrase "dragnet" is a police word, signifying a raid done by a large number of officers. As I understand it, the word came from catching fish with a net in the river. Under the circumstance, fish usually flop around—these are the petty ones. If the fish lie at the bottom of the net without moving at all, then we would call them honorable fish. Unfortunately, most aquatic vertebrates of this kind are petty. That's why they are considered low class. An honorable fish like my uncle would always have some cash on him, which usually came from selling his paintings and would eventually be confiscated by the policemen. If the matter had ended there, it would have been convenient for both sides. But doing things like that would have meant committing errors. The correct procedure was to confiscate my uncle's illegal take first, and then bring him to the police station for education. Since my young uncle was an honorable man, he would go with them without arguing. I always believed if my young uncle had run off then, Uncle Policeman probably wouldn't have chased him—because he had no money on him. My young uncle thought what I said made sense, but still didn't

35

want to run away. He thought of himself as a man with social status, not a little burglar. Running away like that would be beneath him. An honorable man would be taken to the police station and often be badly treated. And a genuine low-down little burglar would feel quite comfortable there, like a fish in water.

Uncle Policeman said even riding a bicycle requires a permit, never mind painting. After hearing this, my uncle said nothing, just puffed up his cheeks and swallowed air. Soon his belly swelled like a balloon. Puffing himself up was his special talent, which had very profound implications. We all know that in the past, when people killed a hog, they always inflated it first, and then used a primitive technique to remove its hair. There is also a saying that a dead hog is not afraid to be scalded by boiling water, which signals stoicism. My uncle puffed himself up in order to show that he was a dead hog, unafraid of boiling water. Afterwards, he squatted by the wall with his belly inflated, waiting for his family member to pick him up. This should have been my mother's job, but she refused to come. So I had no choice. I was a little boy when I crossed the dusty streets of the last century, walking towards the police station to pick up my uncle; I also thought to myself, Hurry up! Or young uncle will explode—it wouldn't look nice if his intestines burst through his belly. Actually, I was worried for no reason: at a certain point of inflation, the pressure inside would be too great and my young uncle would automatically have deflated. Then, with a *puh* sound, all the sheets of paper in the police station would have blown into the air, and with the force of the strong flow, my young uncle's larynx would have emitted the sound of being scraped with a knife. After that, he would have flattened, of course, spreading out on the ground like a fried pancake, making it impossible for the policemen to kick him. They could only stamp on him, and they would have said as they stamped on him: You artists are really low. I'm not just fond of artists; I also like policemen. I always think if either disappeared, art wouldn't exist.

When I was little, we lived near Yuan Ming Garden, where a black market hid in a stand of poplar trees next to the boundary wall. Nearby lay a half-drained pond, with a patch of withered reeds beside it. On summer evenings, the darkness always settled in the woods first because of the lush, dense foliage; in fall, leaves dropped from the trees like heavy rain. To get into the garden required a ticket, but you could save money by jumping over the wall. Packed down by thousands of footsteps, the ground in the woods shone like the surface of porcelain; white cloths with words written in red on them were strung between the trees as signs. The market had the feel of a country village, with peasant-types selling phony antiques there. But if you had a good eye, you could buy the real stuff, just dug out of graves—though I began to feel uneasy about the selling of dead people's stuff. Among these fakers, a few people wore corduroy jackets and sat on folding stools, staring blankly at their own paintings that no one bothered to ask about from morning to evening. That was why they had a melancholy look. People passed by and threw them coins. They didn't move, or thank the passersby. But a few minutes later, the coins disappeared. For a while, I went there frequently to see those people; I liked that sort of mood, believing that the people sitting there with blank looks were all great painters like Van Gogh—this type of loneliness and melancholy I envied to the point of craziness. I wished my uncle could sit with them, because he had that melancholy disposition. He would have looked good sitting there, not to mention that he could have faced a pool of gloomy, stagnant water. When spring came, the lake's surface would grow algae, like a dense, green garbage dump. The water would turn sticky and thick because of this, and waves wouldn't come up no matter how hard the wind blew. I thought he was especially right for the place. Not only would he look good there, but he could also collect some spare change. I neglected to consider whether or not he would like this himself, though.

After I got my uncle, we walked on the street. He let me walk in front of him, which was not a good sign. Then I mentioned the black market for art near my house, and how people sold all kinds of fake antiques, calligraphy, and paintings. Also, there were some street artists who set up their booths on the ground. Moreover, Yuan Ming Garden police station was very close to my house, and it would be much easier for me to pick him up. But I didn't say the words "pick up," afraid that he might not be happy to hear them. He didn't say anything after listening to me, and we walked for another while. All of a sudden, he stuck out a leg and tripped me, letting me fall on the concrete, scraping my knees and elbows. And then he pulled me up and said with phony concern, My good nephew, be careful while you're walking. Afterwards, I learned that the black market in Yuan Ming Garden was very low class. My uncle thought it would disgrace him socially if he sold his paintings there. Always quiet, my uncle was as treacherous as a cobra. But I liked him, maybe because we were alike.

There were many benefits in sending a child to pick up lawbreakers, the most important of which was to reduce the policemen's long-windedness. When a policeman faced such a young audience, his desire to talk would naturally drop off a lot. In the beginning, I rode a mountain bike to get there, calling the policemen "Big Uncle" and filling them with sweet talk until my uncle came out; later, I wore a corduroy jacket, and sat quietly in the reception room waiting for him to come out. I had reached the age where policemen who liked talking finally got their chance, but my silence made them unsure of what to say. When we really had nothing to say, we would talk about how the price of rice was going to rise again, and how the crickets from Wan An public cemetery were pretty good at fighting because they fed on dead people's flesh. I said, of course, crickets couldn't be tougher than mice no matter how good they were at fighting. The policeman said it's illegal to fight mice because they spread disease. Well, since it was illegal to fight mice, I shut my mouth. At first, when my uncle came out, he would pat my head and give me a little bit of money as a tip; later, neither of us said anything; we just walked off in different directions—by that time, I didn't need his money and was afraid of his tripping, too. That period lasted for about five or six years. I grew nine inches and he was unable to pat my head anymore, unless he stood on tiptoe. I used to think that when I was seventy or eighty, I would still have to go to the police station with the help of a cane, to pick up my uncle. But things took a turn for the better—they sent him to the Art Reeducation Institute. The course of study was three years, which meant I wouldn't have to pick up him for at least three years. The Art Reeducation Institute was especially set up for Bohemian artists. They could learn to be engineers or agricultural technicians at the place. Doing so would subtract one troublemaker and add one useful person, society benefiting both ways. I hear that on pig farms, if there are too many stud pigs, they castrate some and turn them into porkers—this isn't an appropriate analogy, of course. I also hear that the genders are out of balance among the Chinese right now; there are more men than women. Some have proposed that the government turn a segment of the male population into females by performing sex-change operations—this also is an inappropriate analogy. Indeed, too many artists are a trouble to society. The numbers should be reduced. But it would be a mistake to subtract my uncle. If there are too many stud pigs, we should castrate some, but we also need to save some for stud; if there are too many men, we can castrate some, but we must save some. If we castrate all of them, we'd have to propagate the race by asexual reproduction, and the entire society would degenerate back into the fungus era. In art, my uncle was definitely a stud. It wouldn't be right to castrate him.

2

Before getting into the Art Reeducation Institute, my uncle had many lovers. I know all the details because I often sneaked into his apartment, hiding myself in the closet to steal a look. I had his key, but don't ask how I got it. My young uncle hung his paintings all over his living room. You couldn't look at them too long, otherwise you got dizzy. This was another error he committed. The leader lectured him: A good piece of work should make people feel happy, not dizzy. My young uncle talked back, saying, Then is a suppository a good piece of work? This was arguing for the sake of argument, of course. The leader was talking mood, not anus. But my young uncle was very good at arguing and could give even the brightest leader a headache.

Each time I went to my young uncle's apartment, I would see a girl I hadn't seen before. The girl would step into his living room, look around, let out a shriek, and collapse. My young uncle then prepared special eyeglasses for his guests: he glued a piece of black paper to the lenses, leaving two small holes in the middle. After putting them on, the guest could keep her feet. She would ask, What have you painted? My young uncle's answer would be, See for yourself. The girl would study them closely, and after a while, her head would whirl again. For this situation, my young uncle prepared another set of special glasses: he glued a piece of black paper to the lenses with even smaller holes cut in the middle. After looking through these glasses for a while, the shaky feeling would return again. Finally, you put on the last set of glasses, which had no holes at all, only black paper. You saw nothing, but still felt dizzy; even with your eyes shut, those dizzying patterns would continue to float in your vision. Overcome with dizziness, those girls all fell in love with my young uncle and began to make love to him. I kept peeping through the narrow crack until the girl wore only bras and panties. And then, I would automatically close my eyes, as required by middle school regulations. Through the sounds of tender moaning, I could hear the girl still pressing, What did you paint anyway? My uncle's answer remained the same, Figure it out for yourself. I guessed that some of them might be virgins, because what they said in the end was this: I've already given myself to you. Hurry and tell me what you painted. My young uncle then said: To tell you the truth—I don't know myself. So the girl would slap his face and then my uncle would say: You can slap me, but I still don't know. So my uncle got another slap, which proved he really didn't know what he had painted. When the slapping began, I thought I could open my eyes to look again. The girls all resembled one another: they had slim figures with slender legs and arms. They all wore matched sets of knitted underwear, the upper part was a bra, and the lower part, panties. The only difference lay in the decorative patterns; some had red dots against a white background, some had green horizontal stripes against a black background, and still others had white stripes against a green background. No matter what they wore, I didn't like any of them. You're not an artist or a cop? Forget about being an aunt of mine!

When my uncle went to the Art Reeducation Institute, I also graduated from high school. I wanted to be an artist and didn't want to take the university entrance exam. But my mother said if I turned into a dubious character like my young uncle, she would kill me. To show her determination, she asked someone to buy six butcher knives in the Hebei countryside, sharpening them until they were snowy bright and imbedding them in a counter in the kitchen. Every morning she made me go to the kitchen to look at them. If the knives grew rusty, she would hone them snowy bright again. Once in a while, she would buy a live chicken and kill it, just to test the knives. After the killing, she would cook the carcass of the chicken and let me eat it. She stayed vigilant until I finished the entrance exam. A hero among women, my mother was always as good as her word. Having been scared out of my wits, I finished the exam in a complete daze and finally got into the Physics Department of Beijing University. The moral of the story is: if you fear being killed, you can't be an artist. You can only be a physicist. As you know, I'm a novelist now, which is also considered a type of artist. But it's not that I'm no longer afraid of being killed—my mother has passed away and no one is threatening to kill me anymore.

Ten years ago, I brought my uncle to the Art Reeducation Institute, carrying his bundle for him. My uncle held a big string bag himself—the sort of thing also called a basin bag. In addition to a basin, it contained a towel, a cup, toothbrush, toothpaste, and several rolls of toilet paper. We walked towards the huge iron gate. It was a cloudy day. I don't remember what we discussed on the road. Maybe I expressed envy at his getting accepted there. Behind the huge gate was a big courtyard encircled by a concrete wall. The iron gate was shut tight, but a small side door was left open. Everyone had to bow in order to get in. A big crowd of students stood in front of the door, waiting to be called in, one by one. By the way, I hadn't volunteered to bring my uncle there, otherwise he would have beaten me to a pulp. The leaders required every student to be accompanied by a relative, or else he wouldn't be admitted. When our turn came, my uncle did something that clearly reveals his character back then. My uncle and I had a bit more than ten years' difference in our ages, which wasn't that much; besides that, we both wore corduroy jackets—ten years ago, people who considered themselves artists wore this type of material—I also had long hair and resembled him, too. To make a long story short, when we reached the small door, my uncle suddenly pushed me on the back, shoving me inside. By the time I realized and tried to turn my head, people inside had already grabbed my collar, yanking me as hard as if I were a stubborn bull. When they yanked me, I instinctively strained backward to get free. As a result, we reached a standoff in the doorway. My jacket seams both under the arms and down the back were ripping; meanwhile, I talked myself hoarse explaining, but nobody listened. I should point out that they grabbed me, thinking they had my uncle, which shows I wasn't the only one crazy about him.

The Art Reeducation Institute was located somewhere in the western suburbs of Beijing. You may gather from what I just said that the address was classified information. Right next to it was a barbed-wire fence surrounding several fish ponds. At the end of winter and beginning of spring, the fish ponds would have no water, leaving only dried, cracked mud and the lingering smell of damp sludge everywhere. A man in a blue uniform stood beside the pond. Seeing the mob, he just gawked open-mouthed, unafraid of his tonsils catching a cold—that was what the place was like. I was trapped in the doorway, with my jacket hiked all the way up and the length of my back exposed. Goose bumps covered me from my ribs to my waist. But I couldn't have cared less how I looked.

Although my young uncle and I resembled one another, there were differences in our builds. Now trapped in a small iron door, with only the upper part of my body in view, these differences became less obvious. At the iron door, I protested, I'm not my young uncle. They eased their grip a little, telling someone to fetch my young uncle's picture so they could compare. After comparing they said, Aha, how dare you say you're not you! And then they yanked even harder. As the result of the yank, my jacket immediately disintegrated. Meanwhile, I began to wonder: What did they mean by "How dare you say you're not you!" The strange part about this sentence was that you couldn't actually refute it. I might have said, "I'm myself, but I'm another person." Or I could have said, "I'm not myself. I'm another person." Or even, "I'm not another person. I'm myself." Or, "I'm not another person, or myself!" No matter what I said, it would have been hard to convince them, and even demonstrated that I deserved a beating.

People grabbing me by the collar in the institute's doorway turned out to be an unusual experience for me. Not only did my heart race and my breath get short, but my face and ears turned all red; and what's more, I got a full erection. The experience was absolutely the equivalent of sex. Still, I didn't want to go in. The main reason was that I didn't consider myself qualified; I was too young, lacked accomplishment, and modesty was my chief virtue. I told the people inside all of this, but they just didn't believe me. Besides, it also occurred to me that if a place was so eager to get you, you'd better not go there. You'd hardly believe it, but inside the door, girls in uniform were lined up along the pathway chirping like little birds, Jolt it with a stun stick—Oh, no, that would make him stupid—Just one jolt. One jolt on it wouldn't make him stupid, and so forth. You may have guessed that the object they were arguing about was my head. With talk like this buzzing in my ears, my head began to pound. The fat girl who held my collar said, Wang Er, why don't you wise up? It's good to be inside. While she spoke, her warm breath, which had a sour smell, blew in my face. I could tell she had just eaten a fruit candy. But I was having a hard time breathing and didn't answer her. One more thing about this fat girl: because I was so close to her, I even noticed the dandruff in her hair. If I hadn't seen that, I probably would have given up and let her drag me in.

Later, the fat girl showed up in my dreams many times, her head big as a bushel, her dandruff flying around as if she had just shaken out the buckwheat stuffing of a pillow. In the dream I make love to her, but as I recall, I was pretty reluctant. Back then I was young and strong and often had nocturnal emissions. No woman had ever grabbed me by the collar before, although now it has become routine. When my wife wants to make love, she comes right up to me and grabs my collar. At home I wear a cowboy jacket, with a cowhide-reinforced collar, which is quite strong.

My young uncle's name is Wang Er, which, of course, was not given to him by my grandfather. Many people tried to persuade him to change his name, but he liked the simple brush strokes and refused. As for me, I wouldn't use such an inelegant name just for the sake of those simple strokes. With my collar in the grasp of those people and being called by that name, I considered myself doubly unfortunate. Finally, it was my uncle who shouted, Let him go. I'm the one you want. Then they set me free. But during the brief struggle, my jacket had been completely torn apart, strips of cloth hanging off my back like flags. My bastard uncle, with a cold grin on his face, took his luggage from my back, straightened my clothes, patted my shoulder, and said, I'm very sorry, nephew. After that, he took a look around, his gaze settling for a moment on the concrete pillars on either side of the gate. They were square pillars with two big concrete spheres on top. He spat through the gap in his teeth, So fucking ugly. Then he ducked and went in. The people inside didn't grab him, and even made way for him—maybe their hands were tired after the battle with me. I walked home alone, with scraps of rags dangling from my back and sore muscles in my limbs and neck. But I felt relieved. After I got home, I told my mother, I've got rid of that god of plague. My mother said, Good, you did me a great favor! Needless to say the god of plague was my uncle, whose whole body carried the plague before he got into the Art Reeducation Institute.

After bringing my uncle to the Art Reeducation Institute, I began to struggle with all kinds of strange ideas: at any rate, from now on he belongs to the institute, and doesn't need me to worry about him anymore. Meanwhile, I would think about the fat girl who grabbed me by the collar, and jealousy would begin to gnaw at my heart. Later, I heard that she used to wrestle stevedores, had married twice, and, now single again, wrote love letters to Japanese sumo wrestlers on a regular basis. Sumo wrestlers are strong and rich—she couldn't have been the least interested in my young uncle at the time. I was way off there. There was another instructor at the Art Reeducation Institute who was about four and half feet tall and as thin as a lath, with pale skin, a sharp nose, a pointy chin and sleep crust at the corners of her eyes, and sparse hair combed into two braids. She wasn't interested in my young uncle either. Fifty-two years old already, this instructor was an old maid, and had made up her mind long ago that she would devote her life to special education in our country. Between these two extremes, there were all sorts of other female instructors, but none of them was interested in my uncle. My uncle was a person of few words, peculiar in many ways. Very few people liked him. His criminal dossier contained photographs of his paintings. To be fair, those photos looked nicer than the originals since they were small, but when it came to making people dizzy they worked equally well. From these pictures alone people concluded my uncle was an obnoxious man. It seemed like no one would like my uncle. I worried too much.

There were all kinds of avant-garde artists at the Art Reeducation Institute; among them were poets, novelists, filmmakers, and, of course, painters. In the moral education class every morning, the students' poetry and prose would be read aloud—if there were no poetry and prose to be read aloud, they would show slides, and then ask the artists to explain what their work meant. Of course, these people were stubborn and wouldn't admit their mistakes: It's art—outsiders wouldn't get it! But the institute knew how to cure stubbornness—for example, beating their heads with a club. Once the artist stopped being stubborn, he began to sweat profusely and go on the defensive, and, humbled a bit then, he would admit he just wanted to impress people with claptrap, so he could get famous. Then the instructor ran a student's movie, which was not just a mess but disgusting. Without being asked, the student already felt embarrassed, and automatically bowed his head for a beating. He said that he had made the movie for foreigners, intending to lighten their pockets. Unfortunately, this tactic didn't work at all with my young uncle. After the instructor showed the slides of his work, he would frankly admit before anyone asked, I don't know what I painted either. That's exactly why I painted them. So other people can appreciate them. After that, all the instructors got headaches trying to figure out how to put him on the defensive. Everybody knew that there must be some meaning in his paintings and tried to force him to say so. He himself also agreed that his paintings must mean something, but he said, I don't know what it is. I'm too dumb. According to the leaders at the institute, all students were fools who thought they were smart. Since my young uncle refused to think he was smart, the leaders believed on the contrary that he was not a fool, but a smart ass.

I often went to the Art Reeducation Institute to visit my young uncle. The leaders asked me to persuade him not to play dumb. Don't play dumb, they told him. They also said, Playing dumb with us won't help you. I defended my uncle saying, My young uncle isn't playing dumb—he was born dumb. But the leaders said, Don't play games with us. Playing games won't help your young uncle.

Aside from my uncle, the only other relative I had was a distant cousin. He was older than my uncle; when I was ten, he was already over forty. He had a groove in his upper lip wider than a playing card, a big hole in the seat of his pants that revealed his pubic hair as well as his balls, and a face very much resembling a bird's. Back then he lived in Sand River Town, often scuffing along in mid-summer in a pair of padded shoes, which were already in shreds and tatters, brandishing a slingshot made from a rubber tourniquet, and, with a broad smile, inviting the passing children to hit the hornet's nest with him—a hornet's nest is a kind of hive built on a tree that looks like a lotus seedpod. My cousin had an earnest, bass voice. He was very popular among the townspeople, always busy going in and out of the police station and the neighborhood committee. If you asked him to push the wheelbarrow or take out your garbage, he would never refuse you. Once, I brought him along to visit my young uncle, just to let the leader see there was another sort of person in our family. Who would have expected the leader to laugh after seeing my cousin? He pointed at my nose and said, You little rascal! You're really slippery! My cousin blurted out in his droning voice, Who's slippery? I'll kick his butt for him! Whenever my cousin came to the institute, he always seemed to be in high spirits; first he took all the garbage out, and then knocked down all the hives, making the hornets fly around so nobody could venture outside. He himself was stung and swelled up as big as a barrel. Despite the fact that he knocked down hives, the people at the institute all liked him very much. Not long after he went home, a passing coal truck hit him and killed him. Everybody felt sad and, from then on, began to hate Shanxi people, because Shanxi province was famous for its coal. While preparing for his funeral, the townspeople invited my mother to attend as a family member of the deceased. She felt slightly uncomfortable, but didn't refuse. Had it been my uncle, my mother might not have gone. I also told my uncle about my cousin's death. He drew a blank—couldn't remember who he was; and then it suddenly dawned on him, Look at my memory! He's been here knocking down hornet's nests. My young uncle also said he really wanted to go to my cousin's memorial service, but it was too late. My cousin had already been cremated.

After the moral education class, my uncle went to his special course. From what I saw through the window, their classroom didn't look much different from the auditoriums in our school—the same bluish fluorescent light bulbs hanging down from the ceiling, and the same long tables and benches arranged in rows, except there were more slogans on the walls. Another difference was that their windows were fitted with iron bars and mesh, along with a sign with lightning bolts on it, warning of electricity. The sign didn't lie—I'd often see a lizard crawling over the window, then, all of a sudden, with a puff of black smoke, the lizard turned into a piece of charcoal; another time I saw a butterfly land on the window and then after a hiss, all that remained was a pair of wings floating through the air. My uncle responded to every question before anyone else, just to show the instructors that he knew none of the answers. So the institute made him wear a straitjacket. After that he could take notes, but couldn't raise his hand and disturb the class. Though he couldn't raise his hand, he still talked too much. Then they put a bandage over his mouth, which he could remove only after class. Pulling it on and off plucked his beard out and made him look like a eunuch. I observed his strange appearance from the window: his left hand was tied beneath the right armpit, his right hand beneath the left armpit, and his whole torso looked just like a canvas bag; but he stared very hard, which made his eyes almost pop out of their sockets. Whenever he heard the instructor asking questions, he would get excited and snort through his nostrils. If he snorted too much, the instructor would come over and give him a shock on the head with a baton. After the shock, he would lie down and doze off. Sometimes, remembering his old habit from the police station, he tried to puff himself up. But the canvas straitjacket was so hard to get inflated that instead it forced his body into a spindle shape—by that time his face would turn the color of liver. The air made him very uncomfortable, and he had to release it—there was a hole in the bandage especially for that purpose—then the person sitting in front of him would turn around and hit him on the head, You smell like a horse, you son of a bitch!

The institute leaders lavished care on their students; they prepared a pair of thick glasses for each student, allowing them to wear the glasses even before they became near-sighted, made them brown wool and polyester suits as the institute's uniform, and equipped everyone with a big leather briefcase, which they were not permitted to hold by the handles but had to carry on their chests. They said the students would appear more sincere by carrying their briefcases that way. The course load was very heavy, eight classes during the day and homework in the evening. To prevent the students from misbehaving, stocks were installed on every desk, in order to force them to bend over the desk. So after a while, all of them looked like bookworms—that is, they all had stooped backs and bent necks, wore brown suits, and held big briefcases in front of them; their glasses resembled the bottom of bottles, their heads were so smooth and shiny that even mosquitoes would slide down the surface—unfortunately, they were studious in name but not in action; what's more, they drooled out of the corner of their mouths. My uncle drooled the most, his saliva gurgling down almost like a stream. Even if the food at the institute hadn't been tasty enough and he were ravenous for steamed buns and meat, he couldn't have drooled any worse. People generally believed that he did this on purpose, trying to blacken the reputation of the institute's food. To stop his drooling, they

were nothing special. However, things were quite different with painters. For instance, if you gave a layman some colors, he didn't even know where to start. Besides, every painter had his own idol, such as the French Impressionists at the end of the century before last and the beginning of the last century. If you called an artist a loafer, he would reply, People said the same thing about Van Gogh. Our country still had diplomatic relations with France, so it was improper to denounce Van Gogh severely. But the institute had its own way of dealing with these people: the instructor collected the students' works from the drafting class, made them into slides, and then displayed them in the moral education class. Meanwhile, the instructor would ask: Convict so and so, what did you paint? The student answered: Reporting to the Instructor, it's a cat! Then the instructor would show a picture of a real cat, and the next sentence would make the convict want to sink through the floor, Now, let's all take a look. See what a real cat looks like! After this sort of reeducation, that student would shed his pride and settle down to drafting. But such tactics didn't work on my uncle. When his ink-wash lotus painting was shown, he stood up and said, Reporting to the Instructor, I don't know what I painted! The instructor had to continue, What are these bright scribbles? My young uncle answered, That's my dried-up saliva. The instructor questioned him again, Does saliva look like this? My uncle replied, Permission to ask the instructor, what do you think saliva should look like? Unable to find a picture of saliva, the instructor could do nothing but put the bandage over my uncle's mouth again.

A month after he got in, the institute tested the students' IQs. The testee was tied to a custom-made measuring apparatus, which was also an electric torture machine. What was tested could be either the testee's IQ, or his ability to withstand torture. The thing consisted of two big iron boxes, one above and the other one below, supported by a steel frame. In the middle was a light stretcher that could be moved on a slide. Some leather straps were attached to the frame of the stretcher. Before the testee got onto it, the stretcher had to be pulled out first and the testee's limbs would be tied with the leather straps, forcing his body into the shape of a cross; then he would be pushed inside—the rectangular steamer in our school's kitchen, with its drawers one over another, looked a little like this machine—if the testee were not tied, you couldn't test his IQ precisely. In order to test the students' IQs precisely, the institute first called a meeting to discuss what scores the students' IQs should be in order to conform to reality. The instructors all agreed that these students were wild and stubborn. If the institute allowed their

IQs to appear too high, it wouldn't advance their thought reform. But my uncle was a special case. He always played dumb. To allow his IQ score to be too low wouldn't advance his thought reform either.

Later, my uncle told me that he'd circled around the measuring apparatus several times, trying to find the plate that indicated which factory manufactured it, but failed. From the crude metal work, he could tell it was made in China. Therefore, he reached the conclusion that the machine used to have a plate, but it was removed—there was the evidence of a mark that supported this idea—for fear the students would blow up the factory after they were released. The machine also had two electrodes, meant to be placed on the testee's body. If the electrodes were placed too low, pubic hair would burn; if too high, the hair on the head would burn. Put simply, some hair was going to burn. When the canteen bought pig's heads and knuckles with the bristle not completely removed, they would send them over and let the machine do that job, too. As a result, the IQ of a pig's head was determined to be higher than an artist's, but a knuckle's was a bit lower. To make a long story short, when the machine operated, it always smelled of burned bristle. Any other smell was caused by the ones who forgot the posted slogan: Toilet before testing. An arrow after the slogan pointed in the direction of the toilet. Like the door of a bank vault, the toilet door was equipped with a timer lock. It would shut you in for half an hour once you entered. A stereo inside played popular music—music of this sort worked to encourage people to defecate and urinate faster.

At the test, the students usually made the request of the instructors: We'll be dating women later, so please leave us our pubic hair. But sometimes the instructor operating the machine would say: I want to leave the hair on your head. This was because the instructors at the institute were innocent and sincere girls. Some of them already had feelings for their students, and hoped to maintain their good looks by saving the hair on their heads, and to prevent them from sewing their wild oats by burning their pubic hair. Besides that, she would advise him outside the machine: Why don't you answer fewer questions right? Don't let the shock make you stupid. To be frank, this advice might not keep his IQ down, because most probably he'd act like a skinny donkey squeezing out a hard turd—determined to play the tough guy. He would rather put up with the electricity than answer the questions wrong. By the time the test was over, the student often collapsed in a ball. There were always touching scenes where an instructor, weeping and sobbing, carried her student out on her back.

The scene of the IQ test was very exciting. From the ceiling an incandescent light hung down, the bulb was very small, but the shade was big, which made it look like a loudspeaker. The light bulb lit the lower part of the room but not the ceiling. The instructor brought her student in, pulled out the stretcher with a bang and gave her terse order: Take off your clothes. Lie down there. Then she turned around and put on her white lab jacket and a pair of rubber gloves. The room was very cold. Taking off clothes caused goose bumps. Some would crack a joke at this moment, but my uncle was a quiet person, always keeping his mouth shut. There were leather belts inside, and the instructor began tying the student tightly, tying him like Jesus on the cross—with his arms outstretched and two legs held together, left foot under the right. A talker would say, Why so tight? I'm not a pig! The instructor would reply, It would save us a lot of trouble if you were a pig. After being tied up, most students would get a hard-on. The instructor would say, Still misbehaving at a moment like this? And the student would argue, I'm not misbehaving. He's always this big! The instructor said, Don't brag! Then she would push him in with a rumble. While lying in the drawer, my uncle would get a hard-on, too. But he wouldn't reply to the instructor's questions. The instructor would smack his belly and said, Hey, Convict Wang, I'm talking to you. Are you always this big? He would close his eyes and say, It's usually smaller. Hurry up! So he was pushed in with a rumble, too. They say the wheels under the stretcher worked really well. When someone was pushed in, he would feel himself in free-fall, completely weightless; then with a huge thud, the top of his head bumped the back wall of the machine, making it ring a little. The scene gave me the creeps—I would have hated to be tied and pushed in. Of course, it would make a big difference if I were the instructor, wearing the white lab coat and tying beautiful girls to the stretcher.

They say that there was a color TV screen installed on the top of the drawer, where the questions were displayed. If the instructor liked the student, she would entertain him with an amusing videotape first, and then shock him half to death, just like a benevolent dentist gives his patient candy before pulling his teeth. However, when my uncle's turn came, there were no videotapes, no questions either, only a sharp shock that made him wail like a ghost. Everyone was a slab of ice-cold meat before being pushed in, with puffs of breath visible between his mouth and nose, and something sticking up out of his crotch like a flagpole; after being pulled out, he was steaming all over as if cooked through, although nothing smelled good in that steam, as if a piece of rotten meat had been cooked; his hair, if he had any, would curl like springs; as for the thing that stuck out, it was down, of course. But it was different with my uncle; he came out still stiff, even two or three times bigger than when he went in, and people simply couldn't stand the sight of it. Some groaned faintly when they came out, as if a horsefly or a dung beetle were buzzing around the room; some kept silent. When my uncle came out, he shouted like a crazy man, Ah, wonderful! Excellent! Very exciting! As mentioned previously, now came the time for the instructor to carry her student on her back. The way she would carry her student was very strange: she laid the student down first, held his feet on her shoulders, gave a little shout and dragged him out with his head on the ground—they say that people in slaughter houses carry dead pigs this way. No one liked to carry my uncle. They would say, Convict Wang, don't play dead. Get up and walk! Everyone else was a dead pig, but not my uncle. My uncle actually stood up with the help of the wall, then, still wobbling, walked away.

Now it's time to talk about their scores. Most of the students scored between 110 and 100. The guy with the highest score got a 115; he bragged that it wouldn't be too difficult for him to get a 120, but he was afraid if he got the 120, he would be made very stupid because electricity could shock people into stupidity. As for my uncle, his IQ was zero—he didn't answer a single question right. This made the leaders very angry: Even a wooden stick could do better than that. So they adjusted the voltage and put him back in for a make-up test. The result of the retest was no more than 50 points. Of course, it could have been higher. But chances are my uncle would have been electrocuted. One thing you probably gathered even though I didn't mention it: other people got their shocks when they gave the right answers, and my uncle got his when he gave the wrong ones. Experienced instructors said that they weren't afraid of students who were tricky and troublemakers, but dreaded dealing with someone like my uncle who played possum.

After the test, my uncle lay on his bed waxy-faced, as if he had hepatitis. I asked him how he felt then. He stared blankly for a while, then a ghostly smile appeared on his face and he said, Very good. He also told me that he had ejaculated wildly in that box. The box was such a mess that it looked like he had thrown jelly around, or a used condom. The next person couldn't help howling from inside, Fuck your mother, Wang Er! Can't you try to collect a little good karma, you son of a bitch? Maybe the guy thought the box was too unsanitary. People said that before getting into the measuring machine, anyone with a social conscience would beat off besides, emptying balls and bowels. They called this jerking off till you were drained, because you might lose control inside the box. But my uncle didn't want to do this. He said he was very excited when he got shocked. If he jerked off till he was drained, it wouldn't be that exciting. I thought he was right. He was a real artist. Real artists were guys who had no regard for anything. But I wasn't sure what was so exciting: was it the questions appearing on the screen of the measuring machine? (He managed to remember one of them: "What does eight plus seven equal?") Or the electric current that went through his body? Or the jelly he shot all over the box? But my uncle refused to answer any of my questions, only closed his eyes.

The day after the test, my young uncle didn't get up for morning exercise, nor did he respond to people calling his name. When they came back from lunch, he was still in his bed. One of his roommates reported this to the instructor. The instructor said, Just ignore him. And don't give him food either. Let's see how long he lasts! So everyone went to class. When they came back in the evening, the room was full of flies. Only then did they find that my young uncle had died and even turned a little green. The smell was really bad after they lifted the quilt. So they got a car and sent him to the hospital morgue. Then they discussed how my young uncle died, whether or not the institute should inform his family and how, et cetera. After serious discussion, they came to the conclusion that my uncle had a heart attack. He had been sent to the hospital before his death, and the doctors had tried to save him for three days and nights, at a cost of tens of thousands. But we didn't need to worry about the money since all institute students had health insurance and could get reimbursed—the advantage of living in a socialist country. Meanwhile, the institute sent a messenger to inform the hospital what they had come up with, in case we inquired about it. By the time all the lies fell into place and they were ready to inform us, the Lijiakou police station phoned, saying that they had arrested my young uncle selling his paintings without a permit at the Great Earth Café again. The institute had better send someone there to collect him. This bewildered everybody at the institute. No one dared to pick him up because there were three possibilities: first, Lijiakou arrested somebody who looked like my young uncle. In that case, the institute would risk appearing stupid by sending someone on this errand, as if they didn't know my young uncle had died; second, the Lijiakou police station was playing a practical joke on the institute. To pick up my uncle in this situation would also appear stupid; last, Lijiakou police station had arrested my uncle's ghost. To send someone there would help promote national superstitiousness. I don't know which genius had the idea of going to the morgue later to check the body. Only then did they discover that my young uncle was made of pork, yellow beans, and flour. At that point the person still alive was in big trouble.

My uncle was a great painter, but this great painter had a bad habit: he liked to draw tickets. Even when he was very little, he would draw movie tickets and bathhouse tickets, anything but money; he knew counterfeiting was illegal. Occasionally he would draw a few valuable stamps. When his permit was canceled, he drew a fake permit. But now with a computer number on every ID, it would be useless for him to draw a fake permit. He could also make all kinds of phony objects. The best example was a piece of shit he made out of laundry soap when he went to a friend's house for dinner. He put the turd on the sofa, and it was so realistic that the hostess fainted at the sight of it. The guy wanted to get out of the institute, and also felt obliged to provide an explanation. So he asked me to buy fifty pounds of pork without worrying about quality. I bought half a diseased pig from the market and smuggled it into him in a sack. However, I had no idea that he was going to make a dead person out of it. If I'd known, I would have suggested he use soap. Putting half of a diseased pig in the dorm was too disgusting.

When I carefully examined the gains and losses of my young uncle's early life, I found that he had made many mistakes. First of all, he shouldn't have painted paintings that people didn't understand. But as he pointed out later, he wouldn't have become a painter if he hadn't painted them; secondly, he should have titled his paintings sea horse, squirrel, and snail. But he also said that he wouldn't have been a real painter if what he'd painted were sea horses, squirrels, and snails; and he shouldn't have played dumb at the institute. According to him, not playing dumb would have given him the creeps. And life would have been intolerable. The next thing he shouldn't have done was running away and putting half of a diseased pig carcass in his bed. But my young uncle also had something to say about that: Should I have hung around waiting for another electric shock? Should I not have faked the corpse and waited till they found me? So these mistakes could be forgiven, but not the last one—he shouldn't have been painting and selling his paintings right after he escaped. If he'd just waited a few days more, only until the institute informed us that he was dead, then everything would have been all right. When Lijiakou police station informed them that they had arrested my young uncle, they might have said nothing but this:

The guy is already dead; you must have arrested the wrong person. I thought my young uncle would come up with some excuses for himself, such as he couldn't wait to get back to his painting, et cetera. Who knew that he would stare blankly? He was in a daze for a long time, and then he smacked himself on the forehead, Really, I'm so stupid!

3

There are many situations in life, and I had more than one young aunt. But the one I'll be talking about here is my real young aunt. I liked my young uncle very much, and hoped that he would marry many different women; I thought of one after another until Marilyn Monroe came to mind. That individual died many years ago, and her flesh and bone have turned to dust. But I hear she had a really big bust when she was alive. As I said before, my uncle had a divergent strabismus problem. So my young aunt had to have a big bust. Otherwise, with part of her bust wobbling outside his range of vision, the visual effect would be too unpleasant. As a matter of fact, I had no reason to worry. My real aunt fixed my young uncle's divergent strabismus in a single night.

A tall and slender woman, my young aunt had fair skin and a supple waist. Whether she sat in a bed or on a sofa, she liked to tilt her head so you could see her shiny dark hair. Besides that, she always seemed about to burst out laughing. The sentence she said to me most often was: Can I help you with something? This usually happened when I pretended to barge into her room by accident, and then she would have that expression on her face. Those incidents happened a lot. However, that was many years ago.

The story began as follows: we used to live on the first floor when I was little, then we moved up to the sixth floor, and the building didn't have an elevator. Inside the building were bare concrete stairs, corridors full of dust and paint peelings, garbage collecting in the corners, et cetera. To be more specific, the garbage consisted of onionskins, eggshells and all kinds of plastic bags, which smelled terrible. Everyone wanted it clean, but whoever did the cleaning would be the sucker. One day, heavy steps came from the stairway; then a woman's voice could be heard from outside, Convict Wang, is it here? A man answered, Yes. As soon as I heard this, I told my mother, Damn, it's my young uncle! My mother didn't believe me, saying my young uncle had a long way to go before he got out. But I believed it, because I had a deeper understanding of my uncle's morals than my mother. We opened the door, and there he was, along with a girl in uniform, who was my young aunt. But she didn't want to let on. My uncle introduced my mother to her, This is my big sister. My young aunt took off her hat and greeted her, Big sister! Then he introduced me, This is my nephew. She said, Oh, really? And then she burst out laughing, Convict Wang, your nephew looks very much like you. The thing I hated most was when people said that I looked like my young uncle, but that time was an exception. I thought my young aunt was a charming woman. If I had known that getting into the Art Reeducation Institute would bring such luck with women, I would have gone instead of my uncle.

Now I want to confess that I didn't like any of my young uncle's girlfriends. But my young aunt was a special case. The first time she showed up she wore a uniform with a peaked cap, and tucked into her wide leather belt was a little pistol. She was in high spirits and looked magnificent. The way she dressed fascinated me. On the other hand, my uncle appeared in a pair of stainless steel handcuffs, holding them in front of his chest like a black bear about to take a bow. Just as there's a difference between cat and mouse, prisoner and guard should also maintain some distinctions. That is why some people wear handcuffs, and others have guns. Once they entered our apartment, my young aunt unlocked one of my uncle's handcuffs, which made me think that she had handcuffed him just to act out their roles. I didn't expect her to cuff him to a handy radiator pipe. And then she said, Big sister, I need to use your bathroom. Off she went. Unable to stand straight or squat, my uncle could only maintain a position halfway between the two, with a rather humiliated look. I was confused and didn't know what was going on. After a while, my young aunt came out, cuffed herself to my uncle, and then the two of them sat on the sofa side by side. They seemed to me to be playing some sort of sexual game. In short, sometimes you need a certain sense of humor to understand life. My mother didn't have that, she understood nothing, and that was why she was often annoyed half to death. I have that sense of humor, and because of it, I found my aunt particularly charming.

As soon as I saw my young aunt, I knew she was a spirited woman who would give my uncle a hard time. But after all, she was still a woman, and thankfully, not a man. On the balcony, I congratulated my uncle, telling him my young aunt was prettier than any other girls he had dated. My uncle didn't say anything, just asked for a cigarette. In my experience, when my uncle didn't want to talk, you'd better leave him alone. Otherwise he'd get you. Besides, he seemed very unhappy that day. Being cuffed to him, I wouldn't have been able to run away if he'd suddenly turned on me. He finished the cigarette and said, I'm not sure whether it's good luck or bad. Then he added, Let's go inside. So we went back to the bedroom, asking my young aunt to take off the handcuffs. She looked us up and down, and said, Convict Wang, this little bad egg really looks like you—maybe he is as bad as you. Usually, an aunt doesn't use that sort of tone to talk about her nephew. Anyhow, my uncle finished the cigarette so completely that he even smoked the butt, which showed how much he needed nicotine. Since he was a popular man, he had never been short of cigarettes any place he went. Now he was even smoking the butt, a very unusual thing. In brief, in all the time I knew him, he'd never fallen so low.

Now I must admit that my political consciousness functioned on a very low level when I was young, no better than the little girl that I met on the bus. That little girl was very clean and only wore underpants, not even a skirt. Her not having a skirt meant her mother thought that her daughter's legs were not enough to give men ideas; her wearing underpants was because the part above the legs would give men ideas. My young aunt guarded my uncle on the bus. It was pretty late, and there were only six or seven passengers. The little girl ran up to my uncle and, staring at the handcuffs he wore, asked my young aunt, Auntie, what's wrong with this uncle? My young aunt explained to her, This uncle committed an error. The child already knew whom to love and whom to hate, and, meanwhile, was aware that my uncle, being handcuffed, couldn't do anything to defend himself. So she asked for the truncheon from my young aunt, wanting to beat my uncle. My young aunt told her, Not everyone can beat an uncle who has committed an error. The girl blinked her eyes as if she didn't understand. My aunt explained again, This uncle committed the kind of error that only this Auntie can beat him for. This time, the girl got it. She screamed at my young aunt, Obnoxious! You're no fun. Then she ran away.

Speaking of political consciousness, the one with the lowest level, of course, was my uncle; next came me since I always saw things from his perspective; then it was my mother, who felt uneasy when she saw my young aunt handcuffing my uncle; next was my young aunt, forever on guard against my uncle; but the most advanced one was that little girl. Wanting to beat someone with low political consciousness was the sign of advanced political consciousness.

The error that my uncle committed might have thousands of strands, but they all came down to one thing—nobody understood his paintings. It wouldn't be too bad if that were the only problem; those paintings appeared understandable. This made people wonder whether the bait hid the hook. Now in writing this story I seem to be committing the same sort of error—the story appears understandable, but nobody can understand it. It's not my fault, but my uncle's, because that's how he was. My mother had a prejudice against my young uncle, believing he was neither like my older uncle nor like her. She thought there must have been a mistake in the delivery room. I look very much like my young uncle, so she said I was a mistake, too. But I don't think everybody can be a mistake all the time. Somebody has to be right sometimes. Anyhow, she always thought that I was the one who knew what was going on with my uncle, but that was wrong—not even my uncle knew what was going on with himself. She called me into the kitchen and said, You two are joined at the hip. Will you just tell me what's going on?

I said, Nothing. It's just my uncle has a new girl. She is a policewoman. He's getting out soon. My mother then started worrying, not about my uncle, but about my young aunt. In her eyes, my young aunt was a good girl and my young uncle wasn't a suitable match for her—my mother always paid attention to the business of mating, as if she worked in a breeding station. However, by evening she no longer worried about my young aunt, because they started to make love—though they were in another room and kept their door shut, we still knew what they were doing. They made noise all night, sometimes screaming, sometimes moaning. The whole building could hear them. This made my mother very angry. She slammed the front door behind her, and went to stay in a hotel, taking me with her. What most angered my mother was that she thought my uncle had behaved himself in the Art Reeducation Institute and was rewarded with an early graduation (or you could call it an early release). But the truth was just the opposite: my uncle had behaved badly there and was to receive a more severe punishment. My young aunt was his escort. They were headed to a labor camp, taking the opportunity to fool around here on the way. For this reason, my mother asked me ferociously, Can you tell me what this is all about? This time even I was confused. So clearly my uncle and I were not joined at the hip.

After getting the notion about my aunt's advanced political consciousness, I was full of questions about her behavior: if you think my uncle is a bad person, why do you still make love to him? Her answer was: It's a waste not to do it—your uncle is a bad egg, but not a bad man. This is called "recycling." But she didn't say so that night. If she did, I would have told my uncle about it, and my uncle would have been on his guard—she said this much later.

The scene of my young uncle and my young aunt's lovemaking was the small sofa in my bedroom. I was certain of this because when I left the apartment the previous night, the sofa was firm and in good shape. By the time I came back, it had been turned into a mound of dough. Besides that, stuck on the wall behind the sofa were three pieces of chewed gum. I removed one of them, tasted it, and calculated that it had been chewed for at least an hour. So you can reconstruct the scene at the time: my uncle sat on the sofa, and my aunt rode him, chewing a piece of gum. Having deduced this, I thought it was such an excellent sight that I cheered, and jumped over to my own bed. It was the only bed in my room, yet it had no trace of being slept in at all. I didn't suspect that my young aunt had a gun on my young uncle. When I found out, I didn't know whether I should have been cheering or not.

Incidentally, my young aunt enjoyed making love to my uncle very much. She would get very excited and cry out every time. Then she would handcuff her left hand to my uncle, hold the pistol in her right hand, pointing it at my uncle's head—it was the real thing in the beginning, and then she switched to a toy gun after quitting her job as a guard. When she caught her breath, she would say, Tell me, Convict Wang, do you love me or do you just want to use me? To be fair, when it came to female government employees, the first thing my uncle did was to use them, and the next to talk about love. But with a gun pointed at his head, of course, he didn't dare tell the truth. Besides, it's really hard to say how much someone can enjoy lovemaking under those circumstances.

My young aunt and my young uncle were not people who spoke the same language. Only people who don't speak the same language could make love that way. While making love to my aunt in our apartment, my uncle stared at the little steel thing and kept wondering: Damn it! Is the safety on or off? Where is the safety? How am I supposed to know whether it's on or not? He could have mentioned it to my aunt, but since they hadn't known each other very long, he was embarrassed to ask. By the time they were sufficiently well acquainted, he learned that the gun didn't have any bullets, which really pissed him off: he would rather have gotten killed by an accidentally discharged bullet than worry for no reason. However, the pistol fixed his eye problem. Before that, it was one eye eastward and the other westward. Staring at the gun so long corrected the problem. Only he was overcorrected and became cross-eyed.

After turning my uncle cross-eyed, my young aunt was proud of herself at first, but soon began to have regrets. She advertised for a cure in a small newspaper and received a folk prescription, which said to get a pair of eyeballs from cattle—whether from a cow or a water buffalo didn't matter, but they had to be an actual pair. Then you marinated them in honey, keeping one here and sending the other to Nanjing. After calculating that the one en route was about to reach Nanjing, you ate the one in Beijing, then hurried to Nanjing to get the other one. My aunt wanted my uncle to try it. But as soon as my uncle heard about eating cattle eyeballs, he said, I would rather die. Because he didn't use this folk prescription, his eyes remained crossed. But what if he tried the cure and the cure turned his eyes into something like a dead cow's, one eyeball pointing south and the other north?

The next morning, my mother said to my young aunt, You're sick. You should go see a doctor. She meant that my aunt came in waves when she made love. As calm as ever, my young aunt went on cracking melon seeds and said, If that's an illness, it's a good illness. Why should I try to be cured? From this answer, I judged my young aunt's mind to be clear and logical. She didn't seem sick. But after she stopped talking, she did something strange: she stood up, buckled her uniform belt, took out the handcuffs and cuffed my uncle in a flash. She then said, Let's go, Convict Wang. It's off to the labor camp for you. No more delays. Wanting to get a few more days off, my uncle began to play for time. But my aunt raised her eyebrows and stared at him, saying, Don't waste your breath! She also said, Love is love, and work is work. She was very firm about this and not wanting to get entangled with a criminal—that was how she took my uncle away. This incident nearly drove my mother mad. She was cut off in her prime, and my young aunt was to blame.

4

In the last century there was a big alkali factory near Bo Sea, famous for its Triangle Brand of pure alkali. To this day when you pass through the Lutai area, you can still see a mass of gray factory buildings. Because the ammonia soda process consumed too much electricity, the alkali factory had closed. Now the alkali people needed had to be dug from the alkali-salt field. It's a hard job, but fortunately, there are people who commit errors and need to be reeducated, so the work is left to them. Besides them, some innocent people are also needed to stand guard. That's the prologue to this story. My uncle survived the labor camp, but what will happen to him is hard to say. Anyhow, my uncle dug alkali on the alkali-salt field, and my aunt guarded him. The alkali field is not far from Lutai. Every time I passed through Lutai, I could see those empty gray factory buildings. Numerous sea birds flew in and out of the big holes left by the removal of the doors and the windows. They blocked the sky and covered the ground. The deserted factory had become a huge birdhouse, and people shaved bald as a gourd and wearing shackles walked in and out, taking shovels and carts with them. This meant that the hard labor not only consisted of digging alkali, but also of scraping up bird shit. I heard that in addition to becoming fertilizer, the bird shit could also be used as a food additive. It needs processing of course—you can't eat it untreated.

Every time I went to the alkali field, I always rode on the bus with the blue roof. The difference between "factory" and "field" consisted of only one word, but they were not located in the same place. The bus clanked along the deserted railroad, with puffs of dark smoke rushing out of its long, thin iron chimney. If the bus broke down halfway, everyone had to get off to push. The passengers walked on the road to push the bus, and the driver sat in the bus to fix the engine. On several unfortunate occasions, we had to push it all the way to our destination. We would pass many empty train stations, shunts not in use anymore, and very ugly rusty rails. The walls of the stations were full of slogans, such as "Protect All Railroad Equipment," "Crack Down on Railway Property Theft," and so forth. But the doors and windows had all been stolen. What was left were the shells of the buildings, like skulls, where bats, wild rabbits, and hedgehogs lived. A hedgehog wears gray and has two pairs of bowlegs. I envy the hedgehog's lifestyle very much: it idles the time away, hunts for food, and, meanwhile, enjoys the sunshine, as long as it avoids its born enemy, the weasel. Every time I visited the alkali field, my socks would turn rusty. I really had no idea how the rust got into them.

When I went to the alkali field to visit my young uncle, I always felt a little awkward. My young aunt and uncle were a couple. Whoever I meant to visit, it wouldn't seem quite right. If I intended to visit both of them it would make me look like a low type; if I went to see neither, why go? My only comfort was that my uncle and I were both artists; for one artist to visit another should be all right. This raised a big problem: I didn't know what art or an artist was. In this case, to claim both my uncle and I were artists wasn't too convincing.

The railroad in the alkali field led all the way to the center of a tent city. Guarded by two wooden watchtowers, the tents were encircled by barbed wire. In the middle of the tent city was a dirt yard, littered with yellow clay and stones. At noon the stones would gleam like glacial debris. The bus drove right into the yard. A wooden platform stood in the very center of the yard. At first glance you wouldn't know the purpose of the platform. As soon as my uncle arrived, they asked him to lie on the front part of the platform and stretch out his legs. Then they got a pair of big shackles and bolted them on his legs. By the time they finished the riveting, the purpose of the platform was clear. The main part of the shackles consisted of an iron chain, about forty pounds in weight and several yards long. Lying on the ground and looking at the big iron chain, my uncle considered it overkill. He also thought the chain was too cold, so he said, Reporting to the instructor, is this necessary? I just painted a few paintings. My young aunt said, Don't worry. Let me go ask someone. A few minutes later, she came back and said, I'm terribly sorry, Convict Wang. There is no smaller chain—you said you had only painted a few paintings. There is someone here who just wrote one poem. Hearing this, my uncle had nothing to say. Afterwards, they shaved my uncle's long hair, which he valued very much, and turned his head into a shiny bulb. Concerning his hair, I need to add something here: though his head was bald in the front at first, the back part remained luxuriant. This made my uncle look like an old fogy from the Qing dynasty, quite a unique style. By the time it was shaved completely bald, he looked like a simple, honest man. In desperation, my uncle cried out for help, Instructor! Instructor! They're shaving me. My aunt shouted back, Be quiet, Convict Wang. Should they be shaving me, instead of you? My uncle had no choice but to shut up. As smart as my uncle was, he should have realized at that point something was really wrong. Right then he needed to stick to his statements about loving my young aunt. If I had been in his place, I would have done the same thing. I wouldn't have changed my words even if they beat me to death.

For my uncle's labor reform in the alkali field, he had to dig alkali everyday. According to what he said later, the scene at the time was as follows: he wore a blue coat stuffed with recycled rags, dragged the big shackle, and carried a pick on his shoulder, walking on the snow-white alkali flat. The wind blew hard, and the sun glared white. If you didn't wear sunglasses, you would go snow-blind—alkali can reflect light as much as snow. From my description above, you know my uncle didn't have sunglasses, so he walked with his eyes closed. My young aunt followed him, dressed in a woolen uniform, with a pair of high leather boots and a gun belt around her waist—all of which added a heroic touch to her bearing. She pulled down her hat string and tied it under her chin. After a while, she said, Stop, Convict Wang! There's nobody here. You can open the shackles now. My uncle squatted to unlock his shackles, and said, Reporting to the instructor, I can't unscrew it. The screw has rusted. My young aunt said, Stupid idiot! My uncle said, Can you blame me? It has both salt and alkali in it—what he meant was that with salt and alkali, any ironware would rust quickly. My aunt said, Piss on it! It will be easier to unscrew when it's wet. My uncle said he couldn't piss. Actually he's finicky and didn't want to touch the urine-soaked screw. My young aunt hesitated for a few minutes and said, As a matter of fact, I have to pee—but never mind, let's move on. My uncle stood up, shouldered the pick, and went on walking. On the snow-white alkali flat, there was nothing but the sparse, withered yellow reeds. They walked and walked and then my aunt let my uncle stop again. She untied her weapon belt, hung it around my uncle's neck, walked towards a cluster of reeds and squatted there to take a pee. Then they moved on. By that time my uncle wasn't just carrying the pick, but also had a weapon belt over his neck, a pistol in one hand, and a cattle prod in the other one, and tottered a lot—an entirely bizarre sight. Finally my uncle found a place where the alkali was thick. He took off his blue coat, spread it on the ground, put the gun belt beside it, then walked away and started swinging his pick and breaking up the alkali. My young aunt paced around him in circles, making constant creaking sounds, weighing the cattle prod in her hand. Then she stopped, taking a red silk scarf out of her left pocket, and tying it around her neck; from her right pocket she took out a pair of sunglasses and put them on. Then she walked to the blue coat, took off all of her clothes, spread out her fair-skinned body and started to sunbathe. Soon her fair body turned red. Meanwhile, my uncle faced the chilly wind with his nose running, swinging the pick to break up the alkali. Every now and then, my young aunt would call out lazily, Convict Wang! He would throw the pick aside, rush over with a series of clanks and say, Reporting to the instructor, Convict Wang here at your service. But my aunt had no real business; she just wanted him to look at her. With his nose running, my uncle had to bend over, squint his eyes in the cold wind, and admire her for a long while. Then my aunt asked him how she looked. My uncle wiped his running nose with his sleeve and mumbled in a low and deep voice, Pretty! Pretty! My young aunt was very content and said, OK, haven't you looked at me enough? Now go back to work. My uncle then ran back with a series of clanks, thinking to himself: What does she mean by "Haven't you looked at me enough?" I'm not the one who asked to look! To save all this running back and forth, I should have brought a telescope with me!

As for observing women through a telescope my uncle had a long history. There were all kinds of telescopes in his place—Zeiss, Olympus, and a Battery Commander bought from the former Soviet Union. He often leaned over the telescope, watching them for half an hour in the manner of Marshal Zhukov of the Soviet Army. They say being under such surveillance frightens and bewilders you altogether. The girls in his neighborhood would often be so befuddled while walking that they would suddenly smack into lampposts. Later, they always used umbrellas when they went out, so my uncle couldn't see them from upstairs. Now my young aunt just lay there letting him look at her, with no umbrella, and my uncle didn't want to look. This is called not knowing when you have it good.

My uncle was depressed in the alkali field, but my younger aunt was just the opposite. After enjoying enough sunshine, she put on her boots, walked into the cold air, came over to my uncle, and said, Convict Wang, you go get some sunshine too. Let me dig the alkali for a while. After saying this, she grabbed the pick and started digging. Meanwhile, my uncle lay down on the blue coat. If an alkali tractor was passing then at a distance, the people on the tractor would shout catcalls at her. This was because my young aunt had nothing on but a red silk scarf around her neck, a pair of sunglasses on her nose, and goose bumps all over. There were quite a few tractors in the field, rolling around on the waste ground and jetting out dark smoke, like nineteenth-century steamboats. The sky was so blue in that place that it almost looked purple, the wind as cold as water, the alkali white and gleaming, and the air dry enough to turn skin into paper. My uncle shut his eyes, wanting to daydream in the sunshine—the defeated always like to daydream. He was thirty-eight at the time. He spread out his limbs and fell asleep.

After a while, my young aunt kicked him and said, Get up, Convict Wang. You won't be able to enjoy sunshine that way! You'll get a rash if you keep yourself so covered up. She referred to the way that my uncle slept fully dressed in the sunshine. Considering it was outdoors and in sub-zero temperatures, what she said was not particularly true. My young aunt bent over, dragging his pants all the way down the shackles. If my uncle ever looked eight yards tall, it was then. Then she bent over again, wildly unbuttoning the four buttons of his ragged coat, and flinging it open. My uncle opened his eyes, and saw a red woman riding on his body with a red silk scarf around her neck and her hair flying like a wild horse's mane. He closed his eyes again. Although these actions had sexual overtones, they could also be interpreted as the instructor's concern for the prisoner—you can be sure the camp food in the camp was not very good. Letting him get some sunshine would provide him with additional vitamin D and prevent him from getting a calcium deficiency. After she finished, my young aunt dismounted from my uncle, seated herself beside him, pulled a pack of cigarettes out of her uniform pocket, and put one into her mouth. Just as she took out a windproof lighter and was about to light it, she changed her mind. She patted my uncle's chest with her palm and the lighter, and said, Stand up, Convict Wang! Don't you know the etiquette? On hearing her voice, my uncle stood up, leaned close to her and lit the cigarette for her. Later, every time my young aunt held a cigarette in her mouth, my uncle would reach out his hand, ask for the lighter and say, Reporting to the instructor, now I know the etiquette!

Afterward, my uncle lay on the alkali flat with his limbs splayed. The wind blew and gathered up the broken bits of alkali, which dropped on his skin and burned as hot as sparks. The bits of white alkali chips disappeared in little red spots all over his body. My young aunt put the rest of the cigarette into his mouth and he continued to smoke after her. Then, she climbed on his body to make love to him, her hair and the scarlet silk scarf flying side by side. As my uncle breathed in and out, smoke came out of his nose and mouth. Later he raised his head to look down, and said, Reporting to the instructor, do I need to put on a condom? But my young aunt said, You just lie there. Mind your own business. So he lay back, watching the clouds scatter in the sky. My young aunt patted his face, he turned around to look at her and asked, Reporting to the instructor! Why did you pat my face?

My uncle had been a frivolous person. After living in the alkali field, he became serious and steady. This had something to do with the story's setting. It was a huge alkali flat, with a muddy black sunken area in the center circled by a barbed wire fence. Inside that sunken area, there were dozens of rows of tents parted by a ditch in the middle, with water pipes lining the end of the ditch. At dusk, my uncle and the other inmates of the labor camp would wash their lunch pails there. The water from the pipes was alkaline, so the lunch pails were easy to clean. My uncle and aunt usually ate their meals inside their tent. It was a thick canvas tent with a light bulb hanging in the center. My young aunt sat commandingly on the bedroll eating her meal; her legs forked and her head held upright; her box lunch contained white rice, hearts of cabbage, and a few pieces of sausage. My young uncle sat on a folding stool eating his meal, his legs crossed, his head lowered, and his bowl containing stale rice and old cabbage, with no sausages at all. My young aunt grunted Moo and my uncle handed over his box. She gave him her sausages and he took the box back, continuing to eat. Then my young aunt glared at him. She hurried to swallow the rice in her mouth and said, Convict Wang, don't you even say 'thank you'? My uncle immediately responded, Yes, thanks! My aunt asked, Thank whom? My uncle hesitated a bit, and then said, Thank you, big sister! My young aunt fell into silence and the reason for that was because my uncle was fifteen years older than her. By the time they finished their meal, my aunt struck her box and said, Convict Wang! I think it would be better if you kept calling me "Instructor." My uncle agreed, took their boxes and went out. My young aunt fell silent again. She felt very good, so good that her sides began shaking with laughter. She thought my uncle very amusing, herself amusing, too, and their life very enjoyable; on my uncle's side, he didn't think himself amusing, nor did he think my young aunt was, and to him this kind of life was a misery. Nevertheless, he still loved my young aunt because he had no other choice.

At this point, my uncle's story ended this way: when he came back from washing their lunch boxes, it was already dark and the wind had started blowing. He put their lunch boxes into a bag, hung it on the wall and then fastened the door flap. The so-called door flap was just a canvas curtain with straps on the sides that could be tied to the tent. My uncle fastened every single strap and turned around, seeing my young aunt's uniform scattered over the ground. He picked the pieces up, folded them one by one and then put them on a wooden shelf in a corner. After that, he stood in the middle of the tent at attention. At that point my young aunt had thrown herself under the quilt, face down, reading a book by a small table lamp. After a while, the light bulb flickered a few times and went out, but my young aunt's table lamp was still on—it ran on batteries. She said, Convict Wang, it's time to go to bed! My uncle took off all of his clothes, including the shackles, which rusted during the day. But my uncle had a small wrench just right for unlock-

On the alkali field, the reason that my aunt kept my uncle and didn't want to release him was also because he was unfathomable. She told me that she met my uncle first in her math class. My uncle had started losing his hair after the IQ tests, and besides, he hadn't found any quick way to get out of there. Because of these two things he was in a bad mood, and the hair on the back of his head stood up like a hedge-hog's. In the class, he glared, gnashed his teeth hard, and often bit off his pencil and ate it as if it were a stick of candy. Then he would wipe the graphite bits left at the corner of his mouth and smear his whole mouth black. He ate all seven of the pencils he got for each class. My young aunt thought he looked scary and often reminded him, Convict Wang, I'm not the one who took your permit away, why stare at me like that? My uncle snapped awake as if from a dream. He stood up and answered, I'm sorry, instructor! You're very pretty. I love you. The last line just occurred to him at that very moment. My uncle always had a well-oiled tongue and couldn't change even after he went to the Art Reeducation Institute. I told my young aunt that she was truly very pretty. She said, Yeah, yeah. Then she laughed, I'm pretty. But it wasn't his place to say so. Later she told me that although she was still young, she was already a wily veteran. At the Art Reeducation Institute, whenever a student complimented an instructor's looks, he'd have something on his mind. As for saying he loved her, he should have been punished for that. I never saw my young aunt hit my uncle, but from the way they talked about it, it must have happened.

My young aunt also said that in the Art Reeducation Institute, bored students often tried to butter her up. She always struck them after she heard that sort of talk. For some reason my uncle seemed different from those others. The two were destined to be together. The evidence of their destiny was that when she looked at his paintings, she felt un-fathomable and very horny. Once the three of us, my uncle, my aunt, and I, lay on the alkali flat. My young aunt was on her belly sunbathing, on a plastic sheet; my uncle lay there with all his clothes on, like a corpse, except his two eyes were wide open, focusing on his nose. My aunt's naked body was very beautiful, but I didn't risk looking at her. I was afraid that my uncle might get jealous. He looked terrible. I wanted to comfort him, but didn't dare, for my young aunt might accuse us of conspiracy. What a strange situation to be dragged into! Just imagining it would be strange.

My young aunt said she liked my uncle's paintings. The Art Reedu-cation Institute had gotten some from Lijiakou police station. But those paintings took up too much space, so the institute decided to throw them into the garbage. My young aunt asked for all of them and stored them in her dorm. When nobody was around, she would look at them. Therefore, it was not by chance that my young aunt escorted my uncle to the alkali field. As the saying goes: Better to have a thief steal from you than keep you in mind. My young aunt had kept my young uncle in mind for a long time. That's my conclusion, but my young aunt had a different opinion. She said: It was the god of art, Apollo, who brought us together. At this point, she nudged my uncle and asked: Is the god of art Apollo? My uncle responded, I don't know who he is. His voice was low and deep, sounding like my dead cousin come back to life.

I often visited the alkali field, and every time, I would tell my young aunt that my uncle loved her. After my young aunt heard this, her eyes would turn golden and she would say, He loves me? Fine! Then she would burst out laughing, which made me doubt whether she really considered it fine. Otherwise, she wouldn't have laughed like that. If it were another woman, how she felt wouldn't matter. But my young aunt had my uncle's life in her hands and I believed it was my responsibility to make her feel good. So I tried to approach her in another way, If my young uncle didn't really love you, how would you feel? She said, He doesn't really love me? That's also very good! Then she laughed again, which to me seemed like mocking. We had come to a deadlock over this issue, so it was time for me to try something else.

One time, I brought all kinds of newspaper clippings to my uncle—the Japanese had taken my uncle's paintings to Paris and arranged a show for him, which caused a sensation. The show was called "2010—W2" and didn't reveal the painter's identity, which was one of the reasons for the sensation. All the newspapers agreed that the visual effect of this set of paintings was amazing; as to whether they were great works, only a few thought so. At the entrance to the exhibit, a painting looking like a crazy donkey dominated the entire show. Even someone with a good inner ear would feel dizzy after looking at it for five seconds. It happened that one person in the audience had Meniere's Syndrome. When he looked at this painting, he felt sky and earth spin to the right while his body fell to the left—a jack couldn't have kept him up. So he was led to another painting that looked like a crazy horse, and then felt the sky and earth spin to the left, so he finally managed to stand straight. Then he turned back and went home; for three days, he could eat nothing and drink only a little ice water. In the center of the exhibit hall a painting hung, which after viewing, people would feel all the blood had rushed to their heads. Whether you were a man or a woman, old or young, your hair would stand up, with the exception of men with crew cuts. Blonde beauties with hair down to their shoulders soon looked like clowns with pointy hats. At the same time, audience members' eyes turned upwards, showing the whites. A man with arteriosclerosis immediately had a stroke. Another painting made people feel that all their internal organs were traveling downward; young men with straight backs would become stoop-shouldered, and men with hernias would feel like they had a hot water bottle hanging from their crotches. People made all kinds of guesses about the identity of the artist named "W2." Some religious leaders had already decided to label him a blasphemer, a minion of Satan, and had ordered his execution. They killed some Williams, Webers, and Willises, and were trying to kill the people who could paint in the World Health Organization (WHO), and even made West Point change its name. At the time none of them got the idea of killing all the Chinese with the surname of Wang. There're one hundred million people named Wang in China, the equivalent of the population of a large country. I don't think they would dare risk it. I showed these clippings to my young aunt, trying to make her understand that my uncle was a great artist and she should treat him well. My young aunt said, Great! Great! If he weren't great, would I be in charge of him? Later, as I was leaving, my uncle took the opportunity to kick me. He used this method of communicating to me that advertising his greatness to my young aunt wasn't good for him. This was the last time that he kicked me. Afterwards, he was sick as a dog and hadn't the strength to kick me any more.

While I obsessed over saving my uncle, he slowly languished in the alkali field. His lips protruded and his cheeks became as hollow as a monkey's. My young aunt also worried and asked me to bring some canned food from town, especially five-kilogram cans of lunch meat. I put them into plastic string bags and hung them on my neck, one on each side, very silly looking. On the bus to the alkali field, people said I looked like Pigsy with a sword strapped on—a slob of a soldier. This lunch meat was mostly used by restaurants in cold dishes, with the meat cut into small pieces; if you ate big chunks, it was very greasy and hard to swallow. As my young aunt opened the can in the tent, my uncle lay beside her and began to throw up. She scooped a piece of lunch meat and forced it into my uncle's mouth. Then she hurried to toss the spoon aside, pressed my uncle's mouth with one hand and choked his neck with the other hand.

She gazed into his eyes and said, One, two, three! Swallow! By the time she finished stuffing my uncle, my young aunt was drenched in sweat. She wiped her hands and said, You, boy, go find out where they sell those machines to force-feed ducks. By then my uncle's lips had swollen and really did look like a duck's bill.

Since he didn't eat well in the alkali field and also felt depressed, my uncle suffered from impotence. But my aunt knew what to do. These anecdotes of my uncle's, he told me himself little by little and somewhat shyly. My aunt added a lot: when he lay on the alkali flat, the thing slouched limply, like a steamed taro. You'd have to shout at him: Attention! Then he would stand up, like a prairie dog, poking his head out and looking around. Of course, you couldn't yell at him unless you were my young aunt. The thing was very good at following orders. He could not only understand "attention" and "at ease," but also knew "right face" or "left face" and "forward march," et cetera. By contrast, my uncle had problems following orders. He couldn't tell left from right; if you told him "turn left," he would surely turn right; when he marched, he would swing the wrong arm. But the thing didn't have any of these problems. My young aunt would laugh whenever mentioning this, saying that his IQ was higher than my uncle's. If my uncle's IQ were 50, his would be 150, three times higher. For a genital organ, the score was pretty unusual. My aunt was teaching him math, but he hadn't mastered it yet. So far, he only knew to nod twice when asked what one plus one equaled. But my young aunt was very confident about his talent for mathematics and resolved to teach him calculus. She had been teaching my uncle the subject, but he hadn't mastered it. She also described in detail how after she gave the order "attention" the little guy staggered up, turned to an exclamation mark from a question mark, and brightened his color from dark gray to scarlet, like an American apple. She said that any woman would feel overcome at the sight. But I thought men would feel the same way.

My young aunt also said: An artist is indeed an artist, even his tool is different from others'—other men definitely don't have this talent. My uncle blushed at hearing this, and he said, Reporting to the Instructor, please don't insult me. You can shoot a soldier but don't shame him. But my aunt just shrugged and made light of the subject, Cut the nonsense! Why would I kill you? Come here, give me a kiss. My uncle had to contain his boiling anger and kiss my young aunt. After the kiss, he forgot about the insult. In my opinion, my uncle didn't have the dash he used to have and had become a little dull, at least around my aunt. I heard that if my aunt shouted "Attention!" at him, he would ask foolishly, Who? If my aunt said, "At ease!" he would also ask who should be at ease. In the tent, my aunt lowered her voice and said, Comrade, you went the wrong way. . . . My uncle would look blank for a moment and ask: Were you talking to me? Did I commit an error? My young aunt mocked him: A human talks to you and you answer like a dog. Sometimes, she talked to my uncle and he made no response at all. She had to pat his face and he would say something like, Sorry, Instructor. I didn't know you were talking to me. The disturbing part was that my uncle and that thing of his were both named Wang Er. My young aunt was confused too and said, The two of you together will be the death of me! Gradually, my uncle didn't know how many selves he had.

My uncle and my aunt reached an impasse in the alkali field. I thought there were two reasons for it at the time. The first was because my young aunt didn't understand art; she only knew how to make fun of artists. If I had known what art was and could have explained it to her, she would probably have let my uncle leave. Since I was unable to, my uncle couldn't get out.

When I first got to college, I was so occupied with the true meaning of art that I constantly forgot about east-west-south-north. People would see me circle around the sports field; if someone tried counting the circles, he'd lose track and walk away. I thought and thought, and then I forgot sunrise and sunset. People would see me sitting on the roof, smoking at midnight, throwing down cigarette butts one after another—the incredible part about my sitting that high was that I had acrophobia. Girls fell in love with me because of this, saying I reminded them of Wittgenstein. But I always told them: Wittgenstein is nobody! After hearing this, they loved me more. But I was too busy solving this difficult problem to fall in love with any of them, letting them fly away from me one after another. Thinking back on this now, I can't help feeling regret, because some of them were very smart; some were very pretty; others were smart and pretty, which was more unusual. As for the true meaning of art, it's why people want to paint, and write poetry and fiction. I believed that as an artist, I first had to think it out clearly. Unfortunately, to this day I still haven't figured out the answer.

I still miss the time I was a freshman at the university. Back then I worked on a physics paper; prepared for the graduate exam in history; visited my uncle from time to time; constantly pondered the true meaning of art; participated in all the discussions on any of the trendy topics in Beijing; and managed to steal some leisure time from my busy schedule to go after a pretty girl in the biology department. During the height of summer, this girl would comb her long hair into a ponytail and wear a white T-shirt and striped culottes; droplets of sweat would often form on her neck and behind her ears. When I met her on campus, I would invite her to go to the pinewoods with me. She would carefully put a handkerchief over the pine needles, sit on it, and take off her leather sandals and knee socks. By then I would get absent-minded, forgetting my intention to use my nose to sniff the sour smell around her neck—the girls all agreed that I had a lovely nose, warm in winter and cool in summer. That was why she didn't mind lifting her ponytail to let me smell the soft hair on the nape of her neck. From this angle, the girl smelled like cheese. Unfortunately, I'd often remember that I had something else to do, so I'd remove my nose from her neck and leave in a hurry. I remember once I detected a heavy scent of something from her breasts. Before I could tell what it was, suddenly I remembered that I had to catch the bus to see my uncle; I hurried away. Next time I saw her, she looked like she was about to cry, and threw the dish she was carrying into my face. The dish contained a half portion of garlic scape and a half portion of tofu, plus several ounces of rice. The garlic scape was overcooked, too soft; the tofu was cooked with five-spice powder that had gone bad, a little bitter; the rice was steamed in a stainless steel tray and then divided into four portions. I hate for rice to be cooked this way. From this incident, I learned about her bad temper and some other things that I didn't like. So I stopped thinking of her, except for occasionally thinking that she might still be thinking of me.

On the alkali flat, when I was considering how to save my uncle, it suddenly dawned on me that the truth of art was unfathomability. However, this answer meant nothing, for nobody in the world knew what unfathomability was. If anyone knew, it wouldn't be unfathomability.

Another reason that my uncle was trapped in the alkali field was that he was not good at love. If he had been good at it, he would have been able to get my aunt to release him. In my opinion, love was a kind of athletics; some people could run a hundred yards in ten seconds, and others needed twenty seconds to finish the same distance. Many of the people who went to the Art Reeducation Institute at the same time as my uncle were already out, strolling the streets holding their former instructor's arm; it seemed they were better at love than my uncle. The secret of athletics is practice. So I started to practice, not only to save my uncle, but also to save myself in the future.

Recently, I met a woman at our class reunion. She said she remembered me, and her memory of me was poetic. First, she remembered a wind at the beginning of this century, full of yellow dust. Below the yellow dust, the leaves appeared unusually green. Between the yellow and the green was a boy, wrapped in dusty corduroy clothes, languidly walking across the sports field as if sick—the boy was me—though I was never sick at the university. I didn't know why she said I looked sick. But judging by what she said, it would have been the period before I started visiting the alkali field.

This woman is my colleague, now living overseas; she smelled like glacial acetic acid from a bottle, almost like an acid bomb. In her poetic reminiscence, the most memorable thing about those yellow-dust days was the leaves dripping with green, the leaves symbolizing sex. Then she mentioned a small room and a window. The window was associated with a mathematical expression—the expression was two times two, which signified the four panes of glass in the window; square, covered by a piece of cloth with a black and red pattern. The wind ballooned the piece of patterned clothes above a wrinkled narrow bed; an indigo wax-printed sheet was spread over the bed. She lay naked on the sheet and tried very hard to stretch her body; in other words, she tried to make her head and her toes separate as far from each other as possible; so her belly sank back into the sheet. Her legs shined with a gray luster. A smell permeated this strange scene, something fishy; in other words, the smell of fresh semen. If you'd told me this smell had something to do with me, I'd have been really surprised. But the room was the dormitory I lived in as a sophomore, and I lived there alone. As for what I did there, I don't remember anything at all.

This woman applied heavy eye shadow, dyed her hair dirty blonde, and now weighed about three hundred pounds. It was very difficult for me to associate her with any girl I had known in the past. Since she knew my room, and even my smell, I couldn't deny our relationship. She also said, at the time we were together, I was a quiet, tense-faced person, often seeming to have something in mind; then all of a sudden, my semen would start jetting, warm as pee. Because I was such an absent-minded bed-wetter, she missed me all the time. But I didn't remember having wet my bed; besides, if you called this love—I would definitely deny it.

At the university, there was a time I took classes like a lunatic, twenty courses one semester. I couldn't attend every class, so I asked my classmates to bring walkie-talkies with them. I myself sat in the dorm, keeping track of the lectures through different earphones. My room looked like a switchboard, and my face got pale. The professors in my department suspected me of taking heroin, and urged me to have a blood test. After finding out that I wasn't a drug addict, they admonished me: Why the hurry to graduate? The most important thing is to be a good student. But I was busy taking finals first, and then busy taking make-ups. When I went to take the medical Latin make-up, I looked like a dead person, and the professor let me pass without asking me a thing. Then I collapsed to the ground and was taken to the school hospital. It was my young uncle's situation that drove me so crazy. Whenever I thought about his predicament, it felt like hundreds of claws scratching at my heart.

During winter vacation, I heard that a girl in the chemistry department had taken twenty-one courses, one more than I did. I fell in love with her because of this, waiting for her in front of her dorm every day with a bouquet. She was a small girl with thick glasses, but the eyes behind the glasses were very large, two Archimedean curves rounding into circles. She had a pale face and a pair of hands like bird's claws, and was a little hunchbacked, too. Later on, I discovered her breasts flat against her chest, no bigger than mine, just a pair of nipples; her shoulders were as thin as mine when I was thirteen. To sum things up, in terms of the parts above her navel and below her knees, she was completely a boy. About things between men and women, she had an academic interest, always asking: Why is it like this? I told her that I loved her and didn't want to love anybody else in this life. She pushed up her glasses and said: Why do you want to love me? Why don't you want to love somebody else in this life? I couldn't come up with an answer, so I suggested we make love. As she said afterward, making love didn't solve the problem. If I really had loved her, I wouldn't have needed a reason. But things without reasons make people suspicious. Therefore, I came to the conclusion that whoever told her he loved her would make her suspicious. After she said what she did, I felt like I didn't really love her. She pushed up her glasses and said: Why don't you love me anymore? Then I fell in love with her again. We seesawed like this. A semester later, her body suddenly began to develop. She bought a pair of contact lenses, and turned into a slender beauty and a dumbbell also. By then there were many pursuers gathering around her and I had lost interest.

6

Once my uncle, aunt, and I sunbathed till dusk. At dusk, my young aunt stood up and looked around. The sunset's red and white colors shone on her body, making her look like a goddess. If I wanted to go into detail, I would say her shoulders reflected like mirrors, and her breasts cast a shadow on her chest. On her flat belly, there was a clump of hair, like a squirrel's tail—I suspect as her nephew I shouldn't be describing her this way—then she bent over to put on her pants, and I had to get back to school. It was the only time that I saw my young aunt in the nude. I never had another chance. If I had known that, I would have taken a good look at her then.

After talking about my young aunt, I should say something about my young uncle. His case was redressed later; the court announced his innocence, and the Art Reeducation Institute declared him a good student. The Oil Painting Association restored his membership and his permit, and even wanted to put him on the Directorate of the Fine Arts Association. But my young uncle didn't collect his permit, nor did he want to join the Oil Painting Association. So the department concerned decided to dismiss my young uncle and revoke his painting permit on the charge of not having the good sense to appreciate when someone is doing him a favor. However, my young aunt objected to their decision and wanted to sue. Her argument was that since my uncle neither rejoined the Fine Arts Association nor collected his permit, how was it possible to dismiss him and cancel his permit? But she lost the lawsuit. The court ruled that as the authority in the painting field, the Oil Painting Association could revoke anyone's membership or cancel his permit, whether he was a member or not, or a painter or not. After the ruling, the Oil Painting Association called a meeting and solemnly decided to dismiss my young aunt. From then on, she could write, but it would be illegal for her to paint. Now, neither my uncle nor my aunt had a permit. Anyhow, he continued painting and selling his paintings to that Japanese. The price had gone down a lot. The Japanese guy said that with the world economy in a slump, paintings weren't easy to unload. Actually, it was a lie. The truth was that my young uncle's reputation had declined—he'd fallen a little out of fashion.

After talking about my uncle, now I should say something about the Japanese—the guy had aged, white stubble grew around his mouth. When I stopped at a red light at an intersection, he'd strut down the crosswalk, open the door of my car, and say, Mr. Wang, paintings! And he took off with the paintings. By the way, my old uncle is called Wang Da, and my young uncle is Wang Er. My mother was such a strong-willed woman that I had no choice but to adopt her last name of "Wang." My young uncle stored those paintings at my place. If the red light were fairly long, the Japanese would chat with me some more. He said that he really missed my young uncle and wanted to see him sometime. I lied to him, My uncle has left to become a nun. He can't break the rules of the order and come out to see you. Put him out of your mind. He corrected me, Monk, you mean monk. Then he closed the door, bowed to me, and walked away. Actually, he knew I was lying. If he hadn't contacted my uncle, how would he find me? On the other hand, I also knew the Japanese was lying. We all lied, nobody trusted anyone else.

Somebody said that the Japanese was actually Brazilian; many people of Japanese descent lived in Brazil. He had a black wife, dark as ink. Once he brought her to China. She wore a green cheongsam while taking a walk with him, which led to a misunderstanding. The police arrested her under the impression she was my young uncle. In the police station, they dipped a towel into water, gasoline and acetone, and scrubbed her face hard. What came off was not black greasepaint, but blood. By the time people from the Brazilian Embassy got word and rushed over, the sign over the station had been changed to "Daycare Center"; all the policemen wore white uniforms, and pretended to be washing the black woman's face. She was about six foot six, almost as tall as a lamppost. The claim that she was a lost child seemed dubious. The Japanese fellow also had a white mistress, white as snow. Once when they walked on the street, there was mix-up again. The policemen took her to the station. The first sentence they said was, Hey! Wang Er, very realistic! How much bleaching powder did you use? Then they pinched her nose, trying to find out if it was plaster, which made her tears pour down like rain; they pulled her hair hard, suspecting it was a wig, and soon her blonde hair looked like a hornet's nest. When the employees from the embassy arrived, the sign over the police station was changed to "Beauty Salon." But it was a little strange for a beauty salon to make her nose look like a drunkard's and her hair like a naval mine. Later, whenever they walked on the street, those foreign women would hang a sign around their necks, which read: "I am not Wang Er."

One day, a policeman seized me, grabbing my tie and dragging me off the ground. Then he said cheerfully, Great, Wang Er, now you don't even try to disguise yourself. I said calmly, Big uncle, you're making a mistake. I'm not Wang Er. I'm his nephew. He stared at me blankly, then put me down and let out a gob of spit, which landed on my leather shoes. He thought for a while, then smoothed my tie, wiped my leather shoes, saluted me, and pretended to walk away. Actually, he didn't walk away but stealthily followed me. Every ten minutes he would rush in front of me and take my pulse, to see if it was racing. I was calm every time, so he didn't dare grab me again. Fortunately, he didn't take me to the police station, otherwise, when the people from my work unit came to get me, the police would have had to switch signs: Judo Studio. The reason that these things happened was because they knew my uncle was still selling his paintings in secret. They really wanted to arrest him, but couldn't catch him. That was not important—the important thing was when they grabbed me, I felt excited and got an erection, which meant that like my young uncle, I had the artistic gift. This probably was beyond question.

So far, I've talked about everyone except me. When I was a little kid, I wanted to be an artist. After witnessing my young uncle's fate, I changed my mind and began to try other things, including working as an attendant at a public toilet. The one I kept watch over was a dark-green building that looked like it was built of glazed bricks, but actually was molded concrete, with a layer of veneer glued to the surface to simulate glaze. Rain showers made it peel so badly that it looked like a turtle with ringworm. There were plenty of long, narrow mirrors inside. Peering at yourself in the mirror, you would feel like you were in a cage. The room smelled of bitter almond, a kind of disinfectant. I stood by the door, distributing bathroom tissue to people. Once in a while I had to clean the inside with a fire hose, turning the people who were sitting on the toilets into drowned rats. One thing I'll never forget was when I asked for tips; if a customer forgot to give me money, I would grab his clothes, and even tear off his pocket. After a while nobody dared not to tip me. I soon got fired because I worked too diligently.

Another time I set up a stall in front of the railway station, repairing watches and lighters. Like other repair stalls, mine was also a glass case, which could be pushed away. Because of the greenhouse effect, it was very hot to sit inside, and I sweated a lot and was thirsty all the time. The watches I fixed wouldn't keep time, but could light cigarettes; the lighters worked as watches, but couldn't strike a light. My customers weren't very satisfied. Another time I wore sunglasses, pretended to be blind, and made a living by singing on the street. Very few people gave me money. For a blind person, my clothes were not dirty enough. They also said my singing was so terrible that I could make children pee faster. Later on, I tried baby-sitting, singing for kids. They couldn't pee at all after hearing my singing. When their parents came home, they would say: Mommy, this uncle sang. Then they began to cry uncontrollably. I tried all kinds of jobs in order to keep stalling and avoid my fate.

Finally I grew up and got a job in the writing department; my uncle also came out of the alkali field and married my young aunt. He still paints. It is my young aunt who changed jobs, working in public relations at a big company. This proves that my uncle and I have no other talents besides painting and palavers respectively. My young aunt had many talents. Sometimes she called me in the middle of the night to complain about my uncle, saying that all my uncle knew was how to play mysterious little tricks in his painting. He had exhausted his talent and couldn't create the kind of paintings that made people dizzy anymore; she also said that one part of his body worked in the old way, she had to give orders to him every day and pretended to like that very much—but she was bored to death. This seems to imply that she got a raw deal by marrying my uncle. But after every conversation, she would always add: Don't tell your uncle what I said. If you dare reveal any bit of it, I'll kill you. As for me, I write stories every day. To tell the truth, I don't even know what I'm writing.

For all we face today, I bear the responsibility. That day, when I returned from the alkali field, I was worried and upset. So I played with my computer, trying to find a game on the Internet. After searching here and there, I didn't find a game, but I came across an electronic magazine called *Physics Today*. Though I majored in physics, I never read anything in physics except textbooks. That day was an exception. The magazine's banner headline read: Who is the greatest painter after Dali—W2 or 486? W2 was my uncle's alias, 486 was a personal computer at the end of the last century, completely obsolete nowadays. You can buy five or six of them for just a dollar. There was an illustration in the article, showing a 486 computer with the hernia-inducing painting of my uncle's on the screen. Of course, it was only a picture of a picture so you wouldn't get a hernia, although it still made you want to shit. After you finished the article, you didn't even want to shit anymore. The article mentioned that at the end of the last century, people began to study physical processes from disorder to order, also known as "chaos." In computer simulation, chaos looks very pretty on the screen. The most famous is the "Mandelbrot Sets," which, magnified, looks like the tail of a sea horse and which I believe everyone has seen. By the way, the "Mandelbrot Sets" didn't make people dizzy and had nothing in common with my young uncle's paintings. But the article's author invented a formula called "Yi Ya Ah La," which uses an obsolete 486 computer to paint and can make people much dizzier than ever. Simply put, a formula plus a junk computer that is cheaper than a box of matches can make paintings like my uncle's. Once you know this you're not going to get dizzy or have a hernia at my uncle's paintings. Obviously, my young aunt wouldn't get horny anymore when she looked at my uncle's paintings. This article gave me a different feeling about my young uncle, young aunt, art, love, as well as the whole world, which is: you open your asshole to fart and nothing much comes out. If I hadn't surfed the net, everything would have stayed the same: my young uncle still as unfathomable as before, and my young aunt still obsessed with him. I am not a boy anymore, why do I still play games?

After reading the article, I hesitated for a long time, and finally made up my mind. I made a hundred copies of the article, attached a letter asking redress for my uncle's case, and sent it to all the departments concerned—after all, my uncle was suffering and I couldn't sit there without lending him a helping hand. The department concerned responded immediately: my young uncle wasn't unfathomable. What he painted were Yi Ya Ah La Sets. Why are we keeping him in prison—Let him go! With this news, I sped to the alkali field and told my young uncle and aunt everything. My young aunt let out a long sigh after she heard this, and said, So that's what they are! I'm sorry, Convict Wang, you've suffered a lot! I'll ask the Institute to pay you some compensation after I get back. You don't have to keep saying you love me anymore. When my young uncle heard my words, he fell to the ground like a dead person; but as soon as he heard those words of my aunt, he came back to life, rose from the ground and said, Reporting to the instructor, I really love you. I was never using you! Et cetera. After my young aunt heard this, her eyes turned a golden color. She grinned at me, Did you hear that? Let's beat this death-before-dishonor guy! But before we could start she changed her mind and heaved a long sigh, Never mind. Don't beat him, looks like he really has fallen in love with me. This seems to imply that if my uncle continued to be unfathomable, it would have been impossible for him to fall in love with my young aunt and she would have had to beat him hard for that reason, but it would also be very enjoyable to make love to him; if he were no longer unfathomable, though he could fall in love with my young aunt, and she couldn't beat him from then on, it would also be very boring to make love to him. My young aunt and uncle left the alkali field, got married, and lived their life; everything became ordinary and predictable.

The year is 2015. I'm a writer. I still think about the true meaning of art. What is it anyway?

Phillip Robertson

In the Mosque of the Imam Ali

When then devil came, he was not red.
He was chrome and he said,
Come with me.

Jeff Tweedy, "Hell is Chrome"

Sungsu Cho

Cho is doing something to a cigarette with his fingers. He's rolling it back and forth until the tobacco falls out onto a sweat damp handkerchief full of black hash. He mixes the tobacco with the stuff we scored in Baghdad and then puts it back in the cigarette like a surgeon. Cho is the acknowledged master of this art and executes his moves with precision. The same fingers that sold vegetables in a market in Seoul. Cho would go anywhere in the war and if he wanted you to stick around, he would say, "Yeah, you stay here, OK?" distracted, tired, then make you dinner with the kimchi he had flown in from Seoul. I wrote the captions on his photographs because it wasn't easy for him. Cho's father is a retired South Korean military officer, and I always wanted to know what happened that sent Cho to war zones, but it was something he and his father never got over. I want to weep seeing him there in the car next to his pile of forgotten Nikons.

Up front, Cho's driver Ibrahim is getting upset. From the back seat I can see him twisting around, trying to figure out what will stop Cho from going through with it but Ibrahim is forced to watch the road for speeding traffic, insurgents hunting the roads and American convoys. We are passing Hilla and Babylon, heading north at eighty miles an hour into a highway of roadside bombs and ten-mile traffic jams. Up front, Ibrahim is spooked out of his mind because his passengers are going to get high and fill his car with smoke. Ibrahim keeps twisting around in the driver's seat to give us a look, but there's nothing he can do. I can tell he thinks that the trip is another bad luck situation from the nervous animal sounds, which keep coming out of him. We speed down the road, Ibrahim swerving away from other drivers and twitching the wheel back and forth. "It's total fucking bullshit," Cho says, and lights up just as we cross into the Sunni triangle. He is referring to everything. Thirty miles south of Baghdad, the highway that runs through the farm towns of Latayfiya and Yusufiya, is the worst stretch of highway in the country, worst meaning highest number of insurgent attacks and kidnappings per tourist mile. Ambushes, executions, and roadside bombs. Firefights and covered in a pall of smoke and fire half the time. American patrols never come close to owning this road, they just roll down it at high speed with their machine guns up, watching and listening for detonations, the high crack of a Kalashnikov, rockets, all the bad spirits of the air.

I watch the low dust-colored buildings reverse along the road, hiding men with rocket launchers and rifles who were watching the stream of cars. We have white rimes of salt under our arms from the sun. It is Friday afternoon, the terminal stages of July, and we are going steadily through light that is gold and then red over the long stands of palms along the Euphrates River, the sun is falling and burning in the West while the groves reverse under the smoldering screen of the sky.

Cho has this handsome Frankenstein face and he takes a drag and lets it out again and the car fills up with the smell of dope. We smoke the joint in the back and laugh and hide our faces from children selling soft drinks by the side of the road. Children work as spotters for kidnappers. When Ibrahim finally cracks a window, the vapors stream out behind us in a comet's tail until and the purified dread washes out of us, a kind of miracle. Oh that road, you never forget. Getting stoned on the road near Latayfiya is like fucking on an altar. Terrible things happened out there, the place gave birth to hundreds of fear myths.

A few weeks before when the war was just starting in Najaf, I found a driver in front of the Hamra hotel, who panicked on the way down south, losing it somewhere on the road near Latayfiya. We had stopped at a U.S. roadblock, which is where Hekmat finally bolted, and said he couldn't go any farther. He was faking car trouble and said he couldn't get the car to start when in fact he had thrown a switch under the dash to keep the ignition from working. I wanted to kill him, and if I'd found the switch I would have stolen the car. Traffic was backed up for miles because of a roadside bomb and the soldiers providing security for the sappers were scared, and they were standing in a row with their weapons up, with rounds chambered. An Iraqi man held his four-year-old kid out in front of him until a soldier lowered his M-16. A young tanker yelled, "Hey how's the sushi in California?" He wanted to know how reporters moved around areas the Mahdi Army controlled. I told him about the safe passage letters and how they didn't work all the time, but the soldiers wouldn't let me through because this unit hated reporters. They wouldn't even let one past the razor wire.

We listened to the sappers detonate the roadside bombs a mile down the highway. While I was trying to talk to the soldiers at the roadblock, Hekmat turned his car around and headed back north. I caught a ride with some laborers in a bus going to Iskandariya. The driver headed off the highway into the network of irrigation canals around the town. A few minutes later, deep in this Euphrates River farmland, I saw a thin kid in a white dishdasha looking in the windshields so he could see the passengers of the cars. The kid had a walkie-talkie he was using to talk to fighters down the road about who was coming through. He missed the foreigner. It was amazing how close you could get to the black edge and survive.

By late July last year, the uprising had spread across Iraq, pulling every village and city into open warfare, bringing in air strikes and heavy armor until you had the feeling that the whole thing was going to end in an apocalypse, a great shout of blood and heat. The ambush road south of Baghdad had rolled all the way out until it was the country itself.

While we drive to Baghdad, twenty miles away, Moqtada al Sadr wrapped in a white martyr's shroud, is about to speak to ten thousand of his followers in the courtyard of the vast Kufa mosque. It marks the place where Imam Ali, the first Shia saint, was murdered. There is no space to move, the courtyard is full of worshippers and ten thousand men cover the flagstones like a sea. They wait until a shattering sound comes from speakers in the minarets, the name of God in a hundred rising and falling syllables. Its carrier wave is the breaking voice of a young man, one of the Mahdi revolutionaries. When the militiamen hear him, they stand absolutely still with their hands at their sides, personalities punched from their bodies by the name of God. Singing and screaming, the muezzin holds them outside time until the voice they hear ceases to belong to someone else, it belongs to the myriad men in black shirts and sandals who no longer want to live in the corrupt world. The voice kills and resurrects. Hearing the call is like having electrical wires run through your veins. It sounds like heartbreak.

After the call, al Sadr begins to speak. Under delicate arches and columns, he promises he will never desert his followers, that he is prepared to die for them. "I will never abandon you no matter what, and I am close to you and living the same life as you," he says like a million other martyrs before him. Al Sadr in his carpenter's Arabic is really telling them goodbye and they are screaming. It's what he wants them to beleive. Al Sadr is urging them forward into the guns of the Americans by throwing out the following chain of associations: I am like Imam Ali, the first martyr of the Shia, I am prepared to die. If you are like me, then you must also be prepared for death.

Death is paradise, freedom from the corruption of the earth, his followers believe. The crowd of young men in their black shirts under the crucible sun shouts at the top of its lungs, straining to see the savior but can't. It's a hundred and fifteen degrees, and the single note they are making with their voices is the human sound reserved only for living gods, the waves of it breaking on the high walls of the mosque. The screaming sound echoes in dark alcoves and stabs at the ears. Al Sadr is also telling them that the war against the Americans is going to begin and he wants them to be ready.

Many of the worshippers believe al Sadr is the disappeared twelfth Imam, returning to deliver them from evil and injustice at the end of the world. "He is just like a lion. He is the Lion of God. Can't you see?" One Mahdi Army fighter once said to me during one of these faith rallies, his eyes ecstatic. They were all thinking the exact same thing, it didn't really matter who you asked. Soon, they would hallucinate. In the Kufa mosque, thousands of young men are kneeling in rows behind al Sadr and praying while other identical men standing on the walls of the Kufa mosque scan the dead horizon with rifle scopes and binoculars. Many of the veteran fighters rose up against Saddam after the Gulf War, spent time in prison. When you met them in their homes, the first thing they showed you were the pictures they took in Abu Ghraib.

The ceasefire that has lasted for nearly a month is on the verge of collapse. It's going to be a matter of days now, but we don't know it yet. There's a feeling of dread everyone has like something is wrong with the air. U.S. forces have demanded that Mahdi Army forces withdraw from

Najaf and Kufa, while the Mahdi Army demands that the U.S. withdraw from Iraq. Ayatollah Sistani and the old sheikhs of the surrounding towns said that they want the Mahdi Army to withdraw. Moqtada al Sadr publicly refused, saying he will only follow the directions of the highest religious authorities. It's a strange statement to make. Sistani is the highest Shia authority there is. The Shia uprising led by Moqtada al Sadr grew out of Shia congregations all over the country. Before the uprisings started, Pro-Mahdi imams urged the young men to join the movement, go to Najaf, and take a stand to defend their religion. Thousands obeyed.

The Well

In the evening, hordes of bats come down from the tops of the buildings in Karrada to swoop down and drink from the Hamra pool. The bats, falling and wheeling through the soft air, nick the glassy surface of the water and then return in a single arc to the tops of the buildings where they live. Every night I watched their trajectories, amazed. The pool was the one place everyone went. It attracted and repelled. I especially loved being there when the power went out. Electricity came and went every four hours and when the city power failed everything went dark except the pool when it radiated a silent blue reactor light.

South African mercenaries ended up there and every time a mortar round went overhead they would take defensive positions in the halls crouching in corners. Some of these men were enormously fat and wore the gregarious faces of men with Down's Syndrome. The older mercenaries had spent serious time in Angola and the rifles in their giant meaty hands were like miniature theater props, useless. They smiled like children. It was surprising that a shell never hit the pool. I wished for one in a perverse way, anything that would shut down the fucked up conversation.

We heard things all the time. "You know, force is the only thing the Arabs understand." Say nothing, let the man go on. "Well, maybe Saddam was right to run the place with an iron fist. I mean look at these people, look at how they live." The guy laughs, drinks his beer. Abu Ghraib torture photographs all over the news in every country in the world. "Now, Ahmed, for god's sake bring some ketchup."

The only thing to do was to find a table far from the mercenaries and pray they would get drunk where they were.

When an attack finally came, it wasn't a mortar. It was a car bomb positioned near the hotel checkpoint that missed the Australian ambassador, but killed a ten-year-old cigarette vendor named Ali. When the bomb went off fifty yards from the Dulaime Hotel, the hallways filled with dust, and the windows facing the street were blown into the rooms. When I opened the door, the hallway stretched away in a long cloud. I thought something was wrong with my eyes. On another floor a woman was screaming. We ran outside and, since there was nothing else to do, watched the car burn. Later that day, a funeral procession for Ali made its way through the Jadriya neighborhood. His family wrapped the body in white for martyrdom while Ali's mother screamed at Bush for doing this to her son.

Everyone had their theories about the Iraqis. A skinny kid in the First Infantry Division told me that summer, "Hell, if it makes sense, Hajji don't do it. But he's getting pretty smart now. He's turning those PVC tubes you see all around here into launchers. I'm saying you gotta watch Hajji real close." Hajji, the honorific for older men or men who have made the pilgrimage to Mecca, has joined *gook, slope, Charlie*.

"You know what Hajji means right?" I asked him.

"Yeah. We like to call 'em Hajjis."

We were on a First Cavalry base in Sadr City, and the skinny soldier pointed at some Iraqi workers milling around the store. "See those guys over there, they are probably spotting for the mortar teams on their cell phones. Shit, here comes another one." There was the cartoonlike descending whistle, the mortar hit near the command center. We huddled in the doorway of the aid station while the shrapnel went through the air. The guys laughed when more mortars came screaming down near the aid station from across the river, and they looked at me as if to say, See what we go through, buddy?

During evening prayers, the imams broadcast bloody sermons, howling that the occupier was an enemy of God. A few weeks later, the same soldiers of the 1-5 Cav were sent down to Najaf, digging into the vast necropolis with a million graves, firing rounds at Mahdi Army positions next to the shrine walls. We were only a few hundred feet apart during the siege, on opposite sides of the lines.

Sitting around the pool, in the warm evening air, Cho brought me a beer. This was about a week before he would be kidnapped by a team of gunmen. Cho sat down next to me and said, "I have a good contact in Sadr City. Maybe he's the best one."

"Sure. I have contacts there too, Cho."

"Yes, but this one is different."

"They are all different."

"No. This guy is a really powerful guy, I call him Little Saddam, you know, as a joke."

"Who is he?"

"He's a journalist but he's more than a journalist. You can meet him if you want, I will arrange it."

"Tomorrow?"

"Tomorrow."

We drank our beers and I forgot about everything and then walked to the Dulaime hotel, a dark, neglected building where second-rate Iraqi drivers waited for customers in its tomb of a lobby. When a wave of kidnappings that targeted Westerners freed up most of the fourth floor, a wire report called the hotel the "Eerie Dulaime." French TV crews came out to investigate. We loved the place. It was a kingdom of stories and near misses. Because the rates were cheap, stringers and freelance photographers filled its rooms. Hamza Dulaime, the sheikh's son, would give freelancers a deal if he saw long-term prospects. When I was broke, Hamza waited for the money, "Don't worry about it," he said to me. This generosity, a willingness to discuss matters, is an Arab trait. It saved us. There were four filmmakers, a few writers, a gang of photographers. We left our doors open, friends stopped by with news, resistance contacts dropped by for coffee. In the hotel, we were all spied upon and cajoled, given incredible information. At night, when the resistance was gone and the work was done, we got high and watched images of burning cars on the BBC. We turned the sound off, replaced it with Led Zeppelin.

I took the elevator to the third floor to room twenty-five. It had windows looked that out over Jadriyah Street, a pale linoleum dance floor, sharkskin-green furniture, a balcony from which one could possibly escape. From the street-facing windows I watched Apaches hunt for mortar teams down in the palm groves. These men would fire volleys of mortars at the Green Zone and vanish. At six in the morning, the thuds of bombs going off under American patrols woke us up.

Fatah al Sheikh

At nine, I met Cho and we drove to the edge of Sadr City, the vast Shia slum named after Moqtada Sadr's father, to meet his special contact,

Fatah al Sheikh. When we arrived at his office in a small Internet café, Fatah, hoarse, barrel-chested, was on the phone arranging a deal. Fatah told us how he had just come back from Iran, showing us a photo album of snapshots. Fatah standing in front of an automated printing press. Fatah staring at the camera in front of a fountain. Fatah talking to a mullah. This man promotes himself, I thought. He gets around. Our first meeting lasted half an hour, and in it I learned nothing, but he learned a few things about us. While he was out of the room, his lieutenants asked me what country I was from, the name of the paper I worked for, going over and over the same questions. "Do you have another job besides journalist?" a man named Basim wanted to know. I said no and explained that I was from Ireland. A lie. I didn't know who they were.

Fatah was interested in talking. When I asked him to give an interview on tape, the sight of the black Panasonic video camera excited him. Fatah went on for a full hour about his persecution at the hands of Saddam. As he spoke, he spooled out his history in a cheerful way, with no inflection, no pause for thought. When he described being tortured in a cell Fatah was upbeat, a sign that he was not telling the truth. Where were the signs of shame and trauma? Nowhere. Fatah seemed to be an intelligent and happy person. No one had tortured him, I thought, so what is missing? He became my primary contact in Sadr City. I introduced him to others, invited him back to the hotel for lunch.

Not long after Cho introduced me to him, I stopped by to give Fatah a copy of his videotaped interview. Just before I left, possibly to return the favor, Fatah went to his computer and said he had something interesting to show me. Fatah printed out a piece of paper with official Mahdi Army letterhead. It was an official mobilization order for the followers of Moqtada al Sadr, which stated that the truce would end in twenty-four hours. Fatah gave me a copy and smiled. It was August 4, 2004. I took the document to a reporter at the BBC, who ran with it in their broadcast that evening. By the following day, the truce that had held for a month had collapsed and there were major battles raging in Najaf and Sadr City. The siege had begun.

On one sweltering day, I was on the way to Fatah's office when I got a telephone call from a colleague who said that Cho had been kidnapped in Sadr City. The only person we knew who had enough leverage to get him out was Fatah. When I arrived at the Internet café, Cho was already sitting in the back room, badly beaten, his face bleeding and his clothes torn. His attackers had destroyed his Nikons.

"What happened?"

Cho shook his head. He was bleeding, didn't want to talk. "I can't tell you here."

Cho's four attackers had fired at him while he was trapped in the car, then they pulled him out, pistol-whipped him. The men said they were going to kill him. After Cho left the café, I stayed because Fatah asked me. Around seven o'clock, just as it was getting dark, a white station wagon pulled up with the men who attacked Cho. I was not allowed to go to the window when Fatah went out to greet them. Fatah had been the one who arranged the attack.

There are several reasons why he would benefit from that act of violence. He was a brutal and cunning man, who used fear to gather information. I learned later that he was not above outright murder. Fatah's methodology was simple: he found weakness and exploited it, then bullied the compromised person to provide information about his friends. It was the signature style of a Baath party intelligence agent, a member of the *mukhabarat*. Blackmail and carefully made threats were his instruments. A day after the attack on Cho, I met Fatah at a restaurant near his office and was interrogated. Precision and thoroughness in the questioning made it seem like a professional job.

"You are from which country? Tell me again."

"Ireland."

Pause.

"I heard that you are an American. Maybe you have dual nationality?"

Pause.

"Who said that?"

"The sheikh said it. He says that I do not know enough about you, that I am spending time with a man who is not truthful, and this was very embarrassing for me."

"Which sheikh?"

"You were acting suspiciously in Najaf and there was an investigation."

"That's ridiculous."

Fatah was angry. "I need to see your passport immediately."

"I don't have it with me."

"No?"

"No. I don't carry it with me because of thieves."

"You can tell me if you are an American, because I am a sophisticated man."

"I am an American."

Fatah smiled, he was genuinely happy. He hated Americans. That was something I knew.

"You must tell me everything."

"That's all there is to tell, Fatah."

"You look sick. Are you afraid of something?"

"No."

"If you are afraid of something, and you run, then I know you are guilty."

Fatah held a cup of water and poured it out in a smear across the table. Dead light came off the surface. "You see? the problem is finished between us. That is how we finish things in Iraq."

It is possible that he had Cho beaten to coerce me into giving him information about our friends and colleagues. This Fatah incident is central to how we got to the Shrine in Najaf during the siege. We went to Najaf because staying in Baghdad was impossible. I felt like I was running from him, the Shia neighborhood and the militia was off-limits to us. Fatah's men controlled access to Sadr city and were running the slum as a private fiefdom. As Fatah portrayed himself as a leader of the uprising, he was carefully working on consolidating power and acquiring armed men to enforce his control of the city. Fatah wanted us to know that if we moved around without his permission, the consequences would be severe.

How did Fatah know so much about us? A few of us at the Dulaime had intelligence files under the previous government. Thorne Anderson, a photojournalist, and a close friend I'd met in Afghanistan, was deported by the *mukhabarat*, during the early days of the of the invasion. His partner, Kael Alford, also a photojournalist, was one of the few westerners allowed to stay. Government minders and intelligence people had watched both of them closely because Thorne and Kael were also Americans. They had covered Balkan wars, lived in impoverished European countries, were fans of literature. We listened to the same eccentric music. Thorne often played Daniel Johnston songs on a ruined guitar by the pool.

After the first session in the restaurant across from the Internet café, Fatah took me over to the Habaibna restaurant for the second phase of his interrogation.

"Now, tell me, who is the woman you were talking to at the Hamra pool a few days ago?"

"Which woman?"

"The pretty one, the blonde one." Fatah was talking about Kael.

"I don't know who you mean."

"I know that you know her, she smiled at you. Remember? I saw you."

"I still don't know who you're talking about, Fatah. I'm sorry."

"Her husband, you know him?"

"No. I don't know them."

"Where are they from? Which country? Who do they work for?"

"I don't know who you are talking about, they are not my friends, Fatah."

"I think they are your friends, she smiled at you, the pretty one at the pool. I saw her."

"Maybe she smiled, Fatah, I say hello to everyone."

"You know her but you will not say." Fatah laughs. His lieutenants are watching me.

"That is not the case. I just don't know her."

"If you are afraid you can leave now. But if you are very afraid, then there is certainly some problem, and then I cannot save you."

"I am not afraid."

Fatah smiles, because he knows fear when he sees it.

"Should we eat?" He calls the waiter over.

When I left Sadr City that night, we drove out through a maze of burning gullies, long lines of burning fuel, which crossed the road at right angles to the direction of traffic. Mahdi Army fighters were out pouring gasoline on the ground and setting it ablaze. When the asphalt melted, they dug shallow trenches and filled them with artillery shells. All the bombs were laid at night. Fighters would wait for a U.S. patrol to drive down the road, then detonate the roadside bomb from a nearby market stall or house. On the way out of Sadr city, I noticed that Mahdi Army checkpoints had appeared at every major street and intersection. We were stopped and questioned by nervous fighters, all of them looking for spies. The Mahdi Army was sowing Sadr City with explosives.

Back at the Dulaime, I spoke to Thorne and Kael about the Fatah interrogation and his involvement in the attack on Cho, as news of the Shia uprising poured out of the television. Cho, recovering from the being pistol-whipped, made plans to leave the country after talking to the South Korean embassy officials. The innocent period in Baghdad was over, and I found that I couldn't write or work. I quickly suspected everyone of spying on us, especially drivers and translators. I stopped talking to Iraqis.

Meanwhile, Najaf was besieged and the few western reporters who had found a way of getting into the old city had left quickly. I drifted around the hotel, falling into a deep depression, which lasted nearly two weeks. It was brought on by guilt over what happened to Cho and a fear that the men at the Internet café in Sadr City had other things planned for us. I felt locked out of Najaf where I had good contacts among the senior leadership of the Mahdi Army and all the time spent in the holy city seemed wasted. I became a prisoner of the Dulaime, paralyzed and bitter.

To the Shrine

After August 5, 2004, U.S. forces closed in on the old city of Najaf, but it was not a lightning attack. Elements of the First Cavalry Division sealed off major roads near the necropolis to the north and began pushing south toward the Shrine of Imam Ali. Marine units moved in from the south and sealed Medina Street. Apache attack helicopters began launching attacks from the floodplain in the west called the Najaf Sea. At the very start of the siege, residents of Najaf heard loudspeaker announcements telling them to leave the city, which sparked an exodus to the outlying suburbs. Within hours, most of the city was empty except for Mahdi Army soldiers and clerics loyal to Moqtada al Sadr and the opposing U.S. forces arranged in a misshapen ring outside. Young men loyal to Moqtada al Sadr poured into Najaf to reinforce the fighters. They had no equipment except their faith in God.

Most of the press was holed up in a hotel outside the U.S. cordon, too far away to see anything but flashes of light from the pitched battle in the cemetery. We watched BBC broadcasts that were little more than a rehash of what U.S. military commanders were saying. What was happening at the center of the Mahdi Army movement, inside the universe of the shrine, was beyond the event horizon. No information was leaving the old city.

When Shia Muslims enter the Shrine, they kiss the doorjambs of the great wooden gates, and greet Imam Ali, whose spirit they believe resides there. Pilgrims speak to him as if he were alive. The shrine is thought to have healing powers and the old, the sick, the mad take shelter within its grounds. I had been there a number of times. In the spring a friend named Abu Hussein had invited me to the tomb. We walked through the gates across a great expanse of polished marble, which reflected the sun, to a smaller building, covered in gold plates. We took off our shoes and walked inside to an antechamber of green marble, whose walls and vaulted ceilings were tiled with thousands of mirrors. Men prayed, edged closer to the tomb. Imam Ali is entombed behind a silver screen, behind glass, in darkness. Pilgrims circle the tomb, running their hands over the silver, while pausing to kiss it and utter prayers. A twelve-year-old boy who was mentally ill chanted verses from the Koran while the Pilgrims assented, prayed with him, kissed the tomb every few steps. This place, which feels alive, is one of the most revered places on earth. Inside the tomb you feel like you are surrounded by complex consciousness, a hive-mind, which is dreaming of the past, reflected in ten thousand mirrors. A few hundred feet away, more than a million people lie buried.

On August 16, Thorne Anderson knocked on the door of room twenty-five. We were restless and sick of being holed up in the hotel. Thorne closed the door behind him and said, "What do you want to do?"

"Fuck it. I think we should go to Najaf."

"How are we going to get in, if we get close enough?"

"There's a safe passage letter from Sheikh Ahmed Sheibani I've been showing around."

Thorne said he wanted to go. We decided to leave the next morning.

We didn't tell anyone about our plans to try to cross the siege lines. Other friends dropped by and asked what we were going to do but we kept it an absolute secret. Kael Alford was already in Najaf, moving around the front lines near the old city but unable to cross because she was continually shot at by snipers. In the morning, we hired a translator named Basim and a nervous driver to take us to Najaf and they were not happy about the trip. Basim said, "Phillip, I really think we should tell Fatah where we're going."

"No fucking way." I said.

"I think we are all going to die," Basim said in his strange high-pitched voice.

"Stop panicking, Basim."

We drove through the southern suburbs of Baghdad, past the black smoke plume of the Doura power station. When Basim finally spoke again, he said, "Phillip, Iraq is like a universe without a god. The result is complete chaos."

No one could argue with that.

In Kufa, a few kilometers from Najaf, a fighter motioned with his Kalashnikov for us to get out of the car. A cleric took us to the mosque, gave us water, and invited us to lunch. They treated us well, and we stuck around in a commander's office for the rest of the afternoon, thinking we might be able to find out about an underground railroad to the shrine, starting at the mosque in Kufa. The commander watched us. We waited in his office for four hours, begged for his help. He said he was sorry, but he couldn't help us. Thorne sat on the floor and made conversation with the commander. We dozed until a fighter came running in to show us a captured American anti-tank weapon. The missile had been fired, but he was proud, he wanted to show us the empty casing. We admired it. Then the fighter showed us his Strela anti-aircraft missile launcher with the missile still in it. He'd come from the old city.

A stream of men arrived with donated food supplies that the commander received graciously and entered into a giant ledger before locking them away. I remember that an old man walked in and told us that he had come from the old city. This was the first break. A few minutes later, an assistant to the Mahdi Army commander of the Kufa mosque offered to take us across the lines. The assistant's name was Talib. A skinny, worried man, a laborer, he seemed honest and straightforward.

Late in the afternoon, as the sun was going down, we took Talib with us and drove toward Najaf, winding our way through the southern suburbs, only stopping when Bradleys were too close or tanks appeared around corners. At the southern edge of the city, we got out of the car and listened to the deafening explosions coming from town. Pressure waves hit us in the chest. It was impossible to go forward. Basim and the driver were panicking, and we retraced our route out of town. Talib told us to stay in a hotel in Kufa run by his friends and said we'd try again the next morning. Talib, the guide, would come for us at seven, when the bombing was less intense. "Don't go outside, don't let anyone see you," he said as we unpacked the gear. A few minutes later, Basim and our driver told us they were driving back to Baghdad without us. "You will die, one hundred percent. If you go in, you won't come out."

"Basim, aren't you a little panicked?" I asked.

"Absolutely not."

Thorne told him to take it easy, but there was no talking to him. Basim was convinced of his own death.

By eight o'clock we were stranded in Kufa without a ride or a translator. We ate a meal of shawarma sandwiches, stayed away from the windows, and felt abandoned.

On the roof of the Kufa Hotel, Thorne put in a desperate satellite call to Mitch Prothero, another journalist at the Dulaime, and told him we were trapped. Mitch said he would send a translator down for us and to expect him in the morning. Around six-thirty, Yassir opened the door of our room and found Thorne and I asleep after being up all night listening to a battle go on outside the hotel. Yassir was ready to go.

Talib, Yassir, myself, and Thorne took a cab to the edge of Najaf, retracing the route of the previous day. In the dusty suburbs of the city we got out to walk three miles to the shrine. Yassir, calm and steady, walked right next to us. We thought there wouldn't be much fighting in the early morning but there was a great deal of it. Tympanum sounds. Tearing noises that went beyond mere machinery. It was the sound of a battle between heaven and hell. I tasted copper in my mouth as we walked. Clouds of dust rose over the warren of houses in the old city. We heard fifty-caliber machine guns, rocket-propelled grenades, and hellfire missiles fired from attack helicopters. We made our way slowly toward the American lines at Medina Street, following a trickle of old men and women. So we walked north, talking to passing Najafis who warned us away from snipers. One middle-aged man offered us water and sanctuary. Men stood outside their houses with their sons listening to the war. A crowd followed us. We continued. Talib told us that if the Iraqi police caught us going into Najaf, they would shoot us. They were worse than the Mahdi Army.

At one dead intersection, another man in Bedouin robes and jellaba said we could cross Medina Street, where the U.S. cordon was, explaining that he had just crossed without any problems. When we arrived at the open boulevard, at a hole between two Bradleys, we held our hands up over our heads in surrender and stepped into the street. It was a weightless feeling.

A block deeper in, the city was ruins. Shards of buildings stood like broken teeth, blackened. All the electrical cables were lying in the street. We'd entered a no-man's-land between the two opposing forces. Cars left in this zone were smoking shells. Talib, our Mahdi guide, left us when he spotted a second Bradley, and some Mahdi children replaced him, leading us deeper into the city. We followed the boys through a burned market, which smelled like death, bordered by the ruined Tho al Fikar Hotel. The boys laughed and ran ahead of us, shouting, "Which channel, which channel?"

When the Mahdi children yelled into the ruins, yells came back from empty windows in the buildings where the fighters were hiding. A head would appear wearing a green band of the Mahdi fighters, then a whole person. Fighters waved to us. We waved to them so they wouldn't shoot us. We came upon a small group of Mahdi Army fighters who offered to help us go to the shrine. I told their commander about wanting to speak to Sheikh Ahmed Sheibani, an advisor to Moqtada al Sadr, and they agreed to send someone with us. Past the hotel we arrived at the boundary of the old city, a wide, open boulevard we would have to cross. When we were halfway to the other side, walking with our hands up, a sniper opened fire on us. Thorne was caught in the middle of the street and had to take cover out in the open, I ran behind a column and listened to the rounds slam into the concrete a few inches away. By the time we were out of the sniper's line of fire, we'd crossed into the old city, solidly inside Mahdi lines. I gave an old letter of safe passage, written by Sheikh Ahmed, to a young man, and he told us to come with him. The shrine's dome glowed in the sun, five hundred yards away. Rows of young men covered in ammunition belts, holding rifles and heavy weapons, hid in the shade of the long street. They shouted and called to us as we passed them. Ammunition and rockets were carefully stacked near their feet. We were at the shrine a few minutes later and, like devoted Shia, when we crossed the threshold, we kissed the great carved wooden gates.

Inside the Walls

The Shrine of Imam Ali is at the center of the old city, a few hundred feet south of the largest cemetery in the world. Its walls, laid out in a perfect square, are a deep red brick and they are at least fifty feet high. The outer walls are imposing. The building is not extensively decorated on the outside, but inside the gates, there is a sea of white marble that reflects the sun. Caretakers continually wash the marble flagstones with water to keep them clean. On the day we arrived, the steps of the south-facing gate were smeared with blood from wounded fighters and the caretakers were busy cleaning it off because blood must not spill on the grounds of a mosque, that is a crime in Islam. They did not have much time to rest. Young Mahdi fighters running down Rasul Street were being blown to pieces by Marine units across Medina Street. Fighters loaded up wounded and dead Mahdi volunteers in wheelbarrows and ran them up to the south gates to a makeshift infirmary in the mosque. Thorne and I stood and watched one fighter bring a dead comrade to the doctors, his severed hand in a cigarette box, a stump of a leg jutting from his clothes. The fighter, losing his mind, screamed at the doctor to save his friend, but the body was a gray dead color. I watched the doctor pretend to take a pulse to calm the fighter down. There was blood everywhere but no weapons.

Sheikh Ahmed Sheibani, the Mahdi cleric and diplomat, was not around and we looked for him around the shrine. The fighters offered us water and allowed us to wait in the Sheikh's office. First Cavalry units were fighting in the cemetery and there was a fierce battle between armored units, aircraft, and young men hiding in underground tombs. With each passing hour, the Mahdi Army was losing territory, their men facing unbelievable weapons with no hesitation. Most of the men who went into the cemetery to fight the Americans didn't come back. An Apache gunner named Joe Bruhl told me about the battle and said, "We'd fly over, and I'd punch off a missile at one of their mortar teams, killing all of them. Then I'd see other guys run in and pick up the weapons the first guys dropped and start firing at me. I didn't know whether to call them crazy or tip my hat. I must have killed dozens of them a day."

Bruhl asked me why they did it, although as a thoughtful fundamentalist Christian, he could have easily answered his own question. It was the Mahdi Army's war at the end of the world.

Moqtada al Sadr, the lion, was not anywhere to be found. I looked, watched for bodyguards and other signs the man was nearby, but there was nothing. We would have known if he was in the shrine. Moqtada was hidden away somewhere, a kind of secret weapon who would never risk being martyred. After all his promises of sacrifice and bravery, he let the other young men walk into the blades of the killing machine for him.

Dead fighters were carried in a slow circuit around the tomb by their friends. Wrapped in white martyr bags, the young men carried their friends and chanted, "There is no god, but God." Because the cemetery was a battleground, the bodies were taken to the Islamic court where they rotted in the basement. These processions happened every few minutes. The cycle was simple: fighters ran down Rasul Street, fought the Americans, were wounded or killed, then hauled back to the shrine.

It was a production line in reverse. The same scene repeated over and over again.

We spoke to Sayeed Hosam al Husseini and made contact with Sheikh Ahmed Sheibani when he returned from the main conference room. His lieutenants brought us lunch, while men poured through the gates of the mosque. As night came on with no pause in the bombing, there were close to two thousand people taking shelter inside the massive walls. Men ate on mats in small clusters according to which group they fought with, the clerics sat with the commanders of the cells and planned the offensive. After evening prayers when the stars came out, they stretched out to sleep. Thorne slept in the office, while I found a place on a mat next to the fighters. All through the night, rounds rushed over the walls making sounds like plucked strings.

The siege of the shrine, which lasted just over three weeks, was a psychological pressure experiment. Deprive men of sleep with constant bombing and soon they start to see visions of their savior. Power failures happened every few minutes when the generator failed. During one of these blackouts, on the evening of August 18, a thin young man began screaming, making a sound halfway between ecstasy and terror. The lights had just gone out and our eyes hadn't adjusted when the young man pointed to one of the archways in the second story of the western wall, the wall which faces Mecca. We thought that Moqtada was going to address the thousands of men in the shrine from a balcony. Yassir helped by translating for the young man, who told us, "I saw a vision of the Mahdi. He appeared there!"

"No, it was Imam Ali," another kid said.

The crowd came and collected around the thin visionary. Dozens of other Mahdi Army fighters claimed to have seen the same image, a flickering saint in an alcove.

"What does it mean when the Mahdi returns?" The Mahdi is the long-disappeared twelfth Imam of the Shia.

"It means he will come to deliver us from injustice and destroy our enemies with incredible weapons. America will be finished."

After some time, the crowd quieted down, but long after that I saw them looking at the balcony for another sign, anything that would have saved them.

C. T. Lawrence

Iris and Me, After the Fall: October 2001

Iris is baby bean, monkey feet, stevie wonder bird, still curled from the womb, singing for milk. I whisper these names in her mouth, insubstantial food; she swallows, opens blues eyes and becomes human, surprised at my offering. I have only words. She has such wide, bright eyes. Here, now, deciduous baby, transparent flakes of skin leave her hands for mine, then shift to the floor. Bones out of nothing girl, not mine.

We sit in a formal living room, clean with lace curtains, Iris in my empty arms. There are dried flowers and dark wood tables you cannot put a coffee cup on. The sun goes down noticeably; the room deepens a few degrees and a lamp arcs a little pool of light around us. The TV is always on. The TV is always on, but the sound is off. And a kind of quiet darkness hangs outside the light like everything has stopped. The place we live, not much goes on; a barrenness still waits beyond the house. Iris breathes. I breathe.

Everything has been so still here, but now I catch the smallest of movements out of the corner of my eye. A shadow runs around the edges of the room, too fast to come in clearly. Then a tiny white plane flies out from under the television cabinet, leaking smoke. It hovers along the floor, as if smelling the carpet, then darts up into the far corner of the ceiling and shivers there, a caught animal. Iris waves a hand at the ceiling. Everything is changing inside of her; she is only Iris of the moment.

Then minutes later, completely new. Hello plane. Hello tiny people, we wave. I think I see them at the windows waving back.

The TV opens up its smoky eye until the black takes over the screen. Then with an electrical snap and a blink the plane is gone, back inside. The lights in the whole house flicker. The TV is dead. The TV is dead. I look at Iris to see what she has seen. Goodbye tiny people! We'll miss you. Where did you go? Iris's eyes, the blue and the holes, reflect nothing. I turn the light out. We sit in the dark, waiting for the TV to come back on.

Pietro Zullino
Translated from the Italian by David Lummus

From Cynthia with her eyes . . . :
An Autobiography of Sextus Propertius

From §§ VII – XIV and § XXXVIII

VII

[. . .]
I have written three books of love elegies. If the fourth is to be published, it will be by others, cut-off and in disorder, half underground. Where I am now, I can't touch it; and if they don't send it to me, I won't even see it.

And everyone will think it's posthumous, since the world no longer has news of me. After all, Maecenas, by the time of the second book, made it clear to the publishers that I had to fade away, vanish: "Don't publish anything else from him! As a flatterer he's untrustworthy, as a poet—useless!" But I've already got out of the way, or rather they made me do it. And since Hostia is dead, I don't care; I hope only to find the courage, in the state I'm in, to leave this life too. He'll have to turn up sooner or later, the poet capable of singing how we rarely ever find the courage to put an end to it all! Everyone who doesn't has his own valid and cowardly reason. Mine has been that, if I killed myself, I would do away with the only person who knew how Hostia really was and who could truly recount it.

Recount it? Why don't I say: confess? Hostia wasn't at all the malicious woman who dominates my songs, she was another person altogether. It's unbearable that she passed to the other world with the bad reputation that I dealt out. With this memorial (I'm writing it in the hope that it will one day come to you) I think that, in the end, I'll have stated the whole truth. "Hostia was good. She had a noble soul" begins my fluvial confession, which I have put off for so many years, because my obligation to produce it keeps me in the realm of the living and so takes away my ability to know if I'd have the courage to do it.

In the meanwhile, my raven hair has fallen away. By now, a formless tuft hangs from my head, to be confused with the gray of this moth-infested beard that I shorten every two months with knife slashes.

And so, for a long time the Princeps had been watching me. Ever since, in my second collection, I published those verses against human reproduction and against war. In the times of the demographic campaigns and of the tax on the unmarried, I declared that I would have never had children, because I couldn't stand the prospect of seeing them in arms: "You'll have no soldiers of my blood," I sang, I who had never even done my military service.

Say *that* in imperial Rome! Blasphemy!

He, the Princeps, almost had a collapse.

At the time he spared me, but held a grudge.

But I was already taken with an severe allergy to politics—like that allergy to fava beans!—when I wrote *Tarpeia*. Standing before the truculence of the Power I instantaneously rejected it. I was full of courage.

My love of Hostia made me feel invincible.

VIII

The years and the pain have made me an expert of myself, and now I see that my political favism was due to my estrangement—how shall I put it?—not only from social life, but from the human species. I have always watched human affairs from the observatory of a faraway elsewhere. I don't know how I ended up in this elsewhere, but the fact is that I'm unable to connect with my peers, to feel empathy. True, I feel enthusiasm about almost every idea and convention, but that doesn't count, because I feel it even about their opposites as well. So what kind of enthusiasm is it? I wouldn't know. I don't take sides or join the crowd; I don't care. Everything slides off me and promiscuous mixing with my fellow man makes me sick.

I'm a man without a party, I can't stand anything in which one enrolls and serves. In politics, if there's something to abhor, then I abhor the arrogance of the plutocrats, but also the weeping of the disinherited; I detest the Senate and the consuls, but, by the same token, I detest the tribunes of the plebs. In my school years, when I was reading the *Iliad*, I didn't know whether to side with the Greeks or the Trojans: all of them got on my nerves, Achilles a little more than Hector and Hector a little more than Achilles.

And if there's something to admire? For example, I admire the martyrs of liberty, but the delirium of tyrants fascinates me too. I can't help myself, that's the way I am. Cicero who saves the republic and Catiline who wants to destroy it, both seem to me magnificent in their respective *perversions*. Caesar who imposes the laws of Rome on the Gauls and Vercingetorix who leads the revolt, I don't know if it's because it all seems to me like theater, but I applaud both, crazily; it's like a joke to me, and at bottom I don't give a damn.

"What kind of fish are you?"

Well, if we must speak of fish, then I'm a fish who doesn't like the water. Is it necessary to force oneself to like the water? *I* don't like it, maybe because of all the dew I got in Bevagna. I have to swim inside it, I'm forced to, but I don't like it. Yet, if we must speak of humans, I get upset with the presumptuous axiom that we are beautiful, intelligent, privileged creatures: in fact I'm completely dismayed by the species I belong to; I think that it's one of the ugliest and most stupid of the entire universe. I especially don't like the human male: I can say it too, since I've always been judged a handsome kid! I don't like the human being when he thinks, but then I don't even like him physically: how he presents himself, how he behaves, how he acts important, even on the toilet. I find his figure monstrous—starting from those deformities that are his feet; his ridiculous erect stance, that disgusting whitish sack of his skin. And if the sack is black. . . .

"You don't like blacks?"

"I already find it bad enough being white."

The created world? A tangled mess of nightmares, sadisms and disease, with the living species that take turns devouring one another below and an unstable, garish, violent firmament above. And they talk of creation! Well the Creator comes out badly. We're in the hands of a deranged maker! The priests say he's in the right, but it's the right of a madman, ripe for exorcism I think. But we who are not priests, why do we keep telling ourselves tall tales? The cosmos is a hell; why do we keep saying "my . . . what a wonder!"?

God is stupid.

Does the idea that he is stupid make you nervous?

Or rather, there is no God and the cosmos is a chaotic mess of particles that chase each other and fall together, as my beloved atomist Democritus taught!

Humanity? A slimy mess of limbs, eyes, and voices, formless and unfinished undergrowth of children in heat, who insist on fornicating and branch off endlessly, only to then endlessly dry up and die! Man? A horrid work of anatomic essence, false knowledge and true arrogance, obtuse drowsiness, insane avidity . . . Well, a good cat is much better!

The Phidiases who want to idealize us in stone, and the Apelles on canvas, only make matters worse, because they think they're adulating us, but in reality they're only representing and passing on our ugliness. If only human thought, since it exists, were real thought, and therefore not a thought within a species, specific, but trans-human! *That* would be objective thought and *that*—making us see our misery—would show us the right way to come out of it! Maybe!

Instead, we only know how to think about ourselves.

That's why we can't solve any of our problems, and why for millennia and millennia—despite every progress—we don't bring about anything but disasters: precisely because we keep thinking about ourselves, we keep wanting necessarily to be that which we are not.

Only in physical love do I glimpse moments of salvation, not because it makes us more beautiful or better, but because it makes us—like Lucretius says—become trans-human. Before an orgasm we are still males and females, lit up with libido; we are still prisoners of our nature and of its *diktat*. Fortunately the payoff isn't only a goal, but is also a means, it's really a way to flee the squalid human condition. In fact, in the moments of maximum pleasure we stop being miserable, we feel free and floating, we start to take part in an alien species, we taste a superior dimension. Lovers melt together in a single block of light.

But it lasts—alas—so little time. Lucretius has sung that

we cannot find a remedy that, stable,
placates the torment and we return to consume
ourselves as if with a secret wound.

"What kind of fish are you?"

I don't know what kind of fish I am, but they don't need to make me choke on my gum, because I am subject to abrupt flares of pride, ruinous above all to myself, let it be understood! Sometimes I act like a dog that barks in church. And the larger the temple is, the more crowded and sonorous it is, the more I bark and enjoy myself. When I frequented the salons, at first they always laughed at my so-called paradoxes, then they looked at me oddly, by the end they turned their backs on me: I would say shocking enormities, I set their evenings off on the wrong foot! But my enormities are only uncomfortable truths, and so may all their evenings go wrong, nasty good-for-nothings!

I've been arrogant with the gods and especially with their deputies on the Earth. Even when I lowered myself to serve them, at the end of my service I always had to turn the tray over on their head, and you can see it from *Tarpeia*.

Not giving a damn about the powers-that-be, offending them (and risking ruin) is the only practice that has given me moments of pleasure in life that are more intense than the sixteen-thousand orgasms reached together with Hostia.

IX

I didn't present *Tarpeia* to the beauty contest, but, like I said, a miracle happened. I gave it to Hostia to sing and at the last verses she stopped singing because she had begun to cry. And when I say that she was crying, I mean that sobs, then rivers of tears came out of her.

Stupefied, I sat up on the sofa. I had never seen her in such a state. I tried to calm her down, but she wouldn't be calmed. Then I took up the papyrus roll in my hand and I reread those ninety-five verses, curious to understand what could have provoked such emotion in my friend. What in hell had I written?

I had written about a certain Roman girl, not even very intelligent, who watches the fires of the Sabine siege from high above the walls of Rome. And, while she is watching, she catches a glimpse, next to one of those fires, of the young enemy king, Titus Tatius, splendid in his brilliant silver armor. She falls hopelessly in love:

> She saw Tatius make war in the sandy plain,
> and lift painted arms on his blond-maned steed

Tarpeia has in her hands a pail full of water from a stream. She lets it fall. It breaks. The loss of water symbolizes the loss of her feminine honor. From this moment, in fact, there will be no more fatherland for Tarpeia; neither friends, nor family, nor shame will exist any longer: she is ready to deny everything that she has held to be sacred up to now. From this moment she lives thinking only of how she can unite herself with the *other* who bewitched her. Things that happen, that have always happened and will always happen in times of war, even in twenty centuries, because there will always be girls who will stain themselves with a collaborationist love and they will always have to pay dearly for it. Tarpeia torments herself, she curses the enchantments of the moon, she wishes she could drown in the Tiber, but she's ready to betray, she will betray . . .

Meanwhile, she hopes that her beloved doesn't come to harm in battle:

> Often she offered silver lilies to the kind nymphs of the stream
> so that the spear of Romulus not harm the face of Tatius.

And she invokes:

> "Fires of the camps, tents of the hosts of Tatius,
> and you, Sabine arms, splendid to my eyes,
> would that I could sit as a prisoner before you,
> that I, prisoner of love, could . . ."

In the dramatic finale there is every bit of the brutality of the male gender. Tatius has deceived the girl and succeeded in getting her to open the gates of the Capitoline with a promise of love and marriage. But it's written in the code of honor of the phatries that you must never reward a traitor, even if they betrayed your enemy. Even if they betrayed because of love for you. And so, Tatius—after the conquest of the hill and the surrender of the Romans—instead of marrying Tarpeia, he has her killed:

> "Marry me—he told her—come to my royal bed."
> And when he had spoken
> he buried her under the shields of his companions.

Hostia wouldn't tell me what had made her cry and why. While I cuddled her in my arms all I could do was puzzle it out. Did she recognize herself in my Tarpeia, for some personal event unknown to me. Was she moved by the role that I had reserved for the delirium of love, that drags us in shackles before the court of men, but absolves us before that of the gods? Or was she able to penetrate the recesses of the female spirit and touch there the cord that, in sounding, says: *love is never ugly?* Maybe she liked my courage to sing of new things and to be myself above all?

Perhaps she had heard the poet Propertius being born?

I'll never know.

"I've had a bout of longing," she said to me.

She soaked an entire handkerchief with tears. When she had dried herself off, she got out of my embrace and, blowing her nose off and on, she looked me over with anxious eyes, full of melancholy.

And this time they were good eyes, like a hyperborean deer.

We didn't make love that day. She wanted to comb my hair. And later, at our parting, she said to me as if I were leaving for the Last Thule:

"Adieu."

X

Why did she say *adieu?* And why did she say it in that way? What an emotional way to say goodbye, I thought. An oddity connected with her tears, a consequence of her enigmatic bout of longing. But it wasn't really so much Hostia's *adieu,* so much as her bitter crying that had intrigued me. Her crying, not the *adieu,* occupied my soaring thoughts all night. I had been able to make that woman melt, who is so in control of herself: unheard of! Unheard of, since the beginning of our relationship! And it had been my poetry that provoked that crying. So, was I really "her one poet"?

I thought of nothing else that night. Was I a poet? I ravenously sought out the certainty of it.

Wild Hostia. But also anxious like a butterfly.

After many years I finally understood her *adieu*. It was a parting with a virgin boy who was about to be deflowered by his future. It was also her own goodbye to a symbolic motherhood that was reached so late, passed by so hurriedly, and failed so early. I was about to compromise myself, I was disappearing. I would return, to see her not as a boy but as a man— that is, never again.

The innocent phase of our relationship was over. She knew that boys die; they die . . . boys. Because every boy flows into and annihilates himself in the unfulfilled man that he almost always will be.

What is a boy? A bewildered creature. He doesn't know anything. He doesn't understand anything about anything. He doesn't know how to gauge the world, nor that it should be gauged. He doesn't even know that he is loved, and by what kind of love, when he is.

But at least he's himself! As long as he's still a boy, he's himself! With his goofiness and his impropriety, but still he's himself!

The unfulfilled man, however . . . Achieved and successful men are exceedingly few, and they live furtively, jealous of their success—in a world that is brimming over with unfulfilled men. Doesn't Epicurus teach it, "live furtively"? Successful men earn the respect, and not the fear, of their women; they are quiet workers, pleasant partners, admirable fathers; they avoid the madness of war, winning with humanity; and when their time is up, they exit on tip-toes, not demanding any monument. . . .

What is the unfulfilled man, then? A boy in ruins. He continues not to understand anything, with the aggravating circumstance that he's no longer himself, because they made him think he could take his destiny in hand, and instead they threw him into a tragicomedy where he will be a puppet in the hands of sclerotic and irascible puppeteers. They'll make him commit one error after another, they'll transform him into a perfect idiot and they'll have him killed in some war.

So it's better to let yourself fall into the hands of a mother!

If no one can understand me, I will have written for myself alone. And for myself alone I will have said: the boy that I was merited more than the man that I have become.

Now I know it's too late.

And if I had known it then?

Unfortunately virginity of the heart is lost in the very instant when that mysterious bell sounds in our head and it flashes through our mind that we can grasp our place in the world. Our place, or another's place, any place, because we crave only one thing: to remove ourselves from the state of not being, from bewilderment.

So we walk on everything without pity, even on the one we love. From bewildered creatures we become senseless ones, and we could even kill.

XI

I started to falsify myself that very night. At home the stench of the Sub-urbis seemed for the first time unbearable. I wanted to get out of there, I wanted some money. I threw myself on the bed and I put out the lantern, but I felt as if I had lizards in my stomach, and in an instant I became malicious.

"If Brimo and Ischomache don't interest her and she wants to cry," I thought, "well, I'll make her cry."

I turned over: "They'll cry."

I couldn't fall asleep, so much did I want to start immediately the deliberate search of emotions to transmit as verses, the verses to then turn into money. So I got my stylus and tablets and I relit the lantern, ready to wager the present against the future.

The fact is that when you start a deliberate search for emotions with the idea of transmitting them, you're already cheating. Emotions aren't transmitted. They're personal and secret feelings; they're felt and that's it. Your emotions remain intimate to your own soul, you can't make them explicit at all. If you try, then you're being an illusionist, like Horace; you look for clever words to stimulate the emotion of someone else, knowing full well that some other person's emotion will remain the emotion of that person in any case, and there will never be any sharing of your emotion— it will be an autonomous, different feeling. Two lovers on the shore of the sea looking at the same sunset? They don't share the same emotion at all, not even if they kiss. He/she feels one thing, she/he another.

Incommunicability makes us like islands. Like stubborn monads.

It can happen that you stimulate an emotion in someone else even without wanting to at all. It can happen that you need to pee and you're thinking of the toilet, when some woman stares at you admiringly and tells you "you're wonderful": who knows what she read in your eyes? Ah, yes! There's a vein of sadness, a bit of unreality, in which every love is imbued!

Me: with *Tarpeia* I had unleashed the emotion of Hostia, but, I assure you, only by chance. It wasn't like it was for so many elegies that I wrote later, the ones that made me cry about myself like a little boy. In writing *The Degenerate of the Capitol* I didn't feel any personal emotion of my own, I swear it by Hercules. From the first to the last verse I remained cold like a lacertus hanging on a hook, I didn't give a damn about Tarpeia, I swear. If anything, I was thinking about Maecenas' frown. I'd go every so often to the window, I'd take another look at the local garbage man and I'd compare myself to a piece of organic waste, and I'd go deaf at the uproar of a gang of rummaging kids: these were the emotions that inspired my *Tarpeia*.

Either that or an attack of cold favism had hit me, and I released it by writing. But Hostia was moved as she read those verses. She had cried and aroused my astonished stupor. All on her own, understand? I didn't do anything at all, I had only found the right words.

And no one knows why. So what is poetry: chance, a game of bowls, pure artifice?

Even Virgil at the Palace, singing the sixth book of the *Aeneid* (where he alludes to Claudius Marcellus, nephew of Octavian Caesar, dead of a mysterious illness at eighteen) made the Princeps and all his imperial court cry buckets: "*Tu Marcellus eris . . .*"

I'm sure that Virgil didn't care at all about Marcellus, but he wanted to titillate. Astutely. He calculated that the memory of Marcellus couldn't help but make his relatives and all the courtesans cry. It had to. I know how it works: I too, on a shitty day, wrote an epicedium for Marcellus; and even though I was already on everyone's bad side and was on the way to disappearing, when it was published I made them cry.

At least that's what I was told later.

So what is poetry? Pure invention of words to make others yearn? Pure induction?

I don't know if I realize what I'm saying.

XII

But passions, those you can communicate, those you *have* to scream because they are suffering; if you don't scream them, you're a fool. But with passions the poet is always secure. Since they're already known and shared by all, it's only a matter of awakening them. They're not like your secret, personal emotions, which only you know. Suffering for love, for envy, for ambition, for destiny, for desire of vendetta, for deluded patriotism, and whatever other passions you want, everyone knows the stuff such suffering is made of. Passions make theater, and theater doesn't induce, it reawakens. Everyone is already disposed to understand Medea. In poetry, however, passions play out poorly. If you don't know how to manage them properly, they can even make people laugh. By contrast, emotion functions well in poetry. But you have to be able to induce it. Always.

Take Catullus: if *he* wasn't passionate! . . . He screamed the *mal d'amour*, the jealousy, the betrayal and the malice of Lesbia, but did his verses ever make anyone cry? I don't think so, because Catullus was only interested in his own business, and he didn't give a damn about you who read or listen, waiting to be infected. He did everything on his own, Catullus, like a masturbator: he didn't see you at all.

And you couldn't help but think, in the middle of reading: "His woman dumped him? Yeah, well, he must've been an asshole!"

In truth, it's a more than legitimate doubt.

The day that Lesbia asked him that surprise question, not the usual "How much do you like me?," but the unpublished "How much do you love me?," Catullus (since in our culture love is a man's thing and among men) answered embarrassedly in verse: "I love you . . . as much as a father can love his son . . . as much as a father-in-law can love his son-in-law . . ."

And it seemed to him, as the sun set on the patriarchy, that he had offered an extremely audacious and heavy simile. Instead, it was the answer of someone illiterate in *eros*. What, he couldn't say, "I love you as much as a man can love a woman"? No, he couldn't. He didn't know how, he didn't get it. Because Catullus—the brilliant, polemical, corrosive, admirable, and, even today, candid Catullus—was in his soul a caveman, or maybe a rabbit in his warren.

Even he didn't succeed in seeing women as an autonomous pole of an amorous relationship. Even for him the female human was still and only what she had been throughout the millennia for all males, poets or not: a pleasurable, but costly freak of nature, a contiguous and ambiguous inferior race, an attraction that it's necessary to succumb to in order to satisfy the species. But at the bottom of the matter, always still a subject all to be defined, all to be named, all to be governed, all to be put up with. And so, put on the spot by such a question, he could only respond with awkward similes.

With the same carelessness he could have answered: "I love you five times as much as my dog!"

And he would have felt himself to be generous!

The very worldly Lesbia must have become disheartened. And why not, why shouldn't she be?

I say it without modesty: since poetry has existed, and after Sappho, I was the first to make a person of a woman. And anyway I did everything I could to mark my planetary distance from Catullus. Not only did I introduce the full bipolarity of love, but I went beyond equality of the sexes. Yes, beyond. And I did it when I glimpsed the true difference that exists between man and woman: that women are born mothers, while men rarely succeed in seriously being fathers, even when they reproduce. I did it furthermore when I gave an adult sex to women and an eternally childlike sex to men. In my poetry I said to Hostia, who could never have children: "I will be your son! And our love will be worth more than the name of 'father'!"

May everyone load these expressions with the meanings that they want.

Did Catullus ever doubt that he could be, in love, an asshole? Yeah, right. *He* thought he was perfect.

But when it came to maturity, he was absolutely at level zero. Nil. Even the lyric about Lesbia's dead sparrow (aesthetically a nice little gimmick, not bad at all), does it stimulate any emotion? The poet is moved or pretends to be, but really, does he infect you? Nil. And you know why? Because of his brutishness, his distance. Because the sparrow he sings about isn't your sparrow, yours, the one that *you* hear. It's his sparrow— *his*—that sings, and what do you matter? But the poet, to make you cry, has to know how to visit your sparrow. And even if you never had a sparrow, he has to convince you that you had one and that he died on you.

But he doesn't care at all about your sparrow, or about Lesbia.

Anyway, at school we would crack up laughing at the idea of a bird that continually pecked at a woman's black camellia. It had to be fat, one or two pounds, what do you think? And the poet could have easily killed it to get it out of that place finally. We'd guffaw.

Still, it's terrible, intolerable, to see our emotions get ignored by others.

I didn't suspect, then, that emotions were such a controversial business.

XIII

That night I tried to evoke some of the emotion I felt on account of Hostia, so that I could come up with some marketable elegies. Damn, I had a lot to choose from.

The time came to mind, when—after a bachelor's party—at night under a full moon that made me a lycanthrope, I came staggering in front of her house to see if the cat's door was open (that's what I called the little back door that the governess left cracked for me when Hostia *didn't* have a guest). Ah, I made some worthless trips to that door of paradise! And how many sighs, how many hand and fist prints, how much spit I left there, since I so often found it bolted! I dedicated an elegy to it, to Hostia's closed door. But that night it was cracked open. And so I slunk inside, happy and drunk.

I arrive immediately.

Only the little night lamps were burning and the whole house was in a half-light. I found Hostia in her room, wrapped in a Greek-style *peplus*, with her hair undone, wonderful in the placid breathing of sleep. But, there and then, I didn't see her beauty and her being-there. Instead I eyed greedily her not-being-there, her sleeping, her remoteness, her being elsewhere with every sense, her momentary reduction to pure object.

And so I was overtaken by lust: because this is the true libidinal drive of males: to possess a female when she is not there. When she's not there with her mind, I mean. When all her defenses are down and she is there as a pure body, unconscious, estranged. Some men massacre women with blows, and they do it impulsively, not out of malice; in the end it's precisely the most carnal lovers who look for violence, because, as Lucretius put it,

> pleasure is not pure: there are dark impulses
> that push you to torture the object from which
> the seeds of fury rise.

Grand lovers beat their women, in my opinion, because terror and pain make females inert: and it's then, when they are reduced to weary flesh or second-hand flesh, it exactly then that you can have a purely masculine penetration. If a child is born, it will be a father's child and that's it! Certain others like to assault them and humiliate them in sordid places. It's a coprophilous version of simple rape, but it's the mental dynamic, the same truth.

Women know it. What, they don't know it? They know it, they know it. They've known it since the dawn of time. Since the age of ages. So they always try to defend against it. And if they dress provocatively and make themselves up and put on an act, it's not to seduce the male more, on the contrary! It's to slow their violent libido. To subjugate it to an erotic ritual made of smells, sights, forms, compliments, colors. It's to put the beast under collar. To make it engage in a liturgy. To arrive at copulation, while avoiding rape, and that's why they use make-up—believe. I don't know if they do it consciously, but, anyway, they do it. The male goes wild for the stench and sweat more than for the perfume, and nothing distracts him from his real goal, nothing diminishes his will for domination, as much as the barricades set up by the rites of seduction.

Rites that intimidate and make you lose your time *and* your head.

They're the sure sign that the woman wants to referee the game or at least play it by rules: a matter that, if we're civil, we have to make ourselves enjoy. But in reality we don't enjoy it.

XIV

I had it nice and hard, and I took a fancy to get into bed with Hostia and to nail it to her without a fuss, but yet again I was afraid. Afraid of her. Neither libido nor my drunken state made me forget how much she didn't appreciate a certain kind of wake-up call. She wasn't the type to let herself submit. To my bravado she would have responded with a horrible scene, so I set myself to thinking about how I could reach my goal without disgusting her too much. I opted for a sweeter technique. Since one of her hands was hanging out of the bed with the palm open and pointed upwards, I ingeniously let my testicles drop in that palm and I left them there, like a pair of freshly-laid eggs.

Everything was silent except a few shrill crickets in the garden, and I felt my heart beat quickly:

in her open hands I gave furtive apples

That cup made of a sumptuous and luxurious hand was gentle and hot. Hostia should have awakened slowly, understood, smiled, closed her hand, hopped up and pulled me into bed by the precious things she had gripped: she should have done this, knowing her. But she didn't wake up. After a few long moments, bored, my stick failed. Then I pulled back the whole limp thing and I stumbled back, perplexed.

I didn't want to go away. I didn't dare to wake her. I cuddled up on the edge of the bed and I started to amuse myself with her soft curves, her hair, the edges of her *peplus*:

And now, from your brow I undid small chaplets
and I placed them around your temples
now I adored recomposing your straying hair

and all the caresses, I gave to your ungrateful sleep
abundant caresses along the curve of your breast;
And when you moved or sighed a little,
startled, I believed vainly in the presages
of a sleep that brought you strange fears
or that as if by force I wanted to make you my own.

Great verses! And for pity's sake, I had never thought about stiffing
her.

Nothing, she wouldn't wake up. And by now the cool, fresh air of
dawn was coming in the big window. The fumes of the wine were thin-
ning and my head became slowly lucid again. I was terribly thirsty.
There was some water on the nightstand and I drank it. At that point
the generous idea came to me, which later—in verse—enchanted so
many female readers all over Rome, and made me popular and for a long
time even rich. At the origin of our fortune there can in truth be a
meaningless event! Really! And I add: remembering those times, it
seems impossible to me that such carnal abandonment was almost simultaneous with a completely pure bridling of the spirit.

Not only the fresh air of dawn was coming in the window. The
beams of the radiant full moon were coming in too. Still oblique, they
weren't touching Hostia's face, but when Cynthia, the moon herself,
as faithful as she was indifferent to her orbit, showed herself in that
room, she would have certainly touched it. Then a prayer came to my
lips, I who consider myself an atheist: "Divine Cynthia, please wake
Cynthia." Anxious as a little boy who has discovered a new game, I
began to wait:

until the moon, the vigilant moon with lingering
light, opened her eyes with gentle beams.

Hostia really woke up at the caress of that moonbeam. And I was
deeply moved by it. A cosmic triad had been activated between me, the
moon, and a woman. Something unrepeatable and magical that can
come true only once, I'm not saying in a man's life, but in the life of one
man out of a thousand. Cynthia who hears your prayer and, with her
gentle beams, wakes for you the woman who sleeps! It's worth a lot more
than an alignment of the planets! And it had been me who foresaw,
wished, invoked, waited, and so who created that sort of miracle, while
the fairy-tale left me and made way for almost angelic intrusions!

But Hostia didn't realize that she had been awakened by the moon.

So her emotion couldn't be, and wasn't, my own. Emotions can't be transmitted, they are induced: the sparrow has to be your own. I tried to tell her: "The moon woke you." But she didn't catch on. She pulled me into bed and we made love intensely, but accompanied by maternal reproaches: "And where have you been at this hour? Why do you present yourself like a beaten dog? What harlot sent you away empty handed?"

God, there was no way that she would understand.

Remembering all this on the night of the *Tarpeia*, I realized that the elegy that I was trying to write had to have a noble end. The greatness of sentiments of my woman had to correspond to the greatness of my own sentiments, otherwise, I thought, it wouldn't work. The poet can't cheat at the game, if he wants to sell. So I idealized and redeemed Hostia and I transformed her rebukes into the lover's laments of a faithful woman, of a Penelope who suspects betrayal:

> "Where have you spent the long hours of my night,
> you, tired out at the vanishing of the stars?
> I would that you, cruel man, endure the vain waiting
> that you force on me, brokenhearted!
> Earlier I kept sleep at bay with purple embroidery,
> then, tired, with the music of Orpheus' lyre
> I lamented gently to myself
> that another love may push you away, till
> lifted by sweet wings I lost myself in sleep.
> And only then did my tears come to an end."

I'm a phenomenon at final couplets, my critics have always given me that. These last two are truly splendid. How they fly high, those in whom is reflected the emotion of the beast that by a marvel becomes human (given that this was really my emotion, and I'm not sure about it at all). But the others? Acceptable in form, but conventional and lying. They didn't represent Hostia, who was the anti-Penelope *par excellence*. Nor her emotion—I don't even know if there was one or what it was. They depict an imaginary woman. Maybe the Hostia that I would have liked her to be? Four o'clock in the morning! *I* liked Hostia in her flesh-and-blood reality, I wouldn't have wanted her any other way.

And then? Then, I was falsifying me and her, I was cheating, I was inventing a model-love and a standard female: a Hostia who was insensitive to bestial strokes but sensitive to the caresses of the moon. She was the Hostia of my very first manner, redeemer and inspirer, capable of teaching men grace and the straight path, just waiting to be defaced. A Hostia like the average imagination of the women of this century and of this city—who aren't women but men—would have wanted to know and see her, so that they could identify with her and obtain the public approval of the toga-wearing males.

A titillating Hostia: for the literary fortune of the kid-poet, who had taken flight that night because he wanted money. And he had become stupid, and half a man.

Since it seemed to me that I had written something worthwhile, and altogether new, I imagined taking *Moonbeams* to be read by Asinius Pollio, the great talent scout, the only literary critic whom you could trust. He's one who's famous for always telling the truth, without mincing words.

I didn't give *Moonbeams* to Hostia to sing.

Who knows why.

It was the first time I hid my verses from her.

XXXVIII

In the first elegy I invented the deplorable situation in which I versify and with the second I begin the narrative of what happened to me. The beginning is soft, there are no sharp rocks under the first steps of my Calvary—it's all serenity, hymns to joy. I'm a gynagogue, I call on Cynthia not to use make-up: "naked is Love and he does not love artificial exteriors . . . If a woman is admired by only one man, she is cared for enough . . ." (a little scholastic matter, I had it on hand . . . it will do). In third position I put *Moonbeams*: love in the state of adoration, a complete idyll. In the fourth I scold an expert friend of mine, from way back, who advises me to leave Cynthia. In sum: "And yet I would die for her . . . For the color of her eyes, for the gifts that the Muses gave her, for the pleasure that we take under the silent sheets . . . The more you try to dissolve our love, the more both of us—keeping ourselves faithful—will avoid you . . ."

Everything proceeds wonderfully. I don't yet know if I'm in love with a woman possessed by the devil . . . But there, in the next elegy, a rumbling of thunder. Maybe my old friend was right—the cruelties have begun: "What are you looking for, madman?" I yell at another such one who has fallen in love, "how many worries can a woman give you!"

116

She will deprive you of sleep, of your eyes,
ah, how many times,
induced by her silence,
will you knock on my door, friend,
and an anxious tremor will open into
violent weeping, and curses will escape
your mouth between sobs, and fear
will mark your face with devastated marks,
and every word will escape you.
What are you looking for, o unhappy man?
You won't know anymore who or where you are!
And many times you will have to return deluded,
many times you won't have to wonder
at my pallor and at my wasted frame . . .
Nor will I be able to console you, who
for my own sickness have no remedy at all . . .

In the next one I speak with an old companion who is going to the
East and would like me to go with him, but I can't leave Rome for faraway countries: "how can I visit Athens and 'the ancient treasures of
Asia' if my Cynthia goes hysterical, despairs, and threatens to kill herself at the very idea that I'm considering a voyage? She blackmails me;
she doesn't want to lose her prey! I'm her prisoner!" This elegy had a
story—a terrible one—so much so that I hesitated much before slipping
it into the collection. And if I finally included it, I did it because I was
short of breath.

In periods of worst misery, as you already know, I had sometimes
asked small sums of money from the usurer Volcatius Tullus—a moral
usurer, I told you. One time, though, I really wasn't able to pay him back,
so he told me, "Maybe I'm going to leave with my uncle who is to be Pro-
consul in Asia. Write me a song in my honor and we'll call it even."

Did you get it? In his honor!

Anyway, I wrote a song, and in his vanity he cancelled my debt. He
never made it to Asia, but the song stuck around. Now I was tempted to
use it for the book.

. . . Let fortune conquer me as she wishes,
let this soul surrender itself
to extreme weakness.
Many have died in the faraway land of Love,
May I too be covered by the same earth.

I was born unfit for arms, unfit for glory:
this is the only militia for which Fate destined me . . .

That way I even included the militia. Of the seventh elegy, dedicated to Ponticus, a smalltime poet, I copy only the central part:

. . . In every way I try to make her happy
even if she subjugates me harshly and even
if she constrains me to serve
not my wit but my sorrow . . .
Oh yes, I regret the hard times
of my first youth! Nonetheless
this life is only a life and it passes,
and my verses will give it fame.
All that I want is to please
my learned friend and to know how
to bear her unjust rancors.
Read here, o you who love:
I want you to know your sickness!
If one day Love wounds you too,
my Ponticus, it will not help you
to write sweet songs: a god will not
have pity; you will weep in your misfortune . . .
And yet I do not consider myself
either humble or beaten, but I shall have
the first place among the bards of Rome.
Weeping on my tomb
young men will say, "You are here,
great poet of our passion!"

In the eighth elegy I reunite the two pieces that I wrote to break up
Cynthia and Hippicus. In the ninth I write again to Ponticus, who, in
the meantime, has fallen in love:

. . . Don't deceive yourself: when she acts like she's yours
she only wants to become your master more sharply,
so that you can no longer take your
by now empty gaze away from her.
Only when he touches the deep fibers of your being
does Love reveal his immense cruelty:
So flee, flee while you still have time,
confess your error . . .

In number ten I describe Cynthia's harsh authority: she has taught me "that which I can ask for and that which I shouldn't," and in addition to bearing in humility her explosions of rage, not to bother her with "silly" words, not to make her promises that I can't keep that instant. All this in exchange for the privilege of serving her in bed and of picking, myself, the sweet fruit of my devotion . . . The eleventh is a letter in verse to Cynthia, while on vacation at Baiae. I really sent the letter and got in return a little postcard that told of the roses and incredible cascades of flowers that were there. My Propertius imagines her "gently posed on that tranquil shore" but exposed to the "whispers" of some seducer. So take my advice, be upset about it: "Leave that place of corruption as soon as you can, it is the enemy of every honest woman," i.e. the place where one goes every summer to enjoy the rich Roman ladies.

Poor guy! my literary double. He doesn't yet suspect the true nature of Cynthia! What everyone else knows: that she is maintained at Baiae by His Excellence Crassus Frugis! He is ingenuous and pure, a true lily. We're halfway through the book anyway, so the storm is still far. But it will come: we who read realize it, though he less so! The trick is exactly this: the readers will have to have understood who Cynthia is and how and from what she lives. That way everyone will wait for the moment of my consternation, everyone will have a foretaste of the catastrophe . . .

In the twelfth something bad really begins to happen. There's a rupture between Cynthia and my Propertius—the first of many. I don't explain the cause. Imagine, though, that the poisons of Baiae have worked; maybe some gossiper had some fun shaking up our overly fragile paradise. You can imagine that some dirty messenger advised the poet of his horns, that he confronted Cynthia on her return and, enraged, she kicked him out . . .

What a love has fled in such a short time! And how serious is the sadness of Propertius, since the dispute doesn't stop his fatal condemnation to love, among women, Cynthia and only Cynthia!

I am not who I was; now I know long
solitary nights and with my sighs
I rack my ears by myself . . .
As women change over a long journey,
that I could have another love!
But it is not given to me. It is not given
that I break from Cynthia and have another:
she was the first and will be the last.

How long has it been that I haven't slept? I've lost the concept of time. I'm tired and half-drunk. My fingernails are black from ink and I feel like dead meat. Ligdamus comes and goes silently with the food; he empties my urinal, serves me food and drink, and tries to wash me. I appreciate what he does; he's discrete and he understands the importance of the moment. He plays his part with comprehension in his eyes. But when he dares to touch the bin full of crumpled paper, I lose the light in my eyes and I slap him one: you don't throw away the crumpled paper, got it? Here there's a continual cut-and-sew; it's a re-exhumation of corpses, don't you see?

From here to the twentieth elegy, Propertius sings his desperation. Cynthia accepted neither his supplications nor his apologies and she keeps him away, but he keeps trying to calm her with his songs (even astute songs, in the sense that they keep the reader's blood pressure high). Take elegy thirteen for example: in declaring all my envy to a friend who enjoys his own better half, I remind him that I saw his fantastic copulation, telling him more or less: "You languished tight on her neck and you fainted on her desired lips! You were about to pass away! I tried to detach you from her, pulling you by your armpits, but only in vain. Your passionate delirium was too vehement! I am silent about the rest, for the sake of good taste, but not even the god Neptune raped the beautiful Tyro with such ability, and not even Hercules was so powerful with Ebis! You bested all the most famous lovers in only one day, my friend, you who were already famous in your youth for the quantity of women you seduced! Well, the one you have now—who demands your fidelity and prohibits other loves—she avenges the unfortunate ones; she'll know how to punish you for the sadness dealt to those you abandoned."

Astute and titillating, because this "friend" is indicated by name and surname, so the song will be on everyone's lips. In the fourteenth elegy one reads that Propertius would renounce any amount of wealth only to have Cynthia, "placated," back by his side. Number fifteen isn't bad; I jotted it down for Hostia after one of our tuffs, but didn't tell her about it then (it could've started up the fight again). Now I reinforce it with horns and I adapt it to her literary double, as if Propertius had definite evidence of a betrayal in hand:

Don't repeat words of perjury Cynthia,
don't call the oblivious gods. Ahi,
you were too audacious. You will understand
what I suffer and you will be sorry, you will be sorry

when you, for misfortune, will have to
suffer worse. The rivers will stop
emptying into the sea, the seasons
will go backwards, a hundred times you can be
as you wish, before I stop loving you,
but one thing I ask of you,
do not be another's. Don't disgrace
with other lies the beautiful eyes
that so often have rendered
the falsehoods credible. You swore
to rip them out if you ever
lied about something, and instead
you watch the sun with them, and arrogant
you do not tremble. Who has ever constrained you
to pale, to cry, to swear?
And yet you did it, and I'm dying of it:
I shall be a warning for every lover.

I spent one day and one night readapting number fifteen and while finish it up I burst into tears and sob, because it suggests that it all really happened and that I am discovering Cynthia's true nature only now. At the last verse I'm exhausted and I roll up on the little bed; my head is empty and I fear that I won't make it to twenty-one pieces. How many are left? My wit is abandoning me! But come on, fall back on expedients, you have to make it. There are only six left, hit the wine again!

I resist the temptation of using *The when and the how* (once *Oracles*), the lyric that has the verse on death that Gallus liked so much. It's too mature; it belongs to another, future phase of love. It would be out of place in this book. But what to do? I dig around in the bin and I find something among the corpses. In the sixteenth position I'm able to stick in the lament about a door that is obstinately closed because the lady of the house won't receive her lover. It's not a bad piece, but it's shamelessly copied a little from Callimachus and a little from Catullus. In the seventeenth and eighteenth elegies I repeat the desperation for the cruel and faraway Cynthia. In nineteen I say that I fear death, but only because she might not cry over my tomb . . .

I really don't know what else to put in. And time is getting short. Time is getting short! Memmius gave me precise instructions and I would like show myself to be at least as precise, but in reality I'm in a panic. My inspiration is completely dried-up and so is the theme . . . So

I save from the bin a scholastic exercise that I've already written: a mythological epyllion about the rape of Ila by the nymphs—Ila, the boy loved by Hercules . . . And a funerary epigram that I wrote at the time for a cousin of mine who had been killed by brigands after having escaped from the war in Perugia . . .

What do they have to do with the *Songs for Cynthia?* Nothing, but at this point I stick them on the end. So what, Horace would say, who's going to notice? That makes twenty-one.

Now I'd give myself twenty-one stabs with a knife! I forgot the rest of the deal that I had with Volcatius Tullus: to cite him in four lyrics to cancel the interest on the loan of four *denarii.* It's true that at Bandusia I told him, "Go fuck yourself for good and forever," but here I am—I pay my debts. But you lost the friendship of a true gentleman, Turdatius.

I turn back through the pages and with a crazed eye I look for a spot where I can shove in three vocative "o *Tullo.*"

I find them and I do it. Screw it, time is short and I'm tired . . . exhausted. I want to sleep. Screw it. Screw all of you.

Translator's Note

Pietro Zullino's *Cinzia, con i suoi occhi* is a novel about the life and poetry of the Augustan elegiac poet, Sextus Propertius. It is written in the form of an autobiography, as the memoirs of a dying man. Propertius, writing in the Rome of Virgil, Horace, and Ovid, was a problematic poet of love in the age of empire and still today Latin scholars have difficulty placing his sensibility among that of his contemporaries. Since the rediscovery of the manuscripts of Propertius' elegies in the fourteenth century by Petrarch, his poetry has served as a source of inspiration for Renaissance poets such as Ariosto, Tasso, and Ronsard, and for Goethe's *Roman Elegies.* In the twentieth century, students of modern poetry will recognize his fortune in Ezra Pound's *Homage to Sextus Propertius,* a translation both of Propertius' language and of his lyric sensibilities into the modern era. Zullino's novel, like his other historical biographies, *Catiline* (*Catilina*) and *The Seven Kings of Rome* (*I sette re di Roma*), seeks to do just that: transfer the sensibilities of a great, incongruous figure onto a modern idiom and demonstrate the relevance of his life and poetry to our age.

Using a variety of registers, from street-talk to discussions in the Roman Senate, Zullino depicts a Rome that is not just marble columns and togas, but that is also-and most importantly-a place where ordinary people, like Propertius, tried to find a life for themselves and even to become extraordinary in that life. Zullino's language is difficult to translate into English for the abundance of dialect and of authorial neologisms as well as for the stream of consciousness style that he uses. The novel covers, more or less linearly, five years in the life of Propertius, in which he rises from a young, unrecognized love poet and law student to the author of an extremely popular book of elegies (Book I of his *Elegies*, also known as the *Monobiblos*) to his decline after the publishing of his second and third collections. The story, like Propertius' poetry, is centered around his lover and muse, Hostia/Cynthia-a courtesan of the Roman Senate. In fact, the novel's title point to her central importance to Propertius' story. It is drawn from the first couplet of the first elegy of Book I, "Cynthia, with her eyes, first ensnared me-a wretch-who had never before been touched by any desires." Self-published in Italy, Zullino's novel is an innovative and creative approach to a poet that has vexed scholars and poets for centuries, from Petrarch to Goethe, from A. E. Houseman to Ezra Pound to contemporary Latin scholars.

* * *

The first of the selections is taken from the beginning of the novel and is a kind of introduction to Propertius' ethics-poetics and to his travails in becoming both a man and a poet. His point of view is removed from the action, as the novel itself is a memoir of the poet, exiled at the end of his life. The second section is a rapid description of the compilation of the *Monobiblos* and of the state of mind of the poet when he must begin writing for others outside his circle of friends. I have followed Zullino's translations of the Latin poetry because he maintains Propertius' difficulty of language and style with a seeming ease of the pen. Nonetheless, I have consulted Latin editions of the poems in order to assure the accuracy of my own translation.

David H. Lynn

Steps Through Sand, Through Fire

When the silver headdress slipped again over Gerald Knapper's eyes, causing him finally to lose the balance he'd been struggling to maintain for
nearly an hour and plummet from the high white horse—an ill-tempered
and ill-treated brute—and into the red Indian dust, the jarring pain in his
left shoulder jolted the breath right out of him. He flailed, wrestling against
the clenched muscle of his own chest. His eyes widened in despair and fear
as he choked. At last, at last, the spasm loosened, allowing him a gasp, a
short breath, a flicker of tears. He lay panting, feeling relief and gratitude
above all. The worst of the humiliation was surely behind him now.

Even through that first flash of pain and of loose grit slamming into
his teeth and nose, he'd heard the ragged cry of merriment from twenty-
five boys and men, most of them hired for the occasion. They were his retinue, what had to pass for his family, his friends. Blowing reedy horns,
beating cymbals, they accepted his embarrassing tumble as merely another
inevitable event in the ceremony. (But certainly also as yet another gaffe
by this ludicrous American, a pale, middle-aged man whom they could
mock even as they cheered him as hero, the conquering bridegroom.)

"Respected sir," said one old man with an extravagant mustache,
gray and coarse as rhino tusks twisting off to either side of his lean jaw.
Roughly shoving his large, gnarled hands under Gerald's arms, he
hoisted him to his feet. In an instant the others had set upon him as
well, patting the dust from his suit, punching at him to demonstrate his
own well being, and shoving the silver helmet back across his brow.

Thus was he planted, sagging but upright, before Ravi Singh, the man about to become his brother-in-law. Ravi wore a casually restrained smile. "Hard luck. No need to worry," said the younger man. His speech was just as perfect though slightly more clipped than his sister's. After college at St. Stephen's in Delhi, Ravi had spent two years in London and Cambridge, whereas Sita had gone to the States. His accent was no more British, however, than hers was American—they spoke the Indian-rooted English of Delhi's new princelings, at home anywhere on the globe.

Gerald sensed not only Ravi's vague amusement but his disdain as well. And for the first time in nearly a month he realized a truth that had been veiled before—that he was in some sort of struggle with this young man, that they were wrestling in the shadow behind word and deed and even his own conscious intention. But this wasn't what he cared about. It wasn't why he was here. He was too old to waste any emotional force on this younger man, the brother of his bride. Patting at the dust on his linen suit, Gerald was perfectly willing to grin and shrug in disarming acknowledgment of the ludicrous spectacle he presented.

No dust dared soil Ravi Singh's double-breasted blazer, nor his tasseled loafers, nor the polished nails on the hand he flicked at the small mob. Instantly, as if the American were no more than a rather rumpled puppet, they heaved him once more atop the garlanded white horse that had already carried him better than a mile from Ravi's house. Hands bolstered him aloft so that he could clutch the headdress in place. Rampant and in artificial triumph, Gerald rode a last few yards towards the high painted gates of the wedding pavilion. It had been erected in the shadows of a nameless emperor's monument, and Gerald assumed that the staging of a private wedding in these otherwise public gardens in the heart of Delhi was one mark of the family's influence.

All evening he'd struggled against a late arrival. It was the one failure, the one mark of bad grace that he dreaded. Hundreds of elaborate crimson invitations had been launched into the world, clearly announcing 6 P.M. as the start of festivities. But the horse hadn't appeared at Ravi's door until nearly seven, and then the procession scudded so slowly through the streets, what with the cheering and braying of horns and the clapping of hand and drum, not to mention his own precarious mount, that at times they seemed to be drifting in hapless ebb rather than toward his Sita. Now, finally, having survived his fall, Gerald prodded his steed through the twenty-foot papier-mache arch festooned with auspicious marigolds. To a last ragged cheer from his distracted cohort— they were already peering towards handouts of wedding food and additional gifts of coin—Gerald Knapper, the groom, did arrive.

No one noticed. A spare spatter of guests who'd come early in order to slip away to other affairs were milling about rather vaguely, attentive only to passing trays of food and drink, greeting each other with caws and kisses. No sign anywhere of Sita or her parents. Once again Gerald felt he'd gone wrong, that he should have known better, that even as he was dismounting he'd stumbled another wrong step in a dance whose proper rhythm eluded him.

Most of his retinue had abandoned him at the scaffolding just inside the ornate movie-set gate. Surprised, alone, he glanced back and saw plastic jugs splashing something clear, no doubt something potent, into their mugs and cupped palms. This, plus handfuls of rupees doled out earlier and hope of more to come, kept a few of these hired friends faithful to their horns and drums, welcoming guests as they appeared. For a long moment, staggering a bit now that he was off the horse, shorn of his make-believe troupe, still balancing Sita and Ravi's great-grandfather's silver helmet, metal tassels and all, on his head, Gerald felt as disoriented as at any moment since arriving in India. He was also struck by his apparent invisibility, given that the elaborate pageant only beginning to gather momentum was in honor of his wedding.

A constellation of enormous tents stretched away to all sides. Carpets large and small were strewn across the dirt and dust and grass, elegant Persian designs next to coir mats and wide strips of green plastic turf.

Not for the first time, Gerald regretted failing to persuade Sita to marry him in Columbus. Larry Tomsich, a friend of many years and local magistrate, would have performed the task simply and tastefully. A few friends in attendance. Perhaps even one of his children might have deigned to come—they'd have thought him merely foolish then, rather than out-and-out crazy. But Sita held fast. She couldn't do such a thing to her parents. Though he sensed even from half a world away that given her age—past eighteen, past twenty-five, even past thirty and fled to America—the family had all but abandoned hope of any proper marriage for her.

Thinking of Sita flooded him with joy like a schoolboy and a first crush. Without warning, it swept over him and rooted him in this moment, this place, glad for the incense in the air, the dust, even the distant waft of burning cow dung in the February night. He loved her with a passion that he'd thought long extinguished. Over nearly a year of dinners and gallery visits and chaste strolls along the Scioto River—and then, finally, when he'd nearly crashed against the limits of what he could endure, the not so chaste retreat into her modest TA-funded apartment at the university, (never, not yet, not until after this marriage, into the far from modest house in Upper Arlington that he'd shared with his wife Margot)—she'd brought him alive again. For this he was willing to travel anywhere, undergo any ordeal, even a wedding like this.

As Gerald stood gazing into the hazy evening, Sita appeared as if conjured by his thoughts from out of the incense and smoke. Her mother in a plum-colored sari on one arm, father on the other, she came gliding toward him, transformed, and Gerald was frightened. This was his first glimpse of her all day. Her eyes were dark with kohl, their lids the blue of a bird. A single diamond stud pierced her nostril. Her own sari was wound tight about her and yet seemed to be flowing all at once, an infinitely fine fabric of gold embroidery on crimson with a single loop covering the back of her head and neck. Her long dark hair was pulled back tight from her face. Looking up from under at him, she might have been ten years younger. She might have been a stranger.

Perhaps she spied the anxiety in his eyes. She lifted her fingers to her mouth, and that little gesture, covering her lips as if with an alarmed modesty, made all the world right. It was something Sita did—a reflex so delicate and personal to her that for him it seemed an intimate signature. Seeing it this evening, spying it here, almost hurt him with gladness. It certainly aroused him.

Her parents relinquished her with looks of mingled relief and concern. "We must greet our guests," she said, approaching him and touching his arm lightly.

He nodded and the silver helmet nearly tumbled into his hands. "When can I take this damn thing off?" he whispered more fiercely than he'd intended. "It weighs a ton. And I feel like the schoolroom dunce." He smiled to make the plea into a joke.

Lips pressed tight, she shook her head. "Stop, please, Gerald. Haven't we been through this? Come, come—there's no taking it off. Family tradition is family tradition. The bloody thing must be endured."

"Only for you," he murmured.

She cocked her head to the side, acknowledging his tenderness with a little smile. It stabbed him with the pain of his own love for her. And it also forced him to dodge once again the awareness that though she loved him—he dared not doubt it—it was not with an intensity that could match his own.

Touching his arm once more, Sita steered him toward one cluster of guests and then another. Although conversation was almost entirely in

English, its sounds had been shaped locally, like the graft of a foreign plant onto sturdy new roots, and Gerald's ear hadn't yet been trained to make sense of them—he missed much of what was said, even when directly to him. On the other hand, no one seemed put off by his awkwardness. They smiled and nodded. They thought it charming that he'd learned to press his palms together and salute them with an earnest *namaste*—charming as a child may be both charming and silly. Like a tolerant, even doting nurse, Sita beamed and steered him proudly about.

Gerald stifled as best he could a swelling resentment. Charming, yes—he'd certainly intended to generate seas of good will on behalf of this woman and her family. But not by being a source of amusement, first for Ravi and now these others. In general, he prided himself on his equanimity, his good will. It had been hard won. Margot's death after five years of battling breast cancer, its remission, its return and blasted triumph, had all but swamped him with despair. To that moment he could trace a chasm spreading between himself and his children, one that had never entirely healed. But his spirits did slowly revive, broadening into an unexpected contentedness in middle age, along with a considerable financial success. Discovering Sita and then persuading her to marry him—these only increased his sense of rare fortune. He was perfectly willing to offer patience and generosity to the world about him. But, but: playing the fool for these wealthy Indians, whatever good will it might earn, was wearing his patience thin.

With a sough like a gathering wind, the crowd's attention swerved away from the bridal couple. Gerald too turned and spotted a silver Ambassador, still the car of official India, with darkened windows and little flags flickering on its fenders, draw to the painted gates of the wedding pavilion. Like an electric spark, word leapt across the sea of craning faces: Gangaswami had arrived! A celebrity among celebrities, the holy man and political guru alone was permitted to be driven this far. Ravi bestowed this honor on him because of the honor that Gangaswami brought in turn to the family by appearing and even participating in the ceremony.

A young boy, fourteen perhaps, with a shaggy head of hair and dressed in a gray jacket and tight pants, scrambled from a front seat and hurried to open the car's rear door. Heavy curtains blocked any glimpse inside. A massive hand thrust out into the night air wielding a heavy black stick, which it planted in the dust. Another hand grasped at the boy's neck and shoulders, part caress and part throttle, threatening to drag him back into the dark maw of the automobile. But the boy braced himself, one hand against the doorframe, legs leveraged into the dirt. Slowly, by stages, an arm, a leg, the gradual shifting of the great bulk of his torso, Gangaswami emerged. Immense in girth, jovial and commanding, he raised a hand in the air and thus allowed the multitude of servants and guests to breathe again. Until that moment they'd been unaware of having ceased in anticipation.

Gerald had first met the god man (as he'd seen him called in the Indian papers, partly in tribute, partly ridicule), shortly after arriving in Delhi. Hurrying to the door of his house, Ravi Singh had grasped the visitor's arm and helped him cross the threshold. As a favor to the rising young political star and scion of one of India's lordliest families, Gangaswami had offered to consult personally on the wedding now being planned. Ravi ushered him through to a salon specially prepared for the audience.

It wasn't until their guest had been settled monumentally onto a vast sofa that the orientation of the room, its deep chairs and other furnishings, came clear to Gerald. He himself had been steered to a solitary, hard settee. Sita was perched across the way, impossibly distant. A family crescent seemed to stretch along Gangaswami's arm span—father and mother, several aunts and uncles and who-knew-else—gathered neatly on either side. Ravi remained standing behind the sofa, sometimes leaning casually to whisper in his guest's ear.

For the sake of politeness, Gangaswami picked at the delicacies and sweets set beside him on a platter, sipped at a glass of water. At last he turned his gaze fully on Gerald Knapper. Behind heavy black spectacles his eyes were small and set too closely together for the amount of flesh about them. Yet they were sharp and full of good humor. He beamed more broadly at the American, and suddenly Gerald was washed by an astonishing flood of warmth. The power of the guru's personality, his sheer presence, was oddly comforting at the same time it was overwhelming. Almost a physical pummeling, it unsettled Gerald in his seat. He felt vulnerable, almost naked before him. Yet he also had to resist an urge to rise and hurry toward the man. This was new—Gerald had dealt with the rich and powerful, but never anyone with such a force. Now he glimpsed how Gangaswami had gathered so much influence, so many protégés among the political elite, from prime ministers to high tech moguls.

"I do not see that it makes any difference," Gangaswami was saying with a toss of his hand, tilting his head first to one side of the family audience and then to other without yet taking his eyes off of Gerald. His voice was itself a surprise: nasal and reedy, almost childishly high-pitched. "If we want to make a proper wedding, there is no reason not to do so. What do the gods of his parents matter so long as he does not reject ours?"

"Sorry?" said Gerald, looking first at the guru and then to Sita. She was staring into her lap. Her parents, the elder Singh and his wife, looked as startled as Gerald. They didn't seem able to respond.

Ravi understood at once. He glanced at his father and then spoke to Gerald. "We of course originally agreed with the notion of a civil wedding, because a traditional one—a Hindu wedding—seemed out of the question. But now that our eminent friend has opened our eyes to what is possible, the family will be happy to welcome you as one of its sons in the traditional way. No one will dare challenge Shri Gangaswami's ruling."

"Sita?" Gerald said. Still she wouldn't face him but blushed deeply and gave the hint of a shrug. "Sorry," he said again. "But this is a little too quick, a little too, well, crazy. You're not giving me a chance to catch up."

"My friend," said Gangaswami with patience and generous good will, "this is a great and unusual honor my friends, Ravi Singh's family, are offering you. We do not say you must give up your gods that you were raised with. Simply that you say welcome to ours, and they will welcome you as well."

Gerald shook his head, but no one seemed to notice. Was this possible? Could he do such a thing? He hadn't been to shul since Margot's death, and never very vigorously before. To what degree did he feel himself bound to have no gods before one who, after all, had been perfectly pleased to keep his own distance? Gerald realized he wasn't much concerned with betraying that God of his youth. Still—he worried whether he might be betraying something of himself in the bargain.

Like moths to a swollen candle, the wedding guests found themselves fluttering toward and about Gangaswami. He was leaning heavily on his cane as he waded through the enveloping crowd. Beaming, his head wagging from side to side, he moved forward, taking notice—making contact, however brief—with apparently everyone. His presence glowed through the throng. The servants, carrying platters of food, circling with beverages, could hardly draw their gaze from the god man.

Gerald's eyes sought out Ravi Singh. Left hand stylishly jabbed in his jacket pocket—who is he, the goddam Prince of Wales? Gerald wondered—Ravi appeared delighted by the delight and distraction of his guests. He was smiling slightly as he observed the melee. Another move in his complicated choreography was playing out as designed. This time he made no move to welcome his eminent guest personally. He was content—more than content—to stand at a distance and savor ripples of excitement radiating through the crowd of politicians, industrialists, artists in dinner jackets, Italian suits, blue silk *kurtas,* the many beautiful women in golden saris and silver *shalwar-kameez.* Such electricity could only brighten Ravi's own star for having arranged it. No doubt the evening was already a grand success for the young man's ambitions. Gerald wondered whether what was to come—a wedding—could be anything more than an afterthought.

For the moment, however, any ceremony seemed far from imminent. And beckoning to Gerald was an entire tent filled with heavily laden tables. He hadn't eaten since midday. As he discovered his hunger it became overpowering. He spied steaming bowls of shrimp in a pungent green mint and chili sauce; roasted chickens sliced on platters; eggplants and mushrooms and spinach. They perfumed the night with ginger and cumin and spices Gerald couldn't identify. He didn't care. Ravenous beyond reason, all he wanted was to stuff his belly. And too, he spied certain gentleman guests who knew how to conjure a magic phrase, sipping tall glasses of whiskey and soda rather than the lemonade and other juices in public circulation. Whiskey, too: he could use a quick dash.

Sita snagged his sleeve as he hesitated. "Come," she said, "come," tugging him away. He resisted, leaning half a step toward the food. But she jerked his arm more sharply. At her touch, the invisibility that had cloaked him since Gangaswami's arrival, and which he'd been enjoying, dissolved like so much mist.

Still the crowd of guests was swelling, hundreds it seemed, surging through tents and across lawns, more and more arriving as the evening grew late. Gerald felt their eyes upon him and Sita as they made their way up toward two high-backed wooden chairs on the terrace of the ancient monument. The grayish hewn stones and few surviving fragments of the emperor's delicate inlay had been incorporated into a high platform overlooking Ravi's party, flowing with explosions of winter flowers—roses, orange and red and peach, purple orchids, strings of marigolds beyond count. Stepping awkwardly, worried about tripping on the uneven stones, feeling that they, he and Sita, were somehow trespassing, Gerald allowed her to lead him along a narrow path that wound toward the throne-like chairs.

"Now what?" he whispered. "Is it time for the ceremony?"

"What a fuss you keep making. One must be patient," she hissed as she turned to sit.

Sita's eyes remained focused on the tips of her toes in their crimson sandals. Faithfully, obstinately, she gripped fast to her role as young bride: joyful, innocent, a tiny bit frightened, she might only have met the man who was to be her husband once or twice during the match-making interviews, and was certainly still a virgin. Gerald didn't know whether to laugh or cry aloud with rage. He was too old for such pretense. *She* was too old.

"What about dinner? I'm starving." Immediately he hated his own voice—whining and petulant.

Sita chose not to answer, but her stiffness and displeasure at his performance thus far were plain enough.

Bravely, as bravely as he could muster, he righted the headdress and prepared himself for what was to come.

What came was slow to the point of madness. While guests plundered food and drink, greeted each other with kisses, slipped off together for urgent consultations or covert assignations—the view from the monument stripped away the feints of ordinary pretense—the wedding couple received tribute. Among the first to rush up toward them, unseemly in their haste and eager enthusiasm, were women who had been Sita's colleagues in the English department at Lady Shri Ram College before she went to America to finish her Ph.D. Gerald was delighted to meet them at last, Kasturi, and Meenakshi and Gopa, so much had he heard about them, though he couldn't begin to match name to face.

Kasturi—it *was* Kasturi?—abruptly grabbed his hand, shook it powerfully in both her own, and looked him straight in the eye in a way that no one, certainly no woman, had done in better than a month. "You are certainly a lucky man, Mr. Knapper. I hope you will be a good one as well. In that case we shall be friends."

Ravi had materialized somehow onto the platform. Sita's friends sensed his presence behind them, and when he leaned ever so slightly in their direction, smiling, they startled into flight with little cries and waves and promises to call on her.

Now the central ceremony of the evening elaborated itself. An old man, perhaps five feet tall, with a heavily pocked face and bulbous nose, slowly climbed the stone steps. He wore an elegantly tailored black Indian jacket. At his hip floated a willowy young woman, perhaps twenty-five and a foot taller than her escort, in a peacock-blue sari. The old man bowed toward Gerald but said nothing, and kissed Sita on both cheeks. He flicked a wrist into the cool night air, and into it a trailing servant placed a thick silken packet. The old man tugged the knot and drew out a single crisp ten-thousand rupee note, one of a thick company. He leaned forward and tucked the bill like a bright kerchief into Gerald's breast pocket. The packet he laid in Sita's lap with another short bow and then turned away. Gerald wondered whether he would go so far as to brush Ravi's shoes with his fingers as he passed.

"Don't touch that," snapped Sita under her breath.

Gerald's own fingers froze. "I can't leave this thing sticking out of my pocket—it's humiliating. I'm not some boy desperate for a buck."

"It isn't about you. They don't know anything about you. Such things are a matter of form."

"It's all a matter of making a fuss over Ravi's sister, is what it is. And of shaming me, or putting me in my place, though I haven't figured out why or what he's after."

"Oh, Gerald." She sighed. She glanced at him despite herself. "He's my brother. He's not after anything except my happiness."

Before he could respond the next pair of guests was already upon them. Two by two they continued to appear, all greeting the couple and bearing gifts. It was hard to tell—and there was no opportunity to ask—but Gerald guessed that most were strangers to Sita as well. Some touched their gifts only at the last instant, receiving the wrapped boxes or stuffed envelopes from a servant and handing them in turn to Sita. Nearly all dropped a few golden coins in their laps or stuck notes of large denomination in pockets and creases and even in the silver headdress. Gerald battled grimly not to blush or shout or stalk off the stage entirely. Sita passed the gifts to a family servant who was constructing a small castle of unopened treasures behind the wooden thrones. And two by two the guests made their way to greet Ravi and be acknowledged for their loyalty and largesse.

Gerald couldn't help but snatch glimpses of Sita's brother as the queue jerked spasmodically along. A prince indeed, it seemed, so at ease was Ravi, so coolly warm in his greetings and deflections. Here was no politician of an American stripe. He received the tributes of these people as his due, for which he was pleased but not indebted.

Well past midnight the last of the visitors paid homage, turning like all the others from wedding couple to host, and then quickly descending into the floodlit darkness below. Gerald rose stiffly. Peering from the lip of the monument, he saw that the tents and tables and buffets of food had grown largely deserted. A general detritus of fallen flowers, of napkins and scattered glasses lay strewn about. Members of the family were gathered in tight fists of conversations. Sita's parents slumped wearily on fabric chairs that had been ferried from the main house, with nieces and nephews, cousins and brothers gathered about for support.

With a daring pat on Sita's knee—and no glance to gauge her response—Gerald rose and strode quickly toward Ravi. He was standing by himself, watching something at the other end of the monument or not watching anything at all. Gerald lifted the silver helmet from his head and thrust it forward.

"Your turn now, don't you think?"

Ravi laughed lightly. "I wondered how long you'd put up with that bloody thing." He made no move to accept this particular gift. "Besides, you haven't finished with it yet. There are still the priests to satisfy."

"Surely your friend Mr. Gangaswami won't fuss if I'm not wearing the family armor." He tossed the headdress toward Ravi, who had little choice but to catch it. His eyes glittered, but the pleasant little smile never wavered.

Out beyond the last of the tents, safely beyond the precincts of the stone tombs of vanished Muslim rulers, flaring tapers kept the night at bay. A larger blaze snapped and smoked in a shallow pit. As Sita and Gerald finally approached the fire, with her family gathered at the threshold of shadows just beyond, Gangaswami lurched up from several large pillows with the help of his young assistant. Plates were scattered on the ground near his cushions. It was unclear how long he'd sought refuge out here in wilderness and exile. Perhaps he'd fled the unceasing homage and pleas for advice or blessing amidst the crowd.

"My friends," he cried in a voice that, nasal and reedy, startled Gerald each time he heard it, "this will be a great moment for you and for your family. And for your friends too, yes, and I am only too happy, so happy, to count myself among the latter."

He grabbed Sita's hand and placed it in Gerald's, drawing them toward the holy fire and the path that twined about it. Gangaswami signaled for two Brahmin priests in attendance to approach. And without another word, the god man turned and strolled heavily away into the night. The practicalities of the affair he would leave to others.

As he trudged the prescribed path around the fire for the third—or was it fourth?—time, Gerald's head was swimming with fatigue and hunger and a faint dizziness, as if a renewed bout of jet lag had swept him up and beyond himself. This woman at his side—who was she?

This disturbing intuition from earlier in the evening, of Sita become someone else, a stranger, had never entirely disappeared. It wasn't merely the kohl around her eyes or the diamond in her nose, nor that he was glimpsing an undiscovered aspect of her character, one he'd never had the chance to encounter in her American exile. No—he'd prepared himself for that possibility before ever boarding the plane for India. No—what unnerved him now in the late blue-black night of these Delhi gardens was the way she carried herself, the different lilt to her voice, an unrecognizable inflection in her eyes. He feared some more profound transformation of her character that he would no longer understand. Yet none of this—not for a moment—lessened his desire for her. And he reminded himself that these doubts and worries might well be simply a measure of his weariness.

Weariness apparently had yet to graze Sita. A gauzy gold-and-crimson *dupatta* was draped over her head and across the lower half of her face. Through most of the months they had all but lived together she'd worn jeans or longish dresses, yet tonight she seemed released by the very constrictions of the tightly wound sari. She floated, she *danced* the prescribed steps around the fire as if she'd trained for this moment all her life, in all her dreams.

Which she had, which she probably had, Gerald silently conceded.

Stranger or lover, both she might be, but her simple presence at his side on the path called to him, bound him, delighted him, stoked him, crushed muscle in his chest and groin with yearning. A thought of what lay ahead in the night once they were finally, finally set free (for this the smoke and strange chants and confusion of dance and dust could all be endured), turned him hard, brilliantly and unreservedly hard, as if he were an adolescent boy again and not a man into his fifties. He was simultaneously proud and a trifle embarrassed. (Surely no one could spy the truth.)

He hadn't slept with Sita in something more than four weeks. Why this was so he hadn't quite fathomed. Ravi had assigned them separate rooms of course, for the sake of appearances. Beyond this formality her brother paid no attention. And whatever their roots in rural Bihar, the elder Singhs were Delhi-wallahs of many decades—more sophisticated, more worldly than Sita had led him to expect. They were under no illusions about the life their daughter had been living, nor were they particularly troubled by it. Yet each night for four long weeks she'd slipped free of his increasingly urgent goodnight kisses—reluctantly, yearningly, but with absolute conviction. He did not understand but was willing to go along with her wishes, her instincts—her playacting, if that's what it was.

In America he'd also been occasionally embarrassed by his passion for this woman. Never in his life (though he wouldn't admit it to his children, or even Larry Tomsich and other pals at the club) had he been so truly intoxicated with love. A glimpse of her, an accidental brush of her elbow or knee, smote him to foolishness. And all he could do was grin and shrug and accept the truth of his foolishness and his delight.

Janice Stein, wife of one of his partners and an academic, had drunkenly accused him one evening of being attracted to Sita because she was exotic—an oriental, full of mystery and potent sexuality. "It's all illusion. It's all in the sick minds of western men," she'd mocked over dinner.

Not intending to make an enemy, Gerald had done the unpardonable: he laughed. A strong deep laugh of astonishment and pleasure in just how silly Janice's notion was. Because that was just it: with Sita he felt a marrow-deep harmony more intense than with any person he'd ever known, even Margot. There was no mystery, nothing exotic, beyond the simple, blissful necessity of there being this woman with whom he could find the best part of himself.

Happily, he'd given up all for her—or, really, given up nothing. His partnership provided money beyond his needs, even with generous tokens of affection (and guilt) to three grown and rather demanding offspring. The work itself no longer provided any satisfaction in itself, rarely much beyond a means to fill his days, which had been so important after Margot died. Better now to let Sita fill his days!

To India then he came.

And came to himself in mid stumble, waking on a narrow serpentine path that wound about the Brahmin flames. His forehead was smeared with orange and yellow paste. Wreaths of marigolds were draped around his neck. Was it Sita who had changed or he himself? The uncertainty rocked him.

He glanced up and in the shadows he made out Ravi watching languorously, hardly paying attention. A sudden searing resentment flared. He grasped with fresh clarity just how Ravi had been twisting and spinning him like a baited animal since his arrival. All while making a pretense of treating him as a new brother, a man to be honored for his own sake, not simply because he was marrying Sita, sister and daughter of the household.

Sacrificing home and family—that had only been an initial gesture, though this too he hadn't properly realized until this moment. They'd forgone a secular wedding in Columbus; he'd agreed to come to India to accomplish the marriage as part of an extended stay (no particular length had ever been mentioned and hadn't concerned him); his children, all the family that remained for him, felt no need to attend a wedding they neither understood nor approved.

As he considered this brief history, humiliations large and small seemed to gather themselves into the ludicrous struggle over the silver headdress. Humiliations large and small—most he hadn't even consciously sensed at the moment, though now they returned with a thousand tiny stings. What had been Ravi's point? What purpose? Merely a rich young man's whim, toying with an American too besotted with his sister to realize the easy sport he made?

No, weighing the past month, Gerald didn't feel that he'd merely been pricked and prodded for sport. He might have been able to laugh that off or arrange a playful revenge. Instead, he'd been stripped and scoured by a thousand goads as by grains of a coarse abrasive. Astonished at himself, that it had taken this long to penetrate his smitten attention, he saw now that Ravi on behalf of his family had undertaken a deliberate process: it was a kind of cleansing, and through it Gerald had been transformed into someone else altogether, at least as far as the world of Sita and her family were concerned. Like some young bride leaving hearth and kin behind, he was being prepared to become part of a new family on its own terms. His wealth—and he grimaced as this occurred to him—was dowry enough for the Singhs to overlook so much else that might compromise the choice of a middle-aged American.

Just as he was reaching the limit of endurance, summoning outrage enough to hurl marigolds from his throat, to cry out some mammoth defiance, to stalk away into a night he didn't begin to understand, the wedding ceremony ended. Sita and he were handed earthenware mugs of holy water. They dribbled some into the fire, which sputtered and sparked. One of the priests followed at their heels and casually dumped out a bucket of less precious liquid. The flame hissed, disappearing into a curl of smoke reeking and fetid.

Guests and revelers had long since departed. A few servants were rolling up carpets, offering token gestures with brooms and wicker baskets, but even Gerald could see that they were only waiting of the Singhs to make their way home. Anything of value had already been whisked away. Just beyond the fringe of shadows he spied, here and there, pairs of eager eyes, young and old, waiting. Once the site was abandoned, the local poor would descend and neatly, precisely scavenge anything abandoned. This was their due.

Strings of electric lights suddenly disappeared into blackness. Only a few torches guttered on wobbly stands.

Sita's mother and father were walking slowly toward a car that would carry them back to the main house. Bent and weary, they seemed oblivious to the world about them. All energy was husbanded for the remainder of this journey. Gerald trailed along after them because he did not know what else to do. Sita had once again disappeared. Nor was there any sign of her brother. Tired, wretched, near tears with frustration, Gerald again imagined himself as a bride learning a first lesson even while being brought roughly into the family: stripped of his past, expected to make a place for himself and be useful. He recognized the absurd self-pity of such an image, but the recognition in no way freed or soothed him.

A sudden clutch at his elbow. He jerked sharply as if bitten. Panting in surprise, he discovered that Sita had magically materialized at his side once more. She slipped her hand through his arm, drawing close. The gauzy *dupatta* had fallen from her head and she smiled up at him as she hadn't been able to smile for weeks.

"Thank you, thank you," she murmured into his ear. "You were wonderful. I'm so grateful."

For a moment it was as if he couldn't quite understand her—what was she chattering about? All the tensions, all the resentments that had been building in him through the evening—for better than four weeks in truth — blistered at this instant, hot to the touch and threatening to burst. His transformation hadn't taken after all. He was fifty-six years old and too old for such a change. Disoriented and miserable, he was swelling with an anger that wasn't like him at all.

He panted, he panted, he wouldn't, couldn't quite look at her yet, but walked along with her at his side. Finally, calming a bit, he had to speak. "What was all this, really? Some kind of test? Or am I initiated good and properly now, a member of your family?" The bitterness naked here was as much an outburst as he'd allow himself.

But Sita wouldn't let him spoil her own sense of relief and release and satisfaction. "My dearest. I told you before—it wasn't about you. Believe it or not. It was for my family. And yes, it was for me too. It was selfish and I'm sorry—oh, but it was fun and wonderful. Believe me, I promise to find lots of ways to make it up to you." She brought her hand to her mouth, but it didn't hide the wicked little smile she beamed at him.

"It won't be easy," he said. He wondered whether she herself had known what Ravi was up to. Was she in on the conspiracy? But already his misery and dourness had been lanced, not by Sita directly but by the joy sweeping up and over him that this woman should love him, that he should know such a love for her. If scouring his allegiances, even his character clean away had been a necessary price to make a new life with her possible, then he was grateful for it.

"We'll have some fun figuring out just how you'll manage it," he murmured.

Meg Mullins

Expecting Glenda

I saw the Pinto before I saw her. It was too old and too ugly to be a sum-mer person's car. But then the girl appeared from around the side of the car and in one look at her denim haltertop and white tennis shorts, those bare feet skipping across the already-hot-at-ten-AM-asphalt, I knew that she wasn't from around here. She started waving her arms, flagging me down. Having just finished the last of the morning's deliv-eries, I had already made up my mind to stop, but the sight of her hop-ping and skipping around, afraid I might drive on by, made something in my throat tighten. It seemed like, just as I eased the truck onto the shoulder behind that sad blue Pinto, there was a part of me that was say-ing, *Hollis, here's the beginning of a mistake.* But like most everyone who's looking back on unhappiness, it's hard to say exactly where it began.

"The gas gauge is broken," she said hopping from one foot to the other, a hint of the South still swimming below her educated Yankee voice.

"You from around here?" I asked, offering her the bandanna from my back pocket to stand on. She laid it over the highway as if it were some antique linen and gently placed her pale white feet in the center. I don't know why, but I couldn't help thinking of the skin on her toes and heels touching that cloth, the one I wipe my face with every God damn day, and I felt dizzy; as if an undercurrent had dragged me down and tumbled me around until I could no longer tell the sea from the sky.

"Born and raised in Montgomery," she said. "Live in Boston now. It's my cousin's car, he lives just over in Fairhope, but the twirp didn't tell me about the gas gauge."

"There's a Texaco over the bridge," I told her. "Check the trunk for a gas can."

She pulled out a yellow container and handed it to me. Then, she slid across the front seat of the car to turn off the radio, which was still playing hard rock, and hopped her way into my truck. I followed her. In the summer, there's nothing special about hauling a summer girl across the bridge for gas, or helping her get into the car she left locked and running, or even loading heavy bags of ice from the vending machine into her trunk just because you happen to walk by with two free hands. These things, I've done all my life.

We drove the quarter mile in silence, the open windows whipping salty ocean air through the cab. I was grateful for that, knowing how I stink every morning after hauling shrimp. She closed her eyes and leaned into the wind, like I've seen some dogs do.

We got the gas and I let her buy me a coffee from the cashier. Going back over the bridge, she hummed a bit looking out at the gulf, then said, "You working today?"

"Just came from my first job," I said. "Started at five this morning."

"Geez," she drummed her fingers against the gas can in her lap, "you must be wiped out. Thanks for stopping."

I smiled, took a gulp of hot coffee. She looked away as I flinched from the burn.

I gently poured the gas into the tank while she watched, again standing on my bandanna and shielding her eyes from the sun. I looked down at her feet, so white the sun was blazing off of them: two pale angels on my dirty black bandanna.

"Down for the beach?" I finally asked as the tank filled up.

She nodded. "Therapy," she said, smiling.

"You know Glenda is headed this way. Don't expect the sun will last much past noon."

There was a pause as she turned and looked out at the ocean. "Sun or not, storm or not, the air can't be beat," she finally said, winking at me as if, after much thought, we'd come to this conclusion together.

She took the gas can out of my hand and threw it back into the trunk. Then she stepped off of the bandanna, folded it into a square and pressed it into my palm. She climbed through the passenger's door, turned the radio back on, and started the car, hanging a thumb out the window as she got herself back into traffic.

I drove the rest of 44 by myself. The sand from her feet seemed like it was buzzing on the floor mat. I had to remind myself that a girl like that, her hip bones like handle bars and her hair, a burning red heat next to me, is just a test. You get so used to the dime a dozen girls with pretty little feet and bare brown backs running around here during the summer that when one of them steps out at you, for some reason looks like something more than just a part of the landscape, it's time to head home as quick as you can and be glad you had sense enough to marry a woman who would never leave the house without putting on a pair of shoes.

The docks are inland from the Gulf, on a bay that is fed by the Intra-coastal Canal. There is a large warehouse with conveyor belts and scales where the shrimpers and other fishermen are paid by the pound for their catch. High school kids get minimum wage for cleaning any fish or crus-tacean that's put in front of them. I load the morning's catch and deliver it to nearly every grocery, restaurant, and market along thirty miles of coast before ten AM.

This morning, Hoang's had been the only boat to go out. All the others were quiet, safely docked and swaying in the choppy current. But there was Hoang, heaving the last of three coolers onto the pier.

"How's the weather?" I'd shouted, only to let him know I was there.

"Is rough. But got nice catch, not bad," he said, pushing his mop across deck.

"Dolly must be worried about you, going out when Glenda is so close by."

"Dolly worry too much. Becky, too, right?" Hoang grinned at me. I didn't like this. I didn't like him making any comparisons between the two of us, and especially not between our wives.

"Becky's got nothing to worry about, Hoang. But you, going out in weather like this, just for, what, fifty pounds of shrimp? I don't know, I think Dolly might have cause for worry," I'd said and walked away from him, towards the warehouse and the familiar smell of fish guts.

Now, as I pulled up under the shade of a pine near the loading dock, my truck empty and trying hard to keep my mind from wandering back to that bridge, I could see Hoang still on his boat. Hosing out his cool-ers, he moved with mechanical precision; a lonely lever bending and lifting, bending and lifting.

Nobody at the docks likes to see him haul in his load of American shrimp, dock his boat, and bicycle home with a wad of dollars in his pocket. But me, I've got to live next door, wave hello to him when he delivers our paper with his big toothy grin, and small talk through his thick accent while our wives trade tips in the kitchen every Sunday night. It's not just that he's an immigrant, it's the way he is so abrupt, so stiff, so busy. He laughs in short hiccups, never sits still, and eats an entire fish, eyes and all. Dolly is the opposite, though, so slow-moving you'd think she were in some kind of trance. The two of them buying the place next door to us was just plain bad luck.

I delivered my receipts inside and when I came out, there was Hoang, standing next to my truck. He'd already put his bike in the back and was shifting from one foot to the next, waiting for a formal invitation to ride home with me.

"Get in the truck, Hoang," I said, without looking at him.

He complied and together we drove through town, past the broods of tanned, wet-haired, long-legged kids coming in off the beach for a fried crab claw lunch basket at Coconut Willie's.

At home, Becky was taking all the good china out of the hutch and wrapping it in towels. Her hair was pulled back into a bun so that her face looked bare, incomplete. Most days, when I drove by her produce stand and saw her with her funny straw hat and the rolled up jeans, I didn't think about how she could look better or be different in any way; I would just honk and wave, letting her know I was headed home to fetch her some lunch. But today, after driving 44 with that girl in my truck, the house felt small and cramped with nothing to look at but Becky's thick hands bundling plate after plate.

"Oh, good," she said, smiling at me. "You're here."

"Are those even worth all this trouble, Becky?" I asked sitting down on the couch.

"How was work?" she said, ignoring my question. "Probably not much this morning, huh?"

"Hoang's fifty pounds of shrimp," I said. I unlaced my work boots and stared out the window at the shirts and panties strung between our two houses. "Except for him I could have slept in," I said.

"He just wants to be your friend, Hollis," Dolly said.

"You have lunch?" I asked, looking toward the kitchen. There is no talking bad about folks with Becky. It took me a while to notice this about her. First off, I noticed her nice white teeth and the way her cheeks flushed when she laughed.

When we were first dating, we'd go to barbecues together, though, and at every one Becky would excuse herself from the circle of folks sitting around a table of dirty dishes, cutting up on people. She'd walk away, around the smoldering grill and stand off in the distance. People around the table would look at me, whisper something about her being a prude and then fall silent when I went after her. She never said anything to me about it, but when I came up on her, saw the mischief in her eyes and the way she said, "Let's go home now," I couldn't ever be sure about her motives. And I liked that about her. She wasn't about to advertise her objection to the kind of talk going on around that table. Instead, she just took my hand and made me feel like there was something much better waiting for us.

"You have lunch yet, Becky?" I asked again.

She looked up at me. "I'm not eating, Hollis, there's lots to do, still. I figured on having catfish for dinner. What do you think about that?"

I nodded and said, "Sounds good." On the counter in the kitchen, there was a basket full of Chilton County tomatoes and peaches. Becky had always done this for Mr. Thompson. No reason to think that his only child wouldn't also have a soft spot for homegrown produce. I was glad that Becky always seemed to know what to do. I was glad I had had sense enough to marry a sensible woman.

I set a sandwich down in front of her, though I knew she would hardly touch it. I couldn't tell whether the storm or Thompson's daughter was worrying her more, but before I went to get cleaned up, she grabbed my hand and said, "Don't worry, Hollis, everything will be fine."

I kept telling myself that if Mr. Thompson had had a son, it would be different. He would have been down as a boy with his father. In his mind, I would already be a permanent fixture in his father's estate. It wouldn't matter whether Becky put catfish or lasagna down in front of him, just as long as there was good beer and lots of bread and I certainly wouldn't be worried about getting a shower before hauling out to the bull pasture to meet him.

Through the lawyer, Mr. Thompson's daughter and I had arranged to meet and walk some property that afternoon, get her acquainted with her new inheritance. Way back, when he moved up to Montgomery, Mr. Thompson's father had hired my father to take care of his property down here. When my father passed, Mr. Thompson's father asked me to continue. And when Mr. Thompson's father passed, Mr. Thompson said I should keep on: tending to fences, auctioning timber, counting cattle. It got to be that I knew the acres and acres of Thompson property better than the couple thousand square feet Becky and I lived upon.

When we were first married, Becky and I would go early each Sunday morning to fish one of his ponds, sit bareback on the aging thoroughbred he kept for his daughter, or just lay on the hood of the truck in the middle of a newly planted pine grove, thinking about where we'd be in twenty years when those same little saplings would be thick and dense as night.

I loaded the new salt lick for the bull pasture in the back of the truck and drove the twenty miles north, away from the gray stretch of clouds that were hovering over the gulf. The wind was blowing a bit and the air was thick as ever, but the sun was still shining. A few carloads of bathers were already heading inland, trailing boats and jet skies. But over the ocean, the planes were still flying, their advertisements of shrimp buffets and live music defying the thick clouds.

Off the highway, on dirt roads overgrown and shaded by kudzu and pines, everything is so green that it tastes something like grass when you open your mouth and swallow a batch of the cool dark air.

When I got to the pasture, I wished again that Mr. Thompson had had a son. The first gate was standing wide open. His daughter must have beat me here and not known to close the gate behind her. I thought about how I'd manage to wrangle that ornery bull and the hundred head of cattle that were probably wandering out over the gully and up the road to Fairhope. But the second gate was closed and there on the other side of it were three young heifers, chewing and blinking at me with indifference. Relieved, I closed the first, opened the second, and drove through before I recognized her.

She was sitting there on a post of the worn down corral where we had kept that old thoroughbred when we had to run cattle between pastures. At first, I thought I'd gone around the bend and was seeing things, but then I saw that sorry Pinto and knew it was for real. She looked at me kind of startled, but then smiled real sly-like and said, "You Hollis?"

"Yes, ma'am, I am." I was still confused, but didn't mind that she knew my name.

"I'm Jenny Thompson. My father was Charles Thompson."

She was wearing the same denim halter as this morning, but now with long cutoffs and sneakers.

"Didn't think she'd make it out here," she said motioning to the Pinto, "but what do you know." She jumped down from the post, swatted at a mosquito, and walked towards me. The truck was still running and she slid right in where she'd been this morning, right where I hadn't dared to think she'd be again.

I latched the second gate and climbed in next to her. Somehow, I had mind enough to offer my condolences. "He was a good man, your father," I said, "I'm real sorry for your loss, ma'am."

She looked past me, at the open pasture and the woods on the other side of it. She nodded, then said, "I like to be called Jenny, OK?"

I put the truck in gear and we headed for the herd of cattle grazing in the middle of the pasture. She fiddled with the threads on the hem of her cutoffs. Then, she hung her arm out the window and smiled. "I was just sitting there thinking about 'Bama," she said. "You ever know her?"

"Why, sure," I said. "Sure I did."

"Of course you did," she said shaking her head. "She was mine, you know. My father bought her for me when I turned ten, but by then I already had more interest in boy-girl parties than I did in long drives with Daddy, even if a horse *were* on the other end."

We were sitting there in my truck, and she was telling me things about herself. She had her legs propped up on the dash, as if she could be at home just about anywhere. The sky was darkening all around us and anything seemed possible.

"She was a fine horse. Gentle and sweet as anything," I said remembering 'Bama's eager lips sucking sweet feed out of my palm and the suede of her muzzle leaning into my chest, asking for more. "She really was."

Jenny smiled at me. "I started coming down once or twice a year back in college. Even thought about taking her back with me, but my father discouraged it, said 'Bama was happier here, in her namesake state, and that you took real good care of her."

I nodded, a rift of guilt cracking open. Six months back, I had been walking the fences, checking for down posts when I came upon 'Bama, caught up bad in a piece of barbed wire I must have left behind when I was patching. The mare lifted her head when she saw me. Her eyes were panicked and I caught that panic like it was airborne. Her back legs were bloody, in a couple of places ripped open to the bone. She'd been struggling hard. I had my shotgun with me, always did when I was walking the fences alone. More to end the wild look in her eye and the senseless jerking of those lame legs than anything else, I pushed the end of my gun right up against her forehead, closed my eyes, and pulled the trigger. I felt her collapse away from the gun before I looked and saw her gone.

I'd seen horses come back from worse and since I didn't want any questions, especially about why the barbed wire was left around, I told Mr. Thompson that night on the phone that 'Bama was bad off with encephalitis and that we should call in the vet to end it for her. He said he trusted my judgment. Right now, that afternoon in the woods seemed like the biggest mistake of my life. To see this girl fix her pretty oval eyes on that horse would make me feel like some kind of a hero.

"That's my bull, huh?" Jenny said pointing, as we drove through the pasture. He stood out in the middle of the cows, grazing.

"Yep, that's him," I said and went on and on about the latest auction and how many calves we were expecting this season and how the price of beef was down.

She finally interrupted. "Tell you the truth," she said, "I'm thinking about selling." Then, when I didn't respond, she added, "All of it."

This was a possibility that had not occurred to me. I had been prepared to argue my experience and skill at managing the property, but I had not counted on not even being given that chance.

To be honest, though, I don't think my first thought had anything to do with our livelihood. Instead, I was thinking about never seeing her again, about never riding slow through the pasture again with her cross-legged beside me and a spattering of rain beginning to fall. Because somewhere in the past five minutes that had become the only part of this life of mending fences and herding cattle that mattered; the only way I could imagine surviving the endless days of hauling shrimp up and down the beach.

There was nothing I could think to say, but when she asked me what I thought about the idea, I swear it was like she was daring me to tell her all the reasons I would trade both my thumbs just to kiss her one time.

"What would you do?" she asked. "Persuade me."

I looked away from her. The rain was turning the pasture into deeper shades of green; the cows' rust-colored coats were darkening. I could sense her breathing next to me. I turned toward her. She had followed my gaze out to the herd beyond us. "It's beautiful land," I said, quietly. "If it were mine, I'd keep it."

She looked at me real hard, like there was something I wasn't telling her. Then she smiled, as if my answer pleased her. "Now I know where you stand," she said as I put the truck in gear and we drove away from the open pasture.

The Pinto didn't start. I thought about tinkering with it, but the winds were picking up and dark clouds were taking over the sky. I unloaded the salt lick and we rode back into town together.

"My wife has planned on supper," I said, only thinking of keeping Jenny with me, not of the actual meal. "It looks like Glenda might actually make an appearance, but Becky's been preparing all day. It's probably the safest place for miles."

"I'd love it," she said, pulling her knees into her chest. The rain was coming down harder the closer we got to town, and the sky was pretty well dark though it was hardly six o'clock yet. A line of cars clogged the highway in the other direction, the hurricane warning now official. "My cousin's going to kill me about that car," she said.

I could see goose pimples crop up across her forearms, "Blame it on Glenda," I said, wishing I had a jacket in the cab to wrap around her shoulders.

"Spoken just like a man," she said and smiled at me.

When we got home the wind had picked up and Hoang's bicycle was turned over on his porch. I could see him in his poncho, carrying the chickens inside. There was something shameful about this. I didn't like having livestock in the back yard, never had. I liked the way the Thompsons kept their livestock: a long drive away from anywhere, a destination.

Becky had boarded up all the windows on our house while I had been gone. The wind was so strong, I felt like I could see it; thick white blasts just like on all the weather maps.

Jenny and I ducked our heads and ran from the truck to the door. She kicked off her shoes, and I put my arm on her wet skin to guide her through the yard.

Inside, Dolly and Becky were shelling field peas and listening to the radio, long patches of static interrupting the warnings. Becky had changed into a skirt and blouse. She had lipstick and earrings on, but still looked plain.

When she saw us, Becky stood up, all the peas she had in her lap scattering across the floor in front of us.

Dolly cursed in Vietnamese. Becky, wrinkling her brow, said, "Hollis?" as if she didn't recognize me at all. "My God, I've been worried sick."

"This is Jenny Thompson, Mr. Thompson's daughter, down from Boston."

Becky was obviously as surprised as I had been that Jenny was Mr. Thompson's daughter. I'm not sure what it was about her that was so shocking. She was pretty, but we get a lot of that down here. Her face had something very angular and serious about it, and she had those perfect oval eyes. They were a thick animal brown, but they shone, almost like small polished magnets. And standing there in the doorway, drenched and disheveled, it looked as if she'd brought all the energy of the storm right inside the house.

"Jenny," Becky finally said, extending her hand. "I'm so sorry, dear. Your father was like family to us."

"Thank you, Mrs. Hollis."

"Call me Becky, please. Come in, come in. Let me get you some dry things. This is Glenda, you know," she said referring to the weather.

"I know," Jenny said, throwing her voice towards Becky in the bedroom, "Hollis said you've been preparing all day."

"Well, we're not taking any chances, are we, Dolly?" Becky said, emerging from the bedroom with a pair of raggedy sweats and my old Army T-shirt. She handed them to Jenny, who took them in her arms and headed for the bathroom.

I changed my shoes and shirt and toweled off in the bedroom. I looked at my wet hair in the mirror, my flushed face. Like a seventeen year old again, I couldn't force a coherent thought through my mind on account of the buzzing between my ears. As a kid, I'd get like this on nights when a summer girl snuck me past the guardhouse, into her condo's private pool, all lit up and empty. I'd wade in slowly, afraid of making waves, afraid of the wall of balconies above us, her family's towels hanging over the railing, watching. She'd sit on the edge, looking sleepy, bored, noncommittal, until I grabbed each smooth brown foot, wrapped each bony knee around my neck and pulled her in with me. We'd hang close to the wall, quickly pawing past each other's swimsuits, licking the ocean's leftover salt from each other's faces, pushing hard and buzzing all over in the blue, blue water.

The kitchen smelled of cornbread and sweet potatoes. Dolly came in behind me, her plastic slides smacking against the linoleum, and started beating an egg as if it were her own home.

"Dolly," I said softly, "why don't you go on home and help Hoang out, huh?"

"We are fighting, Hollis. He's going to let my chickens get thrown away."

"No," I said, "he's out there right now, carting them all inside."

"You lying," she said, lazily turning her head to look out the kitchen window.

"Hollis, what's wrong?" Becky asked, coming into the kitchen with Jenny's wet clothes under one arm.

"I just think Dolly should go home now. We have company," I said, looking at the limp strings of Jenny's halter.

Just then Dolly must have seen Hoang with the chickens because she started babbling in that sideways sounding language and went out into the storm. Becky watched her run across the lawn, then sighed.

"You don't have to be rude, Hollis. Here," Becky handed me Jenny's clothes, "put those in a warm oven. I'll see if she needs a hair dryer."

I spread the halter and shorts out flat on a cookie sheet. Handling them like that seemed somehow shameful. I had to remind myself that Becky had asked me to do this. Feeling the thin, wet fabric, it was so easy to imagine the skin it had been clinging to, shielding, just moments before.

She came out of the bathroom, still on fire in my old T-shirt and sweats. This girl's got something swimming beneath her skin, I thought to myself as she unloaded biscuits into a basket for Becky. I hardly remember tasting anything.

"What is it you do up in Boston?" Becky asked her as we sat down to dinner.

"I'm studying to be a doctor," she said, sweetening her tea.

Becky reached out a hand and covered one of Jenny's. "How wonderful. Your father must have been so proud," she said.

Jenny seemed embarrassed by Becky's touch. She pulled her hand away and buttered a biscuit in silence.

"An M.D., huh?" I said, trying to diffuse the tension.

She looked at me and smiled, crumbs sticking to the corners of her mouth. For once, I felt like I understood people. I know how life gets heavy and all you want is to be distracted, lifted away for a moment. I wanted to give Jenny a boost up and out of this small house. I wanted to follow her out.

"You said it was a heart attack?" Becky asked, her eyes clear and thoughtful.

Jenny put her fork down. "He was swimming. Laps. The heart attack was minor. He drowned."

Becky bowed her head, covered her eyes with the napkin. The terrible thing was, I knew she wasn't being dramatic. She feels things deeply. She looked over at me, her eyes asking for something. A tissue, maybe, a reassuring glance. I looked away. I was feeling less and less akin to her. I didn't want to be akin to her. I wanted to be reckless, unburdened.

"Your clothes," I said to Jenny and excused myself to the kitchen. I pulled her stiff warm shorts and halter out of the oven. They smelled hot, a little singed. With them in my hands, I was powerful. I had ahold of something of hers; something that I could just as easily be handing over to her on a night with no moon and the breeze from the ocean suddenly blowing cold across her skin as she steps from the pool, all pink and spent. I stood there in the kitchen, thinking about this: her nakedness and my arms wrapping her in a towel, and then the moment she would emerge from the towel, leaving my arms and covering herself back over with clothes, but never fully dressed in front of me again.

The boards Becky had nailed against the windows were rattling, fighting hard against the storm outside.

I handed the warm clothes to Jenny, who held them in her lap. I could swear she blushed a little, the way she would if we had just come out of that pool together. "The food was great," she said to nobody in particular.

"Just down home cooking," Becky said quietly, her eyes still red.

The radio had turned entirely to static, but when I went to shut it off, Becky reprimanded me. "Hollis," she said, "leave it alone."

I turned it back on. It was like some sort of strange accompaniment to the distant cracking of tree branches and the incessant shrill of the wind. Jenny stood and walked to the back door. She poked her face into the door's small, uncovered window. "Oh my gosh," she said, looking out.

I stood behind her, our breath mingling on the single pane of glass. Out the window, I saw my shirts, still hanging on the clothesline. In all her fuss, Becky had forgotten the laundry and now it was drenched and being pulled taut, straight up into the strong gusts. One by one, we watched each shirt flap hard against the wind, as if possessed by some spirit, then instantly pull free and be lost to the storm.

So close to her face, I could see Jenny's sparsely freckled ears and her long auburn lashes. Without thinking, I pulled a wet strand of hair away from her cheek. She turned toward me. Her face was calm, unaffected by the fury outside. I smiled and she blinked slowly, as if she understood, and we both looked back out at the clothesline, now bare.

I heard Becky come up behind us. She didn't say anything, but I knew she was waiting for me to step away, turn around. I knew the way her mouth was probably set, her breath short. I knew she needed me to give up on whatever it was that I was hanging onto there in the kitchen.

I stayed at the door, watching Dolly's empty chicken coups knock against the side of the house, splintering open. I imagined the scene next door, the two of them and their chickens inside, eating boiled shrimp and cabbage. Would they be remembering Vietnam, I wondered. Hoang had made mention of the storms they had witnessed, living along the coast there. They would take care of Becky, I said to myself, before I even knew where the thought had come from.

Jenny and I stood there together, watching the storm that was changing the complexion of my backyard. My hand had fallen to her bare arm and it stayed there, far from the innocent gesture it might have been had I let it drop a moment earlier. Then, without a thought, I pushed it up under the sleeve of my T-shirt she still had on, cupping my hand around her shoulder. Her skin felt warm, as if she had just stepped out of the morning sun. I suppose I knew then that I couldn't apologize for or take back the thing I was doing, the choice I was making, but at the same time it didn't feel like a choice at all.

It was, after all, just a moment. But it was the moment that counted—the one that you don't know, couldn't even ask for or dream about, until it's right there upon you. And then, all of the sudden, you have faith in life, in something bigger than your own damn here or there and you've got your hand on her shoulder, holding onto it like she belongs to you. Like she could belong to you. Like you are somebody you are not.

After years of watching summer girls—girls who, in years past, had followed me off their private beaches to the dark corners of the FloriBama for cheap draft and reckless fumblings in the parking lot—return to this place on the arms of their medical school fiancees dressed in crisp white tennis shorts, and cross the street right in front of my shrimp-filled pick-up without a second look, I was finally the one standing next to her, a protective arm on her shoulder. I was the one she turned to and whispered, as if it were the most important thing she'd ever said, "Jesus, Hollis, look at those trees shake."

I don't know how much longer I could have kept my hand there on her shoulder, or where else I might have dared to touch her, because just as she finished speaking, a figure emerged from next door. Dressed in his waders and flimsy dime store sandals, Hoang was suddenly running across the lawn, leaning into the wind, headed for the remaining two chicken coops. Jenny silently put a hand to her mouth.

I watched in disbelief as Hoang bent over in front of one of the coops, apparently checking it for a forgotten chicken. Just as he reached an arm in the open door, a lawn chair came sailing effortlessly across the yard on a strong gust of wind. As if on an invisible track, the chair sliced through the driving rain right into the back of Hoang's neck before being flipped and carried on up again, away from his limp body.

Jenny immediately went for the door handle and without thinking,

I stopped her. She turned and looked at me, her eyes wide, her mouth still open.

"Hollis," she said. "He's hurt."

I held onto her wrist. Her face was close to mine and wrinkled with confusion. She took her free hand and tried to pull my fingers away. I held on tighter.

"Who?" Becky said from behind us, her voice hard and flat. "What's happened?"

There was nothing I could say to explain myself. Becky was standing there with her arms folded, looking at my knuckles whiten around Jenny's wrist.

I let go. Jenny opened the door, the noise of the storm flooding the space between me and Becky, and ran toward Hoang.

Becky looked at me blankly, then looked outside. "Go on, then," she said, raising her voice above the wind. "She can't get him herself." And when I hesitated, her voice turned shrill. "My God, Hollis, go on."

Dolly was already kneeling next to Hoang, talking fast and foreign, spitting rain off her lips. Jenny motioned for me to lift Hoang's torso, which I did as she supported his legs and we ran with him back to the house. Dolly followed behind, her voice now quivering, fading under the wind and rain.

Inside, Jenny and I set Hoang down on the floor. His face was pale, drenched, and a small leaf clung to it, just below his ear lobe. Becky put her arm around Dolly, hushing and cooing her.

Jenny lifted Hoang's wrist, felt for a pulse, then swept the thick black hair away from his forehead, tilting his head back. I watched her hands moving over his skin and then I watched as she lowered her body over him, placing her own wet mouth on top of his. With her first breath, Hoang's skinny bare chest rose. She waited, then blew again, each time his ribs climbing into small ridges across his chest. Finally, his chest heaved, his eyes opened and he gasped for breath.

Dolly, having never stopped chattering, was soon kneeling over him as well. Suddenly she was quiet and he lifted his head. They looked at one another for a moment, then Dolly put her forehead to his in some sort of silent greeting. I watched Jenny, who was leaning back on her heels, pushing her wet hair behind her ears. She was completely focused on Hoang. He finally sat up and Jenny examined his eyes, deciding that he probably had a mild concussion.

Becky turned to me, that black make-up in streaks under her eyes. "Hollis," she said. "Ice?"

Without a word, I went to the bathroom in search of an ice pack. I could hear the mood of the living room change as I dug through the closet—Hoang's sharp laughter traveling through the walls. When I returned, without having found the ice pack, Hoang was sitting on the couch and Jenny had her hand wrapped around his wrist once more. He was telling what he remembered of his trip out into the storm.

"Always, we have twelve chickens. Then, they are running around the house, back and forth, back and forth. We only count ten."

"Your pulse is normal," Jenny said, smiling and gently placing Hoang's hand back in his own lap.

"Thank you, Doctor," Hoang said, bowing his head a little.

"It's Jenny," she said, "and I'm not a doctor, not yet." But she was flattered. Even as Dolly stood over her, stumbling through an endless thank you, I could see that Jenny was taken with the idea of having saved Hoang's life. He had given her something I had not; and only because I had not thought to die. Or I would have. She could have saved me.

Instead, I watched her looking at Hoang as if he were some sort of miracle. This was more than I could take.

Becky looked at me standing in the doorway. "Well?" she said in a voice that was urging me to get over it, to rejoin her as a gracious host of this impromptu gathering.

"No luck," I said. She then assembled an ice pack using a kitchen towel and a plastic sack and handed it to Jenny, who placed it gently on the back of Hoang's neck.

I stood apart from them, unable to move my eyes from Jenny as she allowed Hoang to take the pack from her, resting her hand on the back of his for a moment as they made the exchange.

It looked like Hoang and Dolly had no intention of going home that night.

"Hollis, I need a hand," Becky called out from the kitchen. Slowly, I turned away from Jenny and went to see about Becky. She was busy serving out portions of the still warm peach cobbler.

"That ice cream is hard as a rock," she said without looking up. I knew she was mad and hurt and confused but here she was, ready to go on with life. All I had to do was pick up the big kitchen spoon, run it under hot water and begin to scoop out the ice cream. From there, I would be forgiven.

But all I could see was the storm, framed by that one tiny window. The same view I'd shared with Jenny, the same view that had looked so reckless and stunning before, now looked angry and empty. The trees, shaking with water and wind, were mocking me.

Without a second thought, I left the kitchen. I didn't look at Becky, I didn't explain myself. The good-natured chattering continued in the living room and I didn't want any part of it. I kept walking, unlocked the front door and went out into the storm.

I don't know what I was hoping: That she would follow me out? That I, too, would have to be rescued, resuscitated? That the storm would pick me up and set me down someplace else entirely? Whatever I was thinking, I ended up sitting in my truck, soaking wet and staring at the boarded up windows of my own home. Nobody came after me, but Becky did crack the front door enough to peer out and see me, slouched in the cab. She didn't look surprised or relieved to discover me there; she simply cast her eyes downward, as if in prayer, and then closed the door.

I spent most of the night watching Glenda blow in angry gusts all around me. At first, I worried that the truck would be thrown. I even thought of running back to the house and sitting it out in safety. But then in my mind I'd see Jenny's mouth covering Hoang's, the shivers that had crept up and down his arms as her breath warmed his skin and I knew I wouldn't go back.

As the hours passed, it seemed as though the storm began to move in slow motion. Each hard smack of rain against the side of the truck and every droning gust of wind seemed to last longer and longer. I finally laid down across the seat and slept.

I dreamt of Jenny's clothes, the soggy shorts and halter that I'd so carefully laid out on the cookie sheet and put in the oven to dry. I was alone in the dream. But when I went to pull them out, there was Jenny. She came right out of the oven, her long legs stretching through the warm denim shorts and her red hair oven-dried and smelling of sweet potatoes. It was one of those dreams whose logic stays with you, even after you wake. I had to remind myself, as I sat there, looking at the downed branches and scattered shingles in the morning's first light, that I had no recipe for her; that she would never be the yield of my efforts.

Hoang emerged from my house in his undershirt and waders. He waved at me and approached the truck. I wished I had not still been sitting there, like some kid who tried to run away from home but lost his nerve. He stood next to the door, looking at me until I lowered the window.

"Not too bad," he said, looking around at the changes the storm had made to the yard.

I shrugged.

"No electricity," he then added, nodding toward the house.

I raised my eyebrows and looked at his face. His lips were moving over his teeth, as if practicing certain words. I realized, then, that he had been sent out to deal with me. To tell me, perhaps, that I wasn't welcome, wasn't needed, didn't have a place there anymore. Or, maybe, to tell me that I should come inside and deal with the damage I'd done. Whichever it was, I didn't give him the chance.

I started the truck. The sound of the engine broke through the morning's quiet. Without a word, I put it in reverse and carefully backed out of the cluttered drive. Hoang stood very still as he watched me go.

On the highway, the only other cars were emergency vehicles and utility repair crews. In places, the road disappeared below deep pools of water. As I came to the bridge, I looked at the worn out ocean, now calm and black beyond the shore. I wondered about the night before, why Jenny had let me keep my hand on her, why I'd ever thought that I could. Suddenly, I wished I had told her about 'Bama, about the way, without even thinking, I shot the damn horse. I wanted her to know that I had taken something from her, that I had been close enough, significant enough, to do that.

Colin Dickey

Keeping Times

The blur of night. In California this can sometimes mean a strange kind of heat, one that you barely notice. Their car lays back aways, empty and useless. He walks with his father along the shoulder towards the callbox. The headlights that go by make them angel-bright, and then disappear. The gusts of wind from cars as they slip by hits hard on their backs. His father walks between the passing cars and him, as a gesture of protection, holding his hand. His hand squirms inside of his father's, like a sweat fish in his fingers. He doesn't let go; he tries to tourniquet his father's fingers together.

The air has a dull ache about it, and sighs out oxygen and exhaust into their brains and lungs and the cars all try to outrace it. The boy thinks: *It's like walking on the moon—no one has ever walked here before.* When he steps he looks down at the debris beneath them.

He's afraid his father's hand might slip, so he presses it again with his fingers, though he can already feel the force of wind and gasoline behind them—it takes up the very space of noise and subsumes everything for a moment. Then the engine noise, the flood of lights become distinct, and he doesn't have time to think about this before the car—its driver asleep—cuts them in two, splitting the father and child, the surprised way their hands let go, his father's body lifted up onto the grill of this vehicle, back bent as a bird in space, borne up and lit from the headlights that impale him, a bird moving fast, giant body dwarfed by his assailant, his limbs bleeding into the roar of his murder, they are moving forward, their hands severed, he watches the car and the father move together until the light turns red in brake lights, the tires lock and the car skids to its halt some ways away, his father now just tissues, severed and fragmented, the blood let loose from all its wounds and the heart slowing to rest. He looks at the lines on his palm, in the red lights he looks at the sweat that has collected in the lines of his palms.

It doesn't happen that way. Sometimes he dreams it, sometimes it comes as a waking hallucination. He tells his father he's afraid of the freeway, afraid when he drives fast. He's six years old, seven years old, he doesn't grow used to the road, the dangers it holds.

They live in the mountains, above the Santa Clara Valley, in California. They live in a house his father has built with his own hands, a house older than his child. There's a saltwater aquarium with a lionfish inside. His father does stained glass as a hobby, and the western windows fracture and color the light, spinning it off in blues, greens, deep reds.

In these mountains his favorite trees are madrones. They are the ones he loves first, loves best. When their bark is new, it's slick like wet skin, and it's a fierce neon green. As the bark dries it turns yellow, then a deep rust. It seems impossible that one tree could be so many colors. At night he sees their twisted deranged silhouettes, but though he has nightmares about their shape, he never fears their colors.

When the boy is five or six, his father's head is ripped open by a chainsaw. They'd been out cutting firewood—up in the mountains a neighborhood is communal by necessity, they all help to cut each other's wood. Bruce Bellamy from up the road swings his saw a little too high, lifts it back over his head, and it touches down ever so slightly on the boy's father. Some kiss of the blade, the way an angel might touch down, so quietly.

The father lives. There's stitches, but the blade never touches the bone, never touches what's inside. He heals.

In the afternoons the stained glass walls bleed the house a dozen different colors. The boy walks up and down the room, turning red, turning gold. The father's not home from work—both his parents won't be home until much later. He goes to the glass, presses his hand against the green glass, feels for the heat from the sun on the other side. His hand turns green in the light, and he thinks it might stay this way. A thin film of sweat forms between his hand and the glass, and when he finally drags it away the glass screeches slightly, pulling on his hand as he scrapes it.

He's in the woods, near his house. By the Whale, with another boy named Daniel. Daniel is his first lover, though they'll never touch. The

Whale is a rock that's nothing but a gaping mouth, a smooth hollowed out mouth, ten feet high and fifteen feet wide. He shows Daniel the madrones, shows how you can flake off the red bark and reveal the green skin beneath. While Daniel picks at the bark he lies on the smooth cool floor of the Whale's mouth. He asks Daniel, "If someone who kills is a killer, then what do you call someone who dies?"

Growing up is mostly just giving names to things. You make sense of the chaos by giving names and definitions and you keep giving names until something clicks inside, something works. Daniel shrugs. "A dyer?"

"That's someone who dyes things, changes things' color." He watches Daniel change the bark from rust to green.

"I don't know then."

"If there were a name for those people, the ones who die, then that's what I'd want to be." He waits for the Whale to swallow him up, for the mouth to close down on him. For that old worn-smooth stone to finally move.

When the father does come home from work, the lionfish follows him throughout the room. It sweeps back and forth within its glass walls, eyes always on the father, always trailing him. The boy thinks the fish is like an explosion, ribbons of flesh still kept together, a slaughtered animal somehow still alive. Keeping track of his father.

When he's eight, he's called home from a week-long summer camp, three days early. *Your dad's been in an accident.* River rafting this time. Fell out of the boat, pushed under the water, pressed to the rocky floor. Dislocated shoulder. Lucky to be alive. *They had to airlift him out of the river basin by helicopter.* Dangling from the line, a spinning cocoon like those mummies in the museum.

The boy grows older, the father doesn't die, but he's always bruised, hurt, dislocated, stitched together. When he's healed from this one, the boy hears him talking to his mother, the low, hushed tones behind the bedroom door he's learned to tune his ears to. "Don't you think it's enough of this?" his mother wants to know. "You're over forty, you can't do everything you used to think you could do."

Eventually they'll move back down into the valley, to the suburbs. Eventually his mother will say, "I can't stand it anymore, being so far away from everything." One night, the boy and his father come home to find her sitting on the steps, not moving or talking, staring at the floor. "I've hit a deer," she says. No one speaks. The boy imagines its body flying up onto the hood, into the glass. It smashes so close to you, just on the other side of that glass, but you know it will never touch you. "I'll go find it," the father says, "Take care of it." His father is thinking: *If it lays there, she'll drive past it again on her way to work. She won't want to see it again.* His father knows there is mercy for the killer, not just for the victim. He takes his keys, but she stops him. "No," she says. "Stay here."

When they come down from the mountains, the movers do a sloppy job. They put boxes anywhere, furniture in the wrong rooms. They set the piano—a solid baby grand, a gift from the father to the mother—down on the hardwood floor in the living room. It's on wheels, though, and to keep it from rolling they have to move a carpet under it. The father gets underneath, wedges his back to its belly. He's Atlas in this moment, his arms spread out to brace it, on one knee for support. He knows how to lift it—his back's given out many times, he's slipped a disc once, but it doesn't give now. The boy, still small, still limber, rolls the carpet underneath it as his father presses it up towards the sky. He tries to move quickly, but he really just wants to watch, watch this marvel that is his father, pushing up against this weight of wood, wire and music. A god of strength in this moment. A god of strength.

When he's ten years old, he hears about the dead boy. It's in all the papers—a boy went to out to fish and found the dead body of a kid, also ten years old. No one knows who did it, no one knows who the boy is. Daniel comes to him that night. He hasn't seen Daniel in years, not since he left the mountains, but he hears him in his head, hears him in his thoughts. That night Daniel says, *Don't think of that corpse. You know it's not the corpse you love. It's the other boy, the fishing boy, the one who has to find the body. That's who you love, the discoverer. What are in his eyes at that moment, that's what you want to know. You see a shoe and it's just some shoe someone's left, and then it's not, it's someone's body, it's not just a shoe but a something, a body. How much time passes? These are the questions you want answers to, who cares who the body was. What about the one who lives, who witnesses?* He doesn't believe it, tries to shake it away like a fog. *Where was that kid going, the one who ended up dead? Wouldn't you like to know. You've never even had stitches, never broken a bone. You're whole, complete. You'll never know what makes a kid like that wander, what makes him get in the car, lets somebody touch him. That's not who you are.* But he doesn't believe the voices, not that night. He cries for the dead boy, the boy that could have been him.

⌘

They live in the valley now, but the father keeps going up, keeps driving those windy roads—Highway 9, Skyline Boulevard. Dangerous roads. "Clears my head," he says, the pull of the car as it tries to go over. The boy thinks: *It wants to go over, the car has its own wants, its own ideas of freedom.* Then one day it happens: driving alone, the car finally slips over, pulls the father off the edge of narrow road.

He's still alive. He plunges into a tree; it stops the car. "The tree saved my life," he says. The boy wonders if it still cleared his head, in the accident, if all the thoughts instantly vacated like people jumping from a burning building.

He's in the swimming pool, their backyard, and Daniel's with him, in his head, in his thoughts. Daniel says: *Let's see how long we can stay under.* So they do, they float motionless by the water. He's a dier. He loves this feeling. Then his father's there, shouting his name—"I thought you," he trails off. The boy's fine. He's always fine. This is his sin. The world through a sheaf of water, nothing touches him. Daniel says: *Nothing can harm you.* Daniel says: *Can you live with that?*

He's fifteen, he's learning to drive. His father takes him out on weekends, to empty business parks, loops of road surrounding ghost-still buildings of high tech firms. This is where his father works, moving from company to company, building to building. This is the boom: new companies shoot up everyday, buy up each other, trade work forces, hire people and lay them off. "We'll make a million dollars," the father says. He leaves a place as soon as it's gone public, finds a shakier one that'll pay him more to get it off the ground. He's a problem solver, he gets things done.

The two of them drive in circles around the buildings, gas and brake, turn, signal. The squat towers, gray and black, want to topple over onto them, want to sprint across those too-neat grass lawns. When he drives too close to the curve, the father pushes the wheel back gently, not reprimanding, sure of his son's ability. "This is your freedom," the father says, but the boy doesn't know for a moment if he means the car or the companies in these buildings all around them.

Another year, another accident. The boy is himself almost sixteen, almost driving. "Almost free," his father tells him, but he doesn't think so, doesn't think it is a freedom. A pass through the mountains, dark, and a semi-truck tries to merge into the space where his father is. Again the car takes over, demands this of him, tries to take him off the roads into other places. The car spins, tries to take him elsewhere, but it doesn't kill him, it keeps him safe.

The boy sits in the back of his mother's car, watching his parents watch the car lifted onto a tow truck. He thinks: *Not freedom, you just hold out until you let your guard down, until the car takes over. You're tired, then you yield up to it, and it's over.* His mother drives them back home that night. He sits in the back, watches his father wanting to hold her; the seatbelts, the night, in the way.

Then he's sixteen, and he'll remember this night for years. He's been driving for three months, and he drives some friends out to the reservoir, where a bunch of kids are gathering. Otis Redding's "Love Man," playing loud and he leans out the driver side window, singing it into the air while someone else steers his car. Up at the reservoir some kid takes bets: "I'll smoke this whole cigarette, and the ash won't fall, it'll stay on the end of the cigarette." The boy knows it's a trick: you straighten a paperclip, trim it and slide it into the center of the cigarette. The ash clings to the wire, keeps the ash together. But the kids throw down their money, and he doesn't say anything, watches them watch in wonder as they're duped.

He walks away from them, towards the black expanse of the water. Daniel says, *You remember how to swim, don't you?* He doesn't want Daniel here, not tonight. He wants to fall for the cigarette tricks, drive them around to Otis Redding, he wants to be out of his own skin, he wants not to have to listen to the thoughts in his head. Someone's given him a beer but he can't drink it, he's afraid of its rancid taste. He wishes it was cola, he wishes it wasn't making his hand so cold.

Then he sees her. Up on a hill is Emma, though he doesn't know her name yet. When he hears it, he'll let it roll in his head, thick on his tongue, an anachronism that he loves. A name too old for her lithe body, her broken glass voice. He sees her dancing, some boy's tinny stereo playing music, he sees her body ricocheting in the air. He thinks: *she's made of ash, held together by a thin wire, nothing else.* He nearly runs to join them. But he doesn't dance, he just watches.

In the night like this, without light, everyone's skin is blue. Emma's skin the color of a corpse locked in a freezer, or dug up from a lake. He says to her, "I'm with you all this time." He smells her sweat, he smells the thunder inside himself. "I'm with you." The whole axis of the world spins around him.

He's sixteen. Emma and he drive out to where the city lights die down, a black field of grass. They drive out in his father's car, the one he loves and is terrified of, the one that is always calling to him to leave the road. They stretch out under the night, the stars above them. "Like raindrops about to fall," he says. He reaches for her white skin, skin that smells like coriander—he can't resist. She can; she says, "I don't think I can touch you right now." He tells her to be honest, open. "There is so much trust between us," he says. She tells him, "I'm so goddamn horny, but I can't touch you. I don't feel you like that." Daniel laughs in his ear. The world through a sheaf of glass. Nothing will touch you. Can you live with that?

Two months later his parents are gone. The company his father works for is bought, closed, dismantled. People are offered jobs in Southern California, in the parent company. He thinks: *how can it still be a parent after it's dismantled the child it bought?* They have no choice but to go; there are no other jobs right now. Hard times, his parents tell him, but they give him the choice: follow them south or stay on his own. This is their love, they give him the freedom to make this decision himself. "Our lives are uprooted," his mother tells him, "but that doesn't mean yours has to be as well." So he stays. He doesn't want to leave this woman Emma, who loves him even as he revolts her. That's what real love is anyway, love without pleasure. He doesn't want to start his life over again in a new place. They move him into an apartment, he watches them get in their car and drive south. He paces off the space in his new room, his new life. A box cut out of the world, holding only him. He is not thinking of his parents. He is thinking of Emma, he is thinking of her voice which has always quieted him, he is hoping it will still.

He says to her, "You ever feel like all your atoms are going to fly off, in every direction, explode everywhere?"

She's thinking: *Every second,* but she doesn't say it, he can tell it's waiting behind her tongue, he can tell she can't bring herself to speak to him.

He says, "I just want to be held, to keep myself from going everywhere." But she won't, he can read her too well already. She doesn't think it's her job, she thinks what they have is in their minds and hearts, but not their bodies. She has too many other lovers, too many men that are just sex for her, just the body. He knows she feels too much for him, but he knows she doesn't realize what this means.

The valley is eating itself, slowly from the insides. When the money first started coming in, no one knew what to do with it all. Money was everywhere. Soon there was no one left to work at the McDonald's, the Starbucks, because everyone was making money designing web pages, getting their MBAs. People drove Porsches and slept in housing shelters because no one could afford a house.

He's driving with Emma, tells her, "I'll be gone next week." It's Easter. "Going to L.A., to see my parents." He hears the question she doesn't ask: *Why didn't you go with them? Why did you stay here?* Their house has been sold, but the new owners haven't yet moved in. Escrow. It's empty, but he still has the key. He slips in at night, sleeps on his floor with only a jacket wrapped around him. If someone were to catch him, find him, ask him what he's doing, he'd say: "I just ended up here."

He hears her question, the one she doesn't ask—it eats a hole in him. He says, "I want to hate them. They gave me a choice when they didn't have one. That's what I'm supposed to think. It's my fault I didn't follow. It means that I don't love them, not the other way around. But there's always a choice, there's always a way out." She touches his shoulder; through the cotton, he feels her heat. He wants her hand, wants to hold it, wants to capture her sweat in the lines of his palm.

Lake Forest, California. Orange County. The ground is impossibly bleached white. The taste of decay fills his mouth as soon as the 101 peels away from the ocean and heads towards Los Angeles. He smells Emma on everyone, in the malls and restaurants that comprise the empty land. He wants to be gone immediately. He feels like he hardly knows his parents, sees two strangers across the dinner table. During the day they work and he paces the house mindlessly, unable to wait for them to come home. Then when they do they still don't know each other, they still stare dumbly at each other. The week is painful, slow. He hates them more for their emptiness, their inability to find him where he is. He sees himself on the bottom of the pool; he's waiting for one of them to come rushing out, afraid he might not be okay.

A birthday. He's seventeen. They've been out all night at the beach, and everyone's sleeping on someone's floor, an army of blankets and pillows and limbs. At the end of the night, feigning sleep, he watches Emma with another man. Roger, two years older but the same birthday as him. He watches her slow movements over him, her body again like ash, like it's already burnt out, like it's on the verge of collapse. Earlier that day she asked him to marry her, told him she wanted to be with him forever. Now she bites her lip to keep from making a noise, to keep from being heard. He wants to find that single hard wire, that's holding her together, he thinks he could run his hands up and down it, but instead he hears Daniel's voice again: *Remember that dead boy, that the fisher found? How you wanted so bad to be the corpse, the body? And we both knew you'd never be—you're only here to watch, to discover, to see. That's all you'll ever be.*

He's eighteen, nineteen, twenty. The summer after high school Emma goes to Alaska, gutting fish through the too long days. When she comes back she says, "You're the one I want, I'm tired of fucking around." But even that's a lie: she tries to touch him but recoils, like he's made of fire, like he's burned her. Maybe he is, maybe he has. Maybe that's why she's always been ash, maybe she's already been burned, doesn't want it again. Then he's gone, he leaves the state, he's nineteen, he knows how to live alone, he knows how to hide scars. He's in college, he forgets his parents, he forgets what place they ever had in his life. On the phone he wants to treat them like equals, to him they've lost any power they once had over him. He tries not to think of Emma, of the years spent holding him at bay, teaching him his body was no good. Once she told him, "I love your eyes, your face, your hands." She didn't finish the sentence, but he heard the "but" he knows she has no need for his body, he knows his body is not for this world. It can't be touched, can't be wounded, can't be loved. But he doesn't blame her, he wants to ask her, "Does Daniel visit you as well? Slide into your bed, thin as silver razor, telling you who you are? I think he does." She's been killing him, cutting off the oxygen to his body, but he doesn't blame her. He lets her go, slips into the mist, tries to start again.

Driving home one night, he hits a raccoon. The empty road out before him, and he's lulled by the cones of his headlights in the fog. Then in the corner, the image of the animal, frozen like a film still, mid-run. A noise like a blown tire, and it's over. He hasn't even slowed down. His body shakes and convulses, the steering wheel shivers, but he doesn't slow. It's the road home. He'll see the body, forced back onto the shoulder, everyday for weeks, the slow story of decay being told. But that night he has the dream, the old dream. He and his father on the side of the road, his father borne up by the sleeping driver. But when he reaches the corpse, the body of the dead father, it's not him, it's the deer his mother killed long ago, and his father's standing over him, saying, "I'll find the body, take care of it. You won't have to see it." There's mercy for the killer, too, not just the victim. But the boy knows now why that's not his father's job, why his mother stopped him that night. It's the son's job, it's always been the son's job. His father says, *Go then, find the body. But once you've seen it, when you've found it, will you know what it means? You've seen me die a dozen times, seen me rise up, a walking corpse. And have you ever known what it meant, have you ever put a name to what you've seen?* He knows then, he knows it is never just seeing—it's remembering, it's naming, it's keeping.

He's dreaming, he's remembering, he's trying to find a way back. The boy is lying in bed, in a white room. He is awake and it is the day after Easter, he's in Lake Forest, California, and it's time to drive back. He is sixteen years old. It is early and time for his father to go to work and his father is coming in to say goodbye and both of them feel that the boy is too young for this to be happening.

All this takes place in California. Driving down Highway 101, which is sometimes El Camino Real, the boy thought endlessly of the padres who moved up and down this road, founding their missionaries for Christ, who was the Son of Man.

His father is coming in to say goodbye and it is very early. The boy's father fills the frame of the doorway. The walls of the room are white; the shelves empty. The boy knows there are a million other tragedies in the world. The corporation that's done this to them is not alone or unique in its practices; this is the way of business. The boy does not think this excuses any of what has been done to him. Everyone's life has tragedy in it and everyone must deal with that tragedy to the extent that he or she is able to, but being told of another's misfortune does not somehow nullify your own. The boy does not take comfort in hearing stories of people whose lives are worse, because nothing that has ever happened to him before is as bad as what is happening now. He is sixteen years old, he is full of rage and has no place to direct this rage and this is the way the world works.

When his father comes in that morning and sits down on the boy's bed and begins to cry, the boy understands that something is happening but does not know what it means. Later in his life he will make a list of those things he has been told about fathers and sons:

1. Oedipus left Corinth for Thebes, fearing the oracle, which told him he would kill his father. Despite the distance walked on the clubfoot his father had given him, despite his nomadic journey, the oracle came true after all.
2. God loved us so much that He gave His only begotten son so that we might live.
3. Little boys fear their fathers. They fear their fathers will castrate them.
4. Geza Roheim (anthropologist and psychoanalyst) noted in his studies of primitive societies that the father is always the first enemy and that subsequent enemies become symbolic for the father. In terms of warfare and sacrifice, "everything killed becomes father."

The father is crying and now the son is crying, the son who is still lying in bed, prone and under sheets while his father sits on the edge of the bed and the two of them cry together, the father saying over and over again he doesn't know what happened, somehow his life got out of control and he doesn't know what happened or how to stop, he doesn't know how to stop what's happening, and the boy not knowing how to comfort his father, so he sits halfway up and bed, awkwardly and still his father crying and he reaches out and puts his hand on his thigh, cupping it neatly with his sixteen year old hand just big enough to wrap around the thigh of his father, the skin through the fabric, and his father doing the same now, resting his hand on the leg of his son through the sheets, the two of them together like this on the bed, in tears and out of control, his father's body shaking and the boy trying to keep it still, there is something between the bodies, thin like a sheet like the words of an oracle, the boy still trying to hold in the body of his father, keeping it cupped in his palm, I don't know what's happened to us anymore, I lost track of my life somewhere along the line, the words burrowing in him, staying where they'll hide for years of silence, inside him as he leaves that morning, driving north on the freeways of the great long state of California.

He's twenty-one, he's remembering. He's trying to see. For college graduation his parents come up. They take him to dinner, and he can't remember when they became old. On the freeway, on their way back from dinner, he runs out of gas. Coasting to the shoulder, he remembers the gas in the trunk, knows it will be all right. They land on the shoulder, and he thinks of that word, thinks of his father borne up from the river.

Shoulder. He wants to ask him, "What were you doing on the bottom of that river, letting it push you down against those rocks?" but he knows the answer now, or he thinks he knows. He knows more than he once did.

He opens the door, swings wide into the roar of traffic, and then he's out of the car, and he *sees it*, he can feel the rush of that noise all around him, all that force that's never been harnessed, never been tamed. He wants to lay down in it, wants to let it take him, but he knows he can't—the most anyone can hope for is that it'll touch you without killing you, the most you can hope is that it'll push you against the rock, kiss the crown of your skull, carry you through these black spaces.

Joan Connor

The Folly of Being Comforted

for Jay

Cliff had had it. Since Linda had moved out, there was no one to answer the phone. The phone was always ringing—would he review this
book, write that recommendation, play tennis with some emerging
novelist—soon to be a minor motion picture. He wasn't getting any of
his own work done. Deadline deadzone. He wasn't even getting any of the
work done on the commercial book projects. He was huffy, that's what
he was, and determined to do something about it. So he called the
phone company.

"I would like an unlisted phone," he said.

"Yes, sir. Would you like the forty dollar fee included in your regular monthly billing?"

"Forty dollars? Forty dollars? To not list your phone? Maybe forty to
list your phone, but to unlist it? Okay, what about this. What if I list the
phone but in my uncle's name?"

"There's no fee for that, sir."

"Okay, list the phone under William Butler Yeats." He spelled out
the last name.

For the first two weeks after Cliff listed the phone, the silence stunned
him. He had never worked in such glorious quiet. Before Linda, his girlfriend, had moved out, she would answer the phone. But he could still

hear the phone ring, Linda speaking in hushed tones, Linda scribbling messages. Now he had silence, splendid silence, to work in. No Linda. No ringing phone. Silence, a writer's paradise. Nonetheless his pet commercial project, *The History of Refrigeration*, had stalled, so he turned instead to his second project, *The Secret Lives of Herbs*.

He read what he had written:

Origanum and other herbs cringe at the dreaded cutworm, which pupate in mid-summer. The larvae of the owlet moth end their hibernation in the subfusc bowels of the earth only to creep and teem from their foul snuggery to terrorize the roots of the tender herb.

The prose had a turgid horror-genre cast to it. Cliff shoved back his chair, rose, made tea, stared out the window at the snow ghosts spuming over the field. He selected his tea with finicky indecision—the orange, no the mint, no the orange. Vitamin C. This time of year, a wise choice, an excellent choice. Now which mug? Not the Shakespeare mug. Too much pressure. Maybe the delicate floral one. He drank his tea. Ten more minutes of aerobic staring. He steeped more tea. Yes, yes, the mint this time for a pick-me-up. The wind was whipping the snow into a flurry fury, bruiting the eddies about like brumal rumors. He let the steam of his tea fog the windowpane, and wrote in it with his index finger, "Ah, the writing life." Through the wet letters he watched the snow skirl.

"Basil, borage, chervil, chive," he chanted. "Potherbs keep old Cliff alive."

He could not bear, he could not fucking bear, to go back to the keyboard. Larva of the Painted Lady Butterfly. Parsley worms. He was a serious poet, for Christ's sake, and a fiction writer. Sweet Cicely, what he had to do to pay the bills. He tried singing out loud, "Sweet Cicely Brown." Actually it didn't feel that odd, singing a parody about herbs out loud. It occurred to him that this might not be a good sign.

It was time to get back to staring out of the window. Yep, mighty cold. Veritable wind chill factory today. Hey, one of those snow ghosts bore a surprising resemblance to Harold Bloom. Or more Zero Mostel? No, Bloom. No, definitely Mostel. Was it too early to uncork that little Vinho Verde from Portugal? A light bright little upstart wine with pretensions but no class anxiety. Three o'clock. If he sipped slowly, it would probably be okay.

When the phone rang, Cliff almost kissed it.

"Yes," he said.

"Mr. Yeets?"

"YEETS? Yeets? You want to speak with Mr. Yeets?"

"Yes, Mr. Yeets, I am calling in behalf of the Tru-brite aluminum siding company. How are you today Mr. Yeets?"

"Appalled, that's how I am. Do you know what is wrong with this country? Do you?"

"You can improve the appearance and value of your home, Mr. Yeets, with aluminum siding, professionally installed, while at the same time affording your home, your major investment, additional protection from the weather."

"Do you know who you are talking to? You can't sell me aluminum siding. I am a major poet. I live in a cabin "of clay and wattles made" not waffle irons made. And it's Yeats, not Yeets."

"Yeats? William Butler Yeats?"

"Yes."

"Are you the one who wrote *Sailing to Pandemonium?*"

"Yes, yes."

"We read that in high school."

"Yes, yes, that is mine. 'That is no country for old men,'" Cliff recited.

"Yep, that's it."

"I know that's it. I wrote it. 'Caught in that sensual music all neglect Monuments of aluminum architect.'"

"I can't believe it. William Butler Yeats, the poet. I have to call my English teacher."

She rang off. Cliff rubbed the phone against his cheek. Okay, that was diverting. But no remedy for herbal avoidance.

Aluminum saleswoman, what a dilly. Where there's a dill, there's a way. Lovage conquers all. Lovage makes the world go round. The herb book earned the pennyroyal. Here today and tarragon tomorrow. Cliff slumped into the desk chair.

He wrote, "The heinous Japanese beetle performs karaoke versions of 'All You Need Is Love,' until lemon balm wilts and flags and dies a slow arduous death." Sigh. Winter in Vermont. Snow packed up around the psyche. Invisible snow lizards squiggled through the brain. Day was two hours long. And too long. Maybe he should make a little plate of Ethan Frome fromage and think about that Vinho Verde again. The phone zinged him as if it were wired into his spine. He jingled. He jangled. He sprang from the chair.

"Yes?"

"Mr. Yeats?"

"Yes."

"My teacher says that you're dead."

"I'm not dead."

"She says that you died in 1939."

"You can hear me, right? Do I sound dead? BOO. Shoo. Old clothes upon old sticks to scare a bird."

"You wrote that, too?"

"I did."

"Look, do you want to buy aluminum siding?"

"*Pour moi?* Nope. That is no country for aluminum. Grecian goldsmiths made my home of hammered gold and gold enameling."

"Mister Yeats, it isn't very nice to make fun of someone who's just trying to earn a living. We work for commission, you know."

"Me, too. Want to buy a poem?"

Click.

Okay, in some dim way Cliff hated himself. Okay, she wasn't a member of the gifted and talented class. But he was sick of himself, sick of his meanness, sick of herbs, sick of how he thought. How does one stop thinking how one thinks? He was a total bore, a tidal bore, a wild boar, wild borage. He drank the bottle of Vinho Verde.

Night didn't fall; it fucking plummeted. He stared out the window looking for Zero Mostel, the Mostel of *The Producers*, but he could only see himself reflected. He glared at his shlubby self, body like sausage shoveled into one of those cheap plastic boots you can buy in dismal dime stores. Dime stores? There were no dime stores. His infrastructure was collapsing. He'd lost a briar patch of hair since Linda had moved out. Linda. Bad move to start thinking about Linda, Brer Cliff. He needed to get a dog, something cute and kissy, a Yorkie maybe, a smoochy pooch. He glared at the old man reflected in the window. He raised the empty bottle. "I lift the glass to my mouth. I look at you, and I sigh."

The phone rang. Cliff dropped the bottle. It rolled neatly under the desk.

"Yes? Yeats here."

"You died in 1939."

"In 1942, Zero Mostel debuted at the Café Society."

"You are not William Butler Yeats, Mr. Yeats."

"I am quite sure that I am. I looked myself up in the phone book just last week. And when I called, I answered."

"What was your mother's name?"

"Mom. Tell me what you look like?"

"I beg your pardon."

"Describe yourself."

"Why?"

"Because I dream of a Ledean body." Cliff sat in the desk chair and twirled it slowly around.

"You have no scruples."

"Oh, I don't know. I have one scruple," Cliff said, "maybe a couple of scruples. Scruple, scruple. Have you ever been scrupled?"

"I am sorry, Mr. Yeats, but this is making me uncomfortable."

"How about your name then, just your name?"

"Maude. Maude Gonne."

Click.

The girl was doing her homework. He definitely needed to get the phone re-listed in his own name.

Cliff glared at the monitor. He had pests covered, and was moving on to compost. *Hastening Decomposition.* Cheery thought. Linda had hastily decomposed and been discomposed. The oil man of all things. Of course in Vermont in the winter an oil man was a man of some stature. Slick pumper. An oil man had clout with the frozen few. Cliff could overlook the oil man. But then he found out about the snowmaker. The snowmakers were a weird breed, living in the night, encased in ice, frosted with hoar, they trod the ski areas suffering hypothermal delusions that they were Thor, the winter sports god of thunder, protector of humanity. Cliff had had it when he found one of these snowmakers on his porch, grinning like he'd just invented wood. The oil man, the Valhallan snowman. Talk about the second coming. He started regarding Linda as if she were a bowling shoe. Something that a demographic map of people had shoved their feet into for a lace up. And when he glanced around the alley, the people were sweaty and smelly and had I.Q.'s commensurate to their shoe sizes. Linda didn't like the bowling shoe expression on his face, so she moved on. New frame.

Decomposition. Can one decompose a poem? Decompose love? Toss Linda on top of the coffee grounds and orange rinds and eggshells?

Shit, I have to concentrate. Staring time. Cliff rose and peered out the window. Less wind today. The snow ghosts had danced away to fiddle on a roof somewhere. Ten A.M. Was it too early to crack open that bottle of Sauvignon Blanc, a droll little white from New Zealand, dry but not aloof. Ten in the morning, just an eentsy bit too early.

He really must get back to work on the herb project. I shallot be sage and attack the project. This thyme, I will Burnet up the keyboard. But first he needed to buy a dog. Cliff grabbed his bomber jacket and torpedoed out the door.

Cliff shuffled through the snow on Maple Street to the pet store, Animal Magnetism. The clerk stood with his back toward the door before a tank of Angelfish, whispering to a wispy looking blonde in a trim black coat.

Shit. Linda. Cliff stared. The clerk curved over her as if he were about to slurp her down through a straw like a cherry coke. Cliff felt his face go slack and second-hand, all bowling shoe.

"The lady will have the boa constrictor," he said in a voice that sounded like the cranked up decibels of some enthusiastic over-eager fun-fun-fun soft drink ad for depressives with Tourette's syndrome.

Linda startled, then turned back to the aquarium.

"Sailing to aquarium," Cliff yelled. Why *was* he doing this?

Linda adjusted her coat collar. The clerk whispered in her ear.

"Bowling shoe, bowling shoe, bowling shoe," Cliff yelled. This is what happened when metaphors collapsed, forgot that they were metaphors, when metaphors thought that they were rock stars with addictive personalities and checked into McLean.

"I will be right with you, sir," the clerk said.

Cliff hated him, hated him like one hated divorce lawyers who drove sports cars (it approached magnificent indifference) hated him with his natty mustache and creased trousers. He looked like a waiter in a Van Gogh painting.

"I want a dog," Cliff said. Again with the big voice. The clerk hastened over, looking a little alarmed now, like he was eyeing the phone askance, keeping tabs on it, so that he could make his move, lurch, call 911, and tell them to bring a net before he jumped Cliff and pinned his jugular with a Chihuahua chew toy then hog-tied him with poodle collars till the uniforms showed up.

The clerk pressed his palms together. "You're in luck, sir, because we have dogs. All manner of dogs." He nodded toward the kennels. "What breed are we interested in today?"

"I want a big dog," Cliff said. He suddenly did. He wanted a huge dog, a humongous dog, the world's most enor-fucking-mous dog in the universal pound. "I want a dog big enough to swallow a snowmaker whole."

The clerk tittered. "That *is* a big dog, sir. Follow me, and we will pick out one big dog."

Cliff followed the dapper dogman down the aisle where the dogs crouched under glass like some canine automat. Dachshund on rye. He tramped and stamped as he walked, hoping to force Linda to glance at him, hoping that she would look up and see that he was perfectly okay without her, so okay that he was buying big dogs. Big, bigger, biggest dogs. "That's the one," he said in his over-amplified voice. It bounced off the turtle paradises and fish tanks and ferret cages. It reeled over the hamster wheels. Cliff pointed at a slobbery jowelly weepy-eyed dispirited looking Saint Bernard.

"Excellent choice, sir," the clerk said. "That is most certainly a big dog."

"Want to hear a shaggy dog story?" Jesus, he was ranting now. He couldn't stop. "We had a dog so dumb that it used to sit on one hill every night and bark at the next hill. When the dog on the next hill barked back, he barked again. Haw. Haw. Haw. All night long the imbecile barked at himself. Echolalia. Echolalaia. The little peckerhead was using echolocation to tell himself where he was. Like a bat. Did you know that bats migrate? Someone told me this once. I didn't believe him. Where I asked? Where do they migrate? Mexico, he said. Why, I asked. For some quickie Tijuana divorce? If bats migrate, how come I've never seen them, you know, like birds in a chevron, heading south? My friend said, because they fly by night. Haw haw haw."

"Would you like a seat, sir? A glass of water?"

Cliff heard the little cat bell tinkle on the door as Linda slipped out to the street.

He went home wearing a restless bomber jacket with a Cairn terrier inside it. Shivering. Thank God he hadn't picked the Saint Berrnard.

Four P.M. and already gloaming. Holding the pup at eye level, Cliff inspected the terrier who inspected him. He set him on the coffee table. What to name the little mange-muffin? Linda? Heh heh. How about Peeve? Hi, I'd like you to meet my pet, Peeve. No, too cute. How about Fergus? "Who goes with Fergus?" Why, Cliff of course, no other. He tried it out. "Fergus," he said. The terrier stared at him. "Fergus," he said again, "Fergus, it is four in the afternoon and time for a libation. Maybe that California Chardonnay, vulgar and cloying, but I'd drink paint remover if it had the right vintage—any." He was not going to fribble at the keyboard tonight.

Cliff popped the cork and poured a saucer for Fergus. "Is there a drinking age for dogs?" he asked. Hell, times seven, in dog years, Fergus could pass.

Cliff tilted the bottle and stared out the window. "Fergus, there is no pun for Marjoram." The moon rose full and cut a thin wedge of paler white against the white snow. Small pines dotted the meadow. Sometimes he imagined that they were wee people in camouflage. He swore that they moved, scurrying from one spot to the next in the corner of his eye when he turned his head. Hey, wasn't that one closer? Probably scouting for Linda who had moved into town on Ferry Street two months earlier. One plump tree bore a passing resemblance to Zero Mostel. Zero Mostel sagging with snow, Mostel as snowmaker. In Vermont the snowmaker was the rainmaker. What had Linda been intent on buying at Animal Magnetism, a hamster? A tarantula? A hairy-legged Tarantula. Linda shaved her legs. In the bathtub. He stared at himself in the black window. Age: three-hundred-and-fifty in dog years. He looked it. Every dogday of it.

"I was not in love with her, Fergus, as I told her many times. She is beautiful, mind you, but intellectually we were not compatible. Linda, I told her, we are not intellectually compatible. Your interests are domestic and familial; mine are artistic and intellectual. It would never work, long term. Then I caught the oil man with his nozzle in her fill-pipe. That is not a metaphor, mind you, Fergus. He was really just filling the pipe, but the way that he looked at her like a new Ferragamo turquoise leather loafer . . ."

The phone rang.

Fergus hopped off the coffee table.

"Yes."

"Mr. Yeats?"

"Yes, this is Maude Gonne. I am calling to invite you to the wedding. John, John McBride and I are tying the knot, we are."

"Look, Miss, Miss Aluminum Foil, this ceased to be funny a long time ago."

"We're most serious, Mr. Yeats. You needn't be raising a ruction. Perhaps you're in a tippling way at the moment? I could call back."

"No. Do not call back. Look, Miss. Miss, what is your name really? I've had something of a rough day, and . . ."

"Kathleen Ni Houlihan it is, sir."

"Did Linda put you up to this?" Cliff slammed down the receiver and sank into the couch. He tipped the bottle. "Too much it is, the literary life. It is all simply too much."

Fergus squirmed out from under the couch and watched Cliff roll the empty bottle back and forth with the arch of his argyled foot. "It is just too much, Fergie. How can we tell the caller from the call?"

He rose and crossed to the kitchen and hefted another bottle from the rack without pausing to check the label. He raised the bottle. "Here's to what is past, or passing, or to come."

The phone rang again.

"Yes?"

"Mr. Yeets?"

"Yes?"

"Mr. Yeets have you given any thought to how your loved ones will be provided for should you experience a sudden and unexpected loss of life?"

"Do you know what the problem with the world is? Not enough poetry. People ask me what I do for a living. I say, I am a poet, and they all look at me as if I were vomiting carp onto the canapé tray. So I started telling them, Actually, I am working on a detective novel. *Oh really?* they ask, tilting their champagne flutes against their jaws. *How interesting.* Nobody reads poetry, see, and that is . . ."

Click.

Cliff and the bottle settled into the sofa and brooded gloomily. Fergus scrambled back up on the coffee table and rested his muzzle on his paws, one eyebrow warily raised. Beyond them, beyond the window, the cold, the snow, the darkness settled comfortably in. Far below them blind tubers bided their time, and tiny roots still frozen in fibrillated curls waited to unfurl. It would thaw. It would always and eventually thaw. They had all the time in the world.

Inside Cliff slurred, "I am going to give Linda a call. Who am I kidding. She's an angel, an angelfish. That's what I am going to do. I am going to ask her to move back in. Think she'll come back, Fergus, old boy?"

The phone rang. Cliff lurched. The wine bottle rolled wobbily under the desk.

"Not a chance in hell," Fergus said.

Karen Malpede

Prophecy

The boy walking across the wooden floor of the rehearsal room toward
her, his acting teacher, is beautiful in the way of slim boys about nineteen, angular, delicate, possessing private understanding of the female
without in any way being effeminate—the sort of young man battle-
scarred Greeks mentored and loved. Sara had known one like him in her
youth, even then, many years his senior, she was at twenty-seven, in his
eyes, an older woman.

Her memory boy's blond curls shimmied across his aquiline nose
when he rode on top of her in the dark while her husband, from whom
she was already estranged, did business out-of-town. They had met
blocking traffic in the middle of Broadway during an antiwar protest.
She was a theater school graduate student. He, all of nineteen, a sophomore physics whiz on full scholarship to the Ivy League, had recently
escaped his Irish-Ukrainian alcoholic family and an upstate industrial
town. They made love for hours that first night and for many nights
afterwards, as the protests intensified and the war worsened. He began
cutting classes and his grades started to slip. The study of physics, which
formerly he adored, appeared now to him, under her tutelage, to be
morally indefensible, completely co-opted by the military-industrial
complex. Soon, he could think about nothing but the bombs being
dropped halfway across the world. He looked to be permanently erect,
the outline of his member always distinct inside his worn jeans, long and
slender, like each limb on the slim form she worshiped when he smiled
at her while he scrawled equations on the blackboards of the classrooms

they'd occupied of tonnage dropped on Vietnam villages times body counts and the cost to our inner cities, or if she picked him out of the crowd, smiling back, as she yelled marching routes or the day's chant into her megaphone. Joined at the hip like the primal, androgynous form, they had rolled and tossed through turbulent times.

Today's young man, now standing in front of her chair, is merely getting ready to present his midterm acting project. He hands her the written pages of his speech analysis. He tells the class he is going to perform—rather improbably, she thinks, not simply because of his age, but because she hadn't expected the emotional choice, although precocious surprise is a part of the spell boys like this are forever weaving, impossibly over-reaching themselves, like the memory boy from her graduate school days, feeling more deeply than their years—Teiresias's speech from *Antigone,* in which the prophet succeeds, but too late, in humanizing the king. Jeremy, she checks his name on the paper in her lap just to be certain, moves a folding chair into the center of the space, in front of the seam where the black curtains meet, covering the room's mirrored walls. He sits, shakes his yellow curls over his eyes. This is an aesthetic choice, made because the prophet Teiresias is blind, though it jolts her. His cascading hair is not the result of the motion of the sex act while kneeling over her on the foam mattress in her graduate school apartment. She is only his acting teacher. She leans forward in her chair, clutching the pages of his monologue analysis while Jeremy hunches his back to show how the prophet is bent by the weight of years and his job. He stiffens and curls his long slender fingers. They look the same to her as the ones that, years before, reached all the way up and touched her pale, hard cervix.

In low tones, Jeremy spits the speech's opening words: "Listen, Kreon." Tieresias was sitting alone in his place of augury when the birds started to cackle. Immediately, he detected (Jeremy says in a whisper): "the strange note in their jangling, a scream, (his voice quickens), a whirring fury (he elongates each vowel sound). Teiresias understood, (Jeremy picks up the pace and raises his voice) the birds were "tearing each other, *dying in a whirlwind of wings clashing* (in his mouth, the recurring "w" sounds whip at the "i"s, then the hard "c" crashes down). "And," (speaking softly, again) the boy-prophet says, "I was afraid." He stares through his blond curls at the nothingness in front of his eyes, leaving her breath caught in her chest, so much does she want his next word—it's a surprisingly good acting choice. All of his choices thus far into the difficult monologue have been excellent. She is completely engaged, and his classmates ranged on folding chairs and on the floor in front of him have also stopped fidgeting, drawn along by the simple way he has of saying the words.

Listen, "Instead of bright flame, there was only the sputtering slime of the fat thigh-flesh melting: the entrails dissolved in gray smoke, the bare bones burst from the welter. And no blaze!" She doesn't think he actually *understands* what he is saying. These grizzly sights have been grabbed by him from the sounds of the syllables clashing, liberated from the dusty text by his tongue and white teeth and his almost imperious daring. The boy is possessed by the sounds of the words because how can he, or any of us, here and now, comprehend the terror that must have zipped like an electric shock through the bronzed torsos leaning forward as one on the stone seats as they realized, indeed, they were lost. "The altars of the town are choked . . . the gods will have no offering from us." The boy prophet claws at the curls in front of his face. The altars "are gorged with the greasy blood of the dead man," he shouts. His body turns rigid with rage. Kreon will learn too late, after Antigone has already died, when he holds the corpse of his son. Jeremy's face contorts. He snaps his metal chair out from under him. "Stubbornness and stupidity are twins," he sneers, jerking around. He spots a slice of his face in the mirror where the black drape stops. He waves the chair high above his head, hurls it. With a cackle, his image cracks into pieces. Shards leap off the wall at the audience. The acting teacher watches it happen, unable to change anything. Jeremy runs from the room.

II.

Upstairs in the blood-red Victorian office of the school's director, she stares into a quiet Central Park snow globe while the man finishes his speaker phone conversation with the building's maintenance supervisor. In the moments following Jeremy's (she does not know what to call it) "flip-out," she calmed, reassured and released her students, notified the maintenance staff, oversaw the temporary taping of the mirror. She got down on hands and knees with wet paper towels to blot from the cracks between the wooden floorboards the dangerous invisible pieces of glass and managed to shove a long, sparkling splinter into her right palm. She has a band-aid on the spot. The school's director removes his glasses. With his fat fingers, he drums on Jeremy's file in front of him.

"I believe this young man to be a scholarship student," he pauses to let the impact sink in. "He has destroyed school property and endangered his colleagues. He left the premises and failed to acknowledge responsibility." The heavy director breathes in: "The acting profession for which we have been, in good faith, preparing this young man cannot tolerate those who, for whatever reason, lack the ability to distinguish mimesis from reality." He exhales deeply. "If this same young man were to behave in a like manner in any professional capacity, he would be terminated immediately. Actors' Equity could find no defense for him." He stares at the acting teacher. She has nothing to say. She's an hourly worker here, without benefit of a union, or contract. Beside that, she does not know how to defend the boy. "My first inclination was to expel him immediately," the director picks up Jeremy's file and waves it at her face. "Upon reading further, I noticed, however, that the young man in question is a U.S. Army veteran and is currently a member of our National Guard. His tuition is paid by the GI Bill. Because he has served his country, I have decided to speak with him. I will offer the chance to make full financial restitution to the school. He is to be permanently removed from any class you teach. You are requested to have no further contact. In the future, you will monitor your students' projects far more closely. Performing Greek tragedy is hardly necessary; we train actors for the American stage." He flourishes his glasses in her direction. "Then, again, you should have stopped him the minute you saw he was beginning uncontrollably to shake. Feeling unbounded by form is lethal. Who said that? Walter Pater? Baudelaire?" He asks as he leans across the oaken expanse of his desk, looking down her sweater's v-neck. With a gesture, she is dismissed. The school's director hits the button on his speaker phone, tells his secretary to phone the "disgraced young man."

Why hadn't she asked Jeremy to stop when she saw him begin to shake?

III.

At ten o'clock that night, the acting teacher, Sara, settles into her couch to watch Aaron Brown's CNN news hour, the remains of her take-out Chinese on the coffee table. She is sipping a third large glass of a cheap Merlot when the doorbell rings. She switches the television off. She'd left a message on Jeremy's cell phone asking him to call so they might at least speak about what happened. He must have decided simply to come. Why hadn't she seen him start to fall apart?

"I can't promise much," her message said, but she offered to strategize before his meeting tomorrow morning. She removes the chain from the door. Jeremy is there, twisting a knitted cap in his hands, head bowed, golden curls tucked behind his ears, a palpable sweet young-man smell rising up off of him like invisible steam. She leads him into her living room.

"Thank you," he says in a barely audible voice when she points out a soft chair where he can sit. She perches on the couch. He settles in, stretches out his long legs. He has not bothered to take off his coat, a military issue camouflage jacket in the same fashion worn by her old young lover, except, then, his was green for jungle warfare, not mottled brown for the desert.

"I thought your work in class today was extremely good," she wants him to relax.

"Until," he interrupts with a directness that is admirable, "I totally lost it. Are they going to throw me out?"

"He expects you to make financial restitution." She stops to make her words simpler, "pay for the damage you caused." He groans. "I know you don't have much money, what with living expenses and all. Perhaps, you could offer to pay a little bit every month, and, of course, apologize, even to the class, perhaps. Providing, that is, you want to stay at the school, which I am assuming you do. You should, I mean, although, of course, acting talent is something inborn, and you could, maybe, get along without the training, or study some place else, but you don't want this event to follow you. It would be best to get it expunged, erased, from your record. It all depends on what sort of work you would like to do." She looks at the boy looking at floor. "You have a large talent, you know." He feels so far away from her.

Jeremy mumbles a word or two, which Sara asks him to repeat. "You mean acting work?" She nods. "I don't know what I want to do. It doesn't, anyway, matter very much."

She had been sitting across from her young lover on the foam that served as her couch and their bed, covered with an Indian spread, in her Columbia graduate school apartment when he told her he couldn't continue going to his classes. She had been staring at a shiny brown cockroach walking across the crumb-filled coffee table in front of her, littered with paperback political books and antiwar leaflets. She had passed the hash pipe over to her lanky, blond lover. "Larry" she thinks as she speaks to Jeremy:

"But, of course, it must matter. You're talented."

It was the night the bombing began in Cambodia, and the sturdy roach stepped upon photographs of napalmed children, flames coming out of them, their images sticky from the droppings of take-out food and Cokes. They had just come inside from the protest; they had hurled garbage cans into the streets to block traffic, had yelled obscenities at the police who called in the horses to charge. She'd grabbed a handful of the boy's second-hand fatigue jacket and pulled him out of the fray. "It doesn't do any good to have them arrest you. Not for something stupid like this." And they'd walked with their heads hanging low back to her apartment. Each took another long hit off the hash pipe before he loaded it again and tapped it down with a wooden match.

"The thing just came over me—a rage—I don't know. I couldn't, can't, explain, these days, sometimes, I have no control . . . the words in that speech. I mean, I thought it was awesome. I worked on it for a long time, I wanted to do it ever since we read the play in your class. It made such great sense, I mean, even the gods were repulsed, but then, somehow, it just got away." She can hardly hear Jeremy's rambling response, has to lean forward toward him, put her hands on the coffee table between them, follow his lips. He is also learning forward, shaking his head slowly back and forth, whispering, "I'm sorry, I didn't mean" and his voice trails off, "to get you in trouble."

"You mustn't worry about me."

He had told her that night he was dropping out of school before he flunked out. They had sat silent and apart, she on the foam that served as a couch, he in the second-hand chair with its stuffing coming out, their fingers were touching, both of them were stoned, and shaken, not just by the ugly turn the demonstration had taken, but by their sense of the uselessness of what they were doing, and the mounting devastation of the war. The dead stared at them from newspapers, television screens, and their own mimeographed leaflets, dead children, necks limp, held in the arms of women whose faces were blank with grief. Larry and Sara had walked through the streets of New York, under sheets, wearing papier-mâché masks of Oriental female faces, painted white, constructed larger than life and easy to see. Dozens of demonstrators had walked in straight in rows, down Fifth Avenue from Central Park to the Village, when the protests were always nonviolent, but the napalm kept on being dumped, the jungle was being defoliated. She had reached over and moved a golden lock of his hair back from his forehead, twisting its thickness around her finger, lightly touching his ear. "Fuckin pigs," he muttered, under his breath, "I can't fuckin think anymore." They were still staring hard at the cockroach who seemed to dance a small jig on the sugary stains on top of the torso of the small napalmed girl in the blurry photo. Sara had let go of his curl and touched his lips with the first two fingers of her right hand. It was dark and all they had was a candle. His lips were soft and full, a deep pink, almost as if he had colored them with something. In the dim light, he looked like a girl and she had wanted to fuck him.

"I thought 'wow,'" Jeremy is saying to her now, "when I first read the speech, 'wow' I could really do this. You told us to pick out something we liked, that really meant something to us, something we really felt." Jeremy is looking at her as if because she told him these things she has already done something to him, has already crossed the invisible border that ought to keep teacher and student apart, has already entered his life. "I practiced the speech for days in my room. You know, I felt almost numb, almost like I was flying, I can't describe it. I never felt like that before, with a speech, I mean, like it was so deep inside me but outside at the same time, like I was saying the words, but the words, you know, were really moving through me, almost like they were coming from somewhere else. Like a voice telling me what to say. But, I was in the driver's seat driving some powerful beast. It felt totally awesome. You told us we could memorize the whole thing if we wanted to. You said we could." Sara nods her head.

She had wanted nothing else but her blond lover lying under her to blot out the truth of the war, had wanted to ride his stiff, shiny cock while his yellow hair streamed across the floor, and his amazed face stared up at her, while he moaned in his pleasure. She had needed to forget everything else, had willed herself not to hear the angry shouts still loud on the street below, not to think anymore about the lunatic escalation of the war, the bombs falling half way around the world, and his declaration he was leaving school, or the screams she could hear all night in her sleep of people she didn't know. She had needed to forget. So she dove with her juicy flesh deep into his blond beauty and without thinking she had burst out, the words singing through her as if they were being spoken by someone else: "Never shall a young man, / Thrown into despair / By those honey-coloured / Ramparts at your ear, / Love you for yourself alone / And not your yellow hair." The lovely words rolled from her as she straddled him, both of them naked from the waist down. Her breath came in excited, small spurts. She had been reading Yeats for her seminar, was entranced with how a revolution had been made by poets. She continued, half-singing, half-shouting, the long sounds of the vowels rolling, the consonants striking: "Only God, my dear," thumping, triumphant: "Could love you for yourself alone." He was straight up inside her, but he was bursting. She shouted, "And not your yellow hair." She grabbed it in two great wads in her hands, pulled him up to her, kissed him hard on his full lips, let his head drop to the floor. She got off him, lay by his side, her leg thrown over his wet, pale, limpness, a shining in the dark. "Your yellow hair," she could not rest. Her mouth moved along his spent member, her tongue licked the clear, bitter drops off his spun gold. She watched him straighten again. She wanted only this violence always, of love and of language. She wanted the revelry of sounds. "Only God, my dear," she wanted the madness of rhythm, image, "thrown into despair," to take her out of her self, away from the loss of their innocent youth and the murders being done in their name for no reason she could fathom, away from the screaming in her ears all of the time of the children who were being killed by boys, stoned like he was, only far away from her touch, crouching scared in the jungle. She had wanted to fall across all of them, keep them by her side, her heavy leg on them, safe, their spent, wet members growing, again, to hold them still with her thigh on her floor for as long as it took until the draft ended and the war stopped. But her yellow-haired boy had worked his way out from under her, had gotten on his motorcycle, and had driven away. Gone to join the Weather Underground someone said he said to them before he left, or gone to Canada to avoid the draft. He hadn't even told her that much, had not dared to reveal his plan, had simply been gone one day without so much as word, and the next thing she heard he was dead. In a motorcycle accident on the interstate. Gone from her, gone, and the golden-haired child he had left behind in her belly was also destroyed, a numb look on her face while she lay on the surgical table, legs spread, the small, wet thing was pulled out and she comforted herself with the chant: "Only God my dear / Could love you for yourself alone."

Jeremy is talking to her and she makes herself listen. "I decided to memorize all the words, just like you told us we could. It's odd how it happened. All of a sudden, I couldn't stop saying them. The whole scene began to grow completely clear right in front of me, like I was seeing it all. Teiresias is sitting right there, blind, he can't actually see anything. He can just hear the birds going really crazy. But I saw them. And, slowly, he gets it. The birds are tearing each other apart. Each one has already eaten the rotting flesh of the dead man. The body is lying outside on the ground, unburied. It's being torn apart. The birds are eating from the flesh of the dead man and that makes the gods sick. So they

tional Guard. After the attack on the World Trade Center I was called up. I worked down there for two weeks. The fireman would bring us wheelbarrows full of stuff and we would put them into bags. This one Hispanic guy I worked with, it was a weird conversation, said to me how we kind of deserved this. He was in the whole Cuban revolution with Che, whatever. I kept on asking him, 'How come we haven't really seen any bodies?' He goes 'When you get an onion, and one of those onion dicers? Imagine the World Trade Center, the buildings, as the onion dicer and the onions are the people.'

"When I was saying that speech, I started to remember all this. This Hispanic guy had an ear in his hand and he made a sort of a joke, holding it up, like, 'Oh, I can't hear.' That day, the day that I started bagging was, like, Tuesday, the smell over there—Tuesday, Wednesday, I think I vomited twice on myself, but we all kept on doing what we were supposed to be doing. I didn't want to stop, it was all, like, just keep on, keep on working, but it was the worst. It smelled like rats—like dead rats and stuff like that."

She feels like she's going to gag. She sees what he sees, fleshy fingers with wedding rings, traces of vomit on his desert-fatigue jacket. She shivers against him.

"So, today, saying Teiresias's words . . ."

"Yeah, it was like it all happened again. I didn't know. I had no idea until I got into that room."

He is shaking in her arms. He is so terribly young, younger, even, than the baby she hadn't had who would already have been over thirty if it had been born.

"It wasn't until I got in front with all of those people watching me. That's when I think I really understood what the words said. Even the prophet Teiresias is cut off from the gods' forgiveness, the gods' grace. Because of what fucking Kreon did to everyone, the birds are gorging themselves on unburied flesh. And I got scared. I don't want to be thrown out," he stops, then starts, "from acting school, I mean."

"We'll go together. I'll explain."

He lets her hands drop, starts to talk fast. "I was a real fuck-up in high school. Drugs, booze, turning tricks, petty theft—the usual stuff. The judge gave me a choice, join the army, or go straight to jail. The military straightened me out. I was such a good soldier they made me a member of the President's honor guard. For two years, I stood around looking at Bill Clinton's back." He cannot look at her. He's older than the dead boy she keeps remembering but she's so much older, by now, he seems to her awfully young. "My call-up notice came. I'm mobilized for the war in Iraq. Only, I won't be standing around bagging body parts this time around. I'll be busy blowing some friggen Iraqi bodies apart" He laughs. "And I already know what it's going to look like. I already know how it's going to smell."

After her young lover left her and died, she stopped working on her dissertation. She began working downtown at the Fourth St. Methodist Church, counseling conscientious objectors. Without the Vietnam War, her whole life would have been different. Maybe she'd have tenure somewhere and could afford to be a single mother, would not now be struggling to make ends meet, teaching, without health insurance or retirement benefits, at the second-rate acting school. She would not now be standing here, her hands holding Jeremy's shoulders, remembering how he left her without saying good-bye, raced north to Canada, or to get to Vermont to become a real revolutionary. He blew himself up in a blaze of gasoline on the interstate. His body sliding across the road. His jeans and his fatigue jacket torn. She had never before let herself see the accident happen. His yellow hair matted. She had gotten through the report of his death by letting herself feel abandoned. She got through the shock of losing him by letting herself be opened up so the fetus of their child that wouldn't be born could be suctioned out of her—a whoosh of the vacuum and she was empty.

"You know what got me through those two nights down there?" Jeremy asks her. She is standing behind him, seeing her cold legs stuck into the stirrups. "It was helping the firefighters—which, by the way, I think firefighters are the greatest human beings I've ever met in my life . . . I had never seen so many men cry, just crying like—and then while they were working, they started crying. People just all of a sudden, like, instantly would tear up and have a little breakdown and then keep going. I would get so confused because I would see these big men just, like, frantically freak out and then keep going. Everyone was just about: keep going and keep going and keep going and keep going. I just kept on telling myself: keep working, keep carrying things. Just keep carrying things. I had a Shakespeare due, like on Monday, and I kept on reciting the Shakespeare piece, because it was the only thing I could really remember."

"What was it?" she asks.

"I don't remember."

"It will come back."

"Here it is, it was *Henry V,* the intro to *Henry V.* I have it memorized right now, too. Look, it's all out of my control." he laughs a little bitterly, "I've got my orders right here." He pats his pocket. She sees the envelope sticking out. "I've been re-upped." He moves from her chair. He had never bothered to take off his coat. "My girlfriend is waiting downstairs." Girlfriend. The word comes at her like a shock and with it the thought—this is their Vietnam. The invasion of Iraq is going to start in late-February or March, no matter what any of them do—she has already been marching in Washington, and at the UN—before the desert gets too hot for the American boys to fight. A hundred thousand troops from Houston, Memphis, Omaha, San Diego are already massed in Qatar, Bahrain, Oman, and Kuwait. He's been called up.

O, *for a muse of fire,* the words roll inside her, to ascend the highest heaven of invention. She sees him downtown in a field of pulverized office furniture and loose ears, loping again into battle. She understands this may go on forever, like the loop of a tape constantly replayed, always the same wombish cloud of white dust spitting out pieces of the non-combatants, and Jeremy, come home from the war with a constant twitch, minus some piece of himself, addicted to drugs, coughing up chemicals, without anymore being able to remember his lines. She would so like to save one yellow-haired boy. She would so like to protect him.

"My girl is pretty freaked. The orders came just before I went to your class. My girlfriend thought she was dating the friggen next Leonardo DiCaprio, we'd be moving to Hollywood, get a swimming pool, a couple of cars, have some kids, go to the awards. She's telling me she doesn't want to be a widow before she's even been married." He stands at her door. He is leaving.

"I want you to remember how truly talented I know you are. You are classically talented, really. You can do Shakespeare, the Greeks, you could do Yeats," she realizes he might not know who Yeats is, hardly anyone, anymore, does Yeats's plays. "You could do all the great plays."

"Yeah? Well, thanks for the encouragement," he fidgets a bit. He's so shy, most good actors are. "I hope you don't mind, but I can't get to that meeting at the school tomorrow. I need to pack up my room. I guess I just don't want to be lectured at. I'll get enough of people telling me what to do."

"It's all right. I'll go myself and explain it to him. I'll arrange everything so you can come back. Finish your training."

"Yeah, fine, whatever, someday, maybe. Look, I'm just going down to Fort Bragg, so don't over dramatize," He laughs. "I'll probably be working for Homeland Security."

"Take Sophocles with you, take poetry."

"OK, sure. But, look, I mean, don't you start to shake. Don't throw a chair at that pompous son of a bitch. I'll be all right. I'll probably just end up guarding some airport or bridges or shit." So, he had started to shake and she should have seen it happening. At least, he would not, now, be in disgrace at the acting studio, if she had been able to stop him. "Because, you can bet," he continues, "those poor bastards over there are going to try to hit us again, hard, when we start to bomb them."

She watches his back while he waits for the elevator. "Wait a minute, please." She rushes inside, pulls Yeats's *Collected Poems* off her shelf, hurries back, pushes the worn book into his chest. "Take this. Memorize." His hands are crossed over the book. He smiles at her while the elevator door closes. She does not want him to become a soldier, does not know where he might run to, wants to hold onto him as he is, now, still innocent, somehow, not yet a killer, but a gatherer, inside himself, of body parts and image fragments.

Once he started speaking the prophet's words, she had no longer actually been in the rehearsal room. She had not seen him shaking. She had been on the floor, straddling her yellow-haired boy. She had been trying to forget the war, trying to keep him with her, safe, without thought of the future. She climbs into bed, closes her eyes. He's here with her, now. She can bury her face in his yellow hair.

Anna Smith

Houdini

The year Ronald Reagan was elected president, I fell in love with an actor. I met him in a play about Houdini. He was Houdini.

The audition was at an experimental theater in a garage. That Saturday afternoon in July it was cool inside the theater; the windows had been boarded up long ago. The director, a man in his forties, had me sing "Home on the Range" and fall on the floor several times. He kept saying, "Faster, faster." It seemed that he wanted to know how quickly I could fall on the floor. It turned out that *was* what he wanted to know. Luckily, I was good at it.

Two other people besides me showed up at the audition. We were told we were in. The rest of the cast had signed on ahead of time. They were veterans of the theater and knew what to expect. I was almost twenty and had just moved to this city from the South. I did not know what to expect.

Midway through the audition, a blond man in sunglasses wheeled in a ten-speed bicycle. I knew this was Larry, the theater's star, from having seen him perform the night before in a play about how hard it is to be a man without being a jerk. It was a comedy, in a way. He had written it. He left the sunglasses on for a while after he got inside. He looked about thirty, and even though he had a little bit of a paunch and seemed to have a bad headache, he was gorgeous—like Zeus in army fatigues.

I soon found out Larry had a girlfriend, Margaret. She was one of those women who at that time identified as lesbian for political reasons.

She was up in Minneapolis working in an all women's theater dedicated to dismantling the patriarchy. All the theater old-timers agreed that no matter what else, she was an amazing actress.

In December Larry and I finally got together; it was my idea. We went to a restaurant called the Eggplant. I was amazed that he could eat. At that point in my life, I could never eat in front of someone I was attracted to. He ordered borsht. I'd never heard of it.

Larry had grown up on the streets of Chicago, but sometimes when he was kidding around he had a fancy, highfalutin way of talking. He would use this voice to comment on the intricacies of de-seeding marijuana or his trip to Kmart; it was his way of making fun of anyone professorial, fatherly, British—anyone in a tie. Even people who hated him couldn't help but think he was funny.

I ordered Earl Grey tea. Not because I was a tea drinker, but probably because I thought it sounded Victorian and controlled. I couldn't bear the thought of wolfing down something thick and embarrassing like coffee or hot chocolate. I needed to drink something thin, repressed, British, because inside I was an overweight teenaged maniac from Dixie with an ungraceful lust I just couldn't get rid of. I wanted to make out right then and there, or behind the huge oil paintings in the art museum. He had no idea.

We made a tour of the capitol building and checked out the Civil War museum. From the circular balcony we gazed up at the painting in the dome; there was a scene of angels in flowing robes coming out of clouds. He joked, "What's that? The apotheosis of Wisconsin?" I didn't know what an apotheosis was, so I just shrugged, as if maybe it was and maybe it wasn't.

It was December by this time, but we were both still riding our bikes. The tires slipped as we made our way over the frozen slush on the sidewalks. We parted with no kisses, no hugs, no handshake, just a lot of potential.

One night about a week later he let me come home with him. I had just quit my job at the skating rink so that I could go to the university and not have to work so hard. The girlfriend was still up in Dinkytown dismantling the patriarchy. His apartment was over a laundromat called Ye Olde Laundromat.

He had two huge cats. The living room had an ugly overhead light and smelled like a litter box. I made him find candles to put on the coffee table. He played me radical lesbian feminist gospel music, then an Edith Piaf record. We smoked a joint.

Outside there were snowdrifts; inside there was a couch. He was wearing a collarless light blue shirt and army fatigues; one tooth was slightly chipped and a molar was capped in gold. I was stoned, and every moment had that quality of unfolding amazement that goes with youth, sex, and marijuana.

He had a way of looking at me—shyly, coyly—that made him seem feminine. For a few seconds he would look like a woman, and I wondered if maybe he was gay. After all, his girlfriend called herself a lesbian. I thought, "Larry Fairy," and then, horrified, tried to erase the thought from my mind. He was the biggest person I'd ever had sex with, which at that time was only two other people. He had the short, widening bulk of an ex-football player—which he was—or William Shatner. I was in love and awe to be this close to him. We stayed awake until 4:30.

Opening night was getting closer. The play had been written during the previous six months. It kept getting longer and longer. When the script passed the two-hour mark, the cast started to get scared. We knew we were shooting ourselves in the feet, but no one could convince the writer and director, a guy named Benny from the East Coast. Every evening he brought in new scenes, typed on his ancient typewriter, just that afternoon. People would groan and argue with him. He would assure them that they could quit if they wanted to. All told, the play was three hours and forty-five minutes long. It was to be a musical extravaganza depicting the life of Harry Houdini, who was from Appleton, Wisconsin, which was how Benny got the grant from the State Arts Council.

Benny's plays were always marathons, so he tried to make up for this fact by doing all the scenes in fast motion. People coming to the theater for the first time said it seemed as if all the actors were on speed and the director was a deranged maniac. People who *were* familiar with the theater tended to avoid it. Once Larry accused Benny of deliberately trying to abuse his audiences; Benny went into a tirade about how Americans were all idiots who watched TV all the time and they should all be so lucky to be abused in this fashion. We played an average of ten characters each, and were required to act, sing, and tap dance. Some of us could act, fewer could sing, and only two could tap dance. What we lacked in talent we made up for in mania. One day Benny told me that my characters were not distinct enough. I didn't know right off what this meant. They were distinct to me; they had different names, some were men, some women, they were going to wear different costumes. But Larry said he would coach me.

We went to the theater before rehearsal one night to work on the scene between Houdini (Larry) and Miss Lindemuir (me), the librarian in the Appleton Town Library. He wanted me to change my face, posture, tone of voice. I felt like I had changed all these things already, but he said I was still too *me*. Larry sat on the bleachers in his army fatigues and a light blue shirt. He fiddled with the handcuffs he would wear in the show and leaned back. I began, "Welcome Mr. Houdini. I hope you will enjoy your stay in Appleton. I'm the archivist from the Appleton Town Library. Will you and your wife pose for a few photos?" I had been imagining a friend of my mother's when I spoke these lines, a tiny divorcée who loved square dancing and discussed her relationships with married men in front of me. Until working with Larry, I hadn't even been conscious of it.

"Now." Larry paused from his seat in the bleachers. He ceremoniously placed the handcuffs on the seat next to him. "Now. Could you try to vary your posture, tone of voice, pitch, volume, facial expression so this character will be distinctly different from all your others?"

I tried the lines again. I dropped my mouth into an inverted U. I let my voice quaver like Mrs. Lindemuir's would.

Soon I felt completely stupid. Larry kept saying, "Bigger, bigger," and "More, more."

I was becoming exhausted from saying these lines and looking like a fool in the middle of an empty stage, but the stupider I felt I looked, the more satisfied he looked.

"This isn't realism," he said over and over again. I finally figured out that he meant I was too normal. If I felt like a fool—a shrieking puppet—that was good. That was making me more of an amazing actress. I learned to lose my cool, my dignity, and my reserve, which I'd never had in great supply unless I'd just received a terrible shock. It was a relief to expand the boundaries of my voice. Finally here was a vehicle for the churning angst I'd always carried just below the surface. I learned to call it up at will and use it. After awhile I wondered how I'd ever made it through life without running around and screaming several hours a day. At the next rehearsal the rest of the cast all commented on how much progress I'd made. I smiled.

One night in late March, Larry and I were lying in bed in my tiny room after making love. A candle was burning. We lay like beached whales in the low tide of passion, drinking orange juice from the same mug. Though it was still winter, the room was warm.

Larry talked for a while about the rehearsals for his new play, which would open in a few weeks, after *Houdini* closed. It was about Sigmund Freud and Victor Tausk, a student of Freud's. The plot dangerously resembled Larry's relationship to Benny—an older man obsessed with a younger man he believes is stealing his ideas, and vice versa. The story had a little bit of everything: rape, incest, hysteria, hysterectomy, repressed homosexuality, suicide. Freud was to be depicted as very, very bad. It was somewhat of a comedy.

And then I heard him say that the amazing actress might be coming home soon. It was late, and I was blissfully sleepy. Hearing him yak on about the amazing actress was no skin off my nose that night. She was hardly real. She wasn't on this futon, in this room, this apartment, this town. She had not just had multiple orgasms.

Then he said, "It was a close call the other night on the phone. Apparently some of the cast were a little too forthcoming with the details of our relationship. And it turns out, she was already concerned because of your hair."

"My hair?"

"She is worried about us spending so much time together. And because of your hair she was worried about what kind of person you are."

But I wasn't going to help this along. I said again, "My hair?"

"Well, Sally, you must admit, your hair is somewhat of a standard in male fantasies. But don't worry. I managed to get out of it without her discovering anything."

He presented this last bit casually, as if I were fully aware that I was some sort of a secret.

"Excuse me?" I said, my voice like a baby frog. Larry was gulping orange juice from my mug at that moment. I tried again, "You mean she thinks we're—"

But I had lost my voice.

"Sally, darling. I've always thought it was understood that I was not troubling Margaret with the *specifics* of our relationship. I've told you she is extremely jealous."

I felt a wave of hysteria coming on but couldn't talk or move. I was like a princess who'd been turned into a frog, and now a tiny tadpole. I fantasized briefly that she'd die before coming home, but was fast aware there was something wrong with that. It was impossible to hate her without feeling guilty. After all, she was off in Minneapolis doing her best to dismantle the patriarchy.

I paused for a moment to wonder, just who was the patriarchy in this current situation? Not me, not her. We were female, after all. Clearly patriarchy was this thing with the shrinking penis, pulling on long underwear and army fatigues, as if he'd just remembered an appointment he was late for.

I tried again to say something to clarify the situation. "Just what—who—?"

"Sally, my dear. Please try to understand."

Usually when Larry addressed me as "Sally, my dear," I warmed, smiled, felt in the care of a benign Henry the Eighth, or a severe but kind Henry Higgins who brought a dignity, culture, precision, to the uncertain swamp, the Spanish moss and kudzu, the quicksand, bullfrog, wolf-spider region of my libidinous Southern upbringing. But that night I didn't feel buoyed up, edified, elevated. I was saying to myself, Oh no! Oh no! She doesn't know! And she doesn't like my hair!

I told Patriarchy that this wouldn't do. But I was too calm. I would never make a good guerilla in the war between the sexes because I go into shock. I said, trying not to sound intimidated, that he'd better tell her. I didn't want to be a secret; I'd hoped to be much more than a secret. I was trying to be firm and dignified, not too placating, hospitable, conciliatory—not too bowlegged, backwoods, or bucktoothed. But I was beginning to sense I was out of my league with these folks. After all, the guy I went out with in high school drove an El Camino.

I'd heard Larry talk about monogamy. My understanding of the situation was that monogamy was *bad*. It was a plot by the patriarchy to protect its property. According to Larry, it was an emotional chastity belt. He saw this as explaining why women were usually the ones who were jealous and wanted monogamy, while men more often enjoyed variety. If we could just take off the chastity belt, we'd all be free. I was more than happy to give up the chastity belt. But *my* chastity was apparently not at issue here. If Margaret was the undisputed wife in this scenario, then I was the other woman. Other women don't get to complain about jealousy; they cause jealousy. They recreate the lost lust for the too sedate couple, the couple that would rather watch TV and eat than make love. Other women are expensive aphrodisiacs; less monetarily costly than prostitutes, but more emotionally so. Some folks use them for years—like narcotics—until the system breaks down, the equilibrium destroyed, the immune system worn to a whimper, the adrenals shot.

Patriarchy had the scared look of a little boy who had accidentally bit his brother too hard. He had "no idea." He "doesn't know what he can do now."

I knew I should be angry, but this wasn't easy to put into practice. It was easy to get mad at the men going into the porn shop downtown—their faces were hidden. But getting mad on the spot, at this man on my futon when we were still not yet dry, was something else. The men on the street: that was war; the man in the bedroom: that was murder.

I told Larry before he left that he'd better tell the little lady about me. He said he'd do it.

The next day I started to get hives. They began as tiny red spots on my chest. They were fascinating—until they began to spread, claiming vast territories of my shocked body. Each red spot was like a tiny mouth saying, *Oh no! Oh no!* A thousand red buttons, lit up and ready to be pushed, launching angry missiles to the apartment above Ye Olde Laundromat.

Three days later Larry appeared at my house. We sat on my screened-in porch and smoked part of a very thick joint. We held hands and watched the blue sky beyond the greening trees as he dispatched the news that Margaret would not tolerate an open relationship. Her edict: "Stop fucking that girl." Part of her fury came from the fact that Larry had picked someone so much younger than him—someone who would be in the role of an adoring innocent whom he could count on to think he was a genius.

He spoke. "I am," and while he paused I thought he was going to say, I am a genius, but then he went on to say, "I am insulted by this analysis, but I'm not in much of a position to come to your defense."

So I was not even considered competition, a fact that disappointed and humiliated me. Margaret claimed to be "deeply disturbed" by my lack of assets. She saw me as young, naive, and a bad actress.

"I did try to tell her it wasn't that I was unhappy with her or our sex life, that wanting to be with someone else didn't mean I was bored or dissatisfied with her in any way."

Without a doubt, this speech worked wonders on her. But I was miserable. I could feel my hives getting redder. I showed some of them to Larry. He was appropriately sympathetic, but then went on for five minutes about how Margaret had hardly eaten in the last three days, how every time she ate anything she threw it up. She'd apparently lost five pounds.

She needed to, I thought, then felt guilty. I had never had hives before, but compared to a hunger strike I was small town news.

Larry told me Margaret would be returning to Madison in a few days. He claimed to have mixed feelings about this. He hadn't yet decided what he would do about "the situation." Somehow this conversation was causing me to want to go to the bedroom, hives and all, and fuck our way back to the Stone Age. But Larry said we'd better not. He said he must try to stay clear in order to make his decision. Instead, we relit the joint and listened to a John Coltrane record. Later, I walked him down the stairs, and we kissed for fifteen minutes on the foyer. I wanted to sink down onto the steps, go crazy right there on the dirty carpet, but he resisted, he resisted to the end.

In the daytime I went to my classes at the university. I took courses all more or less on the theme "Dismantling the Patriarchy." I wrote papers on sadomasochism in Shakespeare, sadomasochism in US foreign policy, sadomasochism in the lyrics of Rogers and Hammerstein. I showed my professors my hives, which were now turning into scales. They were sympathetic, though I told them far too much about my love life for comfort. (Their comfort, not mine.) These well-meaning feminist ladies tried to point out the lack of justice in me hating Margaret when Larry ("that scum") got to have his cake and eat it, too. One said simply, "Kill him." But I couldn't figure what good there was in a world where cake wasn't for eating. Neither could I really get behind murdering the very body I was craving, though I'd considered it. But I finally understood that story they made us read in high school. A woman killed her lover and then kept his body laid out on the bed to cuddle with long after it had started to go bad: you've got to do the best you can.

Larry called and offered to pick me up before the final Thursday night run-through of *Houdini*, even though I lived only two blocks away. Before that, he hadn't called in four days. I got in the front seat of his van, looked at him, and said, "You're dumping me, aren't you."

He paused entirely too long before saying, "I don't know if dumping is the right word." Then he shifted gears laboriously, like a general with a burden. He looked at the road, not me. I was quiet. He kept his eyes on the road, looked both ways at the stop sign, and carefully stated his message. "It is not possible for our relationship to continue as it has."

At rehearsal Benny immediately began barraging Larry with questions about his new play. When Benny noticed me crying, he rolled his eyes. I heard him say to Larry, "Don't bring your dirty laundry into the theater."

We had an interesting final run-through with everyone doing the play in German accents, the kind of thing I would have thought witty and fun if I hadn't hated the entire cast by then. In the bathroom some of the women tried to be sympathetic. They had put up with Larry for years and all agreed Margaret was a bitch or, as the pianist put it, "overrated." The value of this assessment was lost on me at the time because it came from the very people Larry had referred to as apolitical and stupid. I was in a hell of a bind. I briefly wanted to switch camps, but then what credibility would I have left with Larry? I couldn't give up hope that he'd change his mind. I was faced with the dilemma of every woman in love with an asshole: no one else seems as interesting. We wait for time to pass until our beloved resumes the stage. We look at him, hear his voice, and then we are awake, then we are paying attention again.

Friday, Saturday, and Sunday night I got bombed after the show with the apolitical and stupid rest of the cast. Larry went out with Margaret and some of the political heavies from the Freud play. When I forgot about Larry, which wasn't often, I had an okay time.

The next time I saw Larry was weeks later at the opening of his play. As Houdini he had had flowing golden curls, but as Victor Tausk his hair was short and brown.

Margaret sat in the front row. The only other time I'd seen her was at the opening night of *Houdini* when she'd hissed at the scenes that objectified women. I stared at her, as if I might learn the secret that would tell me how she managed to win out and have Larry sleeping with her for the last few weeks.

At the end of the play Victor Tausk (Larry) was supposed to shoot himself, and I had the fleeting fear that he was going to really do it. I wanted to cry out, but after the lights came back up, there he was, as the writer and star, waiting for his standing ovation.

The cast party was in a crowded second floor apartment of some of the theater regulars. Everyone was there, even the sworn enemies: Benny and Larry, me and Margaret. There was beer in the bathtub, cocaine in the bedroom, and we were soon all in a frenzy of post-performance drunkenness. It was hard to move. Whenever anyone would turn on a light, someone else would turn it off. Even though the huge windows were open, letting in the night air and the light from the streetlights outside, we were half-blind from tobacco, pot, and clove cigarette smoke.

I spent some time drinking beer and talking to the guy who'd played Freud. It was hard for me to tell if he was interested in me or just felt sorry for me because I'd been dumped by Larry and had lizard skin.

Freud finally floated away, almost as if he'd found out what he wanted to know. Next thing I remember I was in front of Margaret. She'd come up for a beer after having been down on the sidewalk with the members of the cast who considered themselves superior to the apolitical scum upstairs.

I believe my opener was, "Did you hear about my hives?"

She choked slightly on the beer she was swallowing. I noticed she did look thinner in her army fatigues. She said something about how she wasn't going to talk to me, so I should just forget it.

But I wanted to talk to her. It bothered me that she didn't like me— or my hair—that all she knew about me came from other people. I had a fantasy that if I could win her favor she would loosen her grip on Larry. We could share him. It would be revolutionary.

I lit a joint and offered her some. She paused for a second, then accepted it. I guess she figured any disease I had, she had already. Then, in a pot-strangled voice, she started talking. It was as if she couldn't resist or even wait to exhale. "What you don't understand is that I've spent the last eight years with this man." Then exhaling, "I almost went to the hospital. I couldn't eat."

"Well, I have hives. And I'm alone now."

She didn't seem to hear this. "I don't think you really understand what passion is all about. How could you? Passion is separated from love in the patriarchy, but I'm telling you, that's not real passion. Real passion isn't temporary. It's long lasting, deep, and wrathful."

My head was reeling. I was having a hard time following her. "But I thought the two of you were against monogamy." Then emphasizing each word, "I was led to believe this."

Her eyes opened wide for a moment, then she said, "In the right circumstances, of course. Among—" she groped for the word, "equals!"

I exhaled heavily, then belched.

She went on, "How could you have equal power in a relationship with someone over ten years older than you? You couldn't." She took back the joint as if it were settled.

I then asked her why she still wanted to be with Larry if she thought he'd done something so terrible.

Her mouth tightened. "I'm not 'giving in'—I'm surrendering to the passion. That's what I was saying—passion is wrathful and patient." She stared through the smoke at the heaving mass of drunks sinking to the carpet on the song "Rock Lobster," and said, "I'm not willing to be a masochist anymore."

She looked back at me to see if I'd heard her, then wandered off through the smoke.

I was beginning to suspect that I didn't want to be a masochist anymore, either. Until then I'd never identified this as a choice. I resented finding this out so late in the game. I wanted to run down the crowded staircase, push past stoned thespians, find Larry on the sidewalk, grab his arm and say, "I don't want to be a masochist anymore, either." At this point he would say, "And Sally, my dear, you won't have to." Then we would run across the patch of grass to the parking lot, leap into his van, and go find freedom. But he'd probably already heard that line, and not too long ago. I couldn't help but notice that for Margaret to "not be a masochist" meant getting her guy and getting rid of me. I couldn't figure out what not being a masochist would mean for me. It was a puzzle that couldn't be solved, so I decided not to think about it while I was stoned.

During the following summer, I smoked pot out on my screened-in porch every night. Actually, I smoked it in the morning, too. I would stare at the telephone and think of calling Larry. Finally, one night in July at 3:00 AM, I called him. The phone rang seventeen times before he answered, his voice half-drowned in sleep.

I waited several seconds. He hung up.

I called a few more times after that, always after midnight. Larry always answered. All these times I was quick to hang up on him first. These tiny acts of aggression were comforting.

Fall came. I called one night in September.

This time I spit out the words, "Larry, when are you leaving town?"

He hung up.

I gave up acting. I started hanging out with a woman who believed in reincarnation and had a guru with a lot of Rolls Royces. She was a masseuse. I would pay her money to give me long massages with coconut oil. On a wooden table she massaged my shoulders, arms, hands, and feet, then the muscles on either side of my spine. I thought about my parents, about how much they hated each other, and how sad that was. And because I didn't want to think about that, I told her again and again the story of Houdini and Larry and Margaret. How it was hardest to have nothing to say, no way to defend myself. She listened, and when

I would be furious and talking too loud, propping myself up on an elbow to be heard, she would nod and say, "I think they were your parents in a past life. You must have had some bad times together before this one." And then she would say, "Let go. Or else you'll just have to come back and do it all again."

So with that threat looming over me, I tried to let go. And let go, and let go.

Richard Burgin

Jonathan and Lillian

One couldn't really say that Lillian's dinner parties had attained a legendary status primarily because her guests (rarely more than nine and, on this evening, seven) were generally discreet, talking about them mainly to each other. There were several reasons for this. First, at any given party half the guests were as famous, or nearly as famous, as Lillian herself and for them to meet other celebrated people was in the natural course of things. Also, Lillian didn't have dinners exclusively for theater and film people like herself, but always had writers, musicians, or painters and sometimes even businessmen or lawyers among her guests. Consequently, there was no one circle in which news of the parties circulated widely. The lawyers and businessmen talked about them the most, perhaps.

Still, there were any number of people in show business or the arts, or simply moneyed people who knew about them and yearned to be invited to Lillian's—people for whom such an invitation would be the crowning touch of their social year or decade. To see the inside of her storied Santa Barbara house in the mountains was itself an achievement. Then to be able to talk with her and her famous friends and to eat the exquisite food invariably prepared and served by Santa Barbara's finest caterers, was something one might never experience anywhere else. Moreover, there was the sense of history in the paintings, sculptures, and especially the signed photographs of all her friends that adorned the walls. Here was Picasso, there was Judy Garland, Elizabeth Taylor, Barbara Streisand and Tennessee Williams and at the table writers and directors of the first magnitude—it all made one feel slightly dizzy if one were one of the less celebrated guests, and there were always a few of those people at Lillian's dinner parties too.

Finally, Lillian had the inestimable gift of making people feel happy with themselves, so they had little desire to gossip maliciously about her. Nearly everyone thought she was among the nicest people they'd ever met, certainly the nicest famous person they'd ever met. As a result, people truly enjoyed themselves at her parties. They arrived looking as well as they could and stayed as long as possible giving her goodbye hugs and kisses more heartfelt when they left than when they arrived.

How strange that he was now one of Lillian's guests, Jonathan thought while driving to the party. Of course as her latest biographer (the biggest commercial break so far in his writing career in which he'd published only one largely ignored novel and two modestly successful biographies) it was not so wildly strange, he supposed. What was far stranger was that he was apparently going to become her lover—at least she had unambiguously invited him to stay and spend the night with her after her other guests went home. However, there was still the question of her guests and whether he would pass his audition with them. The way she had structured things, he thought this evening clearly represented his coming out party where her Hollywood friends could meet and access him. No wonder he had to take an extra swig of Mylanta before leaving.

It was only a five-mile drive from his little ground floor apartment on West Valerio Street to Lillian's mansion. He began driving up State Street, the glass-enclosed street lamps casting soft light on the succession of elegant restaurants and dress shops, evening clubs and banks. They all seemed to merge together as if connected by the lights and flowers—hibiscus, birds-of-paradise, azaleas and bougainvillea and by the magnolia and palm trees. He saw the clock tower of the courthouse bathed in a lemon-colored light, where people stood on the outdoor balcony looking at the city and at the ocean and mountains. Then, as he started driving uphill, he saw El Encanto, the hotel in the mountains where she'd taken him to lunch on their first meeting. They had eaten outside where the view of the ocean was spectacularly unobstructed but he'd been too nervous to notice. He'd overdressed and drunk too much and felt he'd said too little. Nevertheless, after little more than an hour she'd asked him where he was staying.

"In a hotel on State Street."

"But dearest, I meant where is your home?"

"In New York, in Queens actually."

"An apartment?"

"Yes."

"So you flew here to see me?"

"Yes, I did."

"Well that won't do," she'd said, finally removing her sunglasses and revealing her violet-blue eyes, a startling contrast to her yellow hair. He'd nearly gasped. How could a woman her age look that stunning and young?

"You need to live here, I think, so we can have the kind of talks we've had today in a way that will be convenient for both of us."

"That would be great but . . ."

"Don't worry about the money, that would only get in the way of the book. I'll get you an apartment in town while you're working on it, OK? But please don't look so concerned. I hope you don't think I'm trying to seduce you and will end up asking you to stay with me. I know you writers need your space."

He mumbled a thank you and forced a smile to show he understood her joke and she smiled back playfully but somehow seriously as well. He remembered then that she had a reputation for having affairs with younger men, both in and out of show business, which, these days, was something of a trend in Hollywood. It helped him accept what appeared to be happening between them but he was nervous nonetheless. He had never met, much less flirted, with someone of her stature. He felt he'd had very little success or even excitement in his life and now was suddenly being flooded with both.

"Will that be OK?" she'd wanted to know.

"Of course it's OK. It's incredible really, how kind you are."

"I find I don't spend much time in LA these days. I barely use my house in Beverly Hills anymore. I far prefer my Spanish getaway home in the mountains where . . ."

"It's beautiful."

"Yes, it's beautiful. Here, it's still beautiful. You understand that," she'd said, as if his understanding of the obvious was an achievement. "I'm so happy they picked you to write the book. I think you're an artist—that you have the soul of an artist. I liked the novel you published too. I did my own research on you, you see, and I think you're an artist and those are the kind of people I like to work with and get close to."

He'd thought for a moment that something might happen that day but it didn't. When lunch was finished they walked slowly through the hotel gardens and then in front of her Mercedes she leaned forward and brushed against his lips, her blond hair almost tickling his cheeks. She told him they would meet at her house in a week—she had to go to LA first on business—then gave his hand a quick squeeze and disappeared into her car where her driver was waiting.

During that week he'd tried to stay focused on his book and not attempt to predict the future but she began calling him every day.

"I want to take care of your hotel so I'm going to give you my credit card number and have you put it on my card."

"No, that's not right."

"Don't be silly, Jonathan. It's only fair. You didn't expect to stay this long and I won't have the time to get you an apartment till I get back."

"I don't know," he mumbled.

"I do. So that's settled."

He began thinking a lot about the next meeting at her house where she'd insisted on inviting him for dinner when it could have been for lunch in a restaurant or lunch anywhere. Dinner did have definite connotations that he couldn't deny. Was she planning to sleep with him? Was she waiting for him to make the first move?

Yet it didn't happen that way. First, she surprised him by addressing the issue before the caterer had even brought the main course into her vast, candle lit dining room—a room so large it seemed like a little section of Spain itself.

"You're quite a *young* man to be writing my biography but you don't write like a young man. I think that's the best combination, don't you, maturity in art, youthfulness in appearance. At least I've often been attracted to younger men. My philosophy is if the man *is* younger I promise to *look* younger." She laughed and he quickly joined in. "Tell me, how old are you, Jonathan?"

"Thirty-five," he said, slicing three years off his age and immediately regretting he hadn't said thirty-two.

"That's a good age, Jonathan, very good. Do you think you can handle it if I start to fall for you like I think I already am? And do you think I'll look young enough for you?"

"Oh yes. You look *younger* than me and, of course, infinitely better."

"Thank you angel. When you come to my dinner party Saturday night why don't you plan to stay with me afterwards."

"That would be wonderful," he mumbled into the salmon salad he'd just been served.

"I hope it won't jeopardize your ability to do the book . . . objectively?" she said with a slight smile. He felt frozen and didn't respond, the book suddenly seeming so far away and almost incidental.

"I know," Lillian said. "When we make love we'll use one part of our brain and when we work on the book we'll use the other, OK?" she said, laughing again. "Does that sound reasonable?" she added, extending her hand, which he immediately clutched, then held for a few seconds.

"Sure, it sounds great."

"I don't know about you but I *always* have to be in love. If you're not in love with someone and sleeping with them life is just kind of ridiculous, don't you agree?"

He nodded, not knowing what to say.

"Marvelous, then it's settled."

But a minute after leaving her home he chided himself for his passivity (the same kind of passivity he used to show towards his ex-wife) and for having lost yet more control over his so-called unauthorized biography. Still, the main thing he felt that night and for the next few days before her party was a dreamlike excitement that made it very difficult to sleep. After all, he was about to become Lillian Glass's lover which seemed almost impossible to believe and she had also said she was falling in love with him—or had he imagined that?

Lillian's Spanish "getaway house" had twelve bedrooms and extensive grounds filled with water fountains, flower gardens and a vast swimming pool overlooking the Pacific. Jonathan rang the bell then took a deep breath. A few moments later Kenneth, the butler, opened the door—a good looking man, in a black tux who was tall and blonde like everyone else in Santa Barbara, and who gave him a friendly smile. Gay, Jonathan thought, but the smile was still a nice, unexpected stroke for his ego.

Lillian, dressed in black herself, except for a yellow silk scarf (the approximate color of her hair) met him in the living room. "Hello darling," she said, kissing Jonathan ardently on the mouth. "I'm so glad you could come early."

"You look beautiful, you're amazing," he said, pleased that for once he meant every word of a compliment.

From his position in the hallway Kenneth watched them closely, especially Jonathan, before going into the kitchen again. Look what she's settling for now, he thought with a snicker. This new one was almost frumpy and dull looking with his ill-fitting glasses, receding, thin brown, will-less hair, ten years older, at least, than him; also shorter, less muscular, with a face not even in the same universe as his. Perhaps Jonathan thought writers could get away with looking like that, and maybe they could in New York. But this was Hollywood where a man didn't get any points for looking five months pregnant. Worst of all, perhaps, was how uncomfortable he looked wearing a tie when the whole point of dressing up, of dressing at all was to feel sexy and to show it. Could Lillian possibly become his lover? Could one actually have sex with a mouse like Jonathan? Tonight would probably be their big night. Lillian liked initiating her new lovers on a party or premiere night, something to help remember them by and give the occasion more sentimental value. Even a project like Jonathan could acquire some sentimental value with enough work. Eventually with some new clothes and other beauty aids she could erase the way he truly looked as if he'd never appeared in the universe that way before. It was merely a question of money and Lillian had plenty of that. She had spruced him up too, Kenneth remembered. He still wore the clothes she'd gotten him, though he'd had to integrate them slowly into his wardrobe lest Gina get too suspicious.

He finished his inspection of the refrigerator and closed the door. Amazing how Lillian, how all people repeated themselves, were slaves to their behavior, though they thought themselves so free and au courant. Lillian had saved him for a party too, although he'd had to cater it. Tonight he was the headwaiter and would be paid well (better than Lillian realized, he thought, with another smile). Though she eventually dumped her "civilian lovers," that is, the younger non-stars, Lillian did treat them pretty well financially. But, he didn't like thinking of that. It didn't make the plans for tonight any easier to carry out.

His cell phone rang then from inside one of the pockets in his tuxedo.

"Shit," he muttered, and then quickly discovered that at least the call came from a pay phone.

"What's going on?" a voice said.

It was Hummel.

"Everything's OK."

"Anyone there yet?"

"Her boyfriend, that's all."

"Is he going to stay?"

"Don't know. Probably. He won't be any trouble."

"Why's that?"

"Trust me, he's a real wilted dick. Why are you calling?"

"Don't worry, it's not trouble."

"That's not the point. They could subpoena my phone. They'll be the history of all the calls I've gotten on it then. They can do that now. So, if things don't work out they could . . ."

"Things are going to work out, and you're going to get rid of your phone after your last call tonight."

"I'm not gonna make it on the cell. I'm gonna make it on a pay phone in Santa Barbara. It'll take three minutes longer, maximum, that's all. I'm not negotiating this. I won't put it on the cell. I won't risk that."

"Then throw out the phone after you call me. Drown the fucking phone, OK? I'll get you a new one."

Shit, he said to himself, after the call ended. He hated to get rid of the phone; he hated to get rid of any gift—especially one from her. He heard steps, then saw Lillian.

"Everything going well?" she asked. She always got so nervous before these dinners though she'd done so many of them.

"Everything is perfect."

"Perfect?"

"Couldn't be better."

"OK then," she said, winking at him as she walked out to the hallway to meet Jonathan.

"Everything looks dazzling," Jonathan said and Lillian smiled.

"Kenneth does a marvelous job."

"Was that Kenneth who let me in?"

"Yes, quite gorgeous isn't he? And he's very loyal. Shortly before he died, Tennessee had a big crush on him. Let me show you what we did with the dining room," she said, taking his hand as they walked into it.

"It's magical," he said. "I never realized how many paintings there were before, or how much light."

On the table were more candles in glass holders than Jonathan had ever remembered seeing. The lights danced and half lit the paintings on each sidewall. Again he told her it was beautiful and she gave his hand another squeeze.

"I finished chapter four last night about your early Broadway years. I'm really kind of pleased with it."

"That's wonderful angel. Oh, sweetheart, the bell rang, did you hear it, the bell rang. The guests are coming, the guests are here," she said, leaving him in the room of paintings and photographs and ubiquitous candlelight. Jonathan looked at the shelves and the candles and thought he'd arrived at a strange moment of happiness, that his life had had hideous frustrations to be sure (thinking of his failed career as a novelist and of his being childless), but that he was happy now in this moment at least, and that Lillian always preached that only the moment is real.

He moved out of the dining room into the hallway and saw Lillian embracing Alex Hornstein, the renowned divorce attorney, and his current wife Kathy, who looked like a model. He noticed that Hornstein continued to hold hands with her while talking to Lillian. This will not be an easy night, Jonathan thought. It was never easy to be not only the least wealthy man at a party, but also the least charismatic. To see and feel one's true station in life, one's essential obscurity, was, he supposed, the inevitable result of attending one of Lillian's dinner parties. Denial could only go so far, he thought with a little smile, as he looked out shyly at Hornstein, a man at least four inches taller than him—with a head of convincingly full black hair, a deep confident voice that he modulated with supreme skill during his frequent TV talk show appearances and undoubtedly also in bed with his blonde, outrageously attractive wife.

The bell rang again. Kenneth opened the door and Jonathan recognized Eric West, the movie director, who only a few years ago won an Academy Award and who at the start of his career had directed some of Lillian's best movies. He had a silver goatee and long silver hair and wore a tie and sports jacket but also his trademark blue jeans and black cowboy boots to enhance his western image. Though he'd grown up in New Jersey and lived mainly in New York and Malibu for the last thirty years, West was born in Arizona, or so his bio claimed, and he continued to promote himself as a cowboy director. With him, sporting a huge diamond ring he'd given her when they married last year, was Louise Leloch, the young actress. She was West's fifth wife, by Jonathan's count, and one of his youngest. As Jonathan recalled, she'd appeared in supporting roles in West's last two movies.

Jonathan just had time to finish a vodka tonic before shaking hands with Hornstein and Co. (for an attorney he had quite a macho grip) and then with West and his wife. Then a minute later, Jonathan saw the revered novelist, Margo Garret, with her good friend the gay art gallery owner Maurice Germand.

"Ah, the Great Garret," West exclaimed, turning away from Jonathan to kiss her on the lips. Immediately Jonathan remembered that West had directed at least two movies based on Garret's novels, and that she had co-written the last screenplay with him. The movies had done well at the box office too.

"Eric!" she said, taking his hands, her cheeks coloring slightly after he kissed her.

"This is Louise, fire of my loins, my sin, my soul, Louise—the Great Garret, who deserves to win next year's Nobel Prize and every year's for that matter."

Jonathan was impressed that West knew Nabokov as well as Fitzgerald but he had said it with such grandiloquence that Jonathan cringed. Neither Louise nor Margo seemed the least bit embarrassed, however, as they quickly exchanged kisses on each other's cheeks, and talked about how absurd it was that this was their first face-to-face meeting.

Without any discernable announcement, the guests suddenly began moving to the living room with its enormous array of art and its grand view of the gardens and ocean. Jonathan sat on a chair in the corner by the picture window that overlooked the rose and tulip gardens, and where he soon accepted a new drink from Kenneth. He took a few sips when a thin, balding man with piercing blue, birdlike eyes stood before him.

"I'm Maurice Germand," he said, extending a hand.

"Jonathan Trantnor. I've been to your galleries many times and like the rest of the world admire them greatly."

Maurice inclined his head a little like a swimmer trying to shake water out of his ear and smiled slightly. "Thank you . . . You're writing a biography of Lillian, aren't you?"

"Yes, I am."

"How lucky for you, and her too, I'm sure. Lillian is so divine I just love her to death."

"It is lucky for me, a great piece of good luck especially since she's being so kind to help me with the book."

"Lillian has always taken an interest in people who write about or photograph her," he said, with what Jonathan thought was a slightly ironic smile. He felt a sudden tinge of embarrassment, took another sip of his drink and said, "I think it's one of her gifts to be interested in nearly everyone she meets. That's why so many of them become her friends."

Germand nodded and Jonathan felt he'd recovered nicely.

"Every time I come to Lillian's," Maurice said, "I feel like I'm coming to a familiar but rather fascinating gallery . . . of people as well as paintings."

"A gallery or a museum," Jonathan said. "The range of people that she knows is extraordinary."

"Because she, herself, is so extraordinary. Do you know if she sees Michael these days?" Maurice asked, referring to Lillian's son who reportedly lived in Santa Cruz, as a part-time ecoterrorist, most-of-the-time pot dealer.

Jonathan, somewhat surprised that *he* was being asked this question said, "Not recently, I don't think."

"That's a shame. I think he took the divorce very hard and then got in with some very bad people."

"Yes, it's a real sadness in her life but Lillian is strong and keeps positive about Michael, keeps hoping."

"He's still a young man," Maurice observed.

At dinner, Jonathan was seated next to Kathy Hornstein on one side and Louise Leloch, Eric West's wife, on the other. The food—chicken, fish and pasta, a delicate tomato salad and two kinds of wine—lived up to its reputation, the conversation less so. At least at first. No one topic dominated the table for any length of time—instead everything seemed skittish and a little forced. It reminded Jonathan of an acting troupe improvising from audience suggestions in fitful one or two minute spurts before moving on to the next suggested topic. Finally, the guests found something to talk about that interested them all—the recent, much-publicized wedding of the singer/actress Deanna Russell.

The Hornsteins asked most of the questions about it and Lillian and West, who were at the wedding with Margo, gave most of the answers. Jonathan, making a mental note to not entirely recede into the conversational background, asked some questions too.

The wedding and reception, which about a thousand people attended, had been filmed for a future television show and was covered by much of the nation's (and a good deal of the world's) media. When one movie star found out that a television show was involved she apparently changed her mind and decided to go at the last minute, but demanded, and apparently received, a hundred fifty thousand dollars to attend. She arrived, looking in the words of West, "pale, bloated and horribly depressed." Margo agreed that the actress did have "the worst taste in the western world. What a paradox to have all that beauty clothed in such glaring trash."

There were stories and jokes told about Michael Jackson and Elizabeth Taylor and there was the anecdote about the two actresses who'd had a fight thirty years ago. One approached the other at the reception to make up only to have the latter turn her head and walk away. All the stars were referred to by their first names and Jonathan was not always certain who was being discussed, though he'd immersed himself in show business lore since getting the book contract. Tuesday and Liza he knew, of course, but which Janet were they referring to, which Gary?

Then the discussion turned more to the celebrities at the reception who were ill and to speculation about who might not live long. The brief moments of hilarity were replaced by a somber mood, which got considerably darker when they began discussing what they were doing when 9/11 happened.

"I was writing," said Margo. "I didn't find out for a long time. And then I worried about my friends who worked near there and started calling frantically but by then, it was impossible to get through."

"Was anyone you know hurt?" asked Jonathan.

"A friend of mine who worked at the World Trade Center . . ."

"Yes, Paul," said Maurice quickly. "He unfortunately didn't make it."

"I'm sorry," Jonathan said, "that's awful."

Margo bit her lip and said, "It was very sad, very cruel."

"Margo wrote a beautiful poem about it that the *Atlantic* published," Maurice said.

"No dear," Margo said, "it was actually published in the *New Yorker*."

More condolences and testimonies followed until they led to an uncomfortable silence. Then West began describing a Hollywood birthday party he'd been to that was thrown by a famous director.

"I heard that was a huge party," Lillian said.

"Yes, lots of people, lots of rooms. His house is really extraordinary."

"Does he still supply cocaine to anyone who wants it?"

"I didn't notice any coke, but I'll tell you what I did notice," West said, with a twinkle in his eyes. "I walked into one of the guest rooms to use the john and there was no less a movie star that Brian Kove doing something very strange to some model or other, I think, and damned if he didn't go right on with it. I think he was giving her an enema while dicking her from behind at the same time."

A couple of the guests laughed uncertainly.

"I mean he didn't even stop when I walked in. Just turned his head and looked right at me and continued 'till I left."

"Darling, you probably made his day," said Lillian.

"You probably made him come—which I understand isn't that easy for Brian," said Maurice.

"I mean, I've heard of Hollywood decadence," said West, "but this was ridiculous."

"I know an actress who had an affair with Brian sometime last summer," said Louise. "You know who I mean, Eric, and she told me that all he ever wanted to do, besides watch his own movies, was play games with enemas. Enema love he called it."

A few more guests laughed.

"Well there you have it," said Lillian, "the idea for your next movie."

"Yes," said Eric. "Adultery and drugs are old hat. Everything has to be anal these days to be up to date."

"It's the new intimacy," said Hornstein, clutching his wife's shoulder.

Everyone laughed again, including Jonathan who managed to force a laugh as he squirmed in his seat wondering just what his future with Lillian held for this evening and beyond.

Ridiculous to still be thinking abut the phone on this of all nights, Kenneth thought, but it seemed he couldn't help it. He was even aware of its weight inside his jacket as he served and removed the plates and glasses and tried to avoid any meaningful eye contact with Lillian, who had already smiled at him once. It was not as if it were a little animal he were getting rid of. It was a mineral, he guessed, or at any rate inert, not alive. So why think about it? But given the kind of mind he knew he had he wasn't really surprised. Sometimes he thought of his mind as a department store with a series of specialty sections each devoted to torturing him in a unique way. Once he wandered into one of these sections there was nothing he could do to get out except let the thoughts the section had stored up have their way with him.

She had given him the phone right after the first time they'd slept together so she could call him whenever she wanted him. It was her first gift to him and he used to stare at it, sometimes even with Gina, and say, "This is the phone where I'll get my first part, talk to my first agent, get my first deal." Lillian had said she'd help him (hinted at first but then said it after their second or third time) and she was one of the most powerful women in Hollywood. "With your looks and body you've definitely got a shot. I'll put you in touch with people, angel, don't worry. They'll be impressed when they see you."

But I can act too, he used to say to himself, while they were having sex. And I'm actually a better actor than you, he'd think then in an angry, defiant voice that came from another part of the department store that he couldn't stop, could only hope to control by not saying it out loud, for example, while he was coming.

One time he did tell her about his acting, about studying at the

214

actor's studio and made her listen to him. He read the part of Tom from *The Glass Menagerie* right in front of her wall-length mirror. She'd praised him, of course, though it was impossible to know if she meant it. Yet she *had* done a few things—introduced him to a couple of producers and directors, arranged for an audition or two. Nothing big, probably just the minimum one would expect from a woman in her situation. He did get a small part in a commercial from it, just a few words but it paid well, and then work as an extra in two movies but then it all stopped. She ended their sessions and with them the career favors and of course, the clothes as well. Then the parts stopped, the agent that she'd gotten for him no longer returned his calls and even Gina said he should leave the business. "It's eating you up," she said to him tearfully in bed. Then she went on to cry even more as she started talking again about wanting to have a child, something that was still unthinkable to him.

Lillian's final gift was the offer to be her butler/handyman, somehow even more humiliating than the hustling and small time drug dealing he used to do—but she paid well so he couldn't even say no to that.

The guests were through with dinner and had returned to the living room where the painting was. Even the choice of it, a Diego Rivera, was inspired since seven others in that room alone were certainly worth more. Recently he'd made a point of talking about art to Lillian so she'd know he knew the value of things. All this would help deflect suspicion from him, would make it look instead like the work of a bungling burglar who passed up a Picasso and a Renoir for a Rivera.

He walked in with the tray of cognacs and noticed Louise Leloch talking to Jonathan. In her tight, low cut yellow dress she was showing to maximum advantage her perfectly positioned breasts and ample honey blonde hair, neither of which was probably real, but still, he decided to serve the guests around them and to listen to them talk for a moment, while sneaking in a look at Louise whenever he could.

"So you two met about the book and then it just clicked between you big time, huh?" she said. "I mean, the word is that she really likes you."

"I hope so," Jonathan said shyly.

"Anyway, your book will make you immortal because Lillian is immortal."

"Thank you, that's nice of you to say but I really don't think so."

"But why?"

"I don't think anybody's writing will make them immortal, least of all mine. I know a lot of writers think so, but I think that's just an illusion. I think everyone's art and movies and novels will simply, eventually, be forgotten. You know, I had an editor friend, an editor, you see, not a writer, who once said to me 'art is the last illusion' and I think he was right."

"Art is the last illusion," Louise repeated, "I like that."

"If these artists are so hung up on immortality, I think having children is a much more direct route, a much better solution."

"I sure wish Eric felt that way. I've been trying to convince him to get me pregnant for a year now. Course he's had so many children already but couldn't he give me just one more?" she said laughing. "Do you have any children Jonathan?"

His face reddened.

"No, I'm sorry to say I don't. I wanted to, very badly in fact at one point, but my ex-wife didn't. I used to even have dreams where I'd be talking to my son only to wake up and discover that I'd just had a dream. But no, my ex-wife was really married to her work, and since then there hasn't really been an opportunity."

"What did she do?"

"She was a novelist who *really* wanted to succeed, at least enough to pay any price to do it. I don't think writers like that mix very well with babies."

There was an awkward silence until Louise finally said, "Well, I think it's great and really romantic about you and Lillian. That's the way it was with Eric and me, too. I was just a bit player in one of his movies, I think I said ten words in the picture, but one day during rehearsal our eyes just met in a special way and he invited me to dinner that night and then boom, we just clicked. So, yuh, I was crazy about him right from the start but I also had a lot of hang-ups and insecurities about dating a man who was so world famous and, you know, older."

"But they all went away, obviously. The hang-ups."

"Not completely," she said laughing, as she finished her drink. "I mean you see the nice breasts but behind them beats the heart of a hick."

Jonathan laughed and spilled some of his drink, and Louise laughed too, holding his wrist for a few seconds as if to steady him.

"Excuse me sir, I'll fix that," Kenneth said, removing a cloth from his tuxedo pocket which he kept for this purpose and dabbing away at Jonathan's jacket. He bent down and attended to the rug, catching a glimpse of the Rivera painting on the way down and for a nanosecond on the way up.

"Thank you very much," Jonathan said.

"You're welcome, sir."

Kenneth lingered a little longer, enough to hear Louise add, "But seriously, it gets better, it does. I mean once I went to bed with him the age thing went away pretty quick. And the other stuff, well that maybe takes a little longer. We've been together almost three years now and I still feel in awe of him."

Then Kenneth saw Lillian look at him with her version of a dirty look and he returned with his tray to wait in the kitchen for the guests to leave. It would take one of the confident ones to start the process, then the others would all leave within ten minutes. Perhaps it would be Margo, the "Great Garret," as West had called her, though later at the party Kenneth had heard him diss her writing to Jonathan. Regardless who it was, he would have to spring into action and fetch their coats with a convincing smile firmly in place. Then Lillian would pay him in cash telling him to take the key to open the gate and return it tomorrow. But he'd refuse saying it made him uncomfortable and ask her instead to open and close the gate electronically (only a slight inconvenience) as if he didn't know or want to know the code, which he'd already given, along with copies of the house and gate keys, to Hummel. He also left a living room window unlocked so it could look as if the burglar made a daring climb over the gate by tree, landed in the yard and entered through the window. Yes, he had definitely done his homework.

Lillian, of course, would be hysterical, at first. He would have to spend some time with her and the police too, probably, which would be nerve-wracking and difficult. He couldn't even spend the money right away either but eventually if he kept his cool he *would* get it (he'd tell Gina that he'd won it gambling or maybe the lottery) and then in a few months or so they could leave. That was the thought to focus on, leaving Southern California, the world capital of lies and illusions, that had turned him into a hustler and a slave where he'd once had to let men suck him and where he'd even sometimes had to get on his knees and suck them too, while pretending to enjoy it. He had only to think of that, the old, fat smelly men and young pimply boys he'd done it to to know that tonight was right and was the only thing left he could do.

She was at the door, head inclined slightly, a beautiful slope to her neck, thanking Kenneth for his impeccable job in a voice that was breathy but thrillingly refined. He watched her, feeling like a child who invents and beholds his mother at the same time in a moment of rapture so pure it is almost like terror. He thought, she is truly magnificent, maybe my era of meaninglessness, of being thwarted in everything is over.

She had turned towards him now, the door closing behind her as she embraced him.

"Lillian, you outdid yourself this time. It was the dinner party of all dinner parties."

"Thank you angel. I was waiting so long for this moment when you'd finally hold me. I thought it would never come."

He could feel her trembling slightly against him and her need for him; the incongruous coexistence of her confidence and vulnerability excited him enormously.

They walked into her room holding each other around their waists.

"Let me use the bathroom to take my face off and get ready for you," she said. "My face is only meant to be viewed until midnight."

He laughed, loud enough for her to hear because he knew she liked to hear him laugh, and lay down on the far side of her enormous bed. He saw the light go on in the bathroom. Around him were paintings and photographs of Michael, her only child, as far as he knew. He could feel the Viagra he'd taken (just in case) coursing through his system, already working. God bless those greedy scientists. It was funny how people went to the theater or looked to writers like Margo, who'd been divorced four times, for wisdom but it was the scientists alone who could really make life better for people, who were really the only hope.

He waited and waited barely able to contain his excitement as he continued to sculpt his erection.

"Here I am darling," Lillian finally said, as she emerged from her bathroom in a flowing, yellow silk robe. She lit two pale candles and then shut off the lights.

"Did you have a good time at my party?" she said, as she snuggled against him.

"I had a wonderful time. The pasta was incredible. All of the food was."

"And did you like my friends?"

"They're great—quite an amazing group of people. I didn't get to talk a lot to everybody, of course. I talked mostly to Kathy and Louise."

"I noticed. You were very animated, not at all as shy as you predicted you'd be."

"No. I guess I wasn't. I surprised myself."

"But not me."

"They're both very down to earth. Both really easy to talk to."

"What were you talking about so passionately? I was starting to feel a little jealous. I mean they're both so ridiculously good looking and have these perfect bodies that I've never had and never will have."

"You're kidding, right?"

"About what?"

"Being jealous."

"Not really. Not entirely."

"Well, I mean that's ridiculous."

"So what were you talking about? Something *ridiculous* too?"

"Kind of. Actually, it was a bit philosophical with Louise. We talked about values, believe it or not."

"Did she also talk about babies? Baby Present talking about Baby Future?"

"Yes, she talked about wanting a baby."

"Since she married Eric she's been like a walking commercial for the joys of motherhood, although she's never had one as far as I know. So were you babied to death?"

He laughed. "In a manner of speaking." They were quiet for a few seconds. He was puzzled by her rare use of sarcasm and by her quasi-admission of jealously on this of all nights and wondered if they would end up making love after all, since it was very late. He decided to say nothing. Let her wonder about him for a moment. It seemed it was always the other way around, his always trying to guess her mood and please her. She who had such a full life that his life was now devoted to writing about it.

"Would you like a drink, darling, to recheer you up?"

"Sounds nice," Jonathan said.

"I have a little surprise for you in the refrigerator. There's a bottle opener and some glasses on the counter that Kenneth left for us. Why don't you bring it in, sweetheart?"

"Good idea. I'll be right back."

He felt happy and excited as he walked towards her kitchen, which was larger than some of the apartments he'd lived in. On the counter were the glasses and bottle opener on a tray and inside her enormous refrigerator was a bottle of champagne—Dom Perigon, no less-with a pink heart-shaped card that said "For us, my Jonathan." He read it three times—feeling as if he were tasting the champagne already.

On the way to her room he heard some unsettling noises, the kind of noises a person hurrying and carrying something clumsy would make, but decided not to say anything to Lillian. Not when his consummation was at stake with his first, and undoubtedly last, world famous celebrity, the incomparable Lillian Glass.

... Some things worked out well, others not as well. Despite his anxieties he opened the champagne bottle well, nothing substantial spilled, they laughed, they drank and kissed—it was their happiest moment. His lovemaking, on the other hand, was more pedestrian than he would have hoped, and he had no one to blame but himself—he'd just been too intimidated to be spontaneous. She'd certainly been generous, saying all the right things and more but he didn't think she enjoyed it very much except when he finally allowed himself to come. Still, nothing catastrophic happened, which is essentially all you could hope for the first time.

Afterwards he lay next to her holding her hand, which was nice. They were silent for a minute, he asked her a question then realized she was sleeping and softly, almost politely, snoring. He got out of bed, picked up a candle, carried it to the bed and stared at her. She looked strangely innocent with her eyes closed, her face older looking, of course, without her makeup but still beautiful and mysterious. He suddenly felt ashamed of his spying, returned the candle to the bed table and lay down next to her. The biggest mystery to him was why she wanted him.

Suddenly she opened her eyes and stared right at him.

"Are you alright angel?" she said.

"Yes."

"I dreamed you were looking at me, were you?"

"Yes, I was."

"Was it alright what you saw?"

"Of course it was beautiful," he said. "Go back to sleep." She shut her eyes again.

"Please don't look at me like that again. I told you I'm not to be viewed after midnight—certainly not without my makeup."

"I'm sorry."

"Will you promise not to?" she said with her eyes still shut.

"Yes, absolutely."

"People are so alone when they sleep."

"I know."

"They're alone when they're awake too, but it's worse when they sleep. All their fears multiply, mine do anyway. I think about Michael ... and many things. Sleep has never been an easy thing for me. It's like the hardest part I have to play and really I can't play it at all, not without help from my pillow or from whomever I'm with, angel, because the slightest thing can ruin it. Do you think you understand?"

"You can trust me never to do it again."

"So really, in spite of everything, when you looked at me you saw something that was maybe a little beautiful?"

"Something a lot beautiful."

"That's why we're together don't you think—because you still see something beautiful in me and I do in you too. Isn't that the truth about us, darling?"

"Yes, I think it is."

"Oh thank you, angel. I love you," she said, closing her eyes again.

"I love you, too," Jonathan said.

The phone rang. It was Hummel.

"It's over," Hummel said. "It's all over."

"No interruptions?"

"For a second I heard someone walking."

"Shit!"

"Don't worry, they didn't say anything. It was probably her new screw getting a drink or something but nothing happened. It's all good. Relax."

"OK. Get rid of your keys and your phone."

"Get rid of yours too," Hummel said.

"I'll call you tomorrow from my new one. Adios."

Kenneth opened the window and screamed into the wind, surprised to discover it was misting. It was a happy scream like he used to feel when he scored a touchdown in high school or when Gina did him just right. Well, he wouldn't be playing football anytime soon but he could celebrate with Gina when he got back to their apartment in Oxnard. They hadn't had sex in a long time and besides, that way he wouldn't have to explain anything because he knew she'd sense something and start asking questions, she always did. The only thing that could keep her from talking about it was if he started making love right away. He reached into his coat pocket, withdrew a Viagra and swallowed it. A half hour from now when he got home it would already be working.

Then he felt a panic about what he'd done, as if the wind had blown it into him. He shut the window. He was in the department store again in another special section where he'd have to find the exit sign. Immediately he began reviewing the arguments in his favor. They didn't know he had a key or knew the security combination. He'd refused to take the key from Lillian. Also, he had an alibi for when he wasn't working which the mileage in his car would confirm. He'd driven home after work and his collect call to Gina he'd make as soon as he left Santa Barbara would prove that. Finally, the loss of the painting would only lower her collection a million or two and was undoubtedly insured anyway. She'd still be worth well over one-hundred million so no one would be hurt by this. Even the cops would soon be bored.

Ten miles later he spotted a pay phone in Carpenteria and called Gina collect.

"It's me. The party's over."

"Is everything all right? You sound weird."

"I'm fine. Everything's fine."

"How was the party?"

"Typical."

"Was Eric West there?"

"Yuh, he was there."

"Will you tell me all about it when you get home?"

He promised he would. She loved hearing about what all the movie stars he waited on were wearing or talking about. Then he said, "Listen to me. When I get home I want you naked except for your leather jacket and I want you on your knees in bed."

"Really?"

"Yes, really. I'll be there in twenty minutes, maybe twenty-five," he said as he realized he still had to dispose of the key and the phone. There was a strip of sand and then the ocean about a hundred yards in front of him with no one in it. He may as well do it now.

Things were getting better, he could already feel the wind that had been roaring inside him diminish to a kind of manageable buzz. Good old Gina—by the time he did her and had a glass of wine he'd be out of the department store. He pictured doing her from behind again, imagining he was Brian Kove. He could already feel the first tinglings of his Viagra. So what if he usually thought of her as a young boy? So what if he'd imagined Lillian sometimes as a man too. Who had to know? He didn't have to impress *himself,* did he?

He kicked off his shoes, took off his socks and rolled his pants up to his knees, looking around himself again, as he walked straight ahead into the water. First he threw away the key but held the phone a little longer. Goodbye Queen Lillian, goodbye Hollywood, he said to himself.

Anyway, you couldn't really have a career that meant anything if you died, it was an illusion to think you could. He knew that now. You couldn't have anything, not even a phone, because knowing that you would die drove you crazy, just knowing that you and whatever work you did would completely vanish. He threw the phone as far as he could, watching it sink instantly like a pebble. Lillian knew the same thing as he did—it was one of the secret things they had in common. It was why she kept distracting herself with new lovers like Jonathan, he thought, and with making one movie after another. Workaholics and careerists were just people who couldn't bear thinking. Just addicts like everyone else only with a Good Housekeeping Stamp of Approval.

The black water was surprisingly warm and inviting. It, too, was addictive—maybe the most addictive part of God's department store (the master addict Himself who addicted you to the whole universe). The only difference was God always got His way or at least always called you in. Maybe he'd surprise God for once and come back to His water soon, on his own terms. Come back for good and rest from everything cause the water wasn't an illusion—it was wet and when it was ready it could fold over you forever.

Malena Watrous

November May Day

The day after the funeral our house smells like a florist's shop. Arrangements of flowers cover the kitchen counter so completely that it looks like we must have wiped out the floral stock of the whole town, taken every last rose, carnation, and daisy for sale. The kitchen is pale with autumn morning sunlight. Cut glass vases throw argyle patterns on the wall, and shadowy grids slide out from under baskets. Most of the flowers seem manufactured rather than grown. A fist-sized, silver, helium-filled balloon strains against the ribbon that grips the narrow throat of a vase of carnations. Green wires twist around their stems to keep the dyed buds propped up. I need those, a corset and an anchor, something to keep me upright, something to keep me from wafting away.

My mom doesn't hear me behind her. She stands facing the window that looks out at the front yard, drinking tea from a mug. There's this sleep-flattened spot at the back of her hair, and the hem of her sweater is hiked up, tucked into the back of her waistband, exposing her bottom. I want to go to her and smooth her hair down, pull the sweater out of her pants to cover her up, but she might take this the wrong way, as a sign that she embarrasses me, and she might be right, even though there's no one around to be embarrassed in front of.

She leans on the edge of the kitchen sink and stares out at the garden. The window is open and I can see the patch of sunflowers my father planted a few years ago, standing tall as people, heads angled toward the house as if trying to look in. It's early November and the first frost hasn't struck Oregon yet, so the sunflowers in the yard are wilting gradually, their petals turning stiff and brown. My mother told me once, in confidence, that my father planted that patch of sunflowers just for me, in honor of a sloppy Van Gogh imitation I'd painted. When he was out of earshot, she'd say, "Aren't the sunflowers your father planted for you beautiful? Go tell him how much you like them." She is a natural teacher, unable to turn it off at home. She often told me and my father what to say to each other, which actions and gifts required special thanks and when apologies were due. Now that he is gone, so is our con-versational stand-by. We will have to talk about other things. We will have to learn to talk to each other.

When I flew back from college three days ago, my grandparents met me at the airport, and when the taxi brought us home the house was already filled to bursting with flowers and people, friends and relatives I hadn't seen since I was a kid. They took care of things in shifts, and a larger crowd followed us back home after the funeral. Guests sat on the gray leather couch that I avoided coming close to, its cool skin the last my father touched, and helped themselves to the spread of food covering the coffee table. He'd made that table in his basement shop, and its top, a slab of marble formed around fossilized sea shells, was strewn with cracker pieces, hacked slices of ham and bowls of creamy dip forming thick skins as hours ticked by. "Did you see it coming?" I heard them ask each other. "Did they?" Meaning us. People still filled the upstairs when I went to bed, but this morning they are all gone, the house alarmingly clean, empty of evidence except for all these flowers. This is the first time my mother and I have been alone in the house where my father killed himself. For the first time I can remember, I feel shy around her.

"Mom," I say. "How are you?" Since I came home from college three days ago we have been greeting each other over and over. I don't know what else to say to stir up the molecules of silence that keep settling like dust between us. She turns around, sets her mug down and opens her arms. Our breasts flatten between us, her soft cheek presses against mine, and I smell the tang of her scalp, the chamomile on her breath. I am so completely enveloped that I feel myself disappearing, so that when she says, "You are all I have. We are all we have," her voice comes to me from a distance. She releases me and then grips my shoulders, holds me at arm's length and looks into my face. "I want you to know that I am going to be okay," she says in her most serious, almost punishing ele-mentary school teacher voice. "You need to know that I would never do this. You do not have to worry about me." I am limp, immobilized, a kitten dangled by the scruff of the neck. I hadn't known that I needed to hear her say this. Needles of unexpected relief and shame prick my eyes, but I don't want to cry in front of her. I can cry all I want when I'm alone.

"How are *you?*" she asks, meaning, Are you going to be okay? Meaning, Will I still recognize you after this is over? Of course this will never be over.

"I don't know," I say. "I'm sad."

"I hated calling you so much," she says. "Why didn't he give us warning? Why didn't he tell us how unhappy he was? I keep thinking I should've seen it coming."

"You were gone all summer teaching," I say.

"Not all summer," she says. "Only six weeks. Should I feel guilty for that?"

"Of course not," I tell her. "That's not what I meant. But when you called and you were crying, I knew what you were going to say before you said it."

"You were in shock," she says, and I don't want to argue with her.

When my mom was away last summer, teaching at a history camp for elementary school kids, my dad and I were alone together in the house for the first time. He had retired from his job as a doctor in order to try and be an inventor but he wasn't used to having so much time with nothing specific to do, and he was needy in a way that scared me, unable to be by himself. He followed me around the house, asked for my company on every errand and chore, wanted to come along even when I was going out with friends. Later, in private, they would want to know what was wrong with him. I didn't bother asking what they meant. The blues of his eyes looked shattered and glued back together, his lips and cheeks bleached of color. He was always either too hot or too cold, complaining that he was having difficulty modulating his body temperature. The sadder he got, the more scientific he sounded, the more distant. "Stick to your hypotheses," he'd advise me cryptically. "You could drive yourself crazy questioning every decision you try to make, trying to look into the future to predict the outcome before it happens."

I was working at a movie theater, and on weekday nights I got pairs of free tickets to any show in town, so we saw every movie that came out, even the animated pictures and the NC-17 movies. He was always the one who suggested that we go see a movie, but every time I glanced over at him he'd been looking down, picking out the burnt kernels from the bag of home-microwaved popcorn I hid in my backpack. On our way home, we'd stop at Burger King and order the ninety-nine cent Whopper, no fries or soda because he said that was where they made their money, ripping you off for things that cost them almost nothing. We'd order our Whoppers to-go from a cashier who had been one of his patients and who never forgot to mention how much she'd appreciated the bouquet of flowers that he brought her when she was recovering from surgery. He was famous for his garden. When it was in full bloom, he'd often bring lavish jars of flowers to the hospital where he worked to present to the nurses and decorate the rooms of his favorite patients. He couldn't remember their names but he always knew which flowers they liked best.

A shiny black van pulls up in front of the house and a man in a delivery uniform walks toward the front door, carrying a vase of deep blue irises in one hand and in the other a paper-wrapped spray of yellow and brown orchids, the blooms fluttering on the ends of the stems like moths. "More flowers?" my mom says. "We already have so many, I don't know where to put them all." While she answers the door I stay in the kitchen, opening the refrigerator although I know I won't be able to eat anything. Inside are three large platters, two turkeys and a ham scalloped with pineapple scales. They look like models of ancient mounds, repositories of secrets.

"Sign here," I hear the delivery man say. He sounds like he's in his early twenties, around my age. I don't want him to see me, in case we went to high school together and he wants to know why I'm home from school. I hide inside the refrigerator door.

"I've got two arrangements for you, ma'am," he says to my mother. "You must've done something good."

"No, I didn't," my mother says, but the man won't quit. "Well then, somebody must really love you."

"Yes," my mother says. "I guess that's true."

"Let me guess," he says, "is it your birthday? No? you got a promotion? No . . . You had a grandchild? No?"

"I lost my husband," she says.

"Oh God, I'm sorry," he says. "I feel like an idiot."

"It's okay," she says. "You didn't know."

"What happened? Was he sick?" Don't ask that, I think. Never ask how. You don't want to know the answer. I take another step into the refrigerator, pressing into the cold, breathing in the smell of pineapple and mustard and ham.

"Yes," she says. "He was sick, but he wouldn't admit it. He didn't ask for help." There is a silence, and then I know she's crying because I can hear him offer her a handkerchief.

"He do it himself?" the man asks. How can he know that?

"Yes," she says. "He did." I know that I should go out and wrap an arm around her, shepherd her back in, but my legs are heavy and useless. I have to hold onto the refrigerator shelf to keep myself upright.

"Are you the one who found him?" the man asks.

"Yes," she says. "It was so awful. You have no idea."

"You can't get the picture out of your mind," he says. "I had a brother who did himself. He went to the reservoir and dove off the rocks, even though it was the end of summer and there were maybe three feet of water left where he went it. When he didn't come home, I knew where he'd be. We always went there when we wanted to get away from things. I found him, too."

"What did you do?" my mom says.

"I kept busy," he says. "I took another job."

"Did that get the picture out of your mind?"

"No, but it's faded. Here," he says. "Take my handkerchief. Go ahead and cry if you need to. I've seen it all before."

After a few moments of silence, I look out the kitchen window and see my mom and the deliveryman hugging. She has her head on his shoulder and he is petting the back of her hair, smoothing that sleep-flattened spot, doing the things I should be doing.

"You got someone with you?" he asks. "You need company?"

"My daughter's here," she says, straightening up again. "Thank you." She holds his handkerchief out to him and he says, "Keep it. And don't forget your flowers."

I hear the door close, and when she rejoins me in the kitchen I can't look at her. We both stare out the window and watch the delivery truck as it becomes small, then vanishes over the crest of the hill. It's windy out. The sunflowers sway like buildings in an earthquake.

"Why did you tell that guy what happened?" I say.

"He asked," she says. "Why? Should I be ashamed? Should I keep it a secret?" She's red-faced, angry in a way I've never seen her look before.

"No," I say. "But he was a stranger." She is still wearing the makeup that one of her friends put on her before the funeral yesterday, circles of mauve blush on each cheek. She's holding the vase of roses in one hand and the cone of orchids cradled in her other elbow. I take them from her and look in the cupboard for something to put them in, but all the vases are all already being used. I pull the carnations from their vase, and they come out with a soaking green foam pad clinging to the bottom of their stems.

"I feel invaded," she says, turning to the window. "I can't stand the smell of these funeral arrangements."

"So throw them away," I say. "We don't have to keep them." At first I don't think she's listening to me, but finally she says, "No, I couldn't do that. People spent a lot of money on these flowers."

"He would've despised them," I say. "They're so fake." I stick the orchids into the vase and tweak them in different directions.

"I don't want to be in this house," she says, "but I don't know where to go. What do people do on days like this?"

"I don't think they do anything," I say.

"I'm not good at doing nothing," she says, and she's right. She is not someone who lies on the couch and stares at the ceiling when she's upset. She's a person who takes comfort from routine and activity, often doing more than one thing at the same time, as if her energy, like her capacity to love, were in surplus. She raised me to be the same way, never to be still. When I was a child and I was lonely, or bored, or sad, she'd suggest practical cures. Get a new haircut. Take an art class. How could she understand a depression like my father's? How could she live with it?

"Why don't we give the arrangements away?" I suggest.

"Who could we give them to?" she asks. "Everyone we know gave them to us."

"Let's give them to strangers," I say. "We could drive around the neighborhood and leave them on people's doorsteps, sort of like May Day." I remember celebrating May Day as a kid, getting in trouble for picking neighbors' flowers and then leaving them in front of their own doors. I'm surprised when she looks at me and smiles.

"It might be a good idea," she says. "Sort of a tribute to him. If he were able to see us, he'd have gotten a kick out of something like this, don't you think?" It bothers me to her talk about him so easily in the past tense, but I bite my tongue.

I pack the arrangements of flowers into his hatchback, filling the back seat with baskets and vases, making one trip after another from the kitchen out to the car, which still smells like him, like garlic and sweat and fertilizer. When I run out of space in back, I stash bouquets in the foot space under the dashboard. Bending down, I am startled by a warped reflection of my face in the stainless steel stick shift knob, bulb-nosed and squirrel-cheeked. A year or so ago, my father removed the car's original, leather stick shift knob and replaced it with an artificial hip, a stainless steel ball joint. I remember when he first showed it to me I told him that it was gross. He said, "It's not gross at all. It's extremely elegant." That year, he was trying to invent a new kind of artificial hip, one with a larger range of motion, and he collected used ones to study their designs. My mother had called me at college and reported that she was worried about him, that he wasn't sleeping, that he stayed up all night sketching and welding, that he was spending thousands of dollars to have products designs made and patented and getting few responses from the manufacturers he pitched his idea to. I said that he had always been ambitious, that she shouldn't worry so much. I cover the joint with my hand, blocking my reflection, feeling its cold solidity. I wonder if this knob is one he invented or something he excavated from somebody's body.

Every time I return to the house, my mother is waiting at the front door with two more arrangements in her arms for me. "Don't you want to keep any of them?" I ask.

"No," she says. "Let's give them all away."

By the time we've cleared out the house, the car is so full that its windows are entirely blocked by climbing foliage. Water trickles from baskets balanced on the dashboard, dripping into the glove compartment. A precarious line of vases is tucked in the crack between the two front seats, more at each of our feet.

"I can't see very well," my mother says after she takes the driver's seat. "Can you clear the back window a little?"

"Not really," I say. "There's not any space left. Let's hurry and get rid of some of these arrangements. Then you'll be able to see better."

"We have to go to a different neighborhood," she says. "We have to make sure we're giving them to strangers. I don't want anyone we know to see us doing this."

It's a work day and the streets are empty, quiet. My mother drives down the hill and takes a right onto another residential street where my piano teacher used to live, then another right onto a street that's unfamiliar to me. After a few minutes of driving we are in an unknown neighborhood that looks just like ours but where the streets have new names. Most of the houses are boxy, made of unpainted wood, Frank Lloyd Wright knock-offs designed to blend in with the landscape. The pavement on the street is torn up, an obstacle course of potholes, and as she drives, the water in the vases sloshes and one topples over. I keep my hands on the baskets on the dashboard so that they won't slide into my lap. My feet are clammy from the spilled water that's soaking into my shoes. As we pass a white Victorian with dark green trim and turrets, I say "Let's stop here. I like this house."

"I guess we're far enough from home," she says, shifting the car into park.

I select a small arrangement of purple lilacs and peach roses that stick out from a basket like pins from a pincushion. It looks like something a flower girl would carry, like something someone who lived in a giant dollhouse like this one would love. A porch swing hangs from rusting chains that creak when the wind makes it swing. I tiptoe up the front steps and press my face to the ground floor bay window. There are blue cushions piled from the floor to the window ledge, and on them a magazine and a bowl containing a few bites of ice cream, not yet melted. I leave the flowers balanced on the porch swing's slatted seat, then run back down the stairs.

"Where should we leave the next one?" she asks.

"You choose," I say, and she drives a few more blocks before stopping in front of a bunker of a home, sided with angular stones. It looks like a comic book castle. For this place I select a spiky arrangement of birds of paradise. When I peer into the rectangular window set in their front door, I see stacks of boxes. I hope they're moving in instead of moving out. The flowers could be a housewarming.

My mom and I take turns pointing out houses we want to give flowers to. We avoid the Frank Lloyd Wright knock-offs and stick to the homes that stand out, that don't fit in with their neighbors: an adobe mesa with a matching adobe creche in the front yard, a perfectly square apartment building with three stacked balconies and only sliding glass doors for windows, a turquoise shack guarded by a glossy black dog with angular hips and countable ribs. I am disappointed when he doesn't lunge at me, doesn't even get up, his tail slapping the driveway while I trespass.

"Just think about it," I say when I get back to the car after dropping off one of the last few arrangements. "The people who get these bouquets are going to assume they're from people they already know. Husbands are going to be jealous and think their wives are having secret affairs."

"Not necessarily," she says. "Their wives will probably think that the flowers came from their husbands."

"Right," I say. "And when their husbands come home, their wives will be all thankful, and their husbands will lie and say, 'You're welcome. Happy anniversary, dear,' except they'll be months off. Then their wives will get suspicious."

"I hope not," she says. "Maybe the people who get the flowers won't be married at all. They'll think the have secret admirers."

"Single women are going to wonder about their bosses and leave sexual harassment policies out on their desks," I say. "Widows will write anonymous cards to thank the mailmen, start leaving homemade cookies in their mailboxes."

"That's terrible," she says. "We have to stop doing this."

"I was joking," I say, glancing over at her. "I'm sure people will be happy." She is fingering one of the hammered silver cat earrings that I gave her a long time ago. I wonder if she only puts them on when I'm home or if she really likes them.

"I'm a widow now," she says.

"I'm sorry," I say.

"Widow. What a terrible word."

She brings the car to a stop right in the middle of the street and brings a fist to her mouth, biting her knuckles. "Oh God," she says, shaking her head from side to side, her face bunched in pain. "Please, oh God. No." I reach for her hand but she doesn't give it to me, wrapping her arms around her shoulders instead. "Mom?" I ask. "What's wrong? What?" I brace myself. This is the moment, I think, the one when I see her break for the first time, when I have to take over, take care of her for a change, tell her the right things to put her back together again. For now though I just watch her, trying to think of what those right things might be. She's wearing a sweatshirt covered in appliquéd autumn leaves and the cotton is wet in strange places, stained yellow where she brushed against stamen. Bruised petals are strewn across her lap. She looks beautiful and deranged and I am a little afraid of this new mother.

"The cards," she says.

"The what?"

"The condolence cards. We left the damn condolence cards in the flowers."

"Oh," I say, exhaling deeply. "Well that's not such a big deal. Who cares? They all say the same thing. Sorry for your loss, you're in our hearts, etcetera."

"The thank you notes!" she says. "How can I write thank you notes if I don't know who to write them to?"

"Come on. You don't have to write thank you notes for funeral flowers. You have other things on your mind. People will understand."

"You're wrong," she says. "You do have to write thank you notes. It's a ritual, a way of appreciating what people have done for you. Didn't you get anything from me?" The question stings, even though I know she didn't mean it in that way.

"We have to retrace our route," she says. "We have to try and find those cards. Our names are on all of them. We could get caught so easily."

"Caught?" I say. "This is ridiculous. I can't believe the things you worry about."

"Someone has to worry," she says. As she drives, going only ten miles per hour or so, she sits on the edge of her seat with her face right up against the windshield, looking from the left side of the street to the right, from house to house like she's reading them. We keep coming to dead-ends, having to reverse around cul-de-sacs. We are lost in our own town. Most of the houses were designed to blend in with the hillsides, to lose themselves behind pine trees, so they are set far enough back from the road that we can't even see their front doors, let alone the flowers possibly left in front of them. After five minutes of driving in circles I recognize the green and white Victorian.

"Stop here," I say to my mom, and I jump out of the car as it is still rolling, duck under the first floor bay window ledge and see the basket of lilacs and roses still on the porch swing. I root through the thorny stems and pluck the envelope the size of a business card from a tall, two-pronged plastic fork. I bring the card back to my mother and drop it in her lap. She reads the card, then holds it to her chest as if absorbing its dose of sympathy by osmosis, straight to her heart.

"That arrangement was from one of his patients," she says, starting to drive again. "He gave her a new knee. She hadn't been able to walk for ten years before that. She's just devastated." I don't say anything. Unlike her, I don't feel comforted when other people, strangers, stake their claim to him or share their similar experiences. I want to be alone with mine.

"There's one. I remember this house," she says, stopping in front of a miniature Tudor. A vase is tipped on its side on the welcome mat, and lipstick-colored roses spill across the stoop. "Hothouse flowers," my father would've called them. The card is damp, wavy, but I bring it to my mother anyhow, and she manages to read the blurred writing. "Those were from Señora Pera," she says, her voice high and tremulous. "She was your junior high school Spanish teacher. Remember?"

"Not really," I lie.

"Well you enjoyed Señora Pera's class enormously," she says. "Maybe you could write her thank you card."

"I'm not writing any thank you cards," I say. "I'm not grateful right now."

In fact, I do remember Señora Pera. I'd seen her in the back of the church at the funeral, dressed like an Almodovar mourner in a black lace mantilla and elbow-length gloves. She stood apart from the small Oregon women in their Eastery, floral dresses, and I appreciated her sense of occasion, though I was too embarrassed to approach her afterwards. I remember making fajitas in her Spanish class, roasting peppers over Bunsen burners borrowed from the chemistry labs, then eating them by candlelight until the smoke alarm put a stop to the romantic meal. She was also a Flamenco dancer, and she tried to teach us how, painstakingly coaxing our hands and feet to move in different directions, telling us that it was only this kind of opposition that generated anything real, that love required tension. My mother and father and I had gone to see her dance, once, and she'd told me the next day that my papa was *"muy guapo,"* my mother *"muy simpatica."* I don't want to share memories with my mom right now. If we get started, she'll want to keep going back, and all roads lead back to him, and to share means to give up a portion, and I just can't do that.

Instead, I say to stop in front of a dark wooden house I remember—its siding lacy with lichen—that juts out of the rocky face of the hill like the prow of a ship. I climb a flight of stairs set to the right of the long, steep driveway. At the top, a small, circular window like a nautical porthole is set in the garage door. In front of this door, I see a clutch of sunflowers in a big canning jar. I reach to feel for a card among the stems, but there isn't one. That's when I know for sure that these weren't funeral flowers. They're sunflowers from our own garden, the ones my father planted for me.

I hear a motor turning over inside the garage. The door climbs into the ceiling revealing a speedboat mounted on a trailer, pointy as an arrow, aiming at me. The boat's cherry-red paint is flecked with mica that glitters faintly in the dim garage light. It has creamy leather seats. A man sits in the front seat, turning the key on the ignition. Standing in his path, I feel an irrational surge of relief every time the engine won't start for him. He looks ready to plow me under, make chum of my flesh. He cuts the ignition and says, "Hey there. Whatcha doing with my flowers?"

"Your flowers?" I grip the jar with my left hand, trying to yank it off. "I'm sorry," I say, "but these are my flowers. It must look strange, me being on your property, but these are mine. I left them here a while ago."

"I know," he says. "I was watching you before, through the window, and I thought, hey, what a sweet thing to get pretty flowers from a pretty girl. You made my day. Now you want to unmake it?" One of his front teeth is rimmed in gold, a thin band that wraps around the tooth, and when he grins, it winks at me.

"It was a mistake," I tell him. "I left them here by accident."

"Pretty steep driveway to climb by accident," he says.

This man is in a grounded boat. I could easily get away, without even running, keeping my dignity and the flowers. My mom is sitting in the car at the foot of that steep driveway, barely out of sight. And yet I feel immobilized, my legs stiff, jointless.

"I just hate to part with things," the man says. "What are you going to give me instead?"

"I'm not going to give you anything!" I am suddenly yelling, loud enough that my mom can probably hear me. "You want to know where these flowers came from? Fine. They're condolence flowers. We got them for my father's funeral. You want to know how he died? He killed himself, that's how. He gassed himself in the living room. He filled a scuba tank with gas, I don't know what kind or who agreed to fill it for him, but it worked. He put a bag on his head to make sure none of the fumes went to waste. My mom had to find him lying on the couch when she came home from work. He must've been planning for weeks. You still want the flowers? Fine. Just keep them, you fucking fuck."

"Jesus," he says, holding up both palms in surrender. "I was just playing with you. Just teasing. Take your flowers. Go on. Aw, don't cry."

He starts turning the key in the ignition, drowning out all possible attempts on my part to continue yelling at him. I shake the fist that's in the jar, and finally it falls off of my hand, landing on the pavement and spilling daisies everywhere. I pick up the jar, and when I aim at the man in the boat, he shields his face. At the last moment I throw it low and it shatters against the side of the boat.

Back in the car, my mother takes my face in both hands. It's clear that she heard everything. She kisses my eyelids and I let her. "It's okay," she says. "Shhh." I pull free and stick my head out the window so that the wind will dry my cheeks, but more tears keep leaking out of my eyes. Somehow, the idea of crying together, sharing that too, makes me feel sadder and lonelier than I can stand. "Do you want to drive home?" she asks. "It might make you feel better to do something, focus on something for a moment." I nod. "Just scoot over," she says, sliding her hips to the edge of my seat and pressing down. For a moment, before we finish switching places, I am sitting in her lap again, and it's just as I remember it. For a moment, she wraps her arms around me, pinning me to her, and I can almost believe that I am that small, that everything is still waiting up ahead.

In a week, after I return to school and leave her alone in the house where he died and she found him, some neighbor kid she'll hire to weed the garden won't pay attention when she tells him to keep it the same only tidied up, and he will mistakenly pull the hairy stalks of the sunflowers out of the soil, before the black pelt at the center of each flower has time to unclench and release its seeds. Next summer, when the flowers don't grow back, she will hire the same kid to return and sprinkle drugstore sunflower seed packets into the soil. And when I come home for a visit—which will be unexpectedly harder than the last—feeling shy and apprehensive, withdrawing from her aggressively cheerful advances, she'll just be trying to makes things okay when she says, "Look! The sunflowers you father planted for you came back!" They will have orange petals and brown centers instead of yellow petals and black centers like the ones I remember. I will be outraged by what I'll perceive as her deception, which will seem manipulative rather than generous. I will want to retaliate by saying cruel, regrettable things, by telling her that they were never my sunflowers, that she made up the whole story about him planting them for me because she wanted us to be a closer family than we were, the kind that paid real attention to each other, that talked about real things. I'll want to tell her that she should be more honest and admit that she must have seen it coming, I certainly had, that we were both guilty of pretending, telling ourselves that he was just out of sorts, going through a rough time, a midlife crisis, when the truth was right in front of our eyes. He was shattered and we knew it but we didn't know how to fix him so we just stood by, hoping he'd mend on his own. I will rant. I will say some but not all of these terrible things, and later I won't remember which ones exactly. But no matter what I say, she will not be baited. She will not retaliate by telling me that I was the one who spent that last summer alone with him, that I was the one who should've seen it coming, that at least I was spared the sight of it, of him, laid out on that couch with a tube in his mouth and a bag over his head.

What she will do instead is simply this. She will gesture out the window, to the patch of petite orange sunflowers, heads bright and perky on their slim stalks, and she will say, "I don't know what you're talking

236

about. These *are* the flowers your father planted for you. They came back." Strangely, then, they will begin to look more familiar, and I'll wonder if it's my memory that's been supplanted, not the flowers that I'll never be sure about, whether they're the same ones he planted, or if he even planted them for me to begin with.

Stephen Dixon

Phone Ring Two

Phone rings. What he'd want now was for it to be Dan. "Hello," Stu would say and Dan say "Stu?" with the "u" drawn out. "How's it going?" and Stu would say "As Mom used to say, 'Okay, I guess.'" "Yeah? What's wrong?" I've been in the dumps a bit lately. Sometimes, I'm telling you, hate as I do to say this, but taking care of Janice can get too tough for me. I don't usually mind the day-to-day stuff, getting her up, exercising her in bed, in and out of chairs, getting her on the john and so on, and same in reverse the before-bed stuff, and during the day too, all the work. Cooking, cleaning. Okay, I've got it down to a science you could say. But one mishap, something goes wrong, more work than I'm expecting to do—my science gone awry, I'm saying—and it gets to me, and sometimes I go a little crazy. Let's face it, as Mom also used to say, I get tired faster and I'm weaker because I'm getting old and I know that contributes to the mishaps. I can't lift her or set her down as easily as I used to, for one thing." "Come on, compared to me you're a youngster." "But you're in much better shape. You run and exercise a lot more." "Because I'm retired and have the time and have been running like an idiot the last forty years. But you're in good shape, or last time I saw you, and those things don't change so fast." "I must sound awful; because I don't mean to complain." "Why, why shouldn't you? Let's face it, as you say Mom used to say—I don't remember her saying it but I'll take your word—you've a lot to do. Janice, the kids, house, your schoolwork, writing, and that damnable van. You're doing fine, considering. Just slow down, take a breather now and then. Don't try to get everything done at once when it becomes too hard to and is depressing you. It'd depress me, much worse than you. Little here, there, it all gets done eventually, and if there's anything I can do—anything, I swear to you; I'd love to and I've got all this time—don't hesitate to call me. I'll drive right down. But it's not easy for you, that I know. And how you've handled it so far I really admire you for." "Oh God, I feel like such a drip now, as if I asked you to say that." "Don't be such a dope."

Phone rings. Or he'd want to call Dan. Tell him for one thing how hard things have been for him lately, just to tell someone. Doesn't want to tell his wife because it's mostly because of her he's so exhausted and he doesn't want to make her feel worse than she already does. Guilty; worse. So he calls Dan. If he could he'd say "Hi. Just checking in with you to see how you and your family are." Dan usually said "Great, great, no problems, everything going well," and then would tell him what some of his kids were doing and then a couple of things about himself. Reading a lot. "Mornings, afternoons, evenings till I'm too tired to—it could be the wine—so I take an hour's nap in my reading chair here, and then later in bed before sleep I read some more." "I remember Dad," Dan said recently. "I never saw a book or magazine in his hands except a dental journal till he got sick and was forced to give up his practice. Then he started reading books, mostly novels. It was that or staring at walls and driving Mom nuts. I've always read but nothing as much as I do today. But give Dad a book—any book—and, unlike me, he'd read it through even if he didn't like it. Because if he thought you bought the book—the trick, to keep him reading, was to make him think you did—he didn't want to be wasting good money, as he called it." Finally finished *Gargantua*. He was about three-quarters through it a few days before he died, he said in a phone call. "I started it I don't know how many times in my life. The new translation you gave me worked. It was slow going, though, so I'm not moving on to Book Two. Next up is *Moby-Dick*. Another novel you shouldn't go through life not having read. I better get to it soon because you also shouldn't go through life not having read *Bleak House*, *War and Peace*, *Brothers Karamazov*, Dante's *Inferno*—why is it always Dante's *Inferno* and not Tolstoy's *War and Peace*?—*Ulysses* and *The Golden Bowl*, and how much time does a guy my age have left? Those seven ought to do it. You've read them all?" And he said "Yeah, and *War and Peace* twice," though he'd never read *Bleak House* and the *Golden Bowl* and had only read half of the *Inferno* and neither of the other two in the trio and last year, for the second time, couldn't get through *Don Quixote*, which Dan had read several times, and the *Karamazov* he'd read when he was around eighteen was abridged he learned more than forty years later when he took some of the books from her mother's library after she died. "And what are you talking about? You've plenty of time then, and they all read fast, so add *The Magic Mountain* to your list. By the time you're done with those we should be able to come up with a few more big ones that neither of us has read." Still distributing food to the homeless twice a week. "Gets me out of the house for a few hours, which is good for my marriage, plus short walks and long runs and swimming in the indoor pool in town. And of course, reading the *Times* through every day, everything but the ads and the TV listings." "What about your writing project? Started the book yet?" "Which one? I had so many I wanted to do and a few I even did a little fiddling around with." "*Our Gang.* The one about our old Brooklyn neighborhood and all the friends you left there when we moved to Manhattan. What they did with their lives the last sixty-some years, those still living, and whatever you could dig up about the ones who died. You said it'd be twice as easy to write than the novels you also had all sorts of ideas for, since you'd be using your reporting skills." "Ah, I dropped it along with the others, though that one came as close as any to being written." "Why? You should pursue it. It was a great, and it'd really give you something to do the next few years. And if you put yourself down solely as a writer when you do your taxes, and maybe Melody as you researcher and typist, you can take off all the expenses for the book, travel and otherwise—tell them one old Brooklyn pal you wanted to interview now lived in Paris—on the Schedule C form." "No, I found out I'm no book writer. When I first retired I could have done one. Now, anything that smacks of that kind of labor would cut into the comfortable inertia rut I've finally achieved after around fifty-five years of nothing but working. But what about you? We've only talked of me," and Stu would say "Same as always. We're fine, with occasional major setbacks and lots of minor frustrations, but nothing that doesn't end or we can't live with. And just five more years and three months and I'll be retired too."

Phone. "Will someone answer it?" he yells from his work table in the bedroom. "I'm busy." Nobody picks up the phone. He jumps on the fifth or sixth ring and says hello. "Uncle Stu?" "Say, how's it going, Manny? What's up?" "Nothing good, I'm afraid. I've very bad news to tell you, which I don't want to but it has to come from someone." "It's your dad." He goes through the house after, shouting her wife's name. Opens the kitchen door to the outside and yells "Janice, you around?" Then re-

berry in season. It was always dark by the time they sat down to eat, all of them around a long picnic table behind the house. The steaks cooked just right—medium rare and charred on the outside—and if you wanted more you just went to the steak plate and sliced some. Usually, friends of Melody and Dan's would be over with their kids. All the children would make up a play that day and rehearse it and then perform it for the adults that night by candlelight. His parents always had a great time too. Then he'd walk his father to the bedroom his parents shared—first a long stint on the toilet where Stu would hold him straight so he wouldn't fall off the seat—and say to him when he got him into bed and covered "A good day, huh? Different than the city." His father would say something like "It's always a treat to be here with my kids and grand-children. Dan's a great guy. Very generous, almost to a fault. What these dinners must set him back, not that I'm complaining, for they're deli-cious. But I'll be honest; he's nothing like me. Intellectual—he knows and talks so well about so many things, most of them slipping past me, though he doesn't mean to—and throws money around like it's confetti. Though he has no interest in money—that's the funny thing—but I hear his job pays a bundle, which is what you should be doing. And his wife's very nice. I almost like her more than I do my daughters, terrible as that is to say. You should find someone like her, though Jewish. And the air's so fresh here, the nights nice and cool. It was wonderful sitting outside today under the big shade tree in front. Your mother loves it up here also, I can tell. Dan was smart. Well, when wasn't he smart, but es-pecially with real estate. The Dobbs Ferry house, which I though he paid way too much for, but it now turns out he made a good deal. Then this place when the price was low, and now, he says, these beach houses have shot up sky high. I should've bought something like this forty years ago when you kids were still kids, but on Long Island in a community easier to get to and closer to our own background. Long Beach, which we liked, or a town like that. Could've got one dirt cheap on a nice street and it would've paid off twice over in our just not packing you kids off to camp every summer. Now it doesn't pay, and who's got the money? I'm old and sick and your mother's not getting any stronger, so just com-ing up here with you once or twice for a couple of nights every summer is enough for us. Though it would've been a nice thing to leave to you kids. But there were so many of you then, I thought, or at least we knew we were going to have more, so how would you ever had divided it up?" "We would have. We all got along. And now we're down to four, unfor-tunately, and Dan has his own summer place and wouldn't have liked

then go to the Hungarian Pastry Shop across the street, which I have been to, with you and your girls." Two months ago, during Stu's winter break, they arranged to go to the cathedral, walked around inside, sat up front awhile—"Very nice," Dan said, "and so peaceful for such a big busy place, but unfortunately, no music," and Stu said "What do you mean?" and Dan said "One of the times you were here you said you heard an organ recital and it reminded you of another time in a cathedral in Paris," and Stu said "Right, I forgot; Buxtehude, Bach, or at least I thought so, but why do I think I can recognize Buxtehude?" and Dan said "Why? You know a lot about music, so don't so hard on yourself"—and then went to the pastry shop for coffee. Stu suggested Dan take out food from the restaurant next door. "You love authentic Chinese food and this place is great." So they sat in the restaurant and waited while the food was being prepared. Dan refused a complimentary tea: "The old Riner trait: weak or too small a bladder; I'd have to pee halfway through the short drive home." After about fifteen minutes, when Stu saw Dan check his watch again, he said he felt lousy he'd suggested the takeout idea—"Now you'll probably get caught in rush-hour traffic," and Dan said "No big deal. I'll turn the news on, take my time. It's been worth it, believe me, finally seeing you after so long. And the food's got to be fresh and as good as you say if it takes this long to make." Their father, when Stu was a boy—Dan was already out of the house, in the army, then college—one Sunday a month would order out from a neighborhood Chinese-American restaurant chow mein and chop suey and fried rice and egg drop soup and always asked, or had Stu ask, if he was told to pick up the order, and which would embarrass him, for several extra bags of the dried noodles that came with the soup. Stu didn't like any of it except the fried rice. Too gooey, with vegetables like cooked celery and onions in it. When Dan was working in Washington the first time, he took Stu and several other people to Peking restaurant downtown. Jowses, or however they've spelled—Stu was impressed when Dan asked for them that way, one order steamed, the other fried—moo shu pork with pancakes, Peking duck, a dish with "Mongolian pot" in it, whole rockfish—"Two of you should eat the cheek meat. Go on, it's under the slit in the cheek, the sweetest meat in the fish. "What do I do with this?" Stu said after Dan dropped a pancake on everyone's plate and unfolded and spread it out with his chopsticks, and Dan said "First a little of that hoshin sauce there, spread it around. Next one of these scallion slivers, then the moo shu—serving a spoonful at the most or it gets sloppy—and roll it up this way and eat it with your hands." Japanese beer made from

home and I'll forget we ever spoke about this. Or I won't forget if you don't want me to. We'll talk about it as much as you want, and with anyone else—a friend, a therapist; you choose one and I'll pay for it—but please come home, please. This will kill me, losing you and Isaac both." "You won't lose him. I'm not stealing him. You'll see him plenty." She never came back. He granted her the divorce without a fuss, said he'd give her whatever she asked for—the house, car, half his salary. She said she only wanted a small amount of money for Isaac every month and, way down the road, his college tuition and expenses there. She moved to New Mexico the following year. Dan flew out once or twice a year to see Isaac for a few days. He also saw him whenever she came East to see her parents, and had him two weeks every summer for about fifteen years. Isaac's now forty-four, looks just like Dan, his sister Harriet said. She saw him at the funeral. The memorial, rather, organized by a few of Dan's former colleagues in TV. Stu didn't go, and there was no funeral. Dan was cremated and his ashes were scattered in the Hudson. That's what he always said he wanted, Melody said on the phone. He'd sailed on it a number of times and he loved the view of it from their porch when the trees were bare and he thought scattering them in a river was the best way of not leaving anything behind. Anything physical, she said. The crematory service was private—something else he said he wanted, she said: just her and their children and spouses and Isaac if he could get to New York for it. Took less than fifteen minutes. A couple of short poems chosen and read by the children—Dan didn't read poetry, she said, and he specifically didn't want anything religious at the service—and some hugging, and that was it. Stu wouldn't have gone to the service if he had been invited, for the same reason he didn't go to the memorial: he knew he wouldn't have been able to hold up during it and didn't like the idea of breaking down in front of everyone. Also, the memorial meant coming in by train with his wife—she would have wanted to go—and getting back the same night, since he had classes the next day. The resemblance between Isaac and Dan was uncanny, Harriet said, "even spooky. I almost jumped when I first saw him, for a moment thinking it was Dan, even though he's thirty years younger. I suppose I was just flashing back to what Dan looked like then. But also, Dan looked fifteen years younger than he was, and Isaac looked his age. And their build; the same. And height—relatively short: five-six or five-seven, Dan was, am I right?" and Stu said "He liked to say 'five-six and a half,' or 'bordering on five-seven.'" "Well, Isaac's around that too, maybe an inch taller. But the face: same pug nose, curly light hair and

246

lots of it—Dan never really grayed and you can bet he didn't dye it. High cheeks—you know Dan's; great bone structure there—one I'd love to have—and small ears and mouth. And the blue eyes. I shouldn't forget the blue eyes, the only one in our family to have them. They're supposed to have come from Mom's mother or father—which?" and he said "Grandma Hannah." "Ah, to have those eyes—what I would have given. My lackluster brown eyes, for one thing. But even his voice. Gravelly. You were smart not to come, though. Lots of people getting up and speaking, some of them endlessly. One man—a journalist friend from the Korean War—crying throughout, but he went on till he'd read his whole, what I'd call, speech. Altogether, more than two hours of history and memory, few of them saying anything I didn't know, so for sure nothing you didn't. His capture by the Communist Chinese. One reporter friend gave the name of Dan's boat—so that was new. Years in the Chinese prison and Dan coming out thirty pounds underweight." "Eighteen months in captivity, and two or three prisons. They moved him around." "He said years. His work at PBS, or then it was NET. And CBS, INS, UPS." "UP. United Press." "Sailing across the Atlantic when he was seventy on a boat that was about the size and had the comfort of one of those terrifying river rafts that people pay to put themselves on to risk their lives. And there were three of them but only two berths, since someone always had to be on watch. Here's something I didn't know. That the boat, during a storm near the Azores, almost capsized and would have sunk." "Dan never mentioned that." "This speaker wasn't on it, but that's what he said Dan told him. Dan probably didn't want to worry us, almost losing a second brother like that, especially since he wanted to make the same crossing coming back, not that we ever could have stopped him. His war correspondent days in the Korean War and, approximately five years before that, his service in the army as a paratrooper. He certainly was a gutsy man. What I didn't like about the memorial were these monitors around the room with continually changing photos of him. Dan on a boat, Dan finishing a marathon, Dan after he was released from prison and crossing some Chinese bridge to freedom. Seven or eight monitors, each the size of a large TV screen, so wherever you looked you saw him. I will say it was an impressive crowd, even distinguished looking—quite a number of television news executives were there, I was told—and everyone well dressed. After it was over there was a table of crudités and other hors d'oeuvres and an open bar, which everyone flocked to—something you'd expect from a room mostly filled with ex-newsmen, although by that time and after so many eulogies I

Debora Greger

The Last Dodo of Iowa

In the Midwest of memory,
no fence sags, no sign rusts:
that ear of corn with wings
still flies, but over a field

As black as a blackboard and as empty.
But listen: there's that sound again,
a student poet scratching something out—
the world *silence*—and then, after a spell,

putting it back again.
In the fat Russian novel that was Iowa,
the pages were blank, the wind
blinding one snowy signature to another.

My hand to your cheek—which was colder
that winter, love? You stood at the door,
the Milky Way spilling ancient history on us.
What was it you wanted? I never told you

how, when I should have been writing,
I stood in the homely museum
of natural history on campus,
under the long bones of a right whale

hung like a light fixture from the ceiling.
How had they washed up in a place so wrong?
They floated over a songbird
whose wing bones had been broken,

then folded as flat as an envelope.
A small cloud of cotton oozed from the eye.
A tag tied to the twig of a leg
gave the place of capture: *Yakima*.

Bird, I have been there since you were.
You would find nothing changed.
Orchards, packing houses—nothing
would wake it or you. What were we doing here?

I turned, and looked a dodo in its glass eye.
It was not what it seemed,
having the feet of an ostrich
and a coat of turkey feathers, dyed.

What creature had owned the beak first?
Even in extinction, it was clumsy.
Like me, it longed for a warmer clime.
Was there no record of its cry?

The Middle of Nowhere

Some small hour grew even smaller.
    In the middle of nowhere,
        the bus turned
    from the frayed ribbon of road
toward a patch of street, where the shadow

of a water tower stretched out in sleep.
    Was that tall dark mass
        at the end of the block
    a grain elevator or a volume missing
from a vast encyclopedia of emptiness?

We pulled into what passed for a depot
    in what was barely a town:
        the one filling station.
    A bathtub stood on stout legs
in the ladies' room, ready to bathe the family

who owned the concern. They must have lived
    somewhere in the back because,
        even at that hour,
    a child flitted like a moth
into the light that spread like an oil slick

around the pumps. A woman shook her head—
    at the kid or the driver, it was far
        from clear. In limbo,
    what was one more night
where no one arrived, let alone departed?

Preserves

The past is not open today.
But you may look in the windows,
though the house you grew up in

stands empty. What's in the air?
More invisible than incense at church,
radioactive isotopes drift downwind,

blessing the harvest. On this perfect desert
of a morning, your father's gone to work
at the reactor. Everyone else is in the back yard,

at a picnic table covered with newspaper,
this the season to bottle whatever can be preserved.
And there you are, the eldest child.

Your hand is still so small you're the only one
who can pack the slumped fruits of summer
into the narrow-mouth jar of winter.

It's the beautiful thing about you.
The pinkish blood of a blanched tomato
drips down your arms, stinging as it goes,

yesterday's headlines blurring where it falls.
That was August, late in the age of black and white—
I can just make out a picture of the president

and his brother. Who's in the background
in a dark suit? Is that you, Death?
How young they all look, smudged and innocent.

Christina Pugh

Mercurial (Soap, Glass, Skull)

I.

He's too old for soap bubbles,
but still the boy leans from the sill,
blowing gingerly to the dark,
his lips' duct lofting
a porous ellipse about to break,
his face quiet as a room lit
by a single lamp; and from where I sit,
that light has scrubbed his temple
to a shard—so I hold my breath
and try to read the bubble's
book of blank, lifting to stay
for a moment, perhaps two,
in the air: the boy learning
to exhale, not sing,
his ceremony solemn
as Latin declensions, as paper
flowering in pools: the grindstone
and vertigo of art.

II.

In the factory,
men twirl wands
until the blues
spool and mound:

threads
of hot glass dip
and craze into forms.

Tongs pull a leg,
then a leg
from a liquid
torso, soon
to harden as a horse.

And now a seer
takes to the woods, parting
a branch to make his dream:

four men row a boat
to the darkest
region of the sea.

One looks up
and sees a flock of crows
stilled above him.

III.

If I ever said I loved you,
which I probably
won't, the words might sound
like a pipe
posed under glass,
or a map of some near galaxy:
planets shrubbed
in deepening green,
cress lit
by a starburst
of impulse—
this window box
an artist called
Dream World.

IV.

There's a bubble housed
in the pediment above the skull;
it floats above the frazzle
in the bone.

Then a river of coins
you can never spend:
the balance
of cranium from gable.

The last transformation
is the one
you'll never see:

the lesson is inlaid with gold.

One Thousand Cranes

Pieced quilt (Flying Geese)
ca. 1845–1850

In those days, a couple went to bed with geese—
eight hundred and twenty-six triangles
flown northward in calico, each bird pared
to wingspread and a compass-point of head.

There was a terrain that held them at a distance:
root and tumbleweed stenciled in the chintz
that pieced the unmarked trail beneath their feathers;
sparks of earth that fell away from bird's eye, marrying

geometry and spores—like our digital cameras'
fort-da, or the sudden willows grown behind the blinds
of my youngest childhood home in the Midwest.
The cloth tracks run distant as brooks

seen from the locked towers of dream,
while isosceles rush over the plains' surface,
no shape cut from the same dress or drape:
the triangles are lace, or a tangle of bike spokes;

or three points fence the scalloped
edges of Corinthians. And now her body
stirs beneath the cloth. *Let me see a triangle of sky,*
she told him, *right before I die.* But I think that voice

belongs to a woman who lives here now,
who also asked her husband for the possible:
to watch a stream of birds migrate
on the television propped above her bed;

to return to the seat of her oldest ideas,
where a thousand cranes glide in a girl's
silk pocket: mathematical, sublime, and small—
she almost feels the wings against her hip.

Vicki Hearne

Without Mountains

In a land without mountains
there are no knowing leaners. Sabbath
becomes a day of hiding, the air
loses its canniness, breath
closes, guarding the nature of divinity
from god.

       The mechanics of light
replace light in the sun's refusal
to choose one or the other, showing all
for nothing. Day and night replace
the chiaroscuro of thought and song
splutters out letters to the editor.

Beside me the lean and gracious regard
on my face of a dog reopens the breeze
in which the whisper of mountains begins
to gather. On this new kind
of air, new kinds of life. The animal's gaze
is impudent, love's metaphysics
is its own in a bereft air and compensates
for what the stars used to know. The price.
It is worth the price. It is worth it,
For it must be worth it.

White Out

When the snow busily chews
At the edges of the light,
Catching the eyes up in lace

As in memory, the same old
Glint stings the bones each time but
We admire the distinctions,

Say each one is different,
As though difference were not
The crash of meaning and no

Clarity such as pilots
Wait for, who fly up solo
At times as though time were the

Presence of love, not its drift.
As though snow were a lazy,
Unambitious appetite.

In certain storms each snowflake
Is a heart of light lonesome
For our glow stilly hoarded

Against such luminous greed.
We are not pilots alone
In the storm. The light is ours.

The Old Dog

The old dog
would, as a puppy

would, grab truth, gladdening the air.
There were leaps

that brought the trees to their height
death to its knees. She

lost no time, had nothing

to make up for. Now time
has lost itself

for her and God
did not consult me, God

moved in on her
with assault with intent.

She is limp, there
is no further motive in her.

This love
leaves an iridescent tracery

behind, a veneer that keeps
the distance between me

and the world merely a thing.

Side View (Alumna Report)

The organism bores through,
Has side effects, everyone

Knows all about them, loses
Patience with them and in time

Patience loses too, whether
To love or psoriasis.

My own complaints are private
When no ache loosens my love

Or my astonishment, no
Pain, I mean, or keen startle

Of light such as winter brings
To despised architectures

In strange bleak towns, and I gasp
As though back home with vision

Still intact, but it isn't:
Something one can learn to see

As clearly as if the loss
Of vision were another

Young horse whose shoulders swing out
Suddenly articulate

Covered with gold, suddenly
In the afternoon knowing

Balance and fire, suddenly
Coveting grace and movement

As if they were her own and
Her own news, and lights roll on.

Creatures of the Surface

The dog may be a blue ticked
Coonhound staunch against lamplight,

And mahogany Irish
Gayer than the singing strings.

A terrier, any breed,
Reaching into darkness

With her teeth, thus, naming it
The enemy. A sheep dog,

All made of eye and angles
On the flock. For all we know

A lapdog, free style winner,
Or steady on a man trail.

Always a messenger true
To the world, to us giving

Up the task of the fulcrum
Of lore. We are not ourselves

To know. We are not to name
Any but the exoteric

Creatures of the surfaces.
We are to become pristine.

A tribal song of knowledge
Is the fate that, evaded,

Takes us to the depths, down to
The far and remote regions

Of logic which still demands
that the dog be *this* or *this*

Instead of variously
Emerging into the fields

Of learning as *this* and *this*.
This, and this, and also that

Floatable variation
Of heart, coming home to leave,

Leaving home to come,
Sustaining a merriment

As of a polished fulcrum
Of leg-flash, on which our minds

For bare sustenance depend.
The young Airedale's head tosses

The light and catches it up
On his teeth; laughter's lesson

In the singularity
Of the plural, the many

Birds that on a single wing
Beat their way unwavering.

Knowledge opened. It closes,
Now, on the Old Family.

Other exemplaries of truth.
The nations kick them aside

As is the wont of nations
Greedy to hear a verdict.

Gods do not choose refusal
As an ardent tool fit for

Discrimination. They wait.
They welcome the dogs humbly

Like crumbs poor servants snatch up,
Like worlds wealthy dogs invent.

Wind Rubs Into

Wind rubs into the surfaces
of thorough waters, of sandstone

complete as hope. Wind rubs
against the grain of your life

like hope, wind scares up
the darkness which, left behind,
collects in the corners of knowledge,

nourishes the bright skitter
of those shyer creatures

who dash away with
nearly enough light

from time's skirts. This slows
the roll of seasons

into unknowable ease. Here is how we learn
name after name

for the unpronounceable light.
Whose vice is violence

for the unpronounced
darkness whose vice is peace.

Light and dark, a cross-grained clerk,
bureaucrat at the pearly gates with

a boss. Technophobic, skeptical,
the boss's voice follows

his stomach
into Rome where a single season

brought out the wind, heir
to everything we love.

Imperfection is the toy
of the wind, its vice

and virtue the aroma
of movement, and

don't you cuss that fiddle boy
unless you want that fiddle out of tune.

Mark Strand

Cake

A man leaves for the next town to pick up a cake.
On the way, he gets lost in a dense woods
and the cake is never picked up. Years later,
the man appears on a beach staring at the sea.
"I am standing on a beach," he thinks, "and I am lost
in thought." He does not move. The heaving sea
turns black, its waves curl and crash. "Soon
I will leave," he continues, "soon I will go
to a nearby town to pick up a cake. I will walk
in a brown and endless woods, and far away
the heaving sea will turn to black and the waves—
I can see them now—will curl and crash."

CONTRIBUTORS

Richard Burgin is the author of ten books, including the story collection *The Spirit Returns* (Johns Hopkins University Press, 2001) and the novel *Ghost Quartet* (TriQuarterly Books, 1999). His stories have won four Pushcart Prizes. **Joan Connor** is Associate Professor in Fiction Writing at Ohio University and a member of the faculty at the University of Southern Maine's low residency MFA Program. She has published two collections of short stories: *Here On Old Route 7* and *We Who Live Apart* with University of Missouri Press. Frederick Busch selected her third collection, *History Lessons* (University of Massachusetts Press, 2003), as the AWP Award winner for 2002. **Colin Dickey** received his MFA from California Institute of the Arts and currently teaches at National University. **Stuart Dybek**'s most recent books are *I Sailed with Magellan* (2004), a novel in stories, and *Streets in Their Own Ink* (2004), a collection of poems, both from Farrar, Straus and Giroux. **Debora Greger**'s most recent book of poetry is *Western Art* (Penguin, 2004). **Vicki Hearne** published three collections of poetry, *Nervous Horses* (University of Texas Press, 1980), *In the Absence of Horses* (Princeton University Press, 1983), and *Parts of Light* (Johns Hopkins University Press, 1994). **John Koethe**'s most recent book of poems is

Sally's Hair (forthcoming from Harper-Collins, April, 2006). He is distinguished professor of Philosophy at the University of Wisconsin-Milwaukee. **C. T. Lawrence**'s work has appeared in the *New England Writers Anthology*, the *Connecticut Review*, *Puerto del Sol*, and elsewhere. She is the recipient of awards for short-short fiction from the New England Writers and *Writers Digest*, and for non-fiction from the AWP. **David Lummus** is a PhD candidate in Italian from Stanford University. He holds a B.A. in Classics and Italian from the University of Texas and was the recipient of a Fullbright research fellowship for study in Italy. **David H. Lynn** is editor of the *Kenyon Review*. His most recent collection of stories is *Year of Fire: Stories* (Harvest Books, 2006). **Karen Malpede** is the author of twelve produced plays, including *A Monster Has Stolen the Sun and Other Plays* (Marlboro, 1986) and "Better People," anthologized in *Angels of Power* (Spinifex, 1991). Her short fiction has appeared in *110 Stories: New York Writes after September 11* (New York University Press, 2002) and the journals *Out-of-Line* and *Confrontation*. **Meg Mullins** received her MFA from Columbia University. Her stories have appeared in the *Iowa Review*, the *Baltimore Review*, the *Sonora Review*, and *Best American Short Stories*. Her first novel, *The Rug Merchant*, will be published by Viking in 2006. She lives in New Mexico with her husband and their two children. **Christina Pugh** is the recipient of the Word Press First Book Prize for *Rotary* (Word Press, 2004). Her poems have appeared in the *Atlantic Monthly*, *Ploughshares*, *Harvard Review*, and elsewhere. A recipient of the Ruth Lily Fellowship from *Poetry* magazine, she is currently visiting assistant professor at Northwestern University. **Phillip Robertson** has covered the wars in Afghanistan and Iraq for the news and culture website, Salon.com. He has also reported for BBC radio, National Public Radio, and the *Christian Science Monitor*. He was a finalist for the USC/Annenberg Award for online journalism in the breaking news category. **Donna Seaman** is an editor at *Booklist*, editor of the anthology *In Our Nature* (University of Georgia Press, 2000), and author of *Writers on the Air: Conversations about Books* (Paul Dry Books, 2005), a book of interviews compiled from her show, "Open Books," on WLUW. **Anna Smith** grew up in Greensboro, North Carolina. She lives in Junction City, California. **Jason Sommer** has written three poetry collections, *Lifting the Stone* (Forest Books, London, 1991), and, from the University of Chicago Press, *Other People's Troubles* (1997), and *The Man Who Sleeps in My Office* (2004), nominated for a Pulitzer Prize. **Susan Stewart**'s *Columbarium* won the National Book Critics Circle Award in Poetry in 2003. Her writings on art, *The Open Studio: Essays on Art and Aesthetics*, have just been published by the University of Chicago Press. **Mark Strand** lives in New York City and teaches in the Department of English and Comparative Literature of Columbia University. **Felicia van Bork**, educated at the Ontario College of Art and Design, has exhibited her work widely in one-person and group exhibitions. Her most recent awards include residencies at VCCA (2004) and the McColl Center for Visual Art (2005). She lives in Davidson, North Carolina. **Malena Watrous**'s fiction has been published in the *Alaska Quarterly Review* and *Glimmer Train*, where she was a winner in the Fiction Open Contest. Her nonfiction has appeared in *Lingua Franca, Kyoto Journal*, and on Salon.com. She was a Wallace Stegner fellow at Stanford University. **Wang Xiaobo** was born in Beijing in 1952. He was sent to the countryside for re-education and attended college only after Mao's death in 1976. He studied in the United States from 1984–1988, receiving his MA in comparative literature from the University of Pittsburgh. After his return to China, he taught university before resigning to become one of the country's few freelance writers, until his death. **Hongling Zhang** received her MFA from Washington University in St. Louis. Her work has appeared in *Century China* (published by Hong Kong University) and *World News*, the largest Chinese newspaper in North America. **Pietro Zullino** is an Italian journalist and writer. His works include *Catilina* (Rizzoli, 1989), *The Seven Kings of Rome* (Rizzoli, 1986), and *Judas* (1988).

the strange fruit

Issue 1
NOW AVAILABLE!

the strange fruit

the strange fruit reveres authenticity, preferring
plain-spoken, straightforward language over obscure,
verbose imagery. We aim to present poetry and prose
that examines personal experiences for their
commonality in a way which currently. We gravitate towards
demonstrating a way...
...ta which usu...
...oments whose end
...when we are most...

SUBMIT: Fiction, nonfiction, & poetry. We read year round.
submissions@thestrangefruit.com

SUBSCRIBE: Single issues: $6   One year: $11. Two years: $20.
Credit cards accepted online or send checks to:

300 Lenora Street, #250, Seattle, WA 98121
www.thestrangefruit.com

The Iowa Review

NOW IN OUR 36TH YEAR OF PUBLICATION.

Issues in 2006 include essays by
Albert Goldbarth, Amy Leach, and Ann Copeland;
poems by Stephanie Ivanoff, Arthur Vogelsang, and
Timothy Liu; stories by John Michael Cummings,
Ellen Wilbur, and Susan Harper Martin; and
winners of our 2006 Iowa Review Awards.

THREE ISSUES ANNUALLY.

$24 for one year; $44 for two; $64 for three.
Add $4 foreign mailing.
Single copy, $8.95.

308 EPB, IOWA CITY, IOWA 52242-1408
iowareview.org

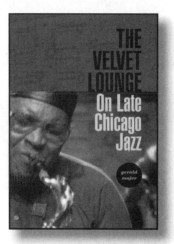